I0831702

THE BRAHMS BUST

Also by Alessandra Comini from Sunstone Press

Schiele in Prison
Egon Schiele's Portraits
Gustav Klimt
Egon Schiele
Egon Schiele: Nudes
The Fantastic Art of Vienna
The Changing Image of Beethoven
In Passionate Pursuit: A Memoir

The Megan Crespi Mystery Series

Killing for Klimt
The Schiele Slaughters
The Kokoschka Capers
The Munch Murders
The Kollwitz Calamities
The Kandinsky Conundrum
The Mahler Mayhem
The Beethoven Boomerang

THE BRAHMS BUST

A Megan Crespi Mystery Series Novel

ALESSANDRA COMINI

SANTA FE

This book is a work of fiction. Names, places, characters, and incidents are either the product of the author's imagination or used fictionally. Any resemblance to actual events or persons, living or dead, is entirely coincidental.

Sunstone books may be purchased for educational, business, or sales promotional use.
For information please write: Special Markets Department, Sunstone Press,
P.O. Box 2321, Santa Fe, New Mexico 87504-2321.

Design › R. Ahl

ISBN 978-1-63293-439-0 (hardcover)

eBook 978-1-61139-651-5

Library of Congress Cataloging-in-Publication Data

Names: Comini, Alessandra, author. | Comini, Alessandra. Megan Crespi mystery series novel.
Title: The Brahms bust : a Megan Crespi mystery series novel / Alessandra Comini.
Description: Santa Fe, New Mexico : Sunstone Press, [2021] | Series: A Megan Crespi mystery series novel | Includes reader's guide. | Summary: "In Vienna, upsetting mishaps occur when a Bruckner/Brahms four-part concert series under the baton of a woman conductor turns deadly"-- Provided by publisher.
Identifiers: LCCN 2021056995 | ISBN 9781632933720 (paperback) | ISBN 9781611396515 (epub) | ISBN 1632933721 (paperback)
Subjects: LCGFT: Detective and mystery fiction.
Classification: LCC PS3603.O477 B73 2021 | DDC 813/.6--dc23
LC record available at https://lccn.loc.gov/2021056995

WWW.SUNSTONEPRESS.COM
SUNSTONE PRESS / POST OFFICE BOX 2321 / SANTA FE, NM 87504-2321 /USA
(505) 988-4418

Dedication

To Mary Dibbern, master vocal coach to generations, Artistic Director of Secular Music, St. Matthew's Cathedral Arts, and Music Director of Education, The Dallas Opera

and

To the memory of Richard R. Brettell (1949–2020), pianist, internationally known expert on French Impressionism and inspiring institution builder, including the Edith O'Donnell Institute of Art History, University of Texas, Dallas

Portrait by Friedrich Kaulbach of the German American sculptor Elisabet Ney (Münster, 1833–Austin,1907) standing before her bust of King George V of Hanover, oil on canvas, 1860, Niedersächsisches Landesmuseum, Hanover.

Photograph of the composer Johannes Brahms (Hamburg, 1833–Vienna,1897) taken around the age of forty before he grew his famous beard in 1878. Photographer unknown.

List of Major Characters

Megan Crespi: retired professor of art history and amateur musicologist, now an international art crimes investigator and older sister of Tina Crespi

Tina Crespi: respected veterinarian known for her fervent animal rights activities and younger sister of Megan Crespi

Jacquelyn McDonald: Director of the Elisabet Ney Museum in Austin, Texas

Edgar Wittgenstein: general director of the Vienna Musikverein with a distinguished heritage

Agatha Endlich: resilient resident conductor of the Vienna Philharmonic

Mario Intagliatore: Hamburg-based sculptor and creator of the Walhalla bust of Brahms

Lukas Eifer: conductor of the Grazer Philharmonisches Orchester, a fervent fan of Brahms, and older brother of Robb Eifer

Robb Eifer: longtime deputy director of the archives, library, and collections at the Musikverein and adoring younger brother of Lukas Eifer

Christian Begeist: conductor of the Bruckner Orchester Linz and a fanatical admirer of the composer Anton Bruckner

Dieter Unfug: former assistant conductor to Christian Begeist, and living now in Wiener Neustadt; also a Bruckner loyalist

Stefanie Schreib: music critic of Vienna's respected daily newspaper *Der Standard* who keeps her ancestry a secret

Peter Heimnis: chief stagehand at the Musikverein

Tönnies Helfer: retired Hamburg ophthalmologist and longtime friend of Megan Crespi

Harry Dunmore: American family physician who has spent his career aiding the sick in India and Africa

Anthony (Tony) Bocello: retired president of the Dallas Symphony Orchestra and former dean of the Meadows School of the Arts, Southern Methodist University, Dallas

Fritz Rahm: grandson five times removed of Friedrich Brahms; a Venezuelan organist attending the Double B Composers concerts in Vienna

Erich Decker: Vienna's Chief of Police who has worked with Megan Crespi on a case concerning Gustav Mahler

Oliver Rologe: a music-loving neurologist and loyal fan of the Vienna Philharmonic for over twenty years

Johannes Brahms's piano room/living room at Karlsgasse No.4, Vienna: 1904 watercolor by Wilhelm Nowak based on the 1897 photograph taken a few days after the composer's death, Wien Museum, Vienna.

1

"A bust of Brahms but a pretty battered bust," mused Megan Crespi out loud, holding up a partly damaged life-size bronze image of the composer Johannes Brahms.

"Come on now, he doesn't even have a beard!" scoffed her sister Tina, who had driven them down from Dallas to Austin for Megan's Sunday evening lecture at the University of Texas Blanton Museum of Art. Entitled "Whoever Heard of a Woman Sculptor?" the lecture was dedicated to the nineteenth-century German-American artist Elisabet Ney, whose Austin home and sculpture-filled studio had been a popular museum and tourist draw for well over a century.

The two sisters could not be more different. Fifteen years separated them. Megan, whose calling had been solving international art crimes since her retirement from teaching, was a daily exercise devotee in her mid-eighties and a "continuous" brunette with sparkling brown eyes. She loved nothing better than researching and writing in her cozy, book-lined home. Tina, a dedicated and respected veterinarian, was blonde, slim, and short in stature, with large, expressive chestnut-colored eyes, and active in all things having to do with animals and the outdoors. Neither one of them had married; both sisters belonged to canines—Megan, to a little Maltese named Button; Tina, to five Japanese Chins whose exotic names Megan could never remember.

"That's the way most people think of Brahms, with a great white beard," Megan was saying, "but, after two skimpy tryouts, he didn't grow a full beard until he was forty-three years old. There is a photo of him sitting with friends on a second-story porch in Pörtschach on the Wörthersee in the summer of eighteen seventy-eight that shows him with a new luxuriant dark beard. And there have been several theories as to why he grew a beard—including that it was a disguise. He himself explained why he had one by saying, 'With a shaved chin, people take you for either an actor or a priest.' But as far as the disguise theory is concerned, yes, after he grew the great bushy thing, he loved to fool people who hadn't seen him in quite some time and see how long it would take for them to discover who he was. He would introduce himself, in a very deep and hoarse voice, as 'Kapellmeister Müller from Braunschweig.' And with his impish love of enunciating things in *Plattdeutsch*—Low German—he probably pronounced the city's name as 'Brunswiek.'"

"Oh, you and your love of dialects!" Tina laughed.

"But seriously, I think he simply felt the need to look as distinguished as his music, which by then was held in great esteem. And also because of his love of alcohol and cigars, he was starting to put on weight and was becoming rather portly and red of cheek." Megan ran her fingers over the sculpted hair circling the bust's neck, long locks that made up for the composer's already receding hair line.

"Okay, but even so, what makes this bust an image of Brahms?" Tina was not convinced.

"Because I *recognize* him! Because Brahms's face was strikingly handsome during his pre-beard years, especially when he was in his twenties. He was charmingly winsome, in fact adorable, and this bust, I'd say this bust was probably made when he was in his mid-twenties, um, thirty at the most."

Megan glanced at the store's owner who was standing at the front counter of his Austin Antiques, absorbed in the morning newspaper. Turning her back to him, Megan produced her iPhone, and spoke to her sister in a whisper.

"Look, Tina, I'm going to show you photos of what Brahms looked like before he grew a beard." She tapped one of the many URLs produced by her online search and pointed to several images of the composer in his twenties and thirties.

"Hmm. I do see what you mean. So sensitive! And already the receding hairline beginning. That narrow bow tie is pretty dashing." Megan typed a new entry into her browser.

"Look here. Brahms in color! See his sensitive blue eyes and dark blond hair? Now watch this." The color image which had been in left profile commenced a slow turn through full frontal face and on to right profile.

"How on earth...?"

"Pretty amazing, huh? A colleague sent it to me recently. It's the work of an Iranian visual artist, Hadi Karimi. He's done the same with lots of nineteenth-century composers, including Clara Schumann."

"Oh, good, he's a feminist!"

"And look here," Megan continued, "this black and white photo of him at the age of twenty, looking a pubescent fifteen at the most, and this one here, in his early thirties, long hair and dreamy look."

"Oh, yes! I think I'm falling in love with him." Tina pretended to swoon.

"Shh! Don't let the owner hear you. I'm going to buy it and I don't want him to think I know what he has here. I doubt he has any idea of what this is." Tina caught on immediately and as they walked to the cash register she pretended to fuss at her sister.

"I don't see why you would want that old, banged up metal head thing."

"It speaks to me somehow, I don't know why," answered Megan as she placed the bust on the counter in front of the man who put down his paper and smiled encouragingly at her.

"So this old bust appeals to you?" he asked.

"Yes, kind of. You don't know who this is supposed to be, do you?"

"No. It came with a bunch of things from the estate of a local woman. Her granddaughter brought the items in to me. But this man must have been important enough to have had a bust made of him."

"Or rich and vain," Tina suggested.

"What are you asking for it?" asked Megan.

"Well, my thinking is that the bust could be of one of the Texas senators here in Austin. Or a judge. If so, that could make it valuable."

"Ha!" Tina laughed. "Don't you think the granddaughter

would have told you if her grandmother was married to or related to a senator?"

"Well, that's true. And I did do some research on her surname. Whalley, it was, and there is no record of a Senator or a Judge Whalley here in Texas."

"So it's an unidentified, badly battered bust," said Megan firmly.

"Well, yeah, if you put it that way," said the man.

"I noticed it because in a way it looks like our father when he was a young man," Megan added, looking meaningfully at her sister. Catching on immediately, Tina nodded vigorously.

"I suppose I could let it go for two hundred and fifty dollars," said the man.

"*That much*?" exclaimed Megan.

"Yes. I think it's worth that much."

"Gosh, as a retired professor I could only offer you at the very most two hundred." There was a long pause.

"Oh, all right," the man said at last. "Two hundred. Here, I'd better put it in something for you." Reaching under the counter the store owner produced an empty cardboard box about fifteen inches square and deep. It lacked a top. He took the bust and set it inside the box, then crinkled up some of the newspaper he had been reading and stuffed it around the head.

"Yes, thank you, that was a good idea," said Megan, handing over her credit card.

Out on the sidewalk afterward, Tina, who had volunteered to carry the bronze booty, congratulated her sister.

"Not for nothing are we half-Italian," she said gleefully. "Congrats, big Sis!"

"I'd credit our Scotch-Irish half for keeping me calm while bargaining," Megan answered, smiling.

They walked to Tina's distinctive Chevrolet truck. The white vehicle was painted with large brown spots to resemble a cow and enhanced by a pair of longhorns mounted on the front. As Tina started to load the bust behind the passenger seat that Monday morning, she expressed surprise that the bust wasn't very heavy.

"Let me see." Megan leaned past her sister and slowly removed the bust from its temporary cardboard home.

"You're right! I hadn't really wondered about that in the shop. But then, of course, the bust is hollow inside. See?" Megan ran the fingers of her right hand vigorously around the dusty interior and then poked her index finger high up, reaching for the nose hollow. As she penetrated one of the nostrils something was dislodged and fell with a clatter to the pavement.

It was an old, small brass key.

2

High above the blue Danube near Regensburg, the white temple of Walhalla honoring historic German luminaries marked the first year of the twenty-first century with the installation of a bust of Johannes Brahms. Effigies of the other two famous "three Bs"—a phrase happily coined by conductor Hans von Bülow—had long been present in the neoclassical shrine. They were Johann Sebastian Bach and Ludwig van Beethoven. A bust of the great sculptor and graphic artist Käthe Kollwitz, admirer of Brahms, had to wait even longer, until 2018.

The creator of the marble Brahms bust was famed Italian artist Mario Intagliatore of Hamburg, and from the moment of its unveiling it was the subject of indignation and dislike. The marble bust didn't *look* like Brahms! It didn't have a beard! Never mind that the master had not grown one until he was in his mid-forties. *Our* Brahms, the public complained, the chubby old man with the great white beard, is posterity's Brahms. In order to leave a protest that all would see, one daring soul had even secreted herself or himself overnight inside the multi-tiered neoclassical building that hosted the glistening white bust with its deep-veined small bursts of black. When Walhalla personnel arrived the next morning to open up the temple, they did not notice anything until a tourist called a guard over to a strange sight. Mounted in place on the pink stippled alabaster wall to the left of the seated marble statue of Walhalla's founder, King Ludwig I, the white bust of Brahms had acquired a flowing white beard. Made of woven straw and spray-painted white, the stiff crisscross ensemble, epoxy-glued into place, appeared perfectly natural and reassuringly familiar from even up close.

The unknown perpetrator of this stunt had been lauded in the local press as restoring to the public the "real" Brahms. A darker Internet reading, however, referred to the composer's "psychotic need for a mask."

3

"Hey, since we found it in Austin, you don't suppose your Brahms head could have been sculpted by Elisabet Ney, do you?" Tina asked her sister as they drove back to Dallas.

Tina was becoming interested in who might have been the bust's creator. Before Megan had given her speech the day before, they had visited Formosa, the Neoclassical-Germanic castle with its two-story crenelated square tower that had been Ney's home and studio. Now, just as the sculptor had hoped, it was the Elisabet Ney Museum. There, led by the museum's dedicated director Dr. Jacquelyn McDonald, they had admired a marmorean-like forest of busts and full-size statues by the artist, from both her European and her American periods. Megan laughed at her sister's enthusiastic question.

"Nothing is impossible, but, for starters, there is no mention of Ney in any biographies of the composer or of Brahms in any biographies about Ney. And it's hardly likely she would or could have brought any of her heavy European work with her when she and her drop-dead handsome physician husband Edmund migrated to America."

"When was that?"

"The very first month of eighteen seventy-one. Right in the middle of the Franco-Prussian war devastating Europe. First they went to Georgia where they had friends, then Minnesota briefly..."

"Oh! Where you were born!" Tina smiled at her sister.

"...and after that they moved permanently to Texas. Where *you* were born."

"You said 'for starters,' Megan, what else?"

"Well, there is absolutely no record of Ney's ever having had Brahms sit for her, even though she did sculpt some very famous sitters: Jacob Grimm, of the Grimm brothers' *Fairy Tales*; the philosopher and misogynist Arthur Schopenhauer, whom she charmed into posing for her; blind King George the Fifth of Hanover; the Italian freedom fighter Giuseppe Garibaldi..."

"So *that's* why you went to the island of Caprera?"

"Yes. I wanted to repeat Ney's courageous boat journey from Sardinia to sculpt a bust of the unifier of Italy. You know he bought half the island and built La Casa Bianca, a grand home which is now a museum."

"And you took photos of all this, of course."

"Of course. Not for nothing are we the daughters of a photographer. But I was telling you whom she sculpted. In Europe she did the Iron Chancellor of Germany, Otto von Bismarck; a life-size statue of mad King Ludwig the Second of Bavaria; a medallion of Cosima Liszt von Bülow, who later dropped poor Hans to become Richard Wagner's wife..."

"Stop! Stop!" Tina said, laughing. "I can't digest all those names and drive at the same time."

They drove in contented silence for a time, then suddenly Megan gasped.

"Tina! I just thought of something! While Ney was still in Hanover sculpting King George the Fifth, he commissioned her to sculpt a bust of the virtuoso violinist and concertmaster of his court orchestra, Joseph Joachim. *Joachim was Brahms's best friend*! And he and his professional singer wife, Amalie Weiss, were both portrayed in marble busts by Ney. You just saw them yesterday."

"Well, there's your connection. I guess."

"Let me check some dates," Megan said, holding up her iPhone. She typed a few words into the Google browser line.

"Hmm. No, that would have been too easy. Wait, I need to check the years eighteen fifty-nine and eighteen sixty, when Ney was busy creating the two busts in Hanover. Did you know Ney and Brahms were almost the same age?"

"Of course, I knew they were the same age," joked Tina, having only learned who Ney was the day before.

"Yes, here it is. I'm checking notes I took from the best modern biographer of Brahms, Jan Swafford. Ah ha! On January eight of eighteen fifty-nine, the twenty-five-year-old Brahms was in Hanover preparing for the premiere of his first piano concerto, you know, the one that begins with that ominous low D minor chord and stormy kettle drum rumbles—fifty or so of them."

"I think it's fifty-one," Tina teased. "So?"

"So Ney was at hand in Hanover, Joachim was at hand in Hanover sculpting King George, Brahms was at hand in Hanover, and it's conceivable that Joachim commissioned Ney to sculpt his dear friend Brahms!"

"Oh, I love it!" Tina exclaimed.

"But now to *prove* it. Considering how meticulously history has detailed the lives of both Ney and Brahms, why hasn't the existence of a Brahms bust ever been mentioned?"

"Aw, does that mean you're ruling out the ID, then?"

"Not on your life! I'm going to hunt this down when I'm speaking in Europe next week." Megan was referring to two lectures she was slated to give, one on Brahms's idols and images at a festival in Hamburg honoring its native son, the other on Gustav Klimt and music at the Leopold Museum in Vienna.

"And what about the *key*? Are you going to take the key that fell out of the bust with you?" Megan shot her sister an exasperated but fond look.

"Of course I am, you sweet idiot sister of mine!"

4

Edgar Wittgenstein was blissful. A slender, tall man in his mid-fifties with curly black hair and perpetually inquisitive eyebrows, he was the multi-talented General Director of the Vienna Musikverein. And now here he was on a Monday evening sitting with eyes closed in a parterre loge of the city's venerable home of the famed orchestra. This was the first evening of a four "Double B Composers" event to be held every other night over one week: Monday, Wednesday, Friday, and then culminating on Sunday. It was Edgar's novel suggestion to pair in one concert symphonies by two nineteenth-century Vienna residents who were contemporaries: the Upper Austrian Anton Bruckner and the North German Johannes Brahms. And to present them in a glutinous sequence. His idea had been eagerly endorsed by resident conductor Agatha Endlich, a slim brunette with sparkling brown eyes, who more than competently took over the baton in the summer months when prominent guest conductors, so far almost all of the opposite sex, did not grace the podium. Edgar's proposal was to present a Bruckner symphony first and then, after intermission, perform a Brahms symphony.

Bruckner was nine years older than Brahms and, all told, had composed eleven symphonies—two of them not numbered—compared to the four written by Brahms, who outlived him by only one year, passing away in 1897 at the age of sixty-three. Edgar decided that the selection of Bruckner symphonies would hopscotch from the Linz version of the First, to the Fourth, then skip the next well-known three, to the colossal Eighth, to the almost completed Ninth to pair with Brahms's four symphonies. Conductor and orchestra were game, and intense rehearsals had taken up the greater part of May for the inaugural presentation at the beginning of June.

And now, with the first concert almost over, the final movement of Brahms's First Symphony, so long in completion, was gloriously resounding throughout the acoustically rich Musikverein's Golden Hall—*Goldener Saal*—with skilled Maestra Endlich at the podium. Brahms himself maintained that the work, from first sketches to final finesses, took twenty-one years, from 1855 to 1876. His endless fussing could be compared to the always insecure Bruckner's continuous revising of his symphonies, but with quite different conclusions. Whereas the final movement of church organist Bruckner's First Symphony was bracing in its use of an almost palpable "pedal" counterpoint to parallel its effusively orchestrated themes, the final movement of Brahms's First Symphony offered two delicacies: an Alpine shepherd's lone horn call, and a grand finale with a heroic melody begging to be sung. No wonder the latter symphony was approvingly referred to as "Beethoven's Tenth"!

5

The sunny breakfast room of sculptor Mario Intagliatore's capacious two-story apartment off narrow Zufallstrasse overlooked Hamburg's newly completed, glistening white promenade along the Elbe River. Just back from selecting a marble block in Italy, the sculptor was shaking his head as he scanned the newspapers that Frau Salem, his devoted housekeeper of many years, had saved for him. There was yet another amusing criticism of his Walhalla Brahms bust that had been in place for well over twenty years now. Apparently an overeager visitor to the site had once again "corrected" the beardless countenance by surreptitiously donating a costume beard strapped to the composer's chin.

The white-haired, black-bearded sculptor looked up from his newspaper to study the images still affixed to his breakfast room wall—enlarged photographs of a young-looking Brahms "*ohne Bart*—without beard." For Intagliatore, Brahms's clean-shaven face was handsome and sensitive and he had tried to convey that in his bust of the great composer. Curious how people did not like to relinquish their preconceptions, even to the point of activist resentment.

Perhaps he would have a chance to talk about this with one of the speakers coming to the Brahms symposium event this coming Wednesday. He would be there because he was lending his new plaster bust of the composer to Hamburg University for the event. It would be interesting to get the speaker's take on that latest vandalism at Walhalla. An art and music historian, she had written an interesting reception history concerning the changing image of Beethoven over the centuries. Intagliatore remembered the author's name because even though she was an American scholar, her surname, Crespi, was Italian. Yes, he would try to speak with the professor after her lecture. It boasted an intriguing title: "The Visual Brahms: Idols and Images."

But now it was time to take to his basement studio the amazing pneumatic pointing machine he had bought in Carrara. The sixty-four-year-old bachelor was still lean and limber. And, having resisted pneumatics for forty years as a believer in literal hand carving of marble, he had tried it out just as a lark in the small Italian town fabled for its high-quality marble and dedicated stone carvers. He was immediately converted by its precision, speed, and light weight.

Intagliatore had always allowed stone cutters to initiate the preparatory process of roughing out a fine block of marble with hammer and chisel, measuring the overall three-dimensionality with calipers. But after that initial step, he himself had always proceeded with the vertical pointing machine that recorded his metal and graphic marks denoting high and low contours of the plaster bust of the sitter he had first arduously modeled in clay. Then the line and dimensions of his plaster model would literally be walked over for transferal to their corresponding positions on the marble block. The process of walking back and forth with the pointing machine would be repeated hundreds of times until the overall form was precisely transcribed onto the marble and Intagliatore could fine-tool the details by hand. But now this amazing pneumatic memory pointing machine transferred all the metal and graphic marks *simultaneously*!

Intagliatore could hardly wait to try it out. The marble block he had ordered in Carrara would take two weeks to arrive. Awaiting him in the spacious basement studio was the finished plaster bust commissioned by a mystery client who had conducted the business through a third party, specifying certain distinct details and paying all costs in cash in advance, including the marble and shipping. Intagliatore's clay bust had been modeled in his basement studio after photographs. Photographs similar in stance to the ones of Johannes Brahms in his breakfast room.

But in these basement studio photographs the composer had a full beard.

6

At the turn of the nineteenth century, the Wittgenstein family in Vienna was one of the wealthiest in Europe. It was also Jewish, which meant that it received its share of prejudice. The pater familias, Karl, was a steel tycoon whose wife, Leopoldine, half-Jewish by blood and Roman Catholic by faith, gave him nine children. The last two were exceedingly famous. Paul, who lost his right arm in World War I, became a celebrated concert pianist for whom noted composers wrote piano concertos for the left hand. Their number included Maurice Ravel, Richard Strauss, Sergei Prokofiev, Paul Hindemith, Erich Korngold, Benjamin Britten, and Lukas Foss.

The last child in the family, Ludwig, was to become a professor of philosophy at Cambridge, known and admired, if not understood, for his *Tractatus Logico-Philosophicus*, written partly in the trenches of World War I. This treatise and his later *Philosophical Investigations* caused many to consider him the greatest philosopher of the twentieth century.

The Wittgenstein Palais at Alleegasse 4, now Argentinierstrasse, was situated a few hundred steps from Vienna's fabled Karlskirche with its green cupola and two great columns. Also, a mere couple hundred steps from the fabled Baroque church, was the old corner building, Karlsgasse No. 4. This address was where Johannes Brahms had lived the last twenty-four years of his life, ultimately moving from a two- to a spacious three-room rented apartment on the third floor. The view from his music room/living room afforded a splendid panorama of the Karlsplatz with its magnificent church. The walk from Brahms's apartment to the Wittgenstein Palais and its legendary music salon took fewer than six minutes.

The decorative panels of the Wittgenstein Palais's darkly tapestried music salon presented minstrels and knights, while Max Klinger's double-fisted white marble torso of a pensive Beethoven rested on a pedestal eyeing two Bösendorfer Imperial grand pianos positioned with keyboard facing keyboard. A two-manual pedal organ faced the back wall. Over the decades, luminaries from the music world attended or performed in the music salon: Clara Schumann, Joseph Joachim, Gustav Mahler, Richard Strauss, Maurice Ravel, Arnold Schönberg, Alexander von Zemlinsky, Bruno Walter, and, of course, Johannes Brahms, for whom a special chair near the exit was furnished so that he could come and go at will. It was here that the composer's velvety Clarinet Quintet was premiered.

And it was *from* here that the afflicted oldest son of domineering Karl Wittgenstein escaped. The musically/mathematically idiot savant Johannes "Hans" Wittgenstein vanished without a trace in America at the age of twenty-four in the year 1902.

7

"So why is Brahms considered as good as Bach or Beethoven?" Tina asked her sister as they neared the outskirts of Dallas. Her forte was animals, not classical music.

"Hmm. That's a biggie. It's not so much a question of being 'as good as,' as it is, how can I phrase it, being a superb master of one's art in one's own lifetime, plus creating original music that lasts and affects others beyond one's own lifetime. So Bach, Beethoven, and Brahms all qualify for that. Not that those other great composers of the past don't qualify as well." Megan smiled, " It's just that their names don't begin with B and they weren't German."

"Well, that's a mouthful," Tina laughed. "I guess all I can say is I know Brahms wrote a lullaby."

"On another topic," Megan said, not wanting to press or embarrass her sister, "I'm thinking that since we found our Brahms bust in an Austin antique shop, and we know that it was locally owned, that possibly it was originally owned by the Ney Museum."

"Oh, and the Museum didn't like the head because it was damaged so they just threw it away? Dumped it in a garbage can? Come on now!" Tina snickered.

"No, no, I don't mean that. I'm remembering that after Ney had been in Texas for a few years and her studio was built, she had some of her busts of German notables sent over to her from her Schwabing/Munich studio, and it could be that the Brahms bust was one of the items sent. But it might have gotten dented in the shipping, so she left it in a storage closet or cupboard or some place and just forgot all about it. On the other hand, the scholarly world would certainly know if a bust of such a famous man had been cast. But perhaps it was sent over in its plaster format and cast in bronze later in Texas."

"So call Jacquelyn and ask her," said practical Tina.

"That's exactly what I'm going to do." Megan pulled her red-cased iPhone out of her shoulder bag and tapped in the Ney Museum's number.

"She might not be there on a Monday," Tina said as the phone rang. But it was Jacquelyn herself who answered. Megan immediately put her phone on speaker so Tina could hear the conversation.

"Dr. Crespi! What can I do for you? It was so much fun being with you and your sister yesterday."

"Thank you, for us, too, and please do call me Megan. I'm so glad I caught you because I have something to tell you and something to ask you."

"Sure, go ahead."

"Okay. This morning, before we left Austin, we drove through the downtown area and stopped at an antique store. I found something unusual and bought it. Now this is hard to believe, but I think it is a bronze bust of Brahms! One from his early years. It's badly battered, as though it had been rolled across a floor, but the features are exactly like the ones we know from photos in his pre-bearded period."

"That's wild!" Jacquelyn exclaimed.

"What's wilder is a fact I just established. Joachim and Ney *and* Brahms were all in Hanover in the year eighteen fifty-nine. If Ney was creating a bust of Joachim for the King, which she finished the next year, she could also have been modeling a clay head of Joachim's best buddy Brahms for Joachim. After all, Ney did create a marble bust of Joachim's wife, a well-known contralto named Amalie Weiss, even though its completion took another eight years."

"Oh, yes. You and Tina saw their busts—Joachim and Weiss—in our museum. I've always felt sorry for Amalie since it must have been so difficult to keep on with her career while bringing up six children."

"I agree. But did you know that after they'd been married twenty-one years Joachim suddenly divorced her? To Brahms's outrage, I can add. And then she got her career back on track. She even toured America."

"Oh, how wonderful! I'll have to add that to her bio here in our Museum."

"Good idea. But what I want to ask you is do you know of or think that there might have been such an object—a bronze bust—in Ney's Texas studio, Formosa, that somehow got sold or thrown out after Elisabet died, or maybe later, after Montgomery died?"

"I really doubt that. Their loyal housekeeper of so many decades, Cenci, would have kept an eagle-eye on everything. And you know Ney's close friend Ella Dibrell and her husband bought Formosa after she died with the express purpose of preserving it intact. They would hardly have thrown any piece of sculpture out, no matter what the condition. Nor would they have sold it. And if it were a head of such an eminent person as Brahms, surely Ney would have mentioned it at least once in the years from eighteen fifty-nine to nineteen seven when she died." Tina, who had been listening intently, nodded affirmation while keeping her eyes on the road.

"Well, tell me this, Jacquelyn," Megan persisted. "What precisely were the artworks she had sent to her from Munich?"

"Hold on. Let me pull up a document."

"Great. Thank you." There was a long pause.

"Okay, here it is. Hmm. Quite a number of them. I'll read you a few of the more important ones. With the exception of the marble busts of her beloved Edmund and herself, all the other busts are in plaster. Let's see. Okay. We've got Jacob Grimm of the Grimm brothers, King George the Fifth of Hanover, Italian Giuseppi Garibaldi, German chancellor Bismarck, mad King Ludwig of Bavaria, contralto Amalie Weiss Joachim, and...wait! Joachim's bust isn't in plaster, it's in gypsum."

"What's *gypsum*?" Tina asked, completely befuddled.

"Nicer than plaster, not as nice as marble," answered Jacquelyn easily.

"Jacquelyn, any mention of an unidentified bronze bust in your document?" asked Megan impatiently.

"Sorry, no, not as such. But I see here we do have Ney's

eighteen ninety-seven draft of a letter she sent to the Houston and Texas Central Railroad complaining of 'irreparable' damage to two busts shipped to her from Munich. Only one is identified: a Count von Werthern."

"All right. Well, that certainly could be a lead. See if you can find out anything more about the unidentified one. The fact that it was damaged is certainly suggestive. Thank you for letting me pick your brain and your archives!" Megan's voice was high with hope.

After the two colleagues said goodbye and Megan had tucked her iPhone away, she turned to her sister.

"I am *not* going to let this matter lie, Tina. This bust of Brahms *had* to make its way to Texas and to Ney's city of Austin somehow. And the key hidden inside it *has* to open *something*. Something either in Austin or Austria or possibly Germany."

8

"That's odd," Intagliatore thought to himself as he started to unlock his basement studio that late afternoon. Without the key having engaged, the door swung open. The shelf-lined interior holding several small clay figure sculptures and some two dozen plaster busts was brightly lit.

"What's this? I *never* leave lights on," the sculptor said out loud. And surely not just before leaving Hamburg for Italy. Frau Salem must have come down here looking for something, he reasoned. But how careless of her to leave the lights blazing and the door unlocked! Not like her at all.

He walked to the center of the long basement room. Everything seemed intact. But then he realized not everything was in place. His painstakingly modeled plaster bust of the bearded Brahms was not where he had left it in the far corner of the room on a worktable. *Diavolo*! Where was it? He began walking around the studio, eyeing each artwork. No, no, no. Not there. Denying reality, he went around the room again. The four photographs of a bearded Brahms were on the wall above his main worktable, but the bust was missing. How could such a thing be? Why was the studio door not locked? His bewilderment gave place to anger. Intagliatore turned off the lights, locked the studio door, and trotted briskly up the stairs. Frau Salem better have a good explanation.

He found the woman in the kitchen, laughing and chatting away with her friend Fräulein Felizitas, the young housekeeper from next door. The two women often shared a cup of tea at this time of day, and after Herr Intagliatore had left for Italy, Frau Salem had proudly shared with her young friend the exciting reason for his trip—a bust of Brahms in *marble*!

But when her employer angrily told her that he had found the door to his studio unlocked and the lights on, Frau Salem did not have an explanation. She was, in fact, flabbergasted. She knew nothing about the door's being unlocked or the lights having been left on. She herself hadn't been to the studio during his absence. Since she had cleaned it the day before the Signore left for Italy, there had been no reason for her to enter the studio. And no, certainly no one had contacted her, asking to be let inside.

Intagliatore was more mystified than ever. Who would specifically want his Brahms plaster bust as opposed to the other busts, many in marble, of famous persons, past and present, lining the walls of his studio? Who, except the eccentric who had commissioned the bust? But who was that? Dealing with a representative was definitely not going to be helpful unless the police were called in. Did he want to do that? Would they be able to ferret out the identity of the anonymous patron who had paid for everything, including the marble, in advance?

Which begs another question, he thought. If it was his mysterious client who had stolen it, why not wait until the bust was carved in marble?

9

"Well, Edgar, dear, your first 'Double B Composers' concert last night was certainly a great success," said Agatha Endlich, coming out of her office and smiling at the man through the open door of his adjacent office on the top floor of the Musikverein. It was close to six o'clock on Tuesday evening and the Maestra was on her way out of the building. This was the first sight she'd had of the General Director since the concert Monday evening.

"Do you think so?" Edgar Wittgenstein looked up from his desk and beamed at the conductor.

"Absolutely! The audience loved it. *I* loved it!"

"Then it's definitely *our* 'Double B Composers' concert. Your interpretations of both symphonies, especially the Bruckner, were instructive and intriguing."

"Why, thank you for that, Edgar! That's so *encouraging*."

"Ha! As if you needed to be encouraged."

"You'd be surprised. I can take all the encouragement I can get nowadays." Her tone of voice sounded a tad forlorn as she continued. "Even if Lukas Eifer and Christian Begeist and even Stefanie Schreib did come backstage to congratulate me," she laughed hollowly without enthusiasm. Agatha was referring to her two fellow conductors who headed the Grazer Philharmonisches Orchester and the Bruckner Orchester Linz, respectively, and the revered music critic of Vienna's daily newspaper *Der Standard*.

A thought struck Edgar. Although the two had known each other for almost three years now, it had always been on a work level. Both were busy bees and had little time for socializing. But it might be nice to relax a bit with the innovative young conductor who was open to unorthodox suggestions such as the one he had made concerning pairing Bruckner and Brahms. Edgar acted on his thought.

"Say, do you have any dinner plans? Or someone to rush home to? I was thinking we might hash over our next concert plans off-site for a change."

"Over some hash? What did you have in mind?" Agatha grinned teasingly.

"Someplace nearby and someplace heavenly," Edgar teased back.

"Now where's that supposed to be in this packed part of town?"

"I'm talking about a certain restaurant of a certain really grand Grand Hotel one block away from us and just across the Kärntner-Ring if we go out the Bösendorfer Strasse exit." Edgar was referring to the historical horseshoe-shaped boulevard that enclosed the inner city and to the palatial old hotel near the Musikverein, built in the 1870s.

"The restaurant there on the seventh floor is called 'Le Ciel,'" proclaimed Edgar, making his point.

"Sounds extraterrestrial. By all means let's ascend," Agatha smiled.

Nine minutes later they were sitting at a table for two underneath the enormous inward slanting windows of the elegantly furnished restaurant. Three large blue ceiling panels confirmed its name.

"We could sit on the roof terrace, should you prefer," Edgar offered.

"Oh, no, no. It's perfect here underneath these celestial chandeliers," protested Agatha, already studying the menu. They both chose Danube salmon, and their discreet waiter recommended a 2017 Villa Tolnay. The white Hungarian wine loosened their tongues.

"Edgar, tell me. How are you related to the Wittgenstein family?"

"Oh dear," he sighed," it's *immensely* complicated. Are you really sure you want to know?"

"Absolutely."

"Well, it goes way, way, way back, and I rarely see any of the present-day members of the clan here in Vienna. Although we all have one thing in common: all Wittgensteins play the piano. My branch originates with the Viennese steel magnate Karl and his wife Leopoldine, both adept instrumentalists, and descends through their fifth child, Helene Wittgenstein, who, like her eight siblings, also played piano. Just before the turn of the twentieth century she married a finance minister in the Austrian government, Max Salzer, and later he oversaw the Wittgenstein family fortune, despite the fact that he was Protestant. So I am the, now hold on, great-great-great-grandson of Helene Wittgenstein. One of her children, Felix Salzer, became a musicologist and settled in America after World War II. But his son, *her* grandson, Frank, wanted to grow up in Austria, took the name Wittgenstein after arriving, and met and married a Jewish woman here in Vienna. Their children had children, and one of them, Patrick, along with his wife Sarah, had me. *Alles klar*?" They both laughed heartily.

"Everything *totally* clear," Agatha finally blurted out.

"So, how much Jewish blood do you think you have in you, Edgar?"

"About a pint." They laughed again.

"And you, Agatha?"

"A little less. I gave at the office."

The joviality continued through dessert as they discussed various characters who had become legendary in the Musikverein world. Finally, over prolonged coffee, Edgar waxed serious.

"So, Maestra, I take it you do not have anyone waiting for you at home?"

"I'll only know that when I'm back home."

"All right. *Be* mysterious if you like. But tell me, how did music come into your life?"

"Do you want the short version, the medium length version, or the long version?"

"Whichever you care to give me."

"Well, it goes back, not as far as you, but to my Bohemian grandfather who was a violinist and who communicated his love of music to his children, and they—my violinist mother, in my case—to their children. I was curious about every instrument in the orchestra and my obliging parents supplied me with a battery of wind, string, keyboard, and even percussion instruments—*they* are what await me at home, incidentally, the instruments," Agatha admitted, laughing. "Plus Fanny, my dog. Named for Fanny Mendelssohn, of course."

"But of course. And how did you move from playing various instruments to conducting them in an orchestra?" Edgar was intrigued on several fronts now.

"My father read about a new two-week seminar based in, of all places, Dallas, Texas: The Dallas Opera's Hart Institute for Women Conductors, and I was allowed to leave Vienna for the Wild West. Wound up staying there for three years, as it turned out, and benefitted enormously. When I returned to Austria I applied for the just-vacated post of conductor of the Bruckner Orchester Linz and won the position! Their first-ever woman conductor, and you can bet the newspapers had fun with my last name, which the approving Dallasites early realized meant 'finally' in English. That was seven years ago, during which I conducted a lot of Anton Bruckner *and* Philip Glass, and now here I am, resident conductor of our Vienna Philharmonic for the past three years, thanks to huge public pressure to admit women to its orchestra! With such a sexist 'tradition' going back to eighteen forty-two when the orchestra was founded, it's been really hard for the nineteen of us females to make our way. And that's in an orchestra of one-hundred-and-forty-five permanent members! But I've gotten off the track, haven't I? Anything else you want to know about me?"

"Are you single?" an admiring Edgar suddenly heard himself asking.

"Yes, I am. Are you?"

"I am a widower. My sweet wife Tanja died five years ago—ovarian cancer. Now work is my life partner."

"Oh, I am so sorry! And it is the same for me, work—my life partner."

"Which direction is home for you?" Edgar asked Agatha as they exited the lobby of the Grand Hotel at a little past nine o'clock. To their joint surprise, dinner had lasted some three hours.

"We left work so quickly that I need to return to my office and pick up a few things."

"Well, I'll walk you back in that case."

The two chatted animatedly and split up only when they reached the Musikverein—Edgar heading for home and Agatha for her office. She was surprised to find the door open. On her desk lay an envelope with her name printed in large letters. Oh? That wasn't there before. Mystified, Agatha used her right forefinger to rip it open. A single page lay folded inside. The Maestra unfolded it and gasped. Printed in bright red letters were the words:

> NEVER PAIR CATHOLIC BRUCKNER AND PROTESTANT BRAHMS AGAIN. YOU HAVE COMMITTED AN OBSCENITY AND IF YOU CONTINUE WITH YOUR TRAVESTY YOU WILL BE PUNISHED.

10

The two Crespi sisters had returned to Dallas on Monday afternoon in good spirits and were delighted to be reunited with their respective doggies, all six of whom had been houseguests of Tina's best friend Bill Frey, who lived near her and was the owner of two Japanese Chins himself. Each sister had tasks to tend to. Tina would be hosting little Button while her sister was away and Megan could always check out what he was up to by connecting with Tina's PetCam system that gave her indoor views and audio of her sister's house. How often Megan had greeted her excited little canine this way while away on trips.

That evening Megan needed to pack for Europe as her flight to Hamburg left the next day shortly after twelve noon and, with plane changes in Washington, D.C. and Frankfurt, frustratingly, did not arrive in Hamburg until ten o'clock the next morning. But that was fine with Megan. She had plenty to keep her occupied with a new book she was writing on twentieth-century women artists and composers in Vienna and Berlin. She also needed to go over the lecture material she was scheduled to present in Vienna, announced as being about Klimt and music.

Megan's packing preparations were unevenly divided among work, clothes, and vitamins. Recently, now that she was in her mid-eighties, she'd had to add a few medications to the pill category, but after all, gotta keep the old body going, she comforted herself. All work-related items were easily contained on her MacBook Air gold laptop, a welcome companion usually inside her slim but expandable black sling travel bag. It had discreet, secure pockets for her iPhone, a wallet containing a small stash of euros, and her passport. Inside a sizable back pocket was a lightweight miniature version of the sling bag for daily use. This smaller beige one she wore suspended in front of her neck so as to have hands free should she fall—something she realized was more likely now if she didn't pay attention to what she was doing. In fact the last time she was in Vienna she had tripped over a bicycle lane curb while crossing a busy intersection and had fallen. It was a miracle she wasn't hurt, since she had landed squarely on her nose and forehead. She somehow attributed this miracle to ballet lessons as a child, but her sister, who was with her on that trip, said, with her usual dark humor, it was just "beginner's luck."

Megan's few articles of summer clothing were divided into two uneven categories: lecture and non-lecture. For the formal events she wore comfortable black Skechers, black socks, black slacks, a black, red, and white striped long-sleeved cotton blouse, and a tailored black vest to conceal the fact that, after retiring from teaching, she no longer bothered to wear a constrictive bra. "Just like Eleanor Roosevelt," she wrongly told herself, judging from her low hanging bosom in photographs.

Non-lecture, everyday wear for Megan comprised two pairs of slacks, one beige, one white, a multi-pocketed beige vest, three T-shirts in black, green, and beige, three long-sleeved blouses in green, beige, and brown, and two elegant long scarves, one in white and beige and one in white and black. In addition, three pairs of white panties and a supply of pads in case of nocturnal leakage, a pair of beige Giesswein house slippers with bluebirds woven on them, long-sleeved dark blue cotton pajamas, and a lightweight tailored black raincoat with its removable hood completed her wardrobe. All fit easily into a tall, black carryon roller bag with two front zipper compartments.

Perhaps the most important wardrobe item, in Megan's eyes, was her fold-up cloth black hat with narrow brim and its matching neck roller band which she wore on all plane flights and in concert halls as a defense against the continuous drafts no one else appeared to feel. To lose her voice on a lecture trip was one of Megan's perpetual fears. Just like Eleanor R. again, or an opera singer, she declared to herself defensively.

Anything else to take to Europe? Well, there was that one thick, 699-page paperback she had begun romping around inside of lately, Jan Swafford's magisterial study of Brahms. Yes, she would download that as an ebook. Airplanes could only take you so far; books could take you to the moon and back.

Megan had finished packing.

11

A frustrated Mario Intagliatore had decided not to contact the police about the theft in his Hamburg studio. His efforts to contact the third party in regard to his commissioned Brahms "with beard—*mit Bart*" bust had been totally unsuccessful. Apparently, the person was as elusive as his unnamed patron. When the prepaid block of marble arrived from Carrara, he would model a second bearded bust of Brahms and carve it into marble with the help of his local German stone cutter and his amazing new Italian pneumatic pointing machine.

One thing he had already done was to set up a security camera in his studio. That made him, to say nothing of Frau Salem, feel better about things. He would be attending the Brahms symposium on Wednesday afternoon with greater peace of mind. Perhaps that *Professoressa* Crespi might have some thoughts on any present-day Brahms zealots, including her colleagues, who might be lustful enough to crave a plaster model of the "essential" bearded Brahms.

12

One person who had never known much about the physical Brahms, other than that he was a habitual cigar smoker and had a luxurious long beard through which he loved to run his fingers, was the offspring, five generations later, of Johannes "Hans" Wittgenstein. In the year 1902, at the age of twenty-four, Hans had mysteriously disappeared in America. In Vienna, the *Neues Wiener Tagblatt* awkwardly reported the event on May 6 of that year thusly: "Industrialist Karl Wittgenstein has suffered a terrible misfortune. His eldest son, Hans (24), who has been in America for about three weeks on a study trip, has had a canoeing accident."

For years afterward the family tried to track down the missing son; theories ranged from abscondence to Venezuela to suicide in Florida's Lake Okeechobee. Karl Wittgenstein forbade the family ever to utter his name again, just as he would when his son Rudolf committed suicide in Berlin two years later, "purposefully also" in the first week of May. The domineering pater familias, who died in 1913, did not live to see another son, Konrad, do away with himself on the Italian Front of World War I in October of 1918.

However, Hans, the wayward son, the idiot savant who was constantly compelled to translate the world around him into mathematical formulae, the phenomenally talented musician limited by his father to playing his instruments—violin, organ, and piano—to only one hour a day, this Hans had not committed suicide; he had not done away with himself. Quite the contrary. He had reinvented himself under an assumed surname that meant "write" in German and he had found employment as a high school mathematics teacher in Virginia City, Virginia. There he married a charming botany instructor and helped identify the more than 350 species of fish in Chesapeake Bay. He entertained his wife with stories of growing up in a Viennese household that had a famous, white-bearded family friend, the great composer Johannes Brahms.

One favorite story was narrated many times. It concerned a visit from the legendary man to the family during which he singled out ten-year-old Hans and asked why his hair was cut so ostentatiously short. The answer was that his nanny believed it would grow again more vigorously if she cut it down to the roots.

"There is a much more feasible method," Brahms had announced cheerfully. "Champagne! It is the best hair restorer in the world. We should apply that now to little Herr Wittgenstein." A bottle of champagne was brought into the room where young Hans stood, the unwilling center of attention. Brahms filled a glass, clicked his tongue approvingly, then dipped his hand into the glass and splashed Hans with three powerful swings as if he wanted to baptize him with holy water. The whole family found Brahms's "baptism" delicious fun, except for Hans, who was greatly embarrassed. But when he was older and Brahms had passed away in 1897, he felt honored to have been singled out by the illustrious old man with the great long beard. And that baptism story was recounted ad infinitum by Hans to his own family.

After the end of World War II, at the age of sixty-seven, although wanting to have nothing to do with the Wittgenstein family, Hans relocated to Vienna under his assumed surname, with his wife, son Herbert, and three grandchildren. One of the grandchildren's grandchildren, a musicologist and pianist with a penchant for Brahms, had made a name in contemporary Vienna of the twenty-first century.

Her name was Stefanie Schreib. As the great-great-great-granddaughter of Hans Wittgenstein, she prized but guarded her secret family history. She was music critic for Vienna's leading newspaper *Der Standard.*

13

It wasn't that he didn't appreciate and adore them. As conductor of the Grazer Philharmonisches Orchester, of course he did. And reviews of his performances of Haydn, Mozart, and Beethoven always valued his understanding of the old masters. No, it wasn't that. Nor was it a case of classic versus romantic periods in music. It was simply a case of loving Brahms more than any other composer. Johannes Brahms! Creator of some of the most poignant, most interesting, most beautiful music written in the second half of the nineteenth century in all areas except opera. And yet he was and remained a conscientious disciple of the classical tradition even if moving on. And wasn't that what all the so-called "Romantic" composers had done, break away from the revered forms of classical music? With Beethoven and even Schubert as the triggering link, hadn't all the great composers of the nineteenth century used elaborate harmonic progressions, considerable ranges of pitch and dynamics, and emotional expression? Wasn't this true not only of Brahms, but also of Schumann, Liszt, Chopin, Berlioz, and Wagner? Yes, certainly, yes, but for the Graz conductor, Brahms's music was the apotheosis of Romanticism.

Maestro Lukas Eifer, a short, heavyset man sporting a white mustache that descended into a great white beard, not only identified with the music, he identified with the man. He too, at sixty-three, was a lifelong bachelor despite occasional infatuations with women; he too, had, despite an often jolly and jesting nature, an inner, overriding melancholia that sometimes made him cranky and even lash out at his closest friends. "Just as Brahms had done with Joseph Joachim and just as Brahms had done with Clara Schumann," Lukas would tell himself in moments of regret. He often thought of how his idol, in a letter to Clara of 1893, wrote of his Intermezzo in B minor Opus 119, Number 1 in terms of melancholy. This had greatly influenced Lukas's interpretation of Brahms's music.

He felt a bond with the composer who had answered a plea from a conductor about to conduct his Second Symphony, to omit the "lugubrious tones" of the trombones and tuba from the idyllic opening of the first movement. Brahms had responded by saying he had indeed tried, but could not, characterizing himself as a severely melancholic person who felt black wings constantly flapping overhead. It was for him an *Et in Arcadia ego* moment, meaning that death is present even in nature's calm bountifulness. He pictured to himself an eponymous seventeenth-century painting he had seen in the Louvre once by Nicolas Poussin showing a scene of shepherds examining an ancient tomb.

"Yes," Lukas told himself out loud, "in my black moods I am like Brahms and he is like me."

Lukas's younger brother, Robb, deputy director of library, archive, and collections at the Musikverein, with whom he was staying for his week away from Graz, agreed. "You are the twenty-first century incarnation of Johannes," he was fond of telling his brilliant brother.

What a farce with the Vienna Philharmonic regarding its juxtaposition of backwoods Bruckner with worldly Brahms, Lukas went on to complain to his adulating sibling.

"I had to pretend enthusiasm with Agatha backstage after the first offense," he confessed, "but, really, only an uncultured or naïve conductor could fall for such an irrational coupling of symphonies. And she's tasteless enough to plan on doing it three more times! It's crazy, I tell you, pitting the two symphonies against each other. Or? And would she really be able to complete such a grueling schedule?"

An adoring Robb had taken every word his older brother said to heart.

14

Stefanie Schreib's *Der Standard* review of Maestra Agatha Endlich's novel concert pairing the first symphonies of Bruckner and Brahms appeared early Tuesday morning. Although usually reserved with her praise, some readers might say even stingy, her approving comments on the conductor's interpretation of both symphonies bordered on extravagance. Schreib had expected the Maestra to conduct Bruckner with authority; after all, she had led the Bruckner Orchester Linz to new heights during her tenure in that old city with its Baroque center spanning the Danube some twenty miles south of Austria's northern border with the Czech. What Schreib wrote about, however, was the conductor's ability to draw out the ebb and flow of tonal ambiguity and her mastery of the stormy intensification passages and their rapid modulations. She "sculpted musical phrases with her baton." And Maestra Endlich's joyous handling of the Scherzo's contagious rhythms animating all sections of the orchestra was matched only by her superb balance of improvisation and drama in the final movement. "Rarely," Schreib declared, "had a conductor honored Bruckner by maintaining such a balance of the ebbs and flows of his musical force."

Perhaps such praise for an experienced conductor of Bruckner was only to be expected by Schreib's readers, but tribute was also enthusiastically and equally paid to Endlich's interpretation of the Brahms symphony with its dense web of musical motives. In her role as conductor-scholar, the Maestra had emphasized the composer's more modern choice of harmonic musical architectures built on the relationship of thirds rather than of fourths and fifths. By the time she ferried her audience to the last movement, listeners were ready for the simultaneously terrifying and sublime effect of a long minor key articulation that gives way at last to the transcendent C major alphorn call. No wonder the audience was on its feet for a second time during the concert. It was not a case of which composer was "better." It was an evening of abundant gift giving. From the two composers and from the conductor. This was how Schreib concluded her article and it triggered a small tsunami of like-minded letters to the editor of Vienna's *Der Standard*.

15

Linz Conductor Christian Begeist's copy of Schreib's Tuesday morning review of Monday's Double B Composers concert had landed in the waste basket behind the couch where he sat in his Wiener Neustadt host's home. It was a good shot, considering that he had suddenly tossed it over his back. A moment later, the robust, clean-shaven man with a prominent nose, dark eyebrows, and a short Prussian haircut doubled over, not in pain but in pure rage.

How could that uninformed, presumptive woman have written a good review of Monday's concert? Didn't she know about his own upcoming Bruckner Series? By god, it must be clear to all music lovers that this ambitious woman conductor was purposefully undercutting him. How many people would want to travel the hundred and fifty kilometers up to Linz now to hear *his* Bruckner performances? Designed to time with the release of his new biography of the master. Of course Maestro Begeist went backstage to congratulate Endlich: she must *know* that he understood exactly what she was doing. And it was obvious she got the message when he looked her hard in the eyes as he "congratulated" her. The exact two words unsmilingly murmured to her were: "Interesting interpretations." What he was really thinking was that this little female bitch, by pairing the composers, was committing an absolute travesty.

Actually his two words to her could cover a bevy of musical sins, but the particular sin in her case was the lack of attention given to straying strings and the sloppy handling of the winds and brass, especially the shrieking trumpets and trombones, to say nothing of her inexplicable pauses. If this was how she could murder Bruckner's First Symphony, what in god's name was in store for the other three?

If a woman could get away with interpreting the master in such a pseudo-dramatic, shrieking manner, then all he held holy in music was in peril.

Maybe Bruckner was lucky never to have married. He knew *he* was. Being a conductor demanded all one's time, all one's experience, all one's mastery of the profession. Just because a woman dresses like a man, wears a pantsuit and resorts to semaphore, doesn't translate at the podium into credible conducting. How painful it must have been for the more experienced musicians in the orchestra. Painful and insulting! This entire spectacle was the result of feminism. The same shrieking feminism that demanded *women* players in orchestras. Thank god the Vienna Philharmonic had held out until 1997, and then, saints be praised, it was only that old Hungarian harpist Anna Lelkes who'd been around since 1974 anyway. At least harpists sit at the edge of orchestras and don't disturb the emotional unity of male players. But now all orchestra sections had women players, including his own Linz Bruckner Orchester. He had been *forced* to audition them. And even worse, orchestras were now being coerced into accepting racial minorities. Think how distracting that is for the *look* of an orchestra! Please god, give me unification, not diversification!

Kudos for Maestra Agatha Endlich from accomplice Stefanie Schreib? He knew that Schreib was filthy rich; lived on the entire top floor of a building she owned just off the Kärntner Strasse in the heart of the city. Probably both women were feminists. Perhaps they were lesbians. Possibly they were both Jewish. He'd check all that out when he had time.

In the meantime he had better get cracking. He needed to call Dieter Unfug, previously his assistant conductor until Linz had cut its budget. With only a part-time job at the moment, Unfug was living with his mother in Wiener Neustadt, conveniently just some forty-five kilometers south of Vienna. Incomprehensively, the talented young man had been passed over in his audition for resident conductor of the Vienna Philharmonic three years ago. The post had gone to Agatha Endlich.

Well, never mind that. Who knows? There might be a light at the end of the tunnel.

16

It had been a long flight from Dallas, with three airport changes, but Megan did not feel at all tired. On the second, overnight lap of the trip from D.C. to Frankfurt, her fold-out brimmed cloth hat, matching warm neckband, and eye mask were all at her side, ready for sleeping. But first, some work on her new book. She wanted to complete a chapter on the women artists and composers in the first fifty years of twentieth-century Vienna and Berlin. The total disruption caused by Hitler and his henchmen had taken its toll, particularly on those women artists who happened to be Jewish. Megan sighed, as she had so many times when pondering that cruel chapter in human history. As a teacher who had lectured for some forty-one years, first at Columbia University in New York and then Southern Methodist University in Dallas, she was determined that her students should know about that still-recent chapter of civilization. The subtitle of any lecture course or seminar she gave was always the same, whether it be on nineteenth or twentieth century art: "The Cultural Content of Artistic Form." Once a year Megan addressed that bleak historic time of the first half of the twentieth century with its two World Wars by teaching about the compelling German artist Käthe Kollwitz, whose life extended from 1867 to eight days before Hitler cowardly committed suicide in his underground Berlin bunker in 1945.

The lecture, she discovered, was needed. Once, after her presentation of Kollwitz, a student from her class of some ninety students came to her office to ask: "Professor Crespi, what is a refugee?" But apparently the lecture took hold. Once when she had finished her Kollwitz presentation and had just left the auditorium, a former student came up to her and whispered triumphantly: "I know who you taught about today—Kollwitz." His answer to her astonished question as to how he could possibly know was: "Because a lot of your students are looking really sad and not even talking to each other." When she glanced around at the students still exiting the auditorium, some of them were wiping their eyes. Behold, the power of Kollwitz!

Megan had had her own experience with refugees. In October of 1956, as a newly inscribed art history student at the University of Vienna, she was witness to the massive flight of refugees to the Austrian capital from their own country during the Hungarian Revolution. She had an Opel Caravan station wagon. She could help. All classes forgotten, she and other university students who had cars did help by bringing Hungarian escapees across the Austro-Hungarian border to Vienna, often three times a day. Empathy. Kollwitz's single greatest command. Empathy had been urged by the artist over a span of some sixty-plus years; pleaded for through pungent, condensed graphics and with compelling images cast in bronze. Now, Megan needed to present a Viennese equivalent to Kollwitz, and she had not yet been able to choose from several worthy female artists.

Reflecting on all of this, she unconsciously raised her shoulders and let out a long sigh. Then she turned her attention to tweaking and finessing the images and audio for her Vienna lecture on Klimt and music. With that task momentarily perfected, she did the same with her Hamburg presentation on the visual Brahms. Although she had printed her texts for both lectures, she was pretty sure she would be inspired to ad-lib a number of humorous aspects. Well, time would tell. It was always reassuring to have the words on paper as well as in her head. Colleagues had told her for years that her impromptu remarks were some of the most memorable parts of her presentations. But she was taking no chances.

The rest of her laptop activity consisted in answering an Everest of email that had accumulated while she was in Austin. Most of them were from former students who kept in regular touch, and she was only too happy to mentor them. She was also still in close contact with her fellow retired colleagues as well as the young ones who had replaced them. They chatted about everything. But it took time. And more and more people preferred communicating via Zoom or FaceTime. She disliked both more than she liked them, because people's faces always seemed distorted, including her own whenever she forgot to hold her head at just the right level and distance from her laptop screen. When she was doing creative work, she loved to listen to music; her favorite providers were Alexa and YouTube. Not that she watched the latter, but she could choose which singers, instrumentalists, and orchestras to listen to as she wrote. The greatest boon to her work, however, was the wealth of information to be gleaned so instantly from the Internet. Information which could be verified or amplified in her huge library of books, lovingly acquired over seven decades. Literally every room in her home had shelves for books, even the kitchen and bathrooms.

That love of books was inherited from her American mother and her Italian father. The two had met and married on the Spanish island of Ibiza and when Megan was due, they made a quick round trip to the home of Megan's mother in Winona, Minnesota, so that, being born in America, she would be an American citizen. Back in Spain— Barcelona this time—the rise of Franco two years later forced the young family of three to flee to Italy, where, after two years of life under Mussolini, the family wisely relocated to America, not to cold Winona, but to warm Dallas, Texas, because of an ad in *The New Yorker* touting its comfortable climate. The single thing Megan's parents had taken with them on all these uprootings was their books. And they had passed that love on to Megan. As she thought about this for a moment on the plane taking her back once again to Europe, she smiled in contentment. A moment later she was sound asleep, her sleeping items still at the ready by her side.

17

For the University of Hamburg's upcoming International Symposium on Brahms, Mario Intagliatore had agreed to the one-week loan of his new plaster bust of the bearded Brahms. A photograph of it had even been used for the symposium's publicity. How could he ever have imagined that the promised plaster bust would be stolen right out of his basement studio while he was away in Italy selecting the marble for it? And he had only discovered the theft two days ago. Fortunately, he was still able to keep his promise to the handsome new all-glass museum of 173 classical plaster casts on the Uni-Campus. But it would have to be the duplicate bronze bust he had cast for himself twenty-some years ago when fulfilling the Walhalla commission for a marble bust of Brahms. And that bust was *ohne Bart*—without beard.

Never mind. At least it was Brahms. Today he had supervised transfer of the beardless bust to the university's popular museum, one of some twenty unique collections housed in various buildings throughout the vast campus grounds. The installation inside the Archaeological Institute of Plaster Casts was simple enough and followed the museum's policy of maximum visual placement that allowed public viewing of some of the collection's sculpture from outside as well as inside. Arranged within a rising pediment with the tallest figure, Apollo, as the central point, are two great centaurs facing each other, kneeling women, ferocious warriors, fallen combatants, and small animals at the two corners. A heavy dark beige curtain, its folds rising from floor to ceiling, enhanced the whiteness of the casts, just as the green garden roof above merged the museum with its environment. Truly a masterpiece of a museum, Intagliatore thought to himself.

The symposium itself would take place behind the great curtain in one of the most novel aspects of the building: an underground auditorium. Decorated to look like the inside of a Greek temple, it provided a most unusual backdrop for individual seminars and classes. A stage was at one end and at the other end was the usual overhead projection booth equipped with the latest technology. Two students had carefully centered and placed Intagliatore's Brahms on a white plinth at the back of the stage. The sculptor was assured that the auditorium would be locked overnight, and he had returned home pleased that his Brahms, albeit the Brahms *ohne Bart*, would be gently presiding over tomorrow afternoon's symposium.

18

"Well, *hello* there!" Edgar Wittgenstein said when he heard Agatha's inquiring voice on the phone. It was nine-thirty Wednesday morning and he was sitting at his desk in the Musikverein.

"Are you all set for this evening's concert?"

"Yes I am, Edgar, but that's not why I'm calling you." Her voice sounded tight, unlike herself.

"Oh?"

"I wonder, it's a strange thing to ask of you, but I wonder if you could possibly come over to my place? Right now?"

"Agatha! Is something wrong?"

"Well, let me just say it could be. Can you come?"

"Of course. I'll be there as fast as I can. You sit tight, okay?"

"Thank you, Edgar, thank you."

"Oh, wait! where do you live?"

"How stupid of me. Sorry! I'm in the ninth district, Porzellangasse Number thirty-three, near the Goldener Drachen. It's apartment six, just ring the bell and I'll buzz you inside."

"Right. I love that Chinese restaurant. Be there as soon as I can." Edgar glanced at his watch as he walked briskly to his Volvo, parked near the Ring on a side street. Because of the usual traffic around the great boulevard, it took almost as long for him to reach his car as it did to drive and park on the Porzellangasse.

"Thank you for coming," Agatha said when he entered her apartment. She was holding back a black and white collie who couldn't wait to sniff out the new arrival.

"Please forgive Fanny," she said. "She has so few visitors. And I feel safer with her here."

"Safer? Why would you need that? This is a great neighborhood, so close to the Ring, and low on crime."

"Yes, I know. But that's why I wanted you to come over. About feeling safe. But here, please sit down, Edgar." Agatha pointed to the couch and easy chair in the room beyond. Once they had been seated and Fanny had tentatively approved of Edgar, Agatha spoke.

"I don't know whether I should be concerned for myself or concerned for tonight's performance. Look at this." Agatha picked up an envelope on the coffee table and handed it to Edgar. It had her name printed on the front and was unsealed. Edgar opened it, drew out the piece of paper inside and read it aloud.

"Never pair Catholic Bruckner and Protestant Brahms again. You have committed an obscenity and if you continue with your travesty you will be punished."

"How did this threat get to you?"

"It was on my desk after Monday's concert. Facing me. I saw it after we split up and I returned to my office."

"Monday evening! And you've been *living* with this ever since? Please tell me you've contacted security."

"No. I haven't told anyone. I guess I thought it was a bad joke. And that it would go away. But now that our concert is tonight, I woke up with the jitters. Perhaps it's an actual threat. To me, to our orchestra, to the building, I don't know what to think. Do you think I'm just being foolish?"

"Not at all, dear Agatha! There are crazies in every profession, and especially in ours. Fanatics who push their wild ideas, from radically reinterpreting the masters to denying the authenticity of authorship, to cruel, domineering conductors—not you, dearie—to nay-sayer critics who never have a good word for any performer. Oh, the music world is full of jealous kooks bent on revenge. This has to be a threat from one of these deranged types—someone who, well, it's hard to tell from the note, isn't it, whether the writer is for Bruckner or for Brahms." Edgar reached over from his chair and gently patted Agatha's hand as she sat next to him alongside the arm of her couch.

"Yes, I hope this is just a kook. But what does he—or she—mean by saying I will be 'punished'?"

"Let's hope, if something does happen tonight, that it's just loud booing, or some attempt to disrupt things between movements."

"That's probably it," Agatha said, not sounding very convinced.

"The longer I look at this threat note the more I have to wonder *which* composer has been slighted. Is the writer pro-Bruckner or pro-Brahms?"

"Yes, I've been wondering about that too. You just can't tell from the sentence. And I even wondered if the note could be from some sort of religious fanatic: someone who thinks it is wrong to play music by composers of different faiths in the same concert."

"Good thinking," said Edgar. There's certainly an emphasis on Catholic versus Protestant."

"Right, but we can't tell if the writer is one or the other. It's all just so mysterious. What worries me most, Edgar, is the word 'punished.' *How*?"

"I don't want you to worry anymore, my dear Agatha. When I get back, I'll alert security. They in turn will advise the ushers when they arrive this evening. And just for our peace of mind, I'm going to ask the police to assign us two officers, one backstage and one at the rear of the auditorium."

"That makes me feel better, Edgar."

"And I'll have our own security officer keep an eye on your office, since someone obviously managed to slip inside after you'd gone down to your dressing room to get ready for the performance."

Agatha sighed and took Edgar's hand, pressing it hard with both her hands.

"Thank you, thank you."

The two sat silently for a minute. Then Edgar stood up, a sense of purpose lighting his face.

"I better get started right away. Do you feel all right being here alone?"

"Yes, yes. I suppose I just needed a little moral support. You've given me that." She walked him to the door, Fanny following closely behind. Just as Edgar stepped across the threshold, he wheeled back toward Agatha, a smile on his face.

"So whom do you prefer? Bruckner or Brahms?"

He could hear the Maestra's melodious laughter all the way to the street door.

19

The pilot's sudden announcement in English and German that they would be landing at the Hamburg International Airport in thirty minutes impinged upon an exciting dream Megan was just concluding and she awoke with a start, never to know its finale. But no mind, she was more than ready to get off planes. There had been too many connecting flights: Dallas to D.C., then overnight to Frankfurt, and only now to Hamburg. She had slept soundly through the night, albeit without her sleeping hat, neck scarf, and eye mask, all of which she found unused by her side when she awoke. That surprised her. This had never happened before. She cleared her throat. Had the hated dreaded overhead drafts given her a cold? No. Thank heavens, she felt all right.

Passport check and transfer to the Hamburg-bound flight had been easy if somewhat rushed. The one-hour flight passed quickly and soon she was gathering up her things and packing them back in her roller bag and large sling purse. As soon as she got inside the Hamburg terminal she would be on the lookout for her longtime friend, Tönnies, who lived in the city and who had offered her his guest room while she was there.

Tönnies Helfer was a retired ophthalmologist and an enthusiastic world traveler whose favorite country was Greece. He had visited Megan in Texas and even stayed in her getaway house on Lake Bonham, some seventy miles northeast of Dallas. Tönnies loved Megan's poolroom and worked out with the weights, the stationary bicycle, and the treadmill. He also swam strenuous, noisy laps in her Endless Pool. Megan, on the other hand, swam stationary laps for a quiet thirty minutes, soundlessly underwater facing the continuous, powerful water stream, while wearing her snorkel. Then they both visited the built-in sauna for fifteen minutes and, after that, it was showers and then collapsing on wooden recliners in front of the poolroom's fireplace, listening to Bach's unaccompanied cello suites. A wonderfully healthy routine much appreciated by her German friend who pronounced it almost as good as being on his favorite Greek island. Tönnies was also an extremely handsome man with a limber mind and genial personality. Megan hadn't seen him in almost ten years and had looked forward very much to enjoying his lively company once again.

The plane's landing was smooth and soon Megan was rolling her travel bag into the huge hall of Terminal 1, its great sloping dome supported with alternating narrow bands of steel and glass opening to the sky. The flight information boards were gargantuan, just as Megan remembered.

She heard her name being called excitedly as she stepped off the escalator into the arrival hall and there he was, dear Tönnies, with his happy, wide smile. They exchanged a long embrace.

"You haven't changed a bit!" Tönnies said at the same moment that Megan declared, "You look just the same."

Arm in arm, with Tönnies easily guiding Megan's roller bag in front of him, they walked past the baggage claim and traversed the airport's grounds to the car park. Tönnies had treated himself to a swank, white Audi A3 convertible and as they drove into the city with the top down, Megan was full of admiration not only for the car's smooth performance but also for the sparkling, greatly modernized area along the river walk.

"Would you like to view it all from atop the Venusberg?" Tönnies asked. There was a brief pause before his guest answered.

"Ordinarily, I would love to, but it's almost eleven and if we get me installed and settled in your place, plus lunch, we won't have much time before the Brahms Symposium begins at two and I do hate the feeling of being rushed just before I give a speech."

"Of course. I understand. Insensitive of me. Perhaps tomorrow on the way back to the airport. I just wish you didn't have to go on to Vienna so soon."

"Oh, me too. My schedule is just crazy this time."

"Ha! When is it *not*?" Tönnies chuckled knowingly.

"What time is our Elphi performance this evening?"

Megan was referring to the sensational new 360-foot-high Elbphilharmonie concert hall in the harbor section of the city. It was situated near visiting cruise liners on the Grasbrook peninsula of the Elbe River, and the towering, sloping-roofs edifice, one-third red brick below, two-thirds glass above, contained the large, five-level auditorium they would enter that evening. It had quickly been judged as one of the most acoustically advanced concert halls in the world. The Philharmonie Orchestra site on the Elbe had immediately been nicknamed Elphi by Hamburg residents. And the Hamburg symphony had changed its name to Elbphilharmonie Orchestra.

"The concert begins at eight," Tönnies answered. "And your Brahms symposium ends at five. So we'll have plenty of time for a relaxed dinner. I've made reservations at an Italian restaurant I'm sure you'll like, and, like the parking, it's inside Elphi."

"*Inside*? Megan questioned unbelievingly. Tönnies laughed merrily and explained.

"Yes, inside. Elphi is a multi-purpose edifice. Not only does it have several restaurants set inside the gigantic glass structure atop the original old red brick warehouse 'plinth,' you could say, but the new structure also has a hotel and forty-something fancy condominiums. Plus, two zippy silver escalators to get you to all these places."

"Well, that's certainly different. I can't wait to see it all. So Elphi's two auditoriums are housed in the new glass building and not below in the warehouse."

"Definitely not down there. Our huge new concert hall, which is literally in the round, and its smaller auditorium partner—the *Laeiszhalle*—are both high up. The acoustics are also excellent in the *Kleiner Saal* with rippled wooden walls. Our string players get a kick out of drawing their bows across them." Tönnies turned to her and made a dramatic gesture as if doing so.

"Tönnies! Please keep your hands on the wheel!"

Ten minutes later the cordial physician was showing his American visitor into the upstairs guestroom of his capacious condominium on the second floor of Klopstockterrasse 2.

20

By the time Maestra Endlich reached the Musikverein staff entrance at Bösendorfer Strasse 12 for her second Bruckner/Brahms performance that evening, her self-confidence was restored and the silly complaint note went quite by the wayside. Fanny's loving canine company and Edgar's supportive visit had done much to calm her anxiety, and her delicious beef stew dinner had left the conductor energized and ready for the evening's work.

A broadly smiling Edgar was on hand to greet her. He had already checked out her office and all was in order, no juvenile threats on her desk this time. He complimented Agatha, as he had two nights earlier, on the discreet elegance of her appearance. Her regular performance outfit was completely white: low-heeled white shoes and white dress pants with a matching white long-sleeved, open-necked blouse. Over the blouse she wore a lightweight white vest in order to deflect audiences from breast size calculations to orchestra size confirmation. The vest was brightened by a discreet sprinkling of Swarovski rhinestones. Critics had already had a field day over this blur of white, accusing her of blinding audiences and of stealing the limelight. But the Maestra remained steadfast in her sartorial choice, and her fans adored her for doing so.

After making her usual brief visit to the musicians lounge to hail her instrumentalists, Agatha retired to her small dressing room, nodding in confirmation at the empty left side of the small dressing table. That was where she kept her baton in its beautiful rosewood case. The chief stagehand Peter Heimnis, who was responsible for bringing it in its case to and from the conductor's podium, had already been there. Agatha liked to have the case open on its own small music stand flanking the podium. Good, all was in order, the baton within easy reach.

Then, assuming a palms-open lotus position on the floor, she briefly meditated on the program at hand. It had been so difficult to "pair" the two composers since Bruckner had written essentially eleven symphonies over a period of forty years and Brahms had written only four, but granted over less a time.

Performance of the Bruckner Fourth Symphony came first; after intermission it would be Brahms's Second Symphony. The Maestra had never been able to decide which work she preferred. Both had such appealing aspects. The Bruckner, in E flat major, she had conducted many times during her years in Linz in its 1878-80 version. The composer himself had given it a subtitle "Romantic." Such a stirring beginning! After a brief horn call alert above shimmering tremolo strings, a six-note descending opening theme beginning with high strings, reeds and full calls on four French horns, is soon joined by trombones, trumpets, tuba, woodwinds, while a vigorous kettle drum underpins four different themes in the dense first movement. So characteristic of Bruckner! No wonder Gustav Mahler paid respectful attention in his own works to the "country bumpkin," as critics called the older composer. Just as Bruckner, in turn, honored Wagner in his compositions. And then after the mournful second movement and a galloping, celebratory scherzo with its horn calls unmistakably announcing a hunt, there was that haunting long finale with its fully articulated rich chord that never seemed to end—one long victorious Amen.

Brahms, on the other hand, with his D major Second Symphony's peaceful, noble first movement with French horn invitations blessed the listener with a light and airy atmosphere recalling, critics liked to point out, Beethoven's "Pastoral," Sixth Symphony. Agatha laughed when she recalled the composer's purposefully deceptive letter to his publisher in which he described the work as so melancholy he wouldn't be able to bear it. The second movement presents its first two themes simultaneously with the bassoons ascending and the cellos descending. A third theme, syncopated and scored for the woodwinds, is lighter in style and character. And then an intermezzo, rather than traditional scherzo, comprised the third movement, its first theme presented by an oboe with pizzicato accompaniment. The final movement's theme began quietly, but its texture would expand to a triumphant setting of the theme for full orchestra culminating, lest the audience forget the key signature, in a fortissimo D major chord sounded by the trombones.

Oh, it was too hard to decide between the Bruckner and the Brahms symphonies! Both were marvelous. How Agatha hoped to convey this to her audience. The first Double B Composers concert had gone so well, been so enthusiastically received. She would try with all her might to make this performance as successful.

An abrupt knock on the door interrupted her reflections. Strange. Staff and players knew this was her quiet time. When she got up and opened the door, a nondescript young boy of no more than sixteen awkwardly thrust an enormous bouquet of red roses at her.

"From your admiring ushers. Toi, toi toi," he yelled quickly over his back as he disappeared down the hall.

Bewildered, and more put out than pleased, Agatha left the door ajar and desperately looked around her dressing room for something in which to put the unwanted bouquet. Finding nothing appropriate, she stood it upright on the floor in a far corner of the small room. Water and vase would have to wait.

"Everything all right, Maestra?" It was the chief stagehand passing by.

"Um. Oh, yes, everything is okay, Peter. Thank you."

Agatha closed her door quickly. Her musical reverie had prematurely ended. She must now pull her thoughts together. The wall clock showed it was nine minutes to eight.

Anton, Johannes, help me do your symphonies proud!

21

Tönnies was as good as his word. While Megan unpacked and changed into her lecturing outfit, he prepared a simple but delicious mixed salad and sliced peaches lunch for them to eat unrushed before leaving for the afternoon event. Megan was the keynote speaker for the opening day of a Brahms symposium at Hamburg University, and she truly regretted not being able to stay for the whole week of talks and music. But Vienna called and its invitation had come weeks in advance of the Hamburg one.

"You've never been to the Archaeological Museum on Uni-campus, have you?" asked Tönnies as they finished lunch.

"No. I've never even been to Hamburg University."

"Well, then, you have an interesting surprise waiting for you."

"I did look up the museum online and am aware that the auditorium is underground, if that's what you mean."

"Yes. I was hoping you'd be surprised, but I should have realized that when you prepare in advance, it includes staking out the guest institution."

"Ha! I suppose it's because once, when I was scheduled to give a lecture at a certain Canadian university, my taxi dropped me at the wrong auditorium on campus. I was twenty-one minutes late to the right one, perspiring like mad, panting my lungs out and facing an angry audience. I never, ever want that to happen to me again!"

Tönnies dropped Megan off at the correct campus museum, the Archaeological Institute of Plaster Casts, then disappeared to find a nearby parking place. The musicologist who had invited her to speak, a Dr. Ernst Erkunden, came to the entrance, beaming at Megan. He led her slowly past the fascinating sculpture-filled, grounded pediment facing the all-glass building façade and down into the auditorium with its painted columns and overhead friezes that so convincingly conveyed the impression of a Greek temple. Megan was pleasantly surprised to see a bronze bust of the bearded Brahms atop a pedestal on the low wooden stage underneath the projection screen. What a fuss had been made when some vandal affixed a fake beard to the un-bearded bust at Walhalla some years ago.

Quickly setting up her MacBook Air laptop and small thermos of water on the lectern and checking the microphone status with a student techie, Megan hastily made the acquaintance of the other three speakers. Out of the corner of her eye she saw Tönnies enter the auditorium and take a seat in the back. After some minutes, with the auditorium completely filled, the speakers took their seats and Dr. Erkunden gave a thankfully short introduction. He mused about how a Texas woman with an Italian surname and the "doyen" authority on the Austrian artist Egon Schiele, came to write a book on the changing image of the German composer Beethoven and then followed up with a volume concerning another German composer, Brahms.

"And so now I give you Frau Professor Doktor Crespi," Erkunden's introduction concluded. Megan quickly walked to the lectern, acknowledge the applause, and at her laptop command, an opening image appeared on the large screen above her.

It did not show Brahms. It was a black and white photograph of his living room/music room.

"I am sure every single person here knows the Vienna address where Hamburg's great composer lived for the last twenty-four years of his life," Megan said, smiling at the audience. Before anyone could answer she flashed the address on the screen: Karlsgasse Number 4. Megan had positioned the words on the upper right of a late nineteenth-century photograph of the old three-story building in which Brahms had lived.

"It was torn down exactly ten years after his death to make way for what became the main building of the Technische Universität of Vienna. The composer's three rented rooms were almost literally within a hefty stone's throw of Fischer von Erlach's majestic Karlskirche with its high dome, framed by two giant columns adorned with helical figured friezes."

On the screen appeared a panoramic image of the great Baroque church and its immense square, the Karlsplatz, with clusters of buildings reaching toward the Ring—all it had looked at the time of Brahms. Megan invited her audience to imagine him in his role as choir master of the Vienna Singverein, and later director of the Musikverein, emerging daily from his Karlsgasse 4 building and striding resolutely, with his hands clasped behind his back, past the front of the Karlskirche and through the Resselpark to reach the Wiener Musikverein building on the far side.

Megan let the pictorial route across the Karlsplatz sink in before proceeding to her next image. One which, taking up the whole screen, left her audience voicing its pleasure and recognition: Rudolf von Weyr's life-size 1908 marble statue in the Resselpark. It presented an elderly, slightly squirming Brahms on a tall plinthed seat. Prostate on a high step to his lower right, a sorrowing woman in drooping classical drapery reaches for an abandoned lyre. Yes, everyone in the audience knew and loved that authoritative image of the master. The monument is directly and equally between his Karlsgasse apartment and "his" Musikverein. The composer would have walked across the site of today's statue every day. So was this going to be about the *visual* Brahms? It was known from her introduction that the speaker had written books on both the visual Beethoven and the visual Brahms. The audience relaxed.

The next image answered that question. Apparently not. It was the photograph of Brahms's living room/music room they had seen before. What was the Frau Professor Doktor up to?

"Yes, we are going to look at the *visual* Brahms today, but not his countenance, which everyone in this hall knows intimately, with and without that luxuriant beard. I want to show you this afternoon a different sort of visual Brahms. *His* idols and pictorial wall images, and what they tell us about *him*. Thanks to photographs *lovingly* taken of Brahms's inner sanctum by his friend and future biographer Max Kalbeck a few days after the composer's death, we can examine centimeter by centimeter Brahms's three rooms: his living room—

slash—music room, his library, and his bedroom. Here on the right, you see his piano, a large J. B. Streicher und Sohn instrument on permanent loan to the composer from the Viennese maker. Note that the pianist from Hamburg did not equip himself with a Hamburg Steinway!"

The knowledgeable audience chuckled quietly. Megan nodded and showed a same-size second image to the right of the photograph. It was a detailed watercolor copy of Kalbeck's photograph by Wilhelm Nowak.

"Brahms used the piano top—adorned with this rich blue cover with fringes—as a counter for his neatly laid out personal belongings. You will note the four ornate oriental rugs on the floor, the animal skin rug on the far left, and the fancy fringed velvet coverlet over that small round table with three thick beveled legs on the right, next to the couch. It was on this sewing table that Brahms laid out his smoking utensils and cigars. Equally important to him was the coffee maker with large brew head on the low table in front of the couch. You can also spot a cup and saucer and containers for cream and sugar cubes. On the wall above we can see the images of some of Brahms's idols. Even though it is high on the wall and to the far right, this idol on a bracket is the first thing we cannot help but spot. Who is it?"

"Beethoven!" the audience shouted, happy to be questioned.

"Yes indeed. Hardly a surprise. It is a sixty-eight-centimeter-high marble bust by the German artist Hugo Hagen, based on Franz Klein's life-size bust of Beethoven of eighteen-twelve. It was acquired when Brahms was forty-two years old. Hardly a surprise since we know how greatly Brahms venerated Beethoven. We can recall how comforted the young Johann had been, years earlier, to see that beloved image in the camp of the musical 'enemy,' Franz Liszt."

Megan's listeners nodded in agreement.

"But Beethoven was not the only great 'B' in Brahms's life. Lower down on the wall, to the left, we see a laurel-wreathed bronze profile of—do you recognize him? Otto von Bismarck, the 'Iron Chancellor' of the newly unified German Empire. A politician on a musician's wall? But this is entirely representative of Brahms—a man of the world who took a keen interest in politics and whose reading matter on trips always included a volume of Bismarck's speeches. The passage of time did not cool his ardor for the politician who would die just one year after Brahms. In the last decade of the composer's life he accepted honorary presidency of the Vienna branch of the *Club Zum Ausspannen der Pferde*—Club for the Unharnessing of the Horses—a zealous society of Bismarck fans who had organized with the express purpose of unhitching the horses of the recently dismissed ex-Chancellor and pulling his carriage themselves to honor his triumphal return to Berlin. Sounds exciting, yes? Well, unfortunately, the plan was thwarted by Kaiser Wilhelm's police."

A sound of surprise circulated through the auditorium. Megan nodded.

"The emperor's extreme conduct leading up to World War I could be a lecture in itself, but let's continue looking at this wall of Brahms's idols and images. Ah ha! There's a framed print of Raphael's *Sistine Madonna* hung in a place of honor right over the couch. Now this Italian ambassador to our Teutonic Kaffeeklatsch reminds us that Brahms was an enthusiastic lover of Italy and Italian Renaissance art. Although he could not be lured to England or America—he had a horror of being on water—he did make *nine* summer trips to Italy, the one country where he purposefully closed his ears—he found Italian music 'ghastly'—and concentrated instead upon the land's natural and artistic beauty. And he loved to rummage through antique shops for old prints."

Megan paused for a quick sip of water and looked out at the audience.

"Ah! But I see some of you are already looking past the two Thonet bentwood chairs and to the left of the Raphael engraving and the rocking chair. Yes, it is a most peculiar sight there on the wall, isn't it?" Megan was referring to a framed portrait reproduction, the right half of which was covered by a curtain.

"The curtain you see was especially made at Brahms's request by his landlady." Megan juxtaposed another image with the Raphael. It was the entire portrait showing a lyre-holding muse.

"Now, just what was it about Ingres's handsome portrait

of *Luigi Cherubini and the Muse of Lyric Poetry* that needed censorship? After all, as you see, the lady was dressed."

A silence prevailed. Megan continued.

"It's just that for Brahms, forlorn but steadfast bachelor and habitual brothel visitor, it was a much too physical presence of the muse of song who dares to crown Cherubini's spiritual accomplishments. '*Dies Froonslüüd mog ik nich*—I don't like this hussy!'"

The audience laughed at Megan's affectation of the Plattdeutsch Hamburg accent. Megan beamed up a second photograph of the room which showed the piano at full-length from the side.

"The artwork you can see reflected in the large mirror over the piano is a reproduction of the extreme left-hand portion of Guido Reni's *Aurora*, yet another print Brahms had acquired in Rome. And to the extreme right you can just catch a glimpse of his desk, so let's look at a photograph taken especially of that modest writing desk and the room beyond, Brahms's library."

Engaged audience members leaned forward in their seats to study such a telling, revelatory photograph of the images on and above the composer's desk and beyond that, through an open door, the books on the far wall of the library.

"You can see that centered on the wall above the desk there's a framed copper engraving of the *Mona Lisa*—not surprising—but look there just under it and at eye-level when Brahms was sitting at his desk. Can anyone see what's there?"

The audience was mute. People were straining to make out what was in the frame beneath. Megan ended the suspense

"It's too small for us to see well in this photograph, but Max Kalbeck identifies it for us: it is a double medallion portrait print of Clara and Robert Schumann."

"Ah!" responded the audience in one breath. Suddenly a man's voice boomed out from the back of the room.

"*When are you going to tell us that Clara and Brahms were lovers*?"

"Not in this lecture, and, as far as I'm concerned, not ever," answered Megan calmly. "I believe they loved each other deeply and had a lifetime of intercourse, but not in the way you imply."

The sympathetic audience, shocked at the rude interruption, spontaneously began to clap at Crespi's artful answer. Most of them were in agreement with the speaker concerning the personal relationship of Clara and Johannes, fourteen years her junior. Yes, it was loving, even adoring on both their parts, and early engendering the intimate *Du* form of address during their forty-year friendship. But their love was not physical, most scholars believe.

"Now then, shall we continue our tour of Brahms's apartment?" Megan asked, sparking some listeners to cry out "Yes!" She circled the beam of her laser pointer around the desk image on the screen. It came to a stop by the library door molding.

"Well, one of the things we all can see hanging on the wall here is a *Bismarck Kalender* for the year eighteen ninety-seven with the page for thirty March exposed—the last day the ailing composer was able to leave his sickbed to adjust the calendar. He would die four days later at the age of sixty-three, just eleven months after the death, at seventy-six, of his beloved Clara." Megan allowed for a moment of silence, then spoke again in a more jovial tone.

"Before we enter the library, look what we can already spot through the entrance. See that tall, narrow wooden structure facing us? That is a standing desk; no chair for that way of working. Something we are coming back to in this age of constant sitting with one's computer. I bet some of you now use a standing desk—a *Stehpult*. Am I correct?"

Encouraging laughter sounded as two of the audience members shyly, then proudly raised their hands.

"Well, standing desks were very popular in the nineteenth century. I can think of at least four famous persons who used them: the Danish writer of fairy tales Hans Christian Andersen; the German theoretical physicist who originated quantum theory, Max Planck; Johann Strauss, Junior; and Kaiser Wilhelm the Second in his summer palace on the Greek island of Corfu, where I once traveled expressly to photograph it. And now we have five, counting Brahms, who stood to work. Does anyone here know of other famous examples?"

Amused silence reigned. Allowing herself a grin, Megan ad-libbed: "Well, for America I could name Thomas Jefferson, Benjamin

Franklin, and Ernest Hemingway. In England, Charles Dickens and Winston Churchill. I've always wanted to write an article on 'those who stood to write,' but I can't find any women who did so and I'm *not* going to write a historical study unless I can include a woman!" Enthusiastic applause came from the women in the audience and was joined by many of the men.

"But now back to Brahms, or have I said that before?" Megan continued, smiling and bringing a new image to the screen.

"This photograph of the library wall that looks out on the Karlsplatz shows us, hung above the side table between the two windows, a large, framed photograph of the Nazarene painter Peter Cornelius's cartoon for *The Apocalyptic Riders*—a really macabre theme that perfectly suits Brahms's musical and personal preoccupation with death."

Appreciative silence followed Megan's words as the engaged audience studied the grim image, an enlargement of which also appeared on the screen.

"Have you noticed the large valise on a chair to the right of the table?" Megan asked. "It calls to mind the idiosyncratic way of packing for one of Brahms's many trips: he simply piled his clothes onto that table-top, then tilted the entire heap into his open suitcase." Amused smiles animated the faces of the listeners.

"The many volumes of Brahms's library have all been studied and catalogued, and I will only say that their subject matters are a rich confirmation of his avid literary interests. Shakespeare was one of them. And the special role that folk music played in his compositions is paralleled by the fact that he owned eighteen well-thumbed volumes of the Arnim-Brentano collections of German folk tales, *Des Knaben Wunderhorn*. Not only Brahms, but, as you no doubt know, a number of composers set poems to music from the series, including...well, you tell *me*!"

The teacher in Megan had slipped out and she opened the palms of her hands invitingly toward the audience. The happily proffered answers included the names of Schumann, Weber, Mendelssohn, Mahler, Zemlinsky, Schönberg, and Webern.

"Excellent!" Megan complimented her happy audience.

"And now let us tiptoe into Brahms's bedroom, where he was

to breathe his last, and respectfully seek to identify the most intimate of his treasures."

Two photographs of the bedroom appeared side by side. To the left on a stove mantelpiece opposite the bed was a porcelain bust of Haydn, a fitting classical pendant to the matted and framed portrait print of Bach that hung in an isolated place of honor over the right side of Brahms's bed. Beethoven and Bismarck in the living room/music room, Bach and Haydn in the bedroom. What greater inspiration could one ask for? Brahms's final work, the eleven chorale-preludes finished in 1896, renders unequivocal homage to Bach. Brahms himself, Megan pointed out, was fond of remarking that the two most important events in his lifetime were the creation of the German Empire by Bismarck and the completion of the Bach Gesellschaft Edition, to which he was an early and ardent subscriber. Bach's scores were frequently to be seen on the music rack of his piano.

"And thus we see the two poles of Brahms's own life—his North German background and his musical heritage," Megan summed up. "If you look at the wall above the linen cabinet there on the left, you will see two more notable images: Shakespeare and, something we would certainly expect, a photograph of Robert Schumann, the man he adored and the husband of the woman he adored."

Now Megan showed her final image, and it was the same one with which her lecture had begun: the composer's living room/ music room.

"In closing, let us return to the living room—slash—music room and glance at one item we seem to have passed by before: the framed print behind the piano under the cherished Beethoven bust." A large image of the print appeared to the right of the wall photograph. Even so, it was difficult to define its subject matter.

"This, unfortunately undecipherable print might be, I suggest, one of the works owned by Brahms by the younger contemporary artist, Max Klinger. The Leipzig-born artist and sculptor—future creator of the famous life-size Beethoven monument exhibited to great acclaim in the Vienna Secession in nineteen-two—this artist had admired our composer from afar, and one day in eighteen ninety-four the mail brought Brahms a most extraordinary homage." Two images appeared on the screen: a red leather album cover and a photograph of the bearded Leipzig artist. Megan continued.

"It was a leather-bound series of forty-one etchings and lithographs by Klinger entitled 'A Brahms Fantasy.' Every note of the composer's *Schicksalslied* had been meticulously rendered on the plates that bore Klinger's fantastic pictorial response to Brahms's setting of Friedrich Hölderlin's fatalistic poem on human destiny. The Leipzig artist had addressed the surrealistic world of imagery conjured by the evocative power of a pianist inspired by his muse. In the opening image, entitled 'Evocation,' which you see here, the commanding muse appears naked—quite a contrast to the curtained-off *clothed* muse of Ingres's Cherubini image!" A close-up of Brahms's curtained Ingres appeared on the screen opposite Klinger's print.

"And at first Brahms had difficulty in appreciating such intensity. But as the magic of Klinger's imagery cast its spell, Brahms relaxed and even found himself experiencing emotions he had thought long since withered. Now think of this: he mailed the Klinger cycle to his dear friend Joseph Joachim with the following exhortation: 'Let yourself sink into the pictures some quiet hour, as high and as far as Klinger's fantasy can take you. Image, work, and sound will unite before you, and you will be, as I was, gripped and enthralled by the beauty and profundity of the pictures.'"

Now Megan showed an ensemble of eight prints from Klinger's cycle and allowed time for audience members to digest the linearly precise, surrealistic images. Then she continued.

"And by the way, Klinger's enchanting gift inspired an elegant, answering gesture from Brahms. In the summer of eighteen ninety-six he published his *Four Serious Songs* with a dedication to Max Klinger."

Noting how earnestly the audience was looking at the Leipzig artist's compelling images, Megan lingered before showing her final image. Filling the screen was the photograph with which the lecture had begun.

"We have looked this afternoon at Brahms's idols and the images he collected. And in doing so we have learned a great deal about Brahms the man. Perhaps the next time we listen to the composer's music we will recall the illuminating idols and images that make up the visual Brahms."

Megan was obliged to return to the lectern twice before the applause quieted down. The other speakers were positively received as well. Last in line to congratulate or ask a question of Megan was a tall, white-haired man with a short black beard. He addressed her in German, but when he identified himself in a melodious accent as "Mario Intagliatore," Megan immediately switched languages and they began speaking in Italian.

"That bronze Brahms bust you see on the stage is by me," he said proudly.

"Oh! Then you must be Mario Intagliatore, creator of the wonderful Walhalla bust of the master!" A new friendship was immediately set and sealed.

"*Grazie mille*, *Dottoressa*! I have a question for you that I hope you can help me with."

Intagliatore told Megan about the break-in at his studio and the stealing of his bought-and-paid-for bust of a bearded Brahms, even though it was just a plaster cast awaiting transformation into marble. And how the curious commission to create the bust had remained an unsolved puzzle.

"What a mystery!" Megan was intrigued.

"*Sì, sì! Esattamente*. What I want to ask you is this: do you know of any crazy Brahms fanatics in America who might be capable of doing such a thing?" Megan thought hard. She did know a few Brahms crazies across the ocean, but she could not think of any who might come to Hamburg, know about, and steal a bust of the master.

"How many people were aware of your anonymous commission?"

"That's the problem. Only my housekeeper who's been with me for years and years. Otherwise only the person who commissioned the bust and his representative who acted as the go-between but never gave me his name. And I was in Carrara recently, choosing marble for the realization of the bust, but certainly none of the stone cutters with whom I worked would have the means or the motivation to come to Hamburg and steal the plaster bust—well, as far as I can imagine, at least."

"Signor Intagliatore, I am so sorry I can't help you, at least not yet. But do give me your card and let me give you mine," said Megan, reaching for one in her sling purse. "If something comes up, I shall contact you *immediatamente*," she said, receiving a sudden parting hug from the lively, interesting man.

The rest of the afternoon passed quickly. Best of all, Tönnies was able to whisk her away in his car from the aftermath of the event and she could relax, even close her eyes for a bit before her host reached their next destination, Hamburg's sensational new concert home, Elphi.

22

Brahms's fortissimo D major chord, magnificently articulated by the trombones, had ended his Second Symphony and brought its discerning Vienna audience to its feet. Applause beckoned the Maestra back to the podium three times. It was apparent to all that the Double B Composers series was a triumphant success.

Edgar Wittgenstein was in the wings and greeted the Maestra after she left the stage and her standing players for the last time.

"Marvelous, Maestra, what a success." He gave his friend an enthusiastic embrace, then stepped back so other insiders could express their congratulations to the smiling, exhausted conductor. She had indeed done Anton and Johannes proud. A few enterprising members of the audience had managed to find their way backstage and were holding up programs for her to autograph. Finally, signaling Edgar to follow her, she broke away and hurried to her dressing room. Atypically, she had not been there to relax during intermission because she needed to boost the spirits of one of her cellists whose bow had escaped his hand and scuttled loudly across the orchestra floor during a stringent Bruckner passage. The cellist was humiliated beyond consolation, and it had taken all of Agatha's gentle energy to calm him.

Now, with Edgar behind her, she turned to address him as she opened the dressing room door, then stopped in her tracks. The disgusting odor of what smelled like feces engulfed them as smoke settled over them.

"What on earth?" Agatha began coughing, waving her hands before her face and turning away.

"It's a stink bomb! Stand back and let the room clear!" Edgar wedged his body between Agatha and the open door. Both were now coughing violently.

"What in god's name is *that*?" It was chief stagehand Peter Heimnis, the person charged, among other things, with bringing the Maestra's baton to and from the podium. A small man in his early sixties with short white hair, he was carrying the baton in its rosewood box back to the Maestra's dressing room and had stopped when he smelled the repulsive odor filling the hall.

"Somebody put a stink bomb in the Maestra's dressing room," Edgar explained angrily.

"Now who would do a thing like that?" Peter was incredulous. "Do you lock your door when you leave to conduct, Maestra?"

"No, never," she coughed, fanning her face.

"Well, we must have a very mean jokester around here." Peter said. "Here, better let me go inside and look around before you go in." He handed the baton box to Edgar.

Vigorously fanning his face, the experienced stagehand strode into the room. The poop smell was overwhelming. He looked around. There wasn't much to see. Just the dressing table and its chair. What was all that clutter in the far corner on the floor? Peter walked over to it and bent down. A big bunch of damaged red roses. Ugh! This was the source of that putrid smell. Wedged down deep underneath the long stemmed roses was a timer attached to a mousetrap, its spring sprung, and a small glass bottle of liquified feces that had been cracked by the spring's action.

"All right," Peter said, standing up and turning to the anxious couple outside the door. "Best not to go inside for a few more minutes until the stink dissolves. Someone has played a nasty joke. There's a huge bouquet of roses on the floor in there and deep down inside them, underneath the stems, is a timer, a sprung mousetrap, and a miniature, cracked bottle—a homemade stink bomb, I'd say. Somebody sure played a bad joke on you. I am so, so sorry, Maestra."

After Peter left them, Edgar pulled a shaken Agatha close to him and smiled concernedly down at her.

"Don't go inside your dressing room tonight. The janitor will take care of things. I'll just get your purse for you and then let's clear out of here."

"I don't carry a purse on performance nights. Just my house keys. They're inside the dressing table drawer."

Edgar turned to get them, but Agatha held him back. Her voice was trembling.

"Don't tell me this is just another juvenile prank. First I get a threat note, and now I get a stink bomb. And there are two more concerts to go." For one of the few times in her adult life, the Maestra broke into tears.

23

"Oh, I so love the Brahms Requiem," Megan exclaimed to Tönnies after they had consumed a delicious dinner at La Favorita, the crowded Italian restaurant inside Elphi's Plaza. It was obviously very popular, and her friend had been wise to reserve a table. Weight-watching Tönnies had ordered vitello tonnato and weight-despairing Megan had done the same, and it numbered among the most delicious either of them had ever eaten.

"My father used to spell out our names on top with capers, if we had it on one of our birthdays," said Megan, picturing to herself how much pleasure it gave him to arrange the black capers on top of the ensemble of flat veal slices covered by a tasty tuna sauce. "My brother especially loved it."

"I was so sorry to hear that he died recently," Tönnies murmured sympathetically.

"Yes. It was so sad. Tina and I flew to see him in Modesto, California, just a few days before he died. He had lost so much weight that, to us, he looked much younger and even good, if you can believe it. He died of lung cancer even though he had given up smoking decades ago. Same thing with my mother, only she never gave up smoking—smoked some three packs a day—Camels, Chesterfields, and Lucky Strikes. She died of *double* lung cancer. To the very last, and *in the hospital if you can believe it*, she was trying to persuade my father to sneak her some cigarettes."

"It was the thing to do in those early years," sighed Tönnies.

"It goes back further than that of course," Megan said. "Brahms, for example, was a chain smoker of cigars and cigarettes.

And think of Freud. He smoked twenty cigars a day!" She suddenly remembered something else concerning smoking.

"You know what? As a warmup with my classes, sometimes I used to show a cigarette ad and ask the students to analyze how well the illustration conveyed the desirability of smoking. I never said anything about the dangers, just let the students figure that out for themselves. And I believe it worked. In fact, I recently received an e-mail from someone I taught three decades ago, and it was a thank you for my 'pictorial anti-smoking propaganda.'"

Over cappuccinos their conversation turned to the program they would be hearing in another half hour. Megan was enthusiastic.

"It's so appropriate they're performing his Requiem here in Hamburg. You know Brahms finished it soon after his mother died," she said, "although composing it was pretty much in his head soon after his hero Robert Schumann's death. But it was the passing of his frail, elderly mother—she was seventeen years older than his father—that triggered its completion. And Brahms was only thirty-four. What a genius!"

"Didn't he specifically call it '*A German Requiem*' in order to make it different from the liturgical Catholic Requiem Mass in Latin?" Tönnies asked.

"That's right," said Megan. "He chose his pungent texts mostly from the Lutheran version of the Bible and the Apocrypha. And because, as an agnostic, he found himself unable either to believe or not believe in an afterlife, he directed his text toward a universal comfort to those who mourn, rather than the *Dies Irae* wrath of a Last Judgment."

"Well, the music *is* a comfort. I've always loved it."

"By the way, Hamburg's orchestra isn't the only one that's performing Brahms this evening. In Vienna they're playing Brahms's Second. And guess what? They are pairing it with Bruckner's Fourth. Such a novel idea, don't you think?"

Tönnies didn't answer. He was checking his watch.

"Hey, we better head to the auditorium; I want you to be able to get the full sense of it before the lights go down." His American guest nodded happily and Tönnies signaled their waiter. While they waited for the bill, Megan pulled the small black case she carried in her purse and inserted her seldom-used hearing aids. She did not want to miss a note of Brahms.

One long and one short silver escalator had already tunneled them up through a continuous narrow white "cave" to the Plaza shops level of the twenty-three-story Elphi building, where the NDR Elbphilharmonie Orchestra was to perform. Now, after two more levels, they entered the great circular auditorium that could hold well over 2,000 people and quickly found their seats. Tönnies had booked them in the area right behind and slightly above the orchestra which itself was situated in the round. Megan was stunned by the great sphere of the interior with its different seating sections and terraced tiers—at least five levels, if she counted correctly. What would that sort of surround sound do acoustically, she wondered. The solid but sensuous white balconies undulating above her were dappled with different sized, small projecting circles, as though they were round pebbles gathered from the seashore.

"This is the most extraordinary auditorium I have ever been in," Megan confessed to Tönnies, who gave her one of his broad smiles in return.

"I thought you might find it rather impressive."

"Impressive? It's more than that. It's unique. I know you cannot qualify the word unique, so I'll just say it's uniquely unique." They took their seats and began looking at the program notes. The cover featured a handsome photograph of Brahms, clean-shaven, as he looked during the time of his composing the Requiem.

"Hey, there's a tragic-comic story about the initial performance of the first three movements in Vienna," said Megan, laughing.

"If it has to do with thankless Vienna, I can understand," Tönnies said. "But tell me the story."

"Well, in the third movement, the percussionist totally misread the score markings. In the pedal fugue section where his repeated Ds were marked 'pf'—piano forte, he read the letters as 'ff,'—fortissimo, and so he continuously and completely drowned out the vocal soloists, the choir, and the rest of the orchestra!"

"Oh god! That's rich," sputtered Tönnies, laughing.

"*Here you are, my dear Tönnies*," a voice suddenly sounded over their heads. They looked up to see a genial looking man in his late fifties or early sixties beaming at them as, holding a ticket in his hand, he stood at the vacant aisle seat next to them. He was tall, with earnest hazel eyes, and an incipiently receding brown hairline. "And, *Megan*, what a coincidence!"

It was Harry Dunmore, one of Tönnies's oldest friends and former husband. A number of years ago Megan had hosted them both for a memorable week at her lake house in Texas: it was the week Michael Jackson died. How could she forget that, or Dr. Harry Dunmore? An American family practice physician with an additional degree in tropical medicines, he was on brief holiday from his current self-posting to Zimbabwe. Harry had devoted his career to helping the poor and the sick in India and Africa. Megan admired him greatly and was sorry to have lost touch with him in recent years. And here he was. Smiling broadly, she looked accusingly at Tönnies, waggling her finger at him.

"*You*! You planned this 'coincidence,' didn't you?" Both men laughed with delight at having successfully surprised Megan.

After a fast catchup, they turned their attention to the orchestra members beginning to gather onstage. Harry pointed out the 'tunnel,' as he called it, on stage right and left from which they emerged.

"Hey, is there an organ in Brahms's Requiem?" he asked.

"No," Tönnies and Megan answered simultaneously.

"There *is* one in Bruckner's early Requiem," added Megan, "but that's no surprise since he was an organist."

"Oh, okay. Because I just realized there's a hidden organ in this auditorium." Neither Tönnies nor Megan had thought about where an organ might be, but as they scanned the walls, they saw what Harry had discovered. Behind them, elegantly integrated into the west wall, were hundreds of long, thin organ pipes.

"I wonder if our programs say anything about the organ," Tönnies said, leafing through his slim program.

"Yes," he said, "here's something. It was built, as was the Elphi, in twenty-sixteen and, get this, there are four thousand, seven hundred, and sixty-five pipes, most made of tin, some four hundred of seasoned wood, plus sixty-nine stops, four manuals, and pedals. And, get this, it has two ship horns and a ship's bell. That makes sense, since here we are, in the middle of Hamburg harbor. Ah ha!

The organ can be played from a mobile console which can be pushed onto the stage for concerts."

"So where is the main console?" Megan wanted to know.

"Program says it's 'directly in front of the organ.'"

"Where the hell is the front of the organ," Harry was mystified.

"I think it must be behind the terraced seats there," said Tönnies, pointing.

"Shush," Megan warned them, "here comes the conductor! And our program says he's American."

The conductor, Albert Sullivan, had recently been plucked from the New York Philharmonic Orchestra. He had a long association with the Elbphilharmonie Orchestra, being its principal guest conductor from 2004 to 2015. And now he was the orchestra's chief conductor. By the sound of vigorous audience applause, he was greatly liked in his new home. He acknowledged his listeners with a deep and long nod of the head, then turned and faced his orchestra, waiting for the strings to fine tune to the oboe's repeatedly prolonged note A. Silence came quickly. Sullivan raised his baton and looked around briefly at the players, a radiant smile on his face. He gave a gentle downbeat, and with his left hand, caressed what slowly rose from the orchestra. Brahms's Requiem had begun.

24

Home again in her spacious top apartment on the Johannesgasse in Vienna's center, Stefanie Schreib was penning the finishing touches to her review of the second Double B Composer concerts. She had praise for both Bruckner's Fourth and Brahms's Second as symphonic masterpieces. Especially concerning the latter, as Brahms was her favorite composer. But she also had a few criticisms this time of Maestra Endlich's interpretations. On the whole, the Bruckner had been taken at much too fast a tempo, while the Brahms seemed almost too cheerful, the tempi of all its movements overemphasized. Stefanie could not quite put her finger on it and she did not want to use the descriptive word that had first occurred to her: desperation. She was searching for a milder term but had not yet found it.

Her mind went back to old desperations, the one that had propelled her great-grandfather, Johannes, "Hans," Wittgenstein to seek refuge in the New World for most of his adult life under the assumed name of Schreib. It was when his grandson, her widowed father, Georg Schreib, reached his mid-sixties that his mind seemed suddenly to have failed. He spoke almost exclusively about his grandfather's life as a child in the famous Vienna family, sometimes speaking to individual deceased members as if they were still alive. Most of all he told the "baptism" story about the family friend, Johannes Brahms. In fact, he had become fixated on this event, repeating the story over and over again, much to Stefanie's exasperation.

Last Christmas she had given to her ailing father eight photographs of the composer showing him both clean-shaven and bearded. He flipped through them without saying a word, then put the beardless images to one side and before anyone could stop him, ripped them in half saying: "This is not Brahms." After that he pressed to his heart the photos of the composer with a beard, and tearfully pleaded: "Oh, do get me frames for these wonderful treasures." A patient Stefanie had fulfilled his request and the framed images of Brahms *mit Bart* now graced the walls of his bedroom in the family apartment. The bearded composer appeared just as he had looked when visiting the Wittgenstein Palais in Vienna.

Just that afternoon the topic of Brahms with beard had come up when Stefanie received an anxious call from her aunt in Hamburg. She wanted to know if "it" had arrived. Yes, Stefanie reassured her, it had safely arrived that morning and she had immediately brought it to her father who, despite the impairment of two recent strokes, was able to convey his joy over the bearded plaster bust. It was now majestically installed on the dressing table opposite his bed in the small top-floor apartment next to her own.

"Well, thank god for that," Stefanie's aunt was saying. My housemaid would never have been able to handle a heavy marble version."

Stefanie's aunt was Margareta Wittgenstein, of the Hans Wittgenstein branch of the famous family, and her irreplaceable housemaid was named Felizitas.

68

That Wednesday evening after the Bruckner/Brahms concert, Maestro Lukas Eifer was pleased he had decided not to return to Graz until the following Monday. There were no concerts scheduled for his own orchestra and the next few days in Vienna he could hear the third Double B Composers on Friday and the culmination concert on Sunday with Brahms's Fourth and Bruckner's Ninth. Yes, the Grazer Philharmonisches Orchester could do without their conductor for a few more days.

And it was actually rather nice to spend more days in Vienna with his morale-boosting, younger brother. For one thing, his violin was still at his brother's place. He simply didn't have the time or even the energy to play it after he had moved to Graz from Vienna. And his brother, who loved hearing him play, urged him to keep it up.

"I do sometimes wish the violin were there for me in Graz," Lukas had once admitted, "but having it here, aside from seeing you, is one of the joys of coming to Vienna and then playing it for you."

Ah, dear, adoring Robb. How often had his doting brother called him the twenty-first century incarnation of Brahms. Such praise made up partly for the fact that the unimaginative Graz public had not received his own First Symphony with any palpable enthusiasm. Didn't audiences and critics realize he was carrying on the musical priorities and innovations of Brahms?

Thank god there were no music critics in Graz who favored the noisy concoctions of that country bumpkin Bruckner, he would fume to Robb. Hell, he understood that an understandably prejudiced Maestra Endlich, with a background as former conductor of the Bruckner Orchester Linz, might wish to present one or even two of the man's pretentious, hysterical, god-fearing symphonies, but to *pair* them with symphonies by Brahms! What was she thinking? And what a setback for the reputation of the Vienna Philharmonic.

Robb had told Lukas gleefully that Endlich's programming blunder might just be the tipping point for hiring a new resident conductor. And as an established Austrian conductor renowned for his interpretation of Brahms in particular, his brother would definitely be in the running. This was a certainty. After all he had guest conducted the Vienna Philharmonic twice in recent years and received good reviews each time. And on the second occasion, Robb had introduced his brother to an important figure at the Musikverein: its General Director, Edgar Wittgenstein. The two men had gotten along well, and the next time Robb passed Edgar in the hall, the genial man had stopped to remark how amazingly similar to Brahms his brother looked. Robb had to laugh. It was not amazing, at all, he confided, it was most deliberate. Then it was Edgar's turn to laugh.

"Ah, so that's why you two attend our summer concerts," the General Director had joked, adding, "What a sensation your brother will make when the Maestra's Double B Composers series begins, since Brahms is one of the two composers!"

"What do you really think are my chances if a replacement for the Maestra opens up?" Lukas asked his brother as they reminisced about the Wittgenstein encounters.

"I think it's more than possible that you might be named," Robb answered reassuringly with a gleam in his eye.

26

"Oh, dear, no, I better not have any more," Megan laughed, holding up her hand to stop Tönnies when he offered to pour her more Bailey's Irish Cream. After the fabulous Brahms concert at Elphi, the trio had headed to his home for a nightcap. Tönnies knew Bailey's was the favorite liqueur of his American friend, as well as almost the only drink she ever partook of, explaining always that she wanted to have a clear mind for work. And since she preferred research and writing to most other activities, she did indeed need to have an unobfusticated brain, as she termed it.

"Well now! How about playing and singing us something?" Tönnies pointed to the old Bechstein piano across the room.

"Yes!" Harry chimed in. "Play us 'Santa Lucia' and sing the words in the original Neapolitan dialect the way you sang it for us at your lake house."

"But I was playing guitar for that."

"Well, can't you do it on the piano too?"

"Yes, but I can do it better on guitar."

"Come on! We just want to hear the song and the words again. Doesn't matter which instrument," Tönnies added his plea.

"Well, all right," said Megan, walking over to the Bechstein and sitting down at the keyboard. She only played by ear on piano; flute was the single instrument for which she could readily read music, and that, therefore, restricted her to the treble clef. But she rolled out a cheery opening C major chord and began singing the lilting song in its charming Neapolitan dialect:

Comme se fricceca la luna chiena!
Lo mare ride, ll'aria è serena
È pronta e lesta la varca mia
Santa Lucia, Santa Lucia!

"Oh, that's fun. I think I got about two-thirds of it," said Harry.

"Me too," Tönnies agreed. "Sing it in Italian, Megan, and perhaps we'll understand all of it, okay?" Megan obliged, warning that the Italian text was somewhat different.

Sul mare luccica l'astro d'argento,
Placida è l'onda, prospero è il vento.
Venite all'agile barchetta mia,
Santa Lucia! Santa Lucia!

"That's great, I got it all," Harry said. "On the sea shines the star of silver, placid is the wave, prosperous is the wind, come to my agile little boat, Santa Lucia! Santa Lucia!"

"Just think. Brahms could have heard this song," Tönnies mused aloud. "He liked to vacation in Italy, didn't he, Megan?"

"Oh, yes, he *loved* spending time in Italy although he thought very poorly of Italian classical music. He went nine times in total, and he did visit Naples. So he could definitely have heard 'Santa Lucia' there. You know how he was fascinated by dialects."

"So, did Brahms speak Italian?" Harry wanted to know.

"Ha. He studied it intensively just before leaving for his initial two visits there, but he just couldn't get the hang of it, and gave up ever mastering it."

"Megan," Harry persisted, "how come you are so knowledgeable about Brahms?"

"'Knowledgeable'? I wouldn't say I was knowledgeable. I just know a lot of odd, peripheral things about composers and about him specifically because I love his music so much; I have a number of biographies about him. And that love for Brahms began very early. When I was at Barnard College I sang in Saint Paul's Chapel choir, right next door on the Columbia University campus.

We performed the Brahms Requiem my senior year under the baton of our wonderful choirmaster and organist, Searle Wright."

"Sometimes I forget you're an art historian by profession and not a musicologist," Tönnies pronounced, looking at Megan assessingly.

"Well, my Italian father played the violin, mandolin, clarinet and saxophone, and my American mother played the harp, so I grew up surrounded by music. And I have to confess I love music even more than art."

"Tell Harry about Interlochen," urged Tönnies.

"Interlochen? Switzerland?" Harry asked. Megan laughed at what to Harry seemed like a non sequitur.

"He means Interlochen, near Traverse City, Michigan and the National Music Camp where I studied two summers before and after my first year at college. The first year I studied art, but I was hugely intrigued by all the instruments the music students left in designated bins when we all gathered in the cafeteria for lunch. I would lag behind, surreptitiously open up the instrument cases, and quietly and quickly, try them all out. So the next summer I went back, not for art, but for music."

"Why did you especially pick the flute?" Harry wanted to know.

"Because it was the smallest instrument there and I realized I could travel with it easily."

"How long did you study flute, then?"

"Only for about a year, but with a famous New York flutist, Frances Blaisdell. That was enough to be able to make music with other students, especially my roommate Isabelle Emerson, who was a fine, as well as patient, pianist. We worked on the Bach flute sonatas and just recently got together in Santa Fe and played through them together. At that altitude you really have to have breath reserves!"

Tönnies stood up abruptly and, before Megan could stop him, poured more Bailey's Irish Cream into her empty glass.

"You naughty boy!" Her reprimand was cheerful and accepting. As she picked up the drink she turned to Harry.

"Harry. I so admire you for your work caring for the poor in third world countries. But tell me, what motivated you to take on such a demanding career?" Harry's answer was immediate and moving.

"Well, as a young man I looked at my life and found that the most ecstatic moments of happiness were when I was helping people, serving others. So I became a physician and was drawn to caring for indigenous peoples worldwide, in war and in peace. I have never looked back."

"And he is greatly loved in turn by hundreds," Tönnies added, smiling fondly at his old friend.

"And what about all the AIDs patients *you* have saved?" Harry asked his host.

Megan nodded in fervent agreement, knowing how personal Tönnies's commitment to fighting AIDs was for him, but she was unable to stifle a yawn. It was almost midnight. Her responsible host noticed the yawn and stood up.

"Come on, Megan, it's off to bed with you. You've had a long day and tomorrow you leave for Vienna."

"I am a bit tired, "Megan admitted. Tönnies and Harry walked her to the stairs and after prolonged hugs she bid them good night. Upstairs, she mechanically went through her bedtime routine and was asleep within a minute of hitting the pillow, the poignant sounds of "Santa Lucia" still in her head.

27

Jacquelyn McDonald, director of the Elisabet Ney Museum, had not let the grass grow under her feet. Intrigued by her friend Megan Crespi's theory that a bronze bust she found in an Austin antique store was that of composer Johannes Brahms as a young man, she had embarked on a thorough search of the museum's file cabinets, looking for any archival documents that might substantiate Megan's theory. And there were lots of file cabinets in the basement offices, all of them full of countless bulging folders.

She had found nothing. She decided to search the building itself. Beginning with the cellar she examined every inch of the floors, walls, and ceilings. Could there be a neglected shelf or nook that might contain something useful? Again nothing. On Thursday afternoon, after the museum had closed for the day, she conducted a search of the main floor, even having a staff member lift each bust and statue on exhibition so she could examine the floor or shelf beneath the heavy objects. Nothing. What was it she hoped to find? She didn't know. But now she was more determined than ever.

The museum's second floor, where more of Ney's work could be seen by the public, took less time to examine, but the persistent director's search was no less thorough. And no more successful. Discouraging.

What about the attic above? The small attic room where Ney slept occasionally? Certainly worth a look. Holding a three-step folding ladder in front of her, Jacquelyn carefully mounted the corkscrew metal stairway on the far side of the room. Once up, she walked over to the three tall interlocked narrow windows lighting the room and looked out over the great expanse of green lawn fronting the museum. Elisabet's view! She felt a brief thrill at the intangible, fleeting connection with the sculptor. Then the director's practical nature took over and she looked up at the wooden ceiling and the molding running along the four walls. Climbing up her stepladder she scrutinized the molding. It was all in good shape and fit tightly against the walls. Nothing. She repeated this process around all four walls. Nothing. Jacquelyn returned to the floor and, squatting down on her haunches, examined each of the wooden floor planks, now bulging with the passage of time, for cracks and crevices. There was definite aging but nothing under which something, a document perhaps, could be stored. Half an hour passed, then forty-five minutes, then an hour went by. Still nothing. Every inch of the area had been examined.

Well, I gave it all I have, Jacquelyn said to herself, standing up and shaking the dust off her clothes. She walked over to the three panoramic windows, with their nine square panels each, for a farewell view. This time her eyes focused not on the sparkling nature outside but on the ancient light brown window trim inside. Its upper left hand corner was the smallest bit out of kilter, leaning forward ever so slightly from the wall. Curiosity's not going to kill *this* cat, Jacquelyn told herself. She reclaimed her stepladder, unfolded it, walked back to the window, and climbed the three steps. With the fingers of her left hand she felt along the back of the slightly sagging wood trim. Her forefinger touched something. It felt like cardboard. Gingerly, she eased it up and out. It was a very yellowed cardboard mailer envelope about twelve inches tall and ten inches wide. Its contents had expanded enough with the passage of time to bulge open its decaying back flap.

Taking in huge gulps of breath and enjoining herself not to do anything in haste, Jacquelyn clasped the envelope with her left hand and carefully stepped back down to the floor. Now she could give her full attention to the envelope and its contents. Should she do it here or down in the light and comfort of her office? No, here! Now!

Sitting down on the floor, legs out in front of her, she stared at the cursive writing on the front of the old mailer. A single faded red and white stamp on the upper right showed the profile of

Emperor Franz Josef of Austria wearing a laurel wreath while the five Kreutzer value of the stamp was clearly indicated on all four corners. Along the broad white medallion rim ran the identifying words *KAIS.KOENIGL OESTERR.POST*—IMPERIAL ROYAL AUSTRIAN POST. The thick black postmark over the stamp read in large letters WIEN and below it the date showed 3. 3. 97. *What*? That was one month to the day before Brahms's death! The envelope was addressed in a very readable cursive: Fräulein Elisabet Ney, Austin, Texas, United States America. The return address on the curling back flap of the mailer read: Dr. J. Brahms, Karlsgasse 4, Wien, Österreich.

Jacquelyn's rapidly beating heart got her attention and she tried to calm down by slowly inhaling and exhaling and talking sternly to herself. I am too excited to draw the contents out of this envelope right now. When I stop feeling the jitters I will collect myself and go back down to my office. There, under a good light and at a clean desk, I shall calmly study this unknown Brahms treasure. But then she exploded out loud:

"Oh my god! *A letter from Johannes to Elisabet*. Hidden at Formosa for all these decades. Wait till I tell Megan Crespi!"

28

Will Fräulein Schreib's review take that miserable woman conductor to task? Maestro Christian Begeist was searching for the review of last night's second unholy Bruckner/Brahms concert in his Wiener Neustadt host's morning paper. He had thrown the Schreib woman's previous approving review of the concert series' first presentation into the nearest waste basket. Would he be doing the same this Thursday morning?

Ah, *here* it is, he murmured to himself, bending the newspaper back on itself. Such under-the-fold placement of text augured well for his hopes of a bad review for Maestra Endlich. He himself, as experienced conductor of the Linz Bruckner Orchester, thought the former conductor of his orchestra, whom he replaced when she moved on to her envied post at the Vienna Philharmonic, had set the tempi throughout Bruckner's Fourth far too fast. All time indications, including the slow second movement which begins as an introspective wordless hymn for cellos in the dark key of C minor. To his critical ears it sounded more like a children's nursery rhyme song.

Ah! Good! Tempo is exactly what Schreib was critiquing: all movements of the Bruckner symphony had been played too fast, and very often too loudly, the brass in particular. What was the Maestra thinking? And the same charge was leveled against her tempi in the Brahms Second, especially the lilting notes of the common link throughout all four movements, all specifically marked by the composer as Allegro non troppo. Endlich's conducting pace was the opposite, it was Allegro troppo—too much. On the other hand, the second movement's Adagio non troppo was *too* slow and its hint of melancholy taken to extreme. What on earth was going on with the capable—he had to give her that—Maestra?

Nevertheless, Schreib's critique of tempi was much easier on her flawed performance, especially of Bruckner, than his had been during the performance. He had taken delight in hissing his indignant outbursts into the ear of his patient companion, his onetime assistant conductor Dieter Unfug, a fellow loyal Brucknerite. Dieter was a slightly overweight tall young man, clean-shaven with exaggerated black sideburns. And Maestro Begeist, whose position as the conductor of the Bruckner Orchester anchored him in Linz, was staying with him while attending the entire Double B Composers marathon. They had much to talk about this sunny Thursday in Wiener Neustadt. Dieter was already out and about on errands for his mother and to pick up a package from the post office, but they had agreed to meet at one o'clock for lunch at the nearby restaurant Am Wasserturm. It was right next to the city's unique water tower that looks every bit like a giant goblet with a closed lid and could be seen from all parts of town.

"You can't miss it," the younger Bruckner aficionado had declared to the older Bruckner aficionado.

There were ideas to discuss, plans to be made.

29

Megan was still sound asleep at eight-thirty that Thursday morning when the cheerful voice of her host sounded outside her bedroom door.

"*Liebling*! I have fresh hot coffee for you and the vanilla creamer you like."

"Oh, wonderful! Come in Tönnies, come in." Megan sat up in the bed. She felt refreshed and a cup of sweetened coffee would do the rest.

"Nice pjs," Tönnies declared, assessing her dark blue cotton pajamas as he handed her not a cup but a very large white mug of cream-colored hot coffee. He sat down on the stool at the old-fashioned vanity opposite her.

"So, what would you most like to do this morning before your six o'clock flight this evening to Vienna?"

"First, eat one of your delicious, healthy cereal breakfasts with the multiple strawberries, blueberries, banana slices, and yogurt you introduced me to years ago." Megan smiled at her old friend affectionately.

"Already done. Everything awaits you downstairs."

"Wonderful. Is Harry here?"

"No, no, he had to rejoin the family he's staying with here—he's the godfather of one of their little girls—but he sends you all best wishes for the next chapter in your busy life."

"Ha! As if *his* life weren't busy and full of chapters."

"And next? What would you like to do next? As if I couldn't guess."

"Well, I haven't seen it since I was last here, and that must have been over thirty years ago by now."

"And you stayed here with me then as well. All right then," her host grinned as he stood up. "Off to the Brahms Museum it will be." Megan dressed quickly, choosing her green T-shirt to go with her beige slacks and vest. A matching green long-sleeve shirt and beige socks and shoes completed her "utilitarian," as she liked to call it, outfit. Her iPhone and the Brahms key were tucked safely in her small beige sling bag which she wore across her front. She packed her bathroom items and slippers and brought her roller bag down with her, ready for the flight to Vienna later that day.

Breakfast was delicious and unhurried. Megan decided to show Tönnies the exciting find she had made inside the Brahms bust she bought in Austin. She went over to her sling bag on the floor next to her roller bag, pulled the key out and placed it dramatically on the table.

"Megan, I didn't know you had your own key to my apartment!" Tönnies joked. "Thanks for returning it!"

"Oh, no, I do want to keep it. Just had to show it to you, it's been so many decades," she sassed back.

"Seriously, what's that key to?"

"I don't know yet. But I was hoping you might have some idea what sort of key it is."

"It looks European," Tönnies held the brass key up to his eyes. "And quite old. But I *might* be able to tell you more. My grandfather was a discriminating collector of old keys and I have part of his collection in my office. Let's go take a look right now."

They pushed back from the breakfast table and Megan followed her host down the hall and into a book-lined room inhabited by a small table and a large computer. Tönnies opened a closet door, bent over, and lifted up a framed four-by-four-foot white board. He carried it over to the armchair at his computer and placed it on the chair arms so Megan could get the full effect. Hanging on the glossy white panel were some thirty keys in six rows, most of them brass bit with solid shanks and a variety of bows with which to apply torque. Each key had a lengthy handwritten label affixed underneath it.

"My grandfather collected mostly German and Austrian keys but there are some French and English ones here as well, right there on the lowest row."

Megan's eyes scarcely glanced at them; she was holding up her Austin-found key and comparing its simple but distinctive oval bow to the keys in the upper rows.

"*Here it is*! Tönnies, look, an exact match!" Megan was holding her key flat alongside one of the keys hanging in the center of the fourth row."

"*Wunderbar*! Let's see what the label says." Megan's excitement was contagious.

"Oh, hell, I need my glasses." Tönnies reluctantly returned to the kitchen.

Unable to wait, Megan slipped her own glasses on and tried reading the script. It was in old-fashioned *Kurrentschrift* but she was used to reading it because of her archival research on Schiele, although it had taken a long time to master the fluid handwriting. She read it carefully out loud to herself just as her host returned.

"*Handschuhfach des Mannes, Wien, achtzehn-neunzig*"

"Ah!" a spectacled Tönnies exclaimed. "'Man's glove box, Vienna, eighteen-ninety,' is it? How interesting. Do you also have the box, Megan?"

"No. Not yet. I found the key in Texas. But at least now I know where to begin my search. Austria, not Germany."

"So what's in the box?"

"That is the problem. I don't know what's in it and I don't know where the box to this key is. I have my suspicions, or rather I should say my hopes, and now, thanks to your grandfather's collection, I know that my key belongs to a man's glove box made in Brahms's Vienna of eighteen-ninety."

Tönnies smiled fondly at his friend. She was always on the track of something, had been when first he met her. But now it was time to get going. Tönnies loaded Megan's lightweight bag in the trunk of his Audi, put the top down, and took the shortest route into the old town and to the many-windowed, multi-storied, red brick museum at Peterstrasse 39. It was just opening.

"You go on in; I see a parking place if I hurry!"

Megan obeyed and entered the historic house. It was not the six-story, multi-windowed "slum" house in which Brahms was born—that had been destroyed during World War II—but it was in the very near vicinity. It was a very similar, if only four stories, many-windowed merchant house dating back to the middle of the eighteenth century.

Once inside, Megan flashed the yellow press pass with her photograph that she had once been issued long ago and which, with the wonders of Photoshop, continued to be updated over the decades. She made up for this small sin by purchasing a ticket for Tönnies. And she waved it at him as he came bolting towards her from the entrance door.

"Thanks! Let's go look at his piano first, please," he suggested. A minute later they were standing before the elegant 1851 Baumgarten & Heins pianoforte known for its intimate, squarish shape and elegant gold trademark above the keys. It was on this piano that Brahms, only eighteen years old himself, taught his young piano students, thus bringing in money for the family whose finances were always wobbly.

"You know it was at that local Hamburg piano firm that Brahms met the talented young pianist Louise Japha," Megan said.

Tönnies made the mistake of saying how nice that was. Encouraged, Megan continued.

"She was seven years older than he, but they got along swimmingly, or rather as well as anyone could with young, introvert Johannes. They studied and played music together, they critiqued each other's compositions, and later they renewed their friendship in Düsselsdorf at the home of the Schumanns. She was studying piano with Clara and composition with Robert. Later Louise Japha concertized around Europe and became quite famous, performing Brahms and other great composers of the day, especially Camille Saint-Saëns and César Franck, *and* she lived until nineteen-ten!"

"Megan, why are you talking about *her* so much when we're here for *him*?"

"Oh! I'm sorry. I guess it's just the eternal feminist in me popping out; can't control it sometimes."

"You are forgiven."

"Good. The thing is, we know Louise Japha composed an *opera*! But no one knows where it is or what it was about."

"Well, I'm glad you explained." Tönnies hid his amusement at Megan's passion. In her next sentence she switched her fervidness to the composer to whom the museum they were standing in was dedicated.

"You know, Brahms had always been goaded to write an opera by his friends so they could see him go head-to-head with what they, and especially his great friend, the Vienna critic Eduard Hanslick, considered Brahms's arch nemesis—Richard Wagner. And many scholars believe he was searching for the right theme and the right libretto, but that he decided none were what he wanted. If he did indeed start composing an opera, he would have destroyed any sketches he'd made for it."

Megan fell silent as they began looking around the first room with its impressive display of photographs of Brahms, musical works, concert programs, letters, and autographs. They separated as they were interested by different objects, then rejoined and entered the next room together.

"Oh! There it is!" Megan exclaimed, pointing to a life-size marble bust of the composer on the far side of the room. It was the bearded Brahms, his smoothly carved head bent down, merging with and supported by a hefty block of white, tooled marble.

"Megan, you know what? I can just *feel* that this bust is by a *woman* artist," Tönnies said, reaching the artwork first and sneaking a look at the didactic label below it.

"Yes, your 'feeling' and your *eyesight* are both good," laughed Megan as she joined him in front of the bust.

"It's by the young sculptor Ilse Conrat, a personal friend of his. She did it in nineteen-three, six years after his death. If you've been to the composer's section in Vienna's Zentralfriedhof, you've seen her work because she's the artist who sculpted his tombstone image. And imagine! She was only twenty-two when she did it."

"Oh! Yes, I've been to the Central Cemetery and I vividly remember seeing that monument above his grave, but I had no idea it was by a woman. Brahms is shown in half torso, looking down at a thick open manuscript and the fingers of his right hand hold his head in thought."

"Correct. Do you remember the large bas-reliefs on the tall white marble slab behind Brahms and what's depicted on it?"

"No. What? Music scores? Cherubs?"

"The lightly curved backdrop slab has two life-size figural images on it, and one of them Brahms would have absolutely *hated*. It's a totally naked woman, her back to us as she holds a soundless lyre high above Brahms's head, and her plenitudinous derriere is at the height of his elbow."

"Ha! He certainly wouldn't have liked *that*. I remember what you said in your lecture yesterday about having his landlady sew a curtain to cover the muse in that Ingres portrait of Cherubini."

"You mean you actually *listened* to my talk?" joked Megan.

"I did. Every word. And now I remember that an equally large, fancy grave and monument to the 'waltz king' Johann Strauss, Junior, is to the left of Brahms's grave. Am I right?"

"Right as rain. Strauss died just two years after Brahms, in eighteen ninety-nine. Oh, I always feel so sorry when people right at the centennial tip don't live into the next century."

"So tell me more about this *woman* sculptor from Vienna," said Tönnies, standing back further from the Brahms bust to admire it.

"Well, she sculpted a number of prominent people in Vienna including Franz Josef's beautiful, anorexic wife, Sisi. Conrat's parents were friends of Brahms and as a teenager she got to know him in the last decade of his life. But her later history was tragic. Although her Jewish parents had converted to Christianity, that didn't do her any good after she moved to Munich. Once Hitler came to power, she was forced to close her large studio in Munich, where she had settled. Then the inevitable happened: in nineteen forty-two she was served a deportation order to the concentration camps, and rather than submit she committed suicide."

"Oh, no! That is so sad. So sad." Tönnies was visibly shaken.

They had completed their tour of the Brahms Museum and, in order to lighten the mood, Tönnies suggested driving them to the Venusberg vista point high above the city. But, after glancing at her Apple watch and seeing they still had ample time, Megan said she would rather take a tour of the port and see the new walkway along the river she had heard so much about.

"Your command is my wish," acquiesced Tönnies. Megan silenced the urge to tell him he had reversed the order in that genial expression. Some five minutes later they had found a parking spot at the end of one of the narrow old streets leading to the broad white promenade that came all the way down to the river at various points.

"We better memorize this undistinguished street so we don't get lost when we want to go back to the car," Megan said, looking up at the street sign that read Zufallstrasse—Chance Street.

"What many visitors don't realize," said Tönnies as they crossed the broad avenue toward the white pedestrian promenade, "is that the planner of all this, Zaha Hadid Architects, was simultaneously adding to a flood protection barrier for the city."

"That's interesting. How clever."

When they reached the top of the river walkway and saw so many people sitting on various levels enjoying the sunny day, they decided to sit down on the steps as well. What a vista.

"And there's one other tiny little fact about the Zaha Hadid Architects you might be interested in."

"What's that?" Megan asked, not taking her eyes off the shifting panorama of people sitting, standing, and walking below her.

"Zaha Hadid was a woman."

Tönnies got the reaction he knew he would get. Megan almost jumped up in her excitement.

"Are you *serious*?"

"I am serious. Unfortunately, she died recently of a heart attack—she was sixty-five—but her firm carries on, as you can see right here." Tönnies spread out his hands toward the curving vista.

Megan was not listening to her friend. She had googled the name Zaha Hadid on her ubiquitous iPhone and was deep into the details of the woman's life.

"So she was born in Iraq, became a British citizen and designed buildings all over the world and they call her 'Queen of the Curve.' Thank you for telling me about her, Tönnies."

"*Professoressa Crespi*?" A man's inquiring voice sounded above them. Looking up toward the source of the deep voice, they both recognized its owner with his short black beard and white hair.

It was the simpatico sculptor from yesterday afternoon's symposium, Mario Intagliatore.

"No, no, please don't get up! I sit here with you," the Italian said, athletically lowering himself down onto the steps.

"What an amazing coincidence that we meet." Megan was genuinely pleased to see the interesting artist again.

"I live very near here, but you, I thought you were leaving for Vienna today."

"That's true, she is, but not until six o'clock," Tönnies informed him.

"What do you have on your agenda next?" Intagliatore asked.

"Nothing, really," said Megan, looking at her host for confirmation. "We might eat lunch somewhere, possibly at that café over there, but we hadn't discussed it yet."

"You haven't had lunch? Then give me the honor of allowing me to host you. There is so much I should like to discuss with you about Brahms. And I can show you my studio, which is very near here."

"Your studio? That would be exciting," said Megan, looking eagerly at Tönnies. "Shall we?" He nodded agreement.

The three of them stood up simultaneously and began walking in two different directions, Megan and Tönnies toward the café, Intagliatore in the opposite direction. As he saw what they were doing, he caught up with them, laughing as he ran.

"*No*, *no*, *no*! When I say 'host' you, I mean at my *home*, not at a café. My house is only two blocks away and I call my housekeeper right now to prepare a little lunch for us, good? Perhaps ham and cheese omelet with an abundance of fresh fruit? You like that?"

The man's invitation was impossible to turn down, and they found themselves following the sculptor across the roadway and down the nearest narrow street.

"But this is Zufallstrasse. This is the street where we're parked," said Tönnies," pointing to his Audi at the far end of the street. This really is quite a *Zufall*!

Megan laughed at the happenstance of parking on a street, the name of which meant "chance."

Yes, indeed, what a happy happenstance.

30

In her small office at the Ney Museum Jacquelyn had at last calmed down after practicing a bit of meditation along with deep breathing while seated at her desk. She believed that the best sort of breathing was to inhale deeply through the nose, filling her lower body before pulling the air upward into her chest, holding it briefly, and then releasing it through the mouth while allowing a soft buzzing sound to vibrate through her lips. She had learned this technique in one of the classes she took at a wonderful health facility just across the border from San Diego in Mexico, the Rancho la Puerta. And just to add a bonus to her deep breathing, she also did her Kegel exercises at the same time.

And now she was ready to open the precious cardboard envelope that lay on the desk in front of her. A letter from Brahms to Ney! How improbable yet possible. She began sliding her fingers into a pair of latex gloves, museum camera at the ready. Just as she lifted the envelope, a strange sound caught her attention. Good god! It was the museum's smoke alarm! Had anyone else heard it? Oh, that's right, nobody's here but me.

Automatically jumping to her feet, the letter falling from her hands, Jacquelyn raced into the hall and toward the large exhibition room. The alarm was louder and seemed to pulsate through her body. And now she smelled smoke. It could be coming from above. Should she race up and look or should she call the fire department? Where was her cellphone? Oh, back in the office. But wait, the museum's smoke detector was monitored, so the fire department should be on its way. In the meantime, she might run upstairs and see if she could spot what had triggered the alarm. Could she possibly have left anything in the attic that ignited something? No, she hadn't had anything with her except the stepladder. And it was made of steel. Then she saw it. A great billow of smoke was pouring into the building from the cloakroom! Cautiously, she moved toward it and at the same time a firetruck pulled up in front of the museum, its siren at full blast. Jacquelyn ran to the entrance, flung the door open and shouted to the firefighter racing toward her. Another one stood at the ready by the truck.

"It's here, it's here! Something's burning in here!" she called.

The fireman ran past her to where she was pointing and entered the cloakroom. He took one look and jumped back.

"Hank!" he called, "we got a little hoverboard situation here. Bring the ABC."

The man named Hank came running with a hand-held fire extinguisher and began spraying the hoverboard. It had not yet caught on fire.

Within a few minutes the smoke had cleared. There was no damage to the cloakroom.

"Sir, *what* is a hoverboard?" Jacquelyn asked.

"It's a skateboard of sorts, Ma'am, a self-balancing foot-size base with two motorized wheels that the rider controls by leaning forward or backward. It runs on a lithium battery pack and it can overheat, it can spark, it can catch fire, it can explode. Some kid must have left it in here. They shouldn't be selling those goddamn things anymore."

"Boy, do I ever agree," said the museum director with relief as she closed the door behind the departing firemen.

Oh my god! *The Brahms letter*! Wait, no, it's all right. Safe in the office, thank god.

31

Frau Salem had provided Mario Intagliatore and his two guests with a delicious lunch of omelet and fresh fruit, and the conversation was lively and interesting. They discussed the theft of his plaster bust of the bearded Brahms and the strange anonymous commission that had initiated the bust. Again, their host asked Megan if she knew of any American Brahms scholars who might be fanatic collectors of Brahmsian paraphernalia, and again, after searching her mind, she had to declare she did not. Then her host changed the subject of their conversation completely.

"Tell me, *Professoressa*, is it true that as a young boy Brahms played piano to earn a living for his family in waterfront dives where prostitutes worked?"

"Yes, that's true, unfortunately, and of course it affected his attitude toward women for the rest of his life. He played a tinny piano in clip joints in the red-light district down by Hamburg's docks where there was a ready supply of horny sailors and accommodating prostitutes. Think of it! Only fourteen or so and he was witness to all sorts of obscenities as well as becoming the object of some teasing sexual attention himself. The same sort of seedy upbringing was given to his brother Friedrich, known as Fritz, and younger by two years. Like his brother, he had perfect pitch and he too became a pianist. He wasn't a bad musician and he also composed, but couldn't hold a candle to his talented, genius brother. In fact in adult life he was known as 'the wrong Brahms.' Can you imagine what *that* felt like?"

"Did he end up in Vienna too?" Tönnies asked.

"Oh, no. First, he fled his brother's fame. At the age of thirty-two he emigrated to Venezuela, of all places, and made his living as an organist in Caracas. But two years later he returned to the parental home and ended up being a piano teacher right here in Hamburg. He also continued to compose, wrote a gargantuan Symphony in D minor that was called by critics '*Die Endlose*—The Endless.' And then a second one which he minimized so much that it was given the name '*Die Allerkleinste*—The Smallest of All' because it was so sparse in theme and orchestration. One composition that caught on, however, was a piano concerto he wrote with the witty title '*Leichtes Konzert für kompetenten Klavierlehrer und Orchester*—Easy Concerto for Competent Piano Teacher and Orchestra.'"

"Oh! That's priceless," laughed Tönnies. "But is this all really true?" He was well aware of Megan's impish sense of humor.

"Yes, it's true. And when he died, at the age of only fifty-one, from syphilis it's thought, he left his small estate to his brother, even though they rarely communicated."

Interesting as all this Brahms family chat was, Intagliatore had been keeping his eye on the clock. He was keenly aware of the fact that the American professor had a six o'clock plane to catch. It was now almost three-thirty in the afternoon and, knowing it usually takes around half an hour to reach the airport, Intagliatore decided it was high time to take his guests down to his studio.

In the hall they passed by Fräulein Felizitas, the housekeeper from next door. She greeted the sculptor respectfully as she quickly stood out of their path. Her face became quite flushed, and Megan momentarily wondered as she passed her whether the young woman had severe allergies of some sort.

Entering Intagliatore's studio was a treat for both Tönnies and Megan. Four large photographs of the bearded Brahms were on the back wall along with four photographs of the sculptor's finished clay model based on those images.

"Would you mind if I took photos of your photographs, Signor Intagliatore?" Megan already had her "iCamera" in her hand.

"Not at all. These are the only proofs that I completed modeling the bearded bust," answered the sculptor morosely.

Two long rows of shelves held some twenty-four or so portrait busts in clay as well as a few clay figurines.

Intagliatore smiled as he watched his guests take in the exhibit.

"Oh my, you have portrayed some of the major German cultural figures of the nineteenth century, haven't you?" Tönnies exclaimed with admiration.

Megan kept her lips pressed together in a tight smile and said nothing about the fact that no women were represented in plaster display of dignitaries. But, after they had discussed a number of the male likenesses, she lost control and spoke up.

"I wonder if you, as a sculptor yourself, Signor Intagliatore, weren't tempted to create the bust of another important nineteenth-century worker in marble?" The twenty-first century sculptor in front of her looked blank.

"I can't think who he would be," he said at last.

"Elisabet Ney."

"Oh? Ney? *Elisabet* Ney? I am sorry, but the name is not familiar to me." Tönnies looked equally blank. Megan hid her disappointment in what she said next.

"Her name may not be known to you, but I would be willing to bet with you that her images are. For instance, a standing life-size figure of King Ludwig the Second of Bavaria, busts of Arthur Schopenhauer, Otto von Bismarck, Joseph Joachim, King George of..."

"*Dio mio*, I *know* those busts! And they are all by this woman?"

"Yes, and just to make you happy, she did the bust of a nineteenth-century compatriot of yours."

"Of an *Italian*?" Both men looked blank.

"Of an Italian. The general who fought for the unification of Italy."

"Oh, you mean Garibaldi," Tönnies answered correctly and in awe.

"But of course!" Intagliatore chimed in. "I did not realize it was she, a woman, who sculpted the head of Giuseppe Garibaldi." Megan smiled her most gracious smile.

"Perhaps if you could stop saying 'woman' and just refer to her name?"

"*Dio*! I see what you mean. Bring attention to her work and not her sex."

"Couldn't say it better myself," said Megan, ever gracious in victory. Tönnies stepped in.

"Your photographs of Brahms *mit Bart* are so interesting; they show him when the beard was brownish black and then later when it, to say nothing of his eyebrows, had turned quite white," he commented, hoping to change the subject.

"Yes, the anonymous commission specified showing him as he looked in his late fifties and early sixties when he had the great white, flowing beard. I did not understand why the specificity, but followed through, modeling with clay, for starters.

"And now my clay bust is stolen! No time to cast it. Right out of my studio. All I have are the photographs I took of it before I left. Here, here they are on my worktable."

"Stolen from your studio while you were away in Italy, you said," Megan confirmed.

"Yes, while I was in Italia."

"I'm sure the police asked you this, but who knew you'd be away?"

"No, *Professoressa*. I did not report this theft to the police. Too complicated, too little to tell them. Only one person knew I would be away and that was my faithful housekeeper, Frau Salem. She has been with me for, let me see, almost twenty-six years now."

"So you trust her completely."

"Absolutely."

"And her friends?"

"Her friends? I do not know if she has many friends. She is here most of the time, from eight to eight. And she lives nearby. I never hear her speak of friends. Come to think of it, I have never heard her speak of having a husband."

"So was she here when you were away in Italia?" Megan persisted.

"Of course. She comes every day here. Only on Sunday not."

"And, of course, she would not have friends over while you were away," confirmed his relentless inquisitor.

"That would be unthinkable." Intagliatore was certain of his housekeeper's loyalty.

"The woman who knew you when we went out in the hall to come down here. Who is she?"

"Megan! You're beginning to sound like the police inquisition Signor Intagliatore wanted to avoid!" Tönnies interrupted.

"No, no, no. *Professoressa* tries to help me. That young woman is housekeeper for family who occupy the other half of this floor. Felizitas is her name. I do not know surname."

"And—I do promise this is the last question—are you friends with the family that lives next door?"

"Only to nod to when passing. They are very wealthy, Jewish, and keep to themselves."

Tönnies glanced at his watch. It was almost four thirty. The time and interesting talk had passed quickly.

"Their surname?" persisted his American friend.

"Megan! You promised that was your last question!" Tönnies intervened.

"It is all right, Doktor Helfer, I do not mind. It is Wittgenstein, answered the bemused sculptor, "the family surname is Wittgenstein."

"I regret, Signor Intagliatore, that it is time for us to leave for the airport." Tönnies took Megan by the shoulders and firmly steered her past the shelves of interesting historical busts to the door.

"I also regret," answered the hospitable Italian sculptor. "God grant our paths cross again."

32

Done at last! Christian Begeist had completed his time-consuming income tax report—Austria's monthly *Einkommensteuer*—which he had brought with him from Linz to work on. It was only then that the Maestro remembered he had agreed to meet his former assistant conductor for lunch at one o'clock. He could just make it in time if he didn't run into his host's mother, the garrulous, nosey Frau Unfug. But luck was against him. Here came the inquisitorial, gabby woman after him just as he had soundlessly reached the front door of her house.

"Ah, there you are, Maestro! I said to Dieter just last night, why in god's name aren't either of you two married? I know you both work very, very hard, but still you need a woman to run your house. My son should be living in his own place with a loving wife. Instead, he refuses to meet any of the local women I have gone out of my way to cultivate. But *he* prefers to be on his own. At least I think so. Tell me, Maestro, is it possible that he has someone in Vienna? He goes there so often. *Says* he has a part time job at a musical instrument store there. Do you know whether or not he sees women when he's in Vienna, if he takes them out?"

"I do not, Frau Unfug. Some men just prefer not to be married."

"Well, but take you, for example. There are all sorts of stories about you being turned down by women you've proposed to. Are the tales true?" Over the years Frau Unfug had heard about her houseguest's failure to find a wife despite proposing to women much younger than he, even teenagers, once even a chambermaid. Gossip easily reached Wiener Neustadt and because her son was a conductor, Frau Unfug followed the music world's personalities with avid interest. The sixty-three-year-old Maestro in front of her surprised even himself with his half honest answer.

"In my case, I know not what women want. I only know they, not you, of course, Frau Unfug, but they make me feel awkward and thus provoke my impetuous conduct toward them. Many acquaintances and friends tell me—I, who in outward appearance so much resemble my musical god, Anton Bruckner—that I am simply destined to lead the same bachelor life he did. And now I am convinced that I shall live to be the age he was when he died—seventy-two."

What Begeist did not say was that he detested modern "liberated" women. Hated their sense of entitlement. Just look at that bitch Agatha Endlich, for example. *He* should have been resident conductor of the Vienna Philharmonic, not she! Rumor had it that the administration had actually been *forced* to choose her in order to bring good publicity to the orchestra. For so many years the Philharmonic had successfully managed not to have distracting female instrumentalists with their hairdos, jewels, and bare legs scattered across the stage.

Begeist stole a look at his watch. Dieter would be waiting for him now. He explained this to the prying old lady in front of him and finally escaped the house.

The Am Wasserturm restaurant was as colorful inside as it was outside. A grinning Dieter was waving at him from a corner table in the back.

"How do you like the décor?" he asked Christian. The Maestro looked around.

"Umm, all these painted giant goblets on the walls certainly encourage visitors to drink, I will say that. So, did you get all your errands done?" Christian asked as he sat down facing Dieter.

"I certainly did. Mother's *and* mine. The package from England has arrived." Dieter smiled triumphantly and pointed to a small carton at his side, the size and shape of a shoebox. He had not opened it yet, but after they ordered their Tafelspitz, one specifying veal, the other beef, they turned their attention to the box. Dieter slit the wrapper open with his dinner knife and lifted the lid discreetly.

He smiled approvingly at what he saw but did not take anything out of the box. Instead, he slid the box across the table to Christian.

"Looks nice and lightweight," remarked the older Brucknerite. He was staring down at a fashion photographer's tool: an Enola Gaye WP40 smoke grenade.

"You can order different colors; I chose smokey yellow, of course."

"Hmm. So what's your plan exactly?"

"Well, of course we let Bruckner's glorious Eighth Symphony sound its splendid course, but after intermission and twenty minutes or so into the Brahms Third—haven't decided exactly when yet—I will jump up from our first row balcony seats, yell 'Fire' at the top of my voice while I'm pointing with my loaded left hand toward the auditorium area beneath us, jerk the cannister ring with my right hand and let it fall while I keep yelling 'Fire!'"

"Sounds effective. How long does the smoke last?"

"From sixty to ninety seconds. Plenty of time for you to spring up along with everyone else and head madly for the exit."

"Well done, my man, well done. Anton will be heard; Johannes not."

The Brucknerites' Tafelspitz arrived and they delved in, both suddenly quite hungry.

33

Their farewells at the Hamburg airport drop-off had been brief, with Tönnies remaining in the car and Megan hoisting her tall, four-wheel roller bag from out of the trunk in one easy motion. She was dressed in her beige and black travel clothes with black sling bag hanging from her neck, facing front. She turned to wave a goodbye kiss to her old Hamburg friend and then entered Terminal One.

It was not as huge as she remembered, but then it was the older of the two terminals. The great curved ceiling created a sense of bouncing light and shadow. Megan made her way slowly past the many beckoning shops to the Eurowings check-in counter.She boarded immediately. Her flight only took an hour and a half, so she would be reaching Vienna by seven-thirty. By eight o'clock at the most, as she had no checked bag to wait for, she should be in a taxi and on her way to her beloved hotel Römischer Kaiser, where she always stayed when in Vienna. Located on the Annagasse, it was literally just about 500 steps to the inner city's main promenade, the Kärntner Strasse, which led from the Opera House to the city's great gothic cathedral, the Stephansdom. When Megan had first lived in the city to study at the University, the Kärntner Strasse was still open to car traffic. Many were the times she had parked her station wagon on the busy downtown street only to be harassed by male passersby excited at the rare sight of a woman parking a car. On the flight to Vienna she reminisced over those old times, picturing some of the people and places that had become part of her daily life. So immersed was she in memories that it was a surprise when she noticed the plane was preparing to land.

"*Annagasse sechzehn, bitte*," she told the taxi driver who pulled up a minute after she exited the airport. During the short ride into town Megan texted the old friend she had planned to meet in Vienna and who was staying at her hotel. Tony Bocello had been her dean at the Meadows School of the Arts at Southern Methodist University until he was plucked to become president of the Dallas Symphony Orchestra. There he had initiated an effective campaign to build the symphony a modern auditorium, and then, when all funds were secured, he worked with the famous acoustical engineer Thomas Hawk to assure the concert hall's auditory success. And now the city of Houston was about to build a new symphony venue and Tony, known as Anthony Bocello in the music world, was brought out of retirement by the Houston Symphony to embark on a one-man tour of acoustically famous concert halls in Europe. He had set up appointments with acousticians, architects, and conductors in Amsterdam, Hamburg, Berlin, Paris, and then finally in Vienna. He and Megan had laughed at the busy schedules of two senior citizens that prevented them from visiting Hamburg at the same time. But at least their calendars coincided and concluded in the Austrian capital. They had even planned to visit one or two of the picturesque Austrian villages where Brahms spent many summers composing. What a treat!

Taxis were among the only vehicles allowed on the one-way Annagasse and as hers turned into and up the narrow street toward the Kärntner Stasse, Megan saw Tony already standing outside the hotel entrance doors waiting for her. His face lit up as he spotted the taxi that had to be Megan's. A dark-haired, blue-eyed energetic man with boundless intellectual curiosity and great sensitivity, Tony was a fine pianist as well as effective administrator. Although as dean he and Megan had not always seen eye to eye as he tried to run an entire school while she single-mindedly championed her department, the passage of time again brought them into each other's orbit. A few years earlier Tony had become a widower and he continued to grieve deeply the loss of his wife. One of his and Megan's fondest memories was when he, as a new dean, came over with his wife Charlotte to Megan's parents' home where, retiring to the kitchen, the two Italian men prepared, hand-rolling dough on two cheese-graters, a delicious gnocchi dinner to everyone's delighted gustation.

And now, decades later, here was Megan's former dean—who once commanded her in writing to "cease and desist"—waiting for her with a big smile on his face in the middle of Vienna. The taxi pulled up to the hotel and Megan emerged with an equally big smile on her face. They hugged each other jovially. Megan pulled out her roller bag, paid the fare, and they proceeded to the hotel desk to check her in. This time she had reserved the "Sisi" Suite, named after Austria's beloved and beautiful Empress Elisabeth, assassinated by an Italian anarchist in 1898. It was larger than the single rooms in the old hotel, and Megan had decided to treat herself for a change. She had usually stayed in one of the small attic rooms, with windows looking down onto the always active Annagasse. It was one of these atmospheric front rooms that she had recommended to Tony and he was delighted with it, he told her, as they took the small, mirror-paneled elevator up to her floor.

"Come on in with me, Tony. I'll just visit the bathroom, leave my bag, and we'll be off for dinner," Megan said as she unlocked the outside door. There was an inner door to the suite and it opened to reveal two rooms—a study and a bedroom—with four large green velvet curtained windows overlooking the street. Tony took an admiring look at the white, rococo-style five-drawer desk positioned between two windows with a straight back chair in front of it and the inviting small couch and coffee table to its side. Before he could try sitting at the desk, Megan had already returned, looking fresh and invigorated.

"Which of our many Annagasse restaurants are you in the mood for?" she asked.

"I'm game to returning to the Italian one you recommended, Salieri, just down at the end of our street. I was there two evenings ago and loved the atmosphere and the food."

"*Perfetto. Andiamo la*!"

34

It was with a huge sigh of relief that the director of Austin's famous Elisabet Ney Museum returned to her office. Her museum had not been burned down by the small fire in the cloakroom. The firemen had arrived in time to put out the flames erupting from a forgotten hoverboard, and what little damage there was could be repaired tomorrow when the museum opened again. But now it was time, uninterrupted time she hoped, to read the contents of the letter she had discovered. Just imagine. Brahms writing to Ney in the year 1896. One year before his death and eleven years before her own. What did the letter say?

"Oh, my god, *where is the letter*?"

Jacquelyn stared at her empty desktop. There was no envelope there. This simply cannot be, she screamed in her brain. It *has* to be here! She fell to her knees in front of the desk and looked underneath it. Oh, thank the lord, *there* it is. She had dropped it when she jumped up to see about the smoke alarm. That seemed ages ago now. Lordy, lord, no more interruptions please, she invoked the powers that be.

Sitting down again, she slipped on the latex gloves she had abandoned, and stared in awe at the front and back of the cardboard mailer. From its noticeable bulge, it could have once certainly contained the key Megan found inside the bust she bought at the Austin antique store. Gingerly, Jacquelyn withdrew what turned out to be five folded sheets of paper and unfolded them on her desktop. Brahms's elegant cursive script met her eyes. It was very small but legible and she translated it to herself out loud.

3 March 1896, Vienna

Elise, my darling, free-spirited, unforgettable Elise!

Do you remember your old Hannes?

Do you remember our week together in Hanover in the winter of 1859?

The night when our dear Joseph Joachim—who is still with us in this world—suddenly had to leave to see his dying mother in Leipzig and you and I, we two, were left alone in his flat? Do you remember how we two discovered we were almost the same age, I twenty-five, but you, four months my senior, already twenty-six? You, my older sister, who told me what we were going to do next?

Do next, but not as sister and brother. No. As woman and man, you said. And how you showed shy, awkward me, no, taught this disbeliever in women what a *pure* woman and an innocent man together can do? The sweetness, the gentleness, the ecstasy! And I was able to forget those other, evil, corrupt women. Those whores who sat me on their laps when I was a boy, whispered horrible things into my ears, covered me with their wet lips, and slipped their hands into my trousers and tugged at the poor, limp organ they found there.

You can understand that as I reached adulthood, the urgings my body felt were confusing. The summer before we met that fateful January, while I was vacationing in Göttingen, those bodily passions overwhelmed me when I met a pretty girl with a beautiful soprano voice called Gathe. A magnet pulled us together. I felt I should marry and that it should be she who would share my life. We secretly bought engagement rings, I had myself photographed wearing mine. But then came the overwhelming realization: she would fetter me. This could not be. I wrote her this and she kindly released me.

But you, great free spirit, who would never think of chaining another spirit, you did not know anything of that; I did not tell you of myself. I simply let myself be guided by you, flourish under your gentle spell, yes, fall in love with you without the words to say so.

I played my heart out to you on the piano. You listened, enchanted. And then you took me to your studio to sit for the image you, with your magic fingers, formed of me out of humble clay, saying it would seal our love in bronze, even if we must soon return to our separate lives. Oh! How I wish I could have seen that bust! The bust that had to remain secret, while the images you made of Joseph and his future wife Amalie could be paraded in public!

And then we had to separate—you, free spirit, to distant Berlin, I, employed court choir master, to nearby Detmold. I, never to see the bust you would cast in bronze, you, never to hear me play again. Our paths did not cross again over our lifetimes—you to distant America, I to nearby Austria. But I knew of you, heard of, saw some of your images—Schopenhauer, Ludwig of Bavaria, and my hero Bismarck! What a triumph for you! I have had my modest triumphs too, but in fleeting sound, not in everlasting form. And you were in possession of an image you dare not reveal to the world, perhaps not even to your "best friend." An image I pray you did not discard but took with you to the New World.

But my darling and now forever far away Elise, I did not despair. Though I suffered in silence, longed for you in secret, adored you and applauded your triumphs from a great distance, I too created something to celebrate our seven days and nights of love, something to declare in the realm of sound my lasting love of you.

What is it, you may ask?

It is something I have never composed before and never shall again.

It is an operetta. Yes, an operetta! It is not a serious, wallowing in heroism or tragic work such as Richard Wagner might have composed. It is an intimate, capricious operetta full of joy, love, and laughter. The enduring joy of our love. I call it *Waltzerfreude bei Wittgenstein*. And this joyous waltzing at the Wittgenstein's takes place here in Vienna with a flank of famous musicians and other notables who come and go. There are children too. And, of course, us. It is in the music salon of the Wittgenstein family in a grand palais some eighty steps from my home, which overlooks the Karlsplatz. Ah, Elise, the beautiful Karlskirche that might have witnessed our marriage, had you not already had your "best friend," as you called him. Even though he was studying medicine in far-off London. You talked so much about him that I remember his name: Edmund. Did you marry him? Does he still live, I wonder?

Our operetta must remain unknown to others and yet, with this letter I send you the key to the humble container in which I have secreted the score. The joyous score that celebrates our love.

I send the enclosed key to you now because my good, honest doctor has diagnosed that I am dying of cancer of the liver, as did my poor father. So if you wish to live our week of love again through music, ask our dear mutual friend Joachim, to whom I have entrusted the whereabouts of the container. A small container to which only you, my eternal darling, have the key. Think of it as the key to my heart.

Your faithful, never-wed Hannes

Jacquelyn had almost forgotten to breathe, so moving and monumental was this find. She must contact Megan Crespi, holder of the crucial key, immediately. What incredible news she had for her. Crespi's business card was in her desk drawer. Jacquelyn slid open the drawer, found the card immediately, and looked at her watch. It was seven-thirty in the evening. Damn! That meant it was two-thirty in the morning, Hamburg/Vienna time. Should she send a text?

No. Jacquelyn wanted to hear the cry of amazement Megan would let loose when she heard the stupendous news. First, before putting it in the museum safe, she would scan the letter to have the copy with her when she called Megan. And she would call her first thing in the morning when she woke up. That would be around seven o'clock her time, around two o'clock in the afternoon for Megan. But would she even be able to fall asleep tonight? Probably not. All right then, she would stay up till midnight and call Megan at what would be seven in the morning her time. No, this cannot wait. Let's make it six-thirty Megan's time.

What an unbelievable, happy discovery for the world of music and for the world of art!

35

As they entered the conveniently located Salieri restaurant, Megan was thrilled to see her favorite table was free. It was to their immediate left, one step down into a small alcove that contained only one table. She steered Tony to it and slipped into one of the chairs against the wall, motioning him to take the chair at the head of the table. This gave them privacy as well as a good view of the restaurant and its patrons. It was a few minutes past nine and the busy place stayed open until ten. Happy, murmuring clients were lingering and a solicitous waiter appeared almost immediately to take their order.

"Megan, what do you recommend?"

"Oh, the gnocchi, without question. And, of course, in honor of our long ago gnocchi dinner with my parents and your Charlotte."

"*Perfetto*." Tony looked at the waiter, smiled, and ordered the pasta dish as well as, after an affirming nod from Megan, small green salads and two glasses of red wine. When the glasses arrived, he raised his to make a toast, but Megan was busy pouring something into her glass from a small blue container.

"What on earth are you doing, Megan?"

"Oh, I like wine and know red wine is really good for us, but I don't like how it tastes, so I just pour a little of this sweetener in when I do drink it. Dasani drops, strawberry kiwi flavor."

"How very un-Italian of you," Tony shook his head.

"I'm sorry. What?" Once again Megan had forgotten to insert her "hear-rings," as she called them. She had taken them out just before boarding her flight to Vienna in order to avoid having to listen to the plane's roar for an hour and a half and had forgotten to reinsert them during the brief time in her hotel room.

"I said how very un-Italian of you," laughed Tony as he watched Megan quickly pull the small buds out of their black case in her purse and discreetly install them.

"Aye, sure an' I dinnae have to be Italian all the time? Och, aye, an' me mither, she be Scotch-Irish. Aye, an' her maiden name were Laird, were it, an laird of our Dallas hame were she." Megan loved to affect accents and had often done so while teaching, hauling in any student whose attention to the subject matter might be straying.

While Tony chortled, Megan took a first sip of the doctored wine and smacked her lips in approval.

"Tell me, Tony, which of the auditoriums, or should I say 'auditoria,' you've visited on this trip did you judge to be the best as far as acoustics are concerned?"

"The one I haven't visited yet," he answered immediately.

"Huh? I don't understand."

"Vienna's own Musikverein. It's still the best in the world."

"With all the modern innovations out there across the world? I don't understand. How can that be? When was that ancient Viennese edifice built anyway?"

"It was completed in eighteen seventy and it seats one thousand, seven hundred and forty-four people. Plus standing room for three hundred. The fabulous acoustics are the result of one, the hall is relatively small in size; two, it's rectangular in shape; and three, it has a very high ceiling—all this gives a long reverberation time. Plus, the interior is plaster and the interior surfaces and sculptures are nicely irregular, which also helps bounce the sound.

"So all those ingredients make for superb acoustics," said Megan, thinking of various rectangular halls in America known for producing great sound. In addition to the relatively recent Meyerson Symphony Hall in Dallas—considered tenth best in the world, and for the success of which Tony had worked—what came to mind was Boston's Symphony Hall, where she had once heard Dvořák's Ninth, "New World" Symphony. Even though the Boston Hall was much smaller than the Musikverein, the sound was fantastic. In Tony's words it had "excellent reverberation time."

"Yes, and that's why I visited Amsterdam," he explained. "To 'feel' the sound. Its Concertgebouw was based on the historic, shoebox hall of the original Leipzig Gewandhaus and opened in eighteen eighty-eight. But a hundred years later its rotting wood pilings were starting to sink under the damp Amsterdam earth, so they had to be replaced with concrete pillars. But the shoebox shape was retained intact, and that keeps its ranking as one of the top concert halls in the world." Tony smiled as he pictured the great halls to himself. Megan was eager to ask a follow-up question.

"All right, Tony, I understand about the importance of the narrow shoebox shape, as you call it, but what about all the newer, circular or oval 'surround' auditoriums? Like Hamburg's Elphi, where we've both just been. And the one you went out of your Germanic route to visit in Paris?"

"Well, the Paris Philharmonie is different, to say the least. And it certainly is a total encirclement. The ash wood platform at the center base of the round hall is rectangular and enveloped by thinly upholstered black orchestra seats on three sides. The fourth side, right behind the orchestra, is capable of holding choirs of immense size, and above that are the organ pipes. And circling above the ground floor there are differently shaped, undulating blond wood balconies. Take all that and the acoustics are, I think, too fractured—too much bounce. The same, in my opinion for the Berlin Philharmonie, which is also surround sound with jutting balcony seating everywhere you look. But, of course, modern architects are not interested in designing traditional shoebox auditoriums any longer. Just think of the Walt Disney Concert Hall in Los Angeles designed by Frank Gehry. I'd call it a surprisingly timid surround sound layout with its balconies gently creating encirclement."

"I've actually been to a concert there but I have to confess I didn't really notice whether or not the acoustics were super."

"They're not bad, just not overwhelmingly good. So now the architectural problem is to achieve excellent acoustics within swirling modern shapes. That's of course what the Paris Philharmonie has attempted to achieve. But for me it was not totally successful. Splintered, as I said."

"Well, I have to admit, I had the same overall impression in the

Hamburg Elphi auditorium with the Elbphilharmonie," Megan said.

"Quite right, not stable enough," agreed Tony.

"What was the program you heard there?" Megan asked.

"It was Tchaikovsky's Sixth and Ravel's *Rapsodie espagnole*. At least the music gave the acoustical configuration a romp for its money," Tony laughed. "And you, Megan, what did you hear?"

"Oh, I was lucky. Brahms's Requiem."

"God, I'm envious!"

"It was a wonderful performance, I can tell you. Musically and acoustically."

"*Any dessert*?" their waiter's voice interrupted. Megan looked inquiringly at Tony who immediately declined, and taking her cue from him she also said no.

"*Café? Cappuccino?*" persisted the waiter. Again the answer from both was no and Tony asked for the check. Then he turned to Megan and spoke in a joyous tone.

"I can hardly wait to experience the perfect acoustics of the Musikverein again tomorrow. Did you know the great conductor Bruno Walter said it was the finest hall in the world? It's been a number of years since I've heard a concert there, but I remember how totally wowed I was at the time."

"Me too, and I've heard concerts in that gorgeously decorated hall since I was a university student here. So I know for sure we really have a treat waiting for us tomorrow night."

"Right. The programming of Bruckner's Eighth and Brahms's Third is certainly a pithy combination. It takes quite a knowledgeable conductor to handle such a contrast and still give his all to both."

"In this case the conductor is a *she*," Megan immediately pointed out.

"Ha! I'm relieved to see you're still a good feminist," Tony laughed, fully aware his conductor comment would tick off his former colleague. Megan continued speaking.

"Actually I know Agatha Endlich from her days at the Dallas Opera's Hart Institute for Women Conductors. She's even been to my house—went crazy over my then baby Maltese, Button. And actually tried out my parents' old Steinway grand—the one you played once, remember? Anyway, that's probably why we're invited to her after-concert reception event Sunday evening."

"Oh, yes, thank you for asking that I be invited too," Tony said. "I intend to recommend several European-based conductors to guest conduct when the Houston Symphony Hall has reached completion. She would certainly be one of them."

"You just said symphony 'hall,' Tony. Does that mean you've already decided to have the shoebox configuration for Houston rather than a circular, shape?"

"You bet I have, Megan, actually, from the beginning. But that's strictly hush, hush. I haven't told our primary benefactor yet—Riccardo Perrotti. Just think. He's already donated millions to the building fund. And although our Dallas Symphony Hall architect I. M. Pei has departed this world, we now have his proven, truly impressive protégé, Scott Cantertold."

"You can't get better than that," Megan smiled.

"You know, one of our problems right now is a fight with the acoustician. Because Houston is surrounded by *three* airports, our acoustician wants to have twelve feet of concrete in the ceiling to keep out airplane noises, but our architect is giving him only six, and he guarantees we won't hear any planes."

"Did you have as many venue visits on your investigation trip for Houston?" asked Megan. Tony laughed.

"No, actually about the same as for the Dallas project. The Birmingham Symphony Hall in England was a fine precedent to ours, with shoebox configuration; the Manchester Symphony Hall had, umm, what I'd call a geometric mix of rectangle and half-moon. And then, of course, the circular, actually ellipsis-shape Royal Albert Hall in London with its glass dome. Lots of history there, with the bereaved Queen Victoria on hand at the opening when the building was dedicated to her beloved Albert's memory."

"I've been there as an admiring tourist after visiting the memorial to Albert just across the street in Kensington Gardens, but not to a concert. What are the acoustics like?"

"Oh, not good! It was instantly apparent that there was a huge echo problem. At first they tried to minimize the cacophony by suspending an enormous canvas awning below the dome. It helped block the sun during daytime performances, but the acoustics have remained a problem all this time. There used to be a famous quip that declared the Albert Hall was the only place where a British composer could be sure of hearing his work twice!"

Discussing the pros and cons of concert venues around the world, Megan and Tony were oblivious to the passing of time and, consequently, were the last to leave Salieri's that evening. The restaurant opened directly onto the Annagasse and as they walked the half-block back to the Römischer Kaiser Hotel at the slow gait Tony had set, the question of whether they could meet in the morning for breakfast arose. Megan spoke first.

"Tomorrow morning for me is a quick check with the Leopold Museum where I'm giving that lecture on Klimt and Music Saturday evening, and then, just for fun, on to a little museum I've never visited before. It's the..."

"Well," Tony interrupted, "I have two different exciting appointments at the Musikverein tomorrow, an early one with the building's acoustician, Leopold Feinstimm, at eight, and the other at one o'clock with the general manager, Edgar Wittgenstein."

"Wittgenstein? As in *the* Wittgenstein family of Vienna?" Megan was impressed.

"Yes, one and the same, I'm told. So that means we'd have to meet for breakfast at seven at the latest."

"Oh, dear. I can't make it. Sorry. It's not that I'm a late sleeper; I just have to get my exercise routine in before I can get dressed and have breakfast. It's sticking to my admittedly strenuous routine that keeps me healthy if not as slim as I used to be."

"What sort of routine is that? We're the same exact age if I'm not mistaken and you do indeed seem somewhat bouncier than I. My only exercises are at the piano. Maybe I'm missing out on something important?" Tony was half kidding, half serious.

"My routine? Do you want the short description or the long description?" Megan laughed.

"Well, seeing we've reached our hotel, and we both need our sleep, perhaps the short version."

"Sure. I call it FSAB—flexibility, strength, aerobic, and balance—and it involves, first on my bed, prolonged sets of head, arm, leg, and torso movements, with face up, then face down. Then, standing, I do an arm circling stepping movement across the room and back twenty times to the words of 'Swing Low, Sweet Chariot.' After that, I lift weights in all directions—here at the hotel I just use water bottles—then elastic cord pulls—always travel with one—then treadmill laps—here, just trotting in place—and finally slow balancing poses while my pounding heart returns to its normal rate. There! Was that short enough?"

"I'd love to hear the long version sometime. Good for you, Megan. So let's meet back here at the hotel tomorrow for dinner around five-thirty, if that's good for you?"

"That's fine."

As they hugged and said goodnight in the elevator, both expressed their highest expectations for Maestra Endlich's performance the next evening.

"*Dormi bene*," Tony called back over his shoulder as the elevator door closed upon Megan. She did not need his exhortation to sleep well. Suddenly the very full day in Hamburg before flying to Vienna overcame her. A double dose of exhaustion and contentment had her sound asleep almost instantly.

36

It was not her alarm, it was the beautiful 'Méditation' orchestral intermezzo from Jules Massenet's opera *Thaïs*, the ringtone on her iPhone, that woke Megan at six-thirty the next morning.

"Hello?" she said weakly, glancing in disbelief at the time.

"Megan! It's Jacquelyn. Jacquelyn of the Elisabet Ney Museum!"

"Oh, hi Jacquelyn," Megan said weakly. "Do you realize what *time* it is here in Vienna?"

"Yes, yes, I do, and I'm sorry about that. But I just had to catch you before you went out for the day. I have incredible news!" Blinking her eyes and hoisting herself up to a half-sitting position in her bed, Megan cleared her throat.

"So, what is so important?"

"*I have found a letter from Brahms to Ney!*"

"What, *what*?" Megan's sleepiness instantly left her and she sat bolt upright.

"Exactly what I said. I have discovered, hidden in the window trim of the museum's attic, a five-page letter to Elisabet. It's dated March, three, eighteen ninety-six and was mailed from Vienna to Formosa."

"Oh, but this is amazing!"

"Yes, and what's even more amazing are the contents of the letter. You're not going to believe what he wrote her about. The whole world of music is going to be blown away!"

"My god, tell me what it says." Megan was fully awake.

"I can do better than that. I can *read* it to you right now and then I can scan the Xerox copy I made of it and send it to you in an email."

"Oh, great, thank you. But *read* it to me, read it to me!"

Jacquelyn's pronunciation of German was excellent and the contents of the letter left Megan practically levitating from her bed. What a find! What a confession! And that an *operetta* by the composer existed! So atypical of him. When Jacquelyn finished her reading of the letter and paused, Megan instantly had a caveat.

"This is going to stun the music world. It stuns me. But just because of that we should go slowly, Jacquelyn. You have been so kind to share this treasure with me, but please, let's think together what should be done next. Let's proceed carefully. I would recommend you verify the date of the paper itself as well as compare the handwriting to known letters in Brahms's small, cursive script. Right? And as for revealing your incredible find to the public, wait until all this is taken care of. Right, Jacquelyn?"

"Absolutely, Megan. I am definitely going to take verification measures and not confide my find to anyone yet, but I absolutely had to tell *you*."

"And I really appreciate your doing so. I'm still tingling with excitement. This is going to bring fantastic publicity to the museum. We should figure out not only when, but how to announce your discovery. Have a co-announcement with the Brahms Society of America, for example. Yes, we, I mean you, must make the most of this extraordinary discovery."

"No, *do not* take yourself out of the picture, Megan. If it weren't for you, I never would have continued searching for a small mailer or package that once could have contained a key! A key hidden inside an unidentified bust of Brahms that *you* found in an Austin antique store here! I want you to share the glory when the discovery is announced. Gosh, I want you to give a lecture on what this discovery means."

"Thank you, Jacquelyn. I can only congratulate you. And I promise that when you send me the scan, I shall keep it to myself, not show it to anyone else no matter how tempting that would be. Especially right here in Vienna."

The two friends, now bonded by Brahms, continued to talk until Megan realized what time it was.

"Yikes! I've got to go. I'll miss breakfast!"

Megan did not miss her hotel breakfast, but she did have to jettison her FSAB routine. And that didn't bother her one whit. Oh, Brahms! Anything for you.

37

On leave from Caracas Cathedral, burial site of the parents and wife of Simón Bolívar, noted Venezuelan organist Fritz Rahm still had two more riveting Double B Composers concerts to attend in Vienna. One was that very Friday evening; the other, the grand finale, would be on Sunday evening. A tall, thin man in his early fifties with wavy blond hair and intense blue eyes, Rahm's sabbatical stay in the Austrian capital had two aims: one investigative, the other explosive.

The first aim had been to ascertain whether any of his great-great-great-grandfather's hand-written scores were in the Austrian National Library or the Vienna City Library, or even in Brahms's extensive estate at the Archive of the Society of Friends of Music in the Musikverein building. The second aim of Fritz, named Friedrich in honor of his great-great-great-grandfather, was to draw public attention to the stolen musical ideas his more famous great-great-great-granduncle had lifted from the unpublished scores of his great-great-great-grandfather, Friedrich Brahms.

The firm that published Johannes Brahms's music, Simrock, had indeed published the scores of a few works by his brother—a piano concerto and two symphonies, one long, one short. That much the present-day Fritz knew. He also knew that in 1866 at the age of thirty-one, his great-great-great-grandfather had secretly married a local woman, Caroline Paasch, a talented pianist who was eleven years his senior. This age difference remarkably followed a pattern set by his and Johannes's own father, Johann Jakob Brahms, who at the age of twenty-four had married a woman who was forty-one, seamstress Christiane Nissen. When Caroline Paasch informed her husband she was pregnant, Fritz decided they should flee Hamburg and his brother's oppressive fame. He chose Venezuela, where he settled as a piano teacher in 1869. Two years later, he abandoned his wife and young son in Caracas and returned to Germany, now that his renowned older brother had permanently moved to Austria.

Back in Caracas, a facility at the keyboard was handed down through the family to the present-day Fritz, who gravitated to the organ with great success. He was extraordinarily sensitive to the Brahms family history, in which the short Johannes Brahms achieved lasting success while the younger brother, dismissed as "the tall Brahms" or "the wrong Brahms," was overlooked and neglected by history. In anger and denial, as soon as he was of legal age, the present-day Fritz—six times removed from Friedrich Brahms—changed his surname by ripping off the first and last letters, becoming Fritz Rahm to the world.

38

Maestro Lukas Eifer of Graz had just been roundly scolded by his younger brother over a prolonged breakfast that morning.

"You've never been to see the Brahms Room upstairs at the Haydn Museum here?" demanded an appalled Robb.

"No, I have not. I didn't know there was one, and I don't have that great an interest in Haydn the man. My trips to Vienna are usually so filled with appointments, I simply don't have the time for visiting composer sites."

"What about *Beethoven*? Surely you've been to his Vienna sites."

"Actually not. I know all about them, of course, but I've never taken the time to visit them in person."

"Well, the Beethoven sites are too far flung for this morning, but guess what we can do today," Robb said firmly, secretly delighted that he could show his big brother something related to his favorite composer.

And since Lukas was actually free for the next few hours, he acquiesced, surprised at his sudden feeling of elation.

"And I'll even drive us there," offered Robb.

"I wonder why a Brahms memorial room ended up in the Haydn Museum," pondered Lukas.

"I'm not sure, but it seems most appropriate to me. Brahms revered him along with Bach, and actually had a bust of Haydn in his bedroom."

Twenty minutes later they were driving up Haydnstrasse looking for number 19.

"Here we are." Lukas pointed to a small building across the street. There was only one tall story above the ground floor, and the central entry door was open showing a small green backyard of grass and fruit trees—a highly unusual sight near the busy, shop-lined Mariahilfer Strasse. They had to drive one parallel block further before a parking space opened up. As they approached the unpretentious building, Robb remembered something he had learned during his previous visit there.

"Hey, you know Napoleon was a great fan of Haydn's, but did you know that during his occupation of Vienna in eighteen nine he heard that Haydn was dying and sent an honorary guard to stand in front of his house. Picture that!"

"Yes, I had heard that once, but I'd forgotten. Thanks for reminding me. Music is indeed universal."

The brothers walked into the museum, paid the entry fee, and began looking first at the exhibition of Haydn items that included not only manuscripts but the composer's fortepiano and his clavichord. In addition to a bust, there was also Haydn's death mask protected in a glass case. Lukas turned away quickly. Such things depressed him.

"Let's go upstairs to the Brahms Room."

They could see its light green walls from the top of the stairs and walked over to a didactic by the entry door. It informed the visitor that the room beyond contained items from Brahms's last apartment: the large linen cupboard in which the composer kept his scores, a round sewing table kept next to his couch, and also a tall black washstand with a white basin. On the walls were a few photographic images of the composer, including one of him very young sitting at a piano, facing the photographer. Another showed Brahms's desk area with a photograph of the now bearded composer, standing superimposed next to it—a misleading image since Brahms had already passed away when Max Kalbeck photographed his apartment. There was also a reproduction of the Nowak watercolor copy of Kalbeck's photograph showing his living room/music room. And that was it. Sharing the small room was a light wood clavichord identified on the cover as having belonged to Haydn. The brothers strode past it.

"I have to tell you, Robb, I don't think much of this museum's

Brahms Room," said Lukas, as they turned to walk back down to the museum entry. Turning too abruptly, he collided with a short woman who was just entering the room. She had brown hair and was dressed in beige slacks, a beige long-sleeved blouse, and matching beige vest.

"Watch it, *Achtung!*" exclaimed the woman, a beige sling bag around her neck hitting Lukas in the stomach.

"*Ach! Entschuldigung!* Please forgive me, Madame, I am so sorry."

"Oh, it's all right. Brahms can *do* that to one," said Megan graciously.

"Ah, you are a lover of the master, then?" Lukas smiled.

"Totally. In fact, he plays a small role in a lecture I'm giving tomorrow evening." Robb looked at the woman with sudden interest.

"By any chance is your name Megan Crespi?"

"Yes, it is."

"Lukas, this is the professor from Texas we're going to the Leopold Museum tomorrow evening to hear speak about Klimt and Music!"

"Frau Professor Doktor Crespi! What a lucky thing to meet you. We are so much looking forward to hearing what you have to say." Lukas was genuinely pleased to meet the author of one of his prized coffee table books, a reception history of the portraits and statues of Beethoven over the nineteenth century.

"Why, thank you. I've just come from the museum, checking the technical setup, as a matter of fact. And because you were just addressed as 'Lukas,' might you, by any chance, be Maestro Lukas Eifer?" The brothers smiled as Lukas answered with a wave of his hand.

"The very same, Frau Professor Doktor, yes," answered the stocky, white-bearded man who looked so much like Brahms. "And this is my wonderful brother Robb, with whom I stay when in Vienna."

The three shook hands and discussed briefly in low voices what little there was to be seen in the Brahms Room. Megan looked past them assessing something, then spoke.

"But how clever of the Museum to use Haydn's piano keyboard

to display the main remnant, after World War Two bombings, of the grand piano that was on permanent loan to Brahms. You know, the one built by the Vienna piano maker Streicher."

The two men's eyes widened in surprise. They wheeled around to look at the previously ignored Haydn piano. There against the simple open music rack was another, very ornate music rack.

"But how do you know this to be so?" asked Lukas, amazed.

"Oh, because it's identified on the didactic there," Megan pointed to the entry door.

"*Ach!*" Robb laughed, walking toward the door. "We only saw the one on the left side of the doorway, we were in such a hurry to get inside the room. Here's the other one." He began to read out loud.

"On the music rack is a printed badge which says Frau Professor Celestine Truxa, the lady who owned the building in which Brahms lived, sold the piano to the Brahms-Gesellschaft in Vienna on thirty April, nineteen four."

"Why, that's fascinating," murmured Lukas. "Thank you, Frau Professor Doktor Crespi. I can't believe we missed it. But it is on the far side of the door."

"Can we drop you off anywhere?" Robb asked as they exited the museum.

"Well, if you're going toward the Ring, yes, that would be very nice."

"That's exactly where we're bound. I'm introducing my ignorant, older brother here, to Vienna's restaurants, visit by visit. He grew up here but knows nothing of eating places. Today we're having lunch at Salieri's by the Annagasse."

"That's amazing! I had dinner there last night." Megan was pleased to have one of her favorite restaurants in Vienna be confirmed by Robb Eifer's choice.

"Might you be inclined to have lunch with us there today?" Lukas extended the invitation, glancing at his brother for agreement.

"Only if you don't call me 'Frau Professor Doktor,'" Megan answered with a twinkle in her eye.

39

"No, there is absolutely no need for that. But thank you anyway. You are too kind."

It was a few minutes before noon when her cellphone rang, and Agatha Endlich was still in her pajamas after having gone over the Bruckner and Brahms scores all morning. It was Edgar again. He had called her the evening before to ask if there were anything he could do for her before Friday evening's performance. Nothing, she told him, and when he asked if he might come over during the day to hold her hand or do anything helpful, she laughed, thanked him, and said there was no need. And here he was again, asking if he could be helpful in any way. If he could come over. She had not known her answer would be so instantly negative. Her nerves were more on edge than she realized. And adding to that was the sudden barking of her dog Fanny.

"But, Agatha, I'm already at your door. One of your neighbors who was just entering the building let me inside after I identified myself as your colleague at the Musikverein."

"What? You're actually *here*!" The Maestra wasn't sure whether she was irritated or touched. But at least she knew why Fanny was barking.

"Yes. You just can't get rid of me. Are you going to let me in?"

Agatha was surprised by her feelings. After the initial jolt, she found herself quite pleased to have Edgar's company. Perhaps, if he hadn't already had lunch, she would fix lunch for the two of them.

"I'm not dressed yet. If you can wait, I'll open the door in a few minutes."

"Happy to wait."

"All right. See you soon." Agatha dashed to her bedroom, ripped off her pajamas, changed into the pants and shirt she'd spent yesterday in, and gave a quick brush to her hair. She would put her makeup on just before it was time to leave for the Musikverein. Not five minutes had passed before she was unlocking her apartment door. A beaming Edgar stood before her with a large sack in one hand.

"You are the most persistent General Director I have ever come across, Edgar," said the Maestra.

"And I have good reason to be so. Look here what I've brought for you." He dove into his sack and held up a small box as they walked to the living room accompanied by an excited canine who showed particular interest in the sack.

"What is it?" the Maestra asked as they sat down facing each other. Edgar handed her his gift and was silent as the woman opened the box which was blazoned with a logo that read Ring Europe.

"But it's *empty*?"

"That's because I've already installed it—a live camera in your dressing room just over the entry door. Open up your cellphone and we'll download the app. Then you can take a look inside the room from any place in the world and at any time you want to, day or night."

"Oh my god! I love it!"

Agatha turned her cellphone on and handed it to Edgar. He downloaded the app, approved payment to the Musikverein's account, and activated it. Within seconds the cellphone's screen displayed a wide-angle view of the entire dressing room. It was reassuringly empty. Agatha was fascinated and she began to enlarge the view.

"Can anyone else use this camera? I mean see inside my room?"

"Only if you allow it. For instance, the Musikverein should theoretically be able to scan the room, but only, and I've made it clear, *only* if you agree. Either way, you can always set the blur mode if you are changing clothes or something private like that."

"A 'blur' mode. I see the sense of that. But what if I forget to set the blur mode?"

"Maybe have a large 'BLUR' sign facing you on your mirror?"

"Maybe." Agatha frowned, trying to visualize where to put such a sign and how large it should be.

"I'm hoping that you'll allow me access as well. Either way, I've arranged it so the Musikverein adds the small monthly cost to its budget."

"That is so incredibly thoughtful of you, Edgar!"

Edgar reached down into his sack again and pulled out a small item, hiding it in his hand, and then pressing it into the palm of Agatha's hand. Two keys lay there.

"From now on, dear Maestra, please *lock* your office door *and* your dressing room door at our Musikverein. I've had new locks installed and here are your keys. Use them! Please put them on your car and house key chain, since that's the only thing you bring with you when you conduct. Promise?"

"I promise. Thank you, Edgar. Certainly helps to know the General Director." The two beamed at each other in silence. The silence continued as they looked happily at each other. Agatha broke it.

"Perhaps I can repay you in small change. Have you had lunch yet? I could fix us something."

"Already taken care of," Edgar dove into his sack again, a pleasant aroma filling the room as he opened up a container with fresh spring rolls and several sauces inside.

"Unbelievable! You know, I could *marry* an ingenious man like you." Agatha could not believe she had just said what she said.

"And I could marry a *helpless* woman like you any time," Edgar responded jokingly. Actually, he thought to himself, Agatha is one of the strongest women I've ever met.

To fill the sudden silence that followed, Agatha reached for the container of spring rolls and marched toward the kitchen.

"Lunch will be served in precisely six minutes. Does the General Director prefer tea or coffee?"

40

Of middle height, clean-shaven, with a short Prussian haircut and prominent nose, Maestro Christian Begeist of the Bruckner Orchester Linz and his former assistant conductor Dieter Unfug, also clean-shaven but slightly overweight, and with ridiculously long sideburns, were in the latter's Volkswagen Golf on their drive north from Wiener Neustadt to Vienna that Friday afternoon. It was a drive Dieter was used to now since finding part-time work at a venerable old store in Vienna, the violin maker and string instrument repair and sales shop known as Atelier im Musikverein Wilfried Ramsaier-Gorbach. The store was actually situated inside the Musikverein on the short Canovagasse. Except for having to walk there from a downtown parking garage, it was most convenient. A further plus was that Dieter could spend time in the Musikverein's Archive researching and studying scores of Bruckner. He would be ready in case Maestro Begeist should ever become incapacitated.

As they drove, the two men were discussing how much Bruckner's initial background as organist at the Abbey of Saint Florian, so close to his hometown, and now part of Linz, had influenced his symphonies, especially the mammoth Eighth Symphony they would be hearing at the Musikverein that evening.

"You know, I think his endlessly revised symphonies often turn the orchestra into a virtual pipe organ," opined Christian.

"Oh, yes, I heartily agree," Dieter said. "There's a sense of effortless modulation. And his orchestration so often doesn't mingle the strings, woodwinds, and brass, but rather features the purity of their distinctive voices. Just like a pipe organ."

"Wouldn't it be wonderful if there were recordings of Bruckner's extraordinary gift for improvisation on the organ?" Christian exclaimed.

"Wouldn't it? When you think of the rave reviews he received, especially during his tours of Paris and London."

"Well, his formative years were spent at one of the greatest organs in Europe. No doubt that helped!"

"And no wonder he asked to be buried under it," quipped Dieter, keeping his eye on the road. Turning serious, he asked Christian whether he thought Bruckner should be credited with eleven symphonies, considering that three of the four early ones— you could call them "tries"—were never given a number by Bruckner. All four were composed while he was still in Linz. And the second Linz symphony, the one in F Minor, was allotted a "Study Symphony" designation by him. Sometimes was referred to as number "Zero Zero."

"But that Study Symphony is indeed a four-movement symphony," Dieter continued, glancing at Christian. "And it really does qualify as a symphony, as does the next one, written in Vienna, the one in D Minor, numbered by Bruckner as Symphony Number 'Zero Zero.'"

"Oh, yes. I know he called it '*Nullte*.' Somewhat confusing."

"So the first two I've mentioned," Dieter persisted, "aren't numbered as symphonies, yet are considered the two symphonies which, added to the nine numbered symphonies, make a grand total of eleven."

"And that doesn't make sense to you, Dieter?"

"Umm, not completely, Maestro."

"I know it can be perplexing. And, because poor, insecure, self-critical Bruckner engaged in so much revision of each symphony, you could almost say he wrote twenty-two symphonies."

"No! Please stop while the stopping's good!" implored Dieter, who had never really thought much about the correct numbering of Bruckner symphonies until Agatha Endlich's Double B Composers presentation. What he really cared about was that it should have been *his* Maestro, and not Maestra Endlich, conducting Bruckner.

"Well, you just haven't had time in your brief career to grapple with the master's early work."

"True, too true. But I have another question for you, Christian. Why do you think Endlich skipped Bruckner's Symphonies Numbers Five, Six, and Seven, and jumped ahead, selecting Number Eight to pair with the Brahms's Third?"

"I can understand why, numerically, she jumped beyond the Fifth with its counterpoint virtuosity as being too complicated for today's audiences. And likewise, she declined presenting the Sixth, with its relentless rhythm of those two quarter notes followed by quarter note triplets—dum dum, da da da, dum, dum, da da da. Or quarter note triplets followed by two quarter notes—da, da, da, dum, dum. She skipped it as too confounding for a modern, mostly ignorant audience. As for the Seventh, Endlich probably realized it's so well-known, after having been initially lauded as the 'greatest symphony composed after Beethoven,' that she decided to leap ahead to the gargantuan Eighth, which is such a showpiece for the orchestra."

"Interesting. Yes, I agree. And he uses Wagner tubas in that one," offered Dieter, proud that he knew at least that about the baffling sequence.

"All this makes sense if you consider that Endlich hoped to benefit the best from what is really the Tenth Symphony even though it's numbered as the Eighth."

Dieter nodded his hard-earned understanding and concentrated on his driving. They had taken the Süd Autobahn/A 4, which was a drive of just a bit under an hour from Wiener Neustadt to Vienna in total. Suddenly he pointed to a sign on the highway.

"Hey, Christian! We've got plenty of time. What say we visit Mödling?" The historic town with its access to the Vienna Woods was just twenty minutes south of Vienna.

"Fine idea. I haven't been there in ages."

In the world of music Mödling had been a favorite retreat of both Beethoven and Arnold Schönberg. It was to the Schönberg-Haus, where the twentieth-century composer lived for seven years and where he conceived the radically new musical system later called the "twelve-tone system," that the two conductors drove. Neither of them had ever been there. The seven-room museum lived up to their expectations, with many of Schönberg's original furnishings and his cello as well as interesting photographs from different phases of his life, both in Vienna and in Los Angeles. And one of the composer's haunting Expressionist self-portraits heads in oil faced a life-size color reproduction of Oskar Kokoschka's 1924 portrait of him in the act of playing the cello, except, with a defiance of mundane reality, the cello is not shown.

This brief visit back into music and art history provided the two conductors a helpful calm before the storm in store for the Musikverein performance that evening. The tempest of Bruckner's mammoth Eighth Symphony pummeling Brahms's anemic Third Symphony, as Christian phrased it.

And then the tornado.

41

Because the weather was so beautiful, Megan's impromptu lunch at Salieri's with Maestro Lukas Eifer and his brother Robb was consumed outdoors at one of the restaurant's sidewalk tables next to a border of boxed green plants. The two men pressed their guest to reveal details of her Leopold Museum lecture, but she agilely avoided specifics by asking them questions in return. One thing she did share in advance with them was that she had just finished writing a book on the changing image of Brahms, and there would be a bit of that in the lecture. When the fellows discovered that she too was attending the Double B Composers concert series, the conversation grew spirited as they discussed the merits of Maestra Endlich, Bruckner, and Brahms.

"Of course it should have been my brother conducting this unusual series of Bruckner and, or versus, Brahms. I guess the kindest interpretation of this lack of recognition concerning my genius brother is that Graz is just too far away. Which, of course, it is not! Why if you take the Süd Autobahn/A four, it's only two and a half hours. No, I think a great mistake, even injustice occurred when this series was planned. Such a snub to my brother should not go unrecognized. And do you think those of us who work at the Musikverein—I'm deputy director of the archives, library, and collections there—do you think any of us were told, informed, or consulted about the Double B Composers series?" Indignation charged Robb's words.

Megan saw that the younger brother idolized his older brother and that this was the motivation for his complaint. "*La familigia é tutto*," she thought to herself.

The two men wanted to know what Megan thought of the Dallas Opera's Hart Institute for Women Conductors, where the Maestra had studied. She couldn't praise it enough and was pleased that Lukas had heard of some of its graduates, now productive conductors around the globe.

"Certainly your Dallas Institute has been successful," Robb commented. His conductor brother nodded, equally impressed. The conversation turned to Brahms, and Lukas held forth with a sudden passion that surprised his brother and his American listener. Megan had been covertly studying the Maestro's amazing resemblance to the composer in height—no taller than five feet, three inches—his portliness, and his sweeping white beard.

"So which of the 'two Bs' is your favorite, Megan," he asked leaning back and stretching his arms out, "now that you know where we stand?" The three had easily shifted to a first name basis.

"What can I tell you? I don't really know Bruckner's symphonies well and so I've been listening with great interest, even though I feel his bombastic universe is not my universe. As for Brahms, I adore his music. My first introduction to him was by way of the Requiem. Eons ago, when I was in a chapel choir in New York, we performed his Requiem. That was one reason I studied German and not Italian in college. The very first two words held me—'*selig sind*'—blessed are they.' So soothing."

"And?" encouraged Robb.

"And I've always loved Brahms, particularly the first and third symphonies and also a lot of the late piano solo music, especially opus one hundred eighteen, and its second piece, the Intermezzo in A major. That surprise high A at the beginning of the third bar really gets me. It gets me every time, even though I know it's coming."

"Ha!" laughed Lukas. "It's supposed to. You know those six introspective pieces were dedicated to Clara, don't you?" A happy smile animated Megan's face.

"Yes, I certainly do. And I have even gone so far as to wonder whether it might be possible that the persistent A in that Intermezzo could be a secret, loving reference to the hallucinatory A-note her husband heard so persistently during his final years." Lukas looked at Megan musingly.

"Do you think Johannes and Clara were lovers?"

Megan felt immediate indignation. Why does everyone always ask that question? She considered what she knew carefully before she answered. And then the words poured out of her.

"I believe it is not possible to come to a final conclusion about that enduring friendship spanning four decades. We know that during Robert's final two years in an insane asylum, Clara was not allowed to visit him until two days before he died, and that a desperately caring Johannes came to live with her in Düsseldorf, console her, and help with her seven children still living at home. Yes, his bedroom was on a separate floor—he later took up an apartment above Clara's— but did he wish to become the eighth child to whom Clara gave her love, some Oedipus-minded smartie might ask? They both adored, cared for, and loved each other and testosterone may have carried the day shortly before or briefly after Robert died. Certainly Clara did not dismiss her bodily urgencies. I'm sure you both know that she and Robert had special diary designations for sexual activity. And later she did have, after all, that brief affair with a musician closer to her in age."

"You're talking about the composer-organist Theodor Kirchner, I take it," Lukas confirmed. "He even looked a bit like Robert!"

"No, actually, in photos of him as a young man he looks like Brahms," Robb intervened. He had been following the spirited conversation between the conductor and the art historian with interest. Megan picked up where Lukas had left off.

"Yes, all three were photographed in the typical poses of the times and all three had similar haircuts. They did have an astonishing similarity of looks in their younger years. But back to Johannes and Clara. I think it was not only financial need but spiritual, or call it psychological, urgency that they split so soon after Robert's death—she to Berlin, he to Detmold. She *needed* the security of the concert stage, *needed* to regain her reputation as one of the greatest pianists of the age, and, of course, *needed* to support her large family. Musical immersion was salvation for them both—permanence as opposed to what might briefly have happened physically between them. And notice I said *might*."

"All right, Megan," an engaged Lukas conceded. "I shall adopt your pronounced uncertainty concerning whether or not they were lovers in the ordinary sense. The fascinating aspect is that their singular relationship, despite regularly perceived slights and disappointments, persevered all their lives."

"Hear, hear!" agreed Robb, holding up his wine glass. The others followed suit, although Megan's glass held only sparkling water.

It had been a lunch to remember.

42

Checking things that afternoon at his beloved Musikverein before the Friday evening performance, Peter Heimnis was shocked to see a video camera had been installed in the Maestra's dressing room. Right above the entry door, providing an almost 360-degree sweep of the room. Once again, it would seem, the upper reaches of the administration had bypassed him. This sort of thing was within his purview and they knew it. Of course he understood why one had been put up, what with the pathetic practical joke that had come the Maestra's way this week. But he should have been the person asked to set up the camera. Setting off a stink bomb inside a bouquet of roses! Why the heck had someone done that?

He could hack into the camera with a config and get the username which, he presumed, would be that of the Maestra. Further rapid churning would likely produce passwords and he could be anonymously sharing the app within minutes. That would give him the same blur capability as the owner, should he wish to avail himself of it. This could be handy if his mysterious employer had further weirdo instructions for him. Initially, it had just been leaving an envelope on the Maestra's office desk during the first of the Double B Composers concerts. This harmless mission had earned him 100 euros for his trouble—welcome funds mailed to his home address. Somehow Herr X, as Peter had begun calling the man to himself, knew he was coping with medical expenses incurred by his wife's recently botched hip replacement. Then, for a second 100 euros, it was directing his sixteen-year-old son Klaus—how did he know the boy's name?—to carry out an innocent enough task. Pick up, forty-five minutes before the Maestra's eight o'clock performance, a large bouquet of red roses from a man with dark hair wearing sunglasses who would be standing in front of the flower shop at the Hotel Bristol on the Kärntner Ring. The caller asked for Klaus's cellphone number in case they missed each other. The boy was to deliver the flowers in person to the Maestra while she was in her dressing room preparing for the Wednesday evening performance. He was to say "toi toi toi," and that the humongous bouquet was from the house ushers, then he was to leave immediately. Heimnis had been as surprised as the Maestra when the bouquet turned out to conceal a stink bomb. He had questioned Klaus at length as to whether he was the prankster, but the boy was genuinely shocked that a bouquet from the fancy Bristol flower shop could contain anything like that.

Should he share the Maestra's dressing room surveillance camera just to be sure nothing else went on there that could be more than a practical joke? Indulging in a sip of whiskey from his hip flask, he typed several instructions into his computer. Done. He could check out the room any time he wished.

43

Lunch with the Eifer brothers did not break up until almost three o'clock, and as Megan walked back to the Römischer Kaiser, the attractive idea of taking a short nap came to her. Not that she was tired, it was just that fifteen or twenty minutes stretched out on her very comfortable hotel bed seemed a wise thing to do.

"Oh, Frau Doktor! An envelope was just left for you," the receptionist said, as Megan passed him on her way to the elevator. Herr Amt, whom she knew from numberless stays at the hotel, quickly pulled a large envelope out from one of the mail slots behind him and handed it to her.

The elevator was in use so she opened the envelope on the spot, right at the desk. It contained a long handwritten note over two sheets of paper, and a photograph. Megan looked at the photograph first. It was of a colored drawing. Realistically rendered, it showed a small group of women standing and singing on the far right and opposite them on the left, a man playing a concert grand piano, his right hand raised toward the choir. The angle of the drawing was from right of center, the somewhat look-alike singers were in profile while the clearly articulated features of the pianist's bearded face showed him looking commandingly at his choir. He looked to be in his early forties perhaps. At the bottom right of the drawing in miniscule hand was the date 1878 and above that was an extended, capitalized single letter: K.

Gustav Klimt? Interesting. That artist was born in 1862 so he would have only been sixteen that year. Megan turned to the accompanying letter. Written in a very readable, if small hand, it was in almost perfect English:

Honorable Mrs. Professor Doctor Crespi,

I look forward so to your lecture at the Leopold Museum tomorrow evening on Gustav Klimt and Music. Perhaps it interests you to see this depiction of a choirmaster and his choir drawn by my ancestor, Ernst Klimt. He was the younger, by two years, brother of the famous Gustav Klimt. In 1877 he joined his older brother to be student at Vienna Kunstgewerbeschule. Unlike Gustav, who was studying architectural painting, Ernst studied engraving in order to become engraver, like their father. Both Ernst and Gustav also loved music and after school they would often sneak into the nearby Musikverein in order to listen to and watch rehearsals of the Women's Choir held in the smaller auditorium there. They would sneak down and in the darkened auditorium give themselves front row seats, unbeknownst to the choir director or singers. My great-great-granduncle Gustav had his unquenchable interest in women even then, although he was only sixteen in 1878, the date of the drawing of which I enclose a photograph. As you, a renowned Klimt expert, certainly know, he later fathered fourteen illegitimate children.

When I inherited this drawing, about the size of a book, even though it is in bright colored pencils, I did not think it interesting enough to hang on my wall and so I put it away in a drawer with other inherited small items that went back to the nineteenth century. However, recently my granddaughter Lisl, who is now also a student at Kunstgewerbeschule, asked to see the drawing and she thinks it might be valuable.

I have waited to ask experts here because I do not know of any, or how to contact them, but upon learning in the paper that you, an authority on Gustav Klimt, will be speaking in our beautiful city, it seemed to me to be a good idea if I leave you this note and a photograph of the artwork that has been in our family so long. The Leopold Museum kindly informed me where you are staying. I hope to speak to you after your lecture if you are not too busy. I will bring my granddaughter and the drawing with me to your lecture.

In the hope that you find the drawing interesting, and, perhaps even valuable!

With kindest regards,
Margret Klimt Grainer

Oh, what fun! Megan's first reaction triggered one question and affirmed one certainty. Which brother actually did the drawing? Based on the precociousness of the work, it had to be Gustav. Gustav, who early in his career had created several different what could be called homages to music. Megan would be handling them in her lecture.

The certainty? The certainty was wonderfully obvious. The choirmaster with receding hairline and long, dark-blond hair, looking to be in his mid-forties in the year 1878 could only be one person.

The recently bearded Johannes Brahms.

44

Edgar's lunch with Agatha in her cozy apartment had been long and lively. She practiced looking into her dressing room via her new Ring Europe app camera. When Edgar left to tend to things at the Musikverein, it was already half past three.

"Things will be just fine tonight, so don't you worry," were his parting words. And Agatha felt new strength flowing through her veins as she returned to her scores to Bruckner's Eighth and Brahms's Third. The massive Bruckner symphony she knew extremely well, having led several performances of it in her previous post as conductor of the Bruckner Orchester in Linz. She had delighted in emphasizing to her instrumentalists that, other than his contemporary César Frank, Bruckner was the first important composer since Bach whose main instrument was the organ. And that was why, perhaps, she was able to pull such a thickly woven tapestry of sounds from her brass section. She hoped to do the same this evening with the Wiener Philharmonic.

The regular 145-piece orchestra had been augmented for the occasion with a second harp and four Wagner tubas—those horns combining the tonal properties of French horn and tuba, with its smaller bell held upright. What a sound was achieved with these instruments that could be intimate or thunderous! Ideal for the mysterious opening and closing of the first movement and for the savage scherzo of the second, the heart-rending theme of the third movement's immense adagio, and the fourth movement's swelling grandiosity—just like a full organ.

Yes, she believed she would be able to pull all this out of

Bruckner's Eighth again. More challenging for her, only because she had conducted it fewer times, was Brahms's Third Symphony in F major. She loved the musical cipher present in the opening, with its three powerful chords underscoring the notes F-A-flat-F. Brahms cognoscenti agreed the chords were an intended variant on what the composer had once expressed in music as his life maxim: "*frei aber froh*"—"free but happy." This had been summed up early by the notes F-A-F, Brahms's cipher response to his friend Joachim's musical motto F-A-E, standing for "*frei aber einsam*"—"free but lonely." Unlike Joachim, *he* had declared himself not lonely but happy. These two differing statements were purposefully introduced into the "F-A-E" violin and piano sonata co-written in Düsseldorf by Robert Schumann, his student Albert Dietrich, and Brahms for Joachim to play when he arrived in town. Agatha understood that in Brahms's Third Symphony essentially all of the melodic ideas were related to this simple musical motif. The motif, displayed in vibrant orchestral colors, was handled with the organic development and metrical flexibility for which Brahms was known. Agatha felt humbled by the responsibility involved in conveying all this, but also honored. As she leafed through the score once more, she felt up to it. She would give Brahms her all.

45

Dogged days of research in Vienna's rich Archive of the Society of Friends of Music at the Musikverein had finally paid off. And handsomely. After weeks of work looking through the unpublished scores of his great-great-great-grandfather, Venezuelan organist Fritz Rahm had come upon with what he was looking for. Proof of plagiarism.

In his beloved ancestor's clearly recognizable notation for the third movement of his Fifth Symphony was definite proof that the high and mighty Johannes had stolen a thematic idea from his younger brother. How? Because his great-great-great-grandfather's score was an enunciation of what the world thinks is one of Johannes Brahms most famous melodies—a slow, sad *waltz*, introduced by cellos and then taken up by violins and eventually by flutes, then oboes, and finally horns. All this occurs at the beginning of the third movement of melody-lifter Johannes's Third Symphony, completed in 1883. But Friedrich Brahms, already up to his *Fifth* Symphony by then, had composed a third movement to this opus that began with the same mournful waltz! The date of Fritz's great-great-great-grandfather's unpublished Fifth Symphony? The year 1879—*four years earlier than Johannes's Third!*

At last he had accomplished the first of his two aims while in Vienna. Neglected in the Archive of the Society of Friends of Music, to which Johannes Brahms had given his musical legacy, he, the modern day "wrong" Fritz, had discovered proof that his great-great-great-granduncle was a *musical thief.* A colossal, undeniable example of the evidence lay in front of him. Slipping his cellphone out of his pocket, Fritz quickly took several detail photos of the document in front of him.

Tonight's Double B Composers concert would be featuring his great-great-great-grandfather's plagiarized Fifth Symphony.

He would be there in his front-row orchestra seat, within lunging distance of the conductor. His second aim, revealing the man's musical theft to the world, would also be realized. All he needed was to purchase one single item and smuggle it into the concert hall with him.

46

Tony Bocello's day had gone exceptionally well. That morning he had met with the Musikverein's Leo Feinstimm, one of the most knowledgeable and articulate acoustic engineers he had ever encountered. Once again Tony was impressed with the amazing near-perfect, long reverberation time of the venerable concert hall. It had all the proven requirements: its relatively small size, an optimum audience of no more than 2,200 people, a raised stage, irregular interior surfaces, plaster interior, and details such as the hollow golden caryatid statues lining the ground floor that created multiple reflections in a plane just over the heads of the audience. This allows, Feinstimm explained, sound reflections to be sustained without being absorbed by the audience. Tony had to admit to himself that he was always so intent upon the music being performed that he had not attentively studied those life-size gold caryatids or the numerous plaster statues that reclined on the many ornamental pediments lining the two long walls of the hall. And he was surprised to learn that the great organ pipes behind the orchestra were fakes, allowing for repairs to be made to the real ones without affecting the hall's acoustics. Feinstimm sent out for lunch when their meeting stretched past noon, and Tony's question about reverberation times was answered in excruciating detail.

Thus it was an almost too well informed Tony Bocello who staggered out of the majestic Musikverein building at two forty-five and hurriedly made his way to meet his old friend Edgar Wittgenstein in the colorful Fleischmarkt area of the inner city. They had planned to meet at three o'clock at Vienna's oldest restaurant, the historic Griechenbeisl, dating from the middle of the fifteenth century. The reason for their choice was not its antiquity, but rather the fact that it was a favorite locale of Beethoven, Schubert, and Brahms. How appropriate, considering the quartet of symphonies by Brahms being performed over a single week at the Musikverein. Miraculously, Tony got to the front garden, enclosed by a hedge of green, just at the very moment the hour struck three. And there he was! Edgar, vigorously waving at him from a white-clothed table close to the restaurant's simple entrance. He was sitting right under a large striding figure of the legendary seventeenth-century ballad singer and bagpiper Augustin who entertained at local Viennese inns and restaurants during the Great Plague. Edgar could clearly see the huge identifying gold letters circling around him that proudly stated: "*HIER SANG SEIN LIED ZUM 1. MAL DER LIEBE AUGUSTIN.*" Greatly amused, Tony translated the words to himself: "Here sang his song for the first time the dear Augustin."

Edgar stood up as Tony approached him intoning the well-known song "O Du Lieber Augustin, Augustin, Augustin,"—once ostentatiously if dissonantly used by Schönberg in the second movement of his second quartet—and the two friends hugged. They had met years ago during Tony's first trip to Vienna when he was scouting out the best European auditoriums for acoustical emulation at Dallas's Meyerson Symphony Center. By closely emulating the fundamental features of the Wiener Musikverein hall, the Meyerson had been a crowning success.

"So, Tony! You are looking as young as ever," said Edgar, looking at him up and down.

"And you are still the great fib teller! I really do look and feel my great age now."

"Ah, I did not fib to you about our Musikverein, did I? Now tell me: would you rather talk out here where it's a bit noisy, or retreat indoors to the Mark Twain Zimmer?"

"What? A Mark Twain room? Are you kidding?"

"Not at all. Don't you ignorant Americans know that Mark Twain was here in Vienna for almost two years?"

"I did not. When was that?" Tony was amazed he didn't know that about the creator of the still-subject-to-discussion characters Huckleberry Finn and Tom Sawyer.

"*Ach*, I don't remember the exact dates but it was in the late eighteen nineties if memory serves me right. With his whole family. The headlines were full of him and even the emperor wanted to meet him and did. So, where shall we sit? Outside here, or indoors where you can see his signature."

"I'd rather stay out here," Tony said, welcoming sunshine after his many hours inside one of the dark upper offices of the Musikverein.

"Your choice, my friend, your choice." They both ordered a refreshing Berliner Weisse, that low alcohol beer which came, in Vienna, with a raspberry syrup. Tony had had enough of acoustics for the day and instead asked about the performances of the Double B Composers concerts he had missed.

"So far they have been quite a success. Audiences seem to love the pairing idea, and our radiant, resident conductor, Agatha Endlich, has shown adroitness and sensitivity in communicating the two very different styles of Bruckner, the musically bloated, spectacular Wagnerite, some say; and of Brahms, the abstractionist who united classical form with romantic expression if I can put it that way."

"You certainly can with me," smiled Tony, taking a sip of his refreshing Berliner Weisse.

"We began this past Monday evening with each composer's First Symphony, of course, and it was clear to see that our audience was fascinated by the two contrasting characters of the music. It's interesting that both Bruckner and Brahms spent so much time revising their symphonies, especially their first ones. They were each in their very early forties when they pronounced them done."

"And Bruckner was what—nine, ten years older than Brahms?" Tony asked.

"Yes, nine years older. And yet they died within seven months of each other, both here in Vienna."

"And how did the Wednesday evening concert go?"

"Well, that was a little problematic. Not with the music so much, although in certain spots the Maestra did exaggerate various tempi ever so slightly. But the two symphonies in their expansive, for Bruckner, and pastoral, for Brahms, manner were a big success." Edgar said no more. A shadow had crossed his face.

"Is something wrong?" asked Tony, surprised by his friend's sudden silence." Are you worried about tonight?"

"Not so much worried as slightly apprehensive."

"Apprehensive?" Tony was genuinely concerned, and Edgar suddenly needed an outsider to talk with. Kindly, older, and wiser Tony Bocello filled the need.

"A few very strange incidents have been triggered by our concert series. And they've been *mean* incidents, really mean. The first one was simply scary. When the Maestra returned to her office after we'd had dinner together a few evenings ago, she found an envelope on her desk with a message that said, and I remember the message word for word: 'Never pair Catholic Bruckner and Protestant Brahms again. You have committed an obscenity and if you continue with your travesty you will be punished.'"

"How weird! And as you say, how mean. But what does the writer wish to convey by calling the pairing of Bruckner and Brahms a travesty? He emphasizes their religion, and certainly Bruckner was an almost overly fervent Catholic. And Brahms, of course, had a Protestant background. But why would playing a symphony by each composer in a single evening's program constitute a travesty? A mockery of what? Or of whom? I understand your concern, Edgar. And to threaten punishment! Oh, the poor Maestra. She must have been terribly upset and frightened."

Edgar was absorbing his friend's flood of outrage and alarm. It was good to hear his own feelings expressed by someone else.

"This is what is so amazing about our Maestra, about Agatha. She was actually able to brush it off as a poor joke. I was far more concerned than she seemed to be."

"But now you're halfway through the series and nothing bad has happened, right?"

"Nothing really bad, but there has been another incident. Preparing for her second concert in her dressing room, Agatha answered a knock on the door and it was a young boy who thrust an enormous bouquet of roses at her, said it was from the ushers, and then immediately disappeared down the hall. There was no accompanying card and since it was almost time to mount the podium and she had no vase in the room, Agatha just stood the inconvenient anonymous gift in a corner of the room and left to conduct."

"And?" Tony could see the story had more coming.

"And when I accompanied her to her dressing room after the concert was over, we opened the door to discover that someone had outfitted the rose bouquet with a timed stink bomb! The billowing smell was disgusting."

"Disgusting. Yet so childish. Do you think this was done by the same person who left the threat note?"

"I haven't really decided whether it was one and the same person or if it was two different people, since the first act was vicious and the second childish. What do you think?" Edgar asked almost imploringly.

"I'm not sure. The two acts are so different. As though conceived by different minds. How is the Maestra taking it?"

"Well, she's holding up but it's definitely had an effect on her. Her conducting of the Brahms wasn't up to par, I hate to say. And even her Brückner had some weak spots as far as tempo was concerned. I believe the threatening note left on her desk has affected her more than even she realized."

"Of course. Things like that can deepen with time. Have you had a chance to talk with her today?"

"Actually, I dropped by her place late this morning just to check on her as well as tell her something which I hoped would comfort her. On my own, I installed a Ring Europe surveillance camera in her dressing room that she can check via her cellphone. I downloaded the app and we tried it out on the spot. I tied into it as well and that seemed to comfort her a lot. There's a blur capability that she can flip to if she's changing clothes or just wants privacy while in the room, and she liked that. Plus I even got the Musikverein to pay for it."

"Well, what a grand idea, Edgar. That should give her a good degree of confidence. I know how much those surveillance cameras have meant to my children and grandchildren. You feel so much more secure knowing you can check on things even while you're away."

"I think so. We've got the motion detector on so we'll both be notified should anyone enter. Although that should be difficult now as she's begun locking her door—something she had never bothered to do before. Such a trusting nature."

"I am so looking forward to meeting her in person Sunday evening after the final performance," Tony said sincerely. "I remember she was one of the awardees of our Dallas Opera's Hart Institute for Women Conductors, but unfortunately our paths never crossed."

"How about another Berliner Weisse?" a smiling Edgar asked, looking at his watch and seeing that it was only a few minutes after four, plenty of time before returning to the Musikverein to supervise preparations for tonight's third Double B Composers Concert.

"Great suggestion," responded Tony. Edgar raised his hand and caught the attention of their waiter and pointed to their empty glasses. Almost instantly a new round of Berliner Weisse was placed in front of the two men. They lifted their glasses and smiled at each other.

"To the Maestra!" said Tony.

"Oh, yes, to our Maestra!" said Edgar.

47

The two Brucknerite conductors, one employed, the other seeking an orchestra position, were enjoying an early dinner at Vienna's renowned Hotel Sacher, just off the pedestrian Kärntner Strasse and a convenient ten-minute walk to the third Double B Composers Concert at the Musikverein.

"Are you having any second thoughts about the little incendiary drama?" asked Christian.

"Not yet. I'll be judging the distance and the people in the seats around us as well as directly below our balcony seats, of course, but I'm definitely still game," Dieter answered. His great hope was that the distraught Maestra would be too nervous to continue the program and that *his* Maestro would be called to the podium. He had made sure that it was known to the general director that the Maestro from Linz was attending these Double B Composers concerts.

"And when exactly do you plan to trigger the device and yell 'fire'? At what musical moment in the Brahms Third?"

"Tell me first where in the symphony *you* would create havoc," smiled Dieter challengingly.

"Hmm. I don't want the poor audience, still so full of our magnificent Bruckner sound, to hear any more of Brahms than it must. So I guess I'd yell 'fire' on that third hysterical opening chord of F major," answered Christian.

"Ha! That's what I initially thought of doing too," Dieter laughed. "You know when the thing was first performed by the Boston Symphony in eighteen eighty-four, while Brahms was still living, *several hundred* people walked out. I'm pretty sure that news reached even Vienna."

"Or maybe they kept the news from him," Christian reasoned. "So when would *you* yell 'fire'?"

"You're not going to like this, perhaps, but I'd let the poor beleaguered audience sit through the entire first two movements, the Allegro and the Andante with their excessive light-headedness. By then they'll have snoozed right into the calm, insipid third movement, so about thirty measures before the end when sound asleep, they will be wrenched awake by my horrified cry of 'fire' which I'm sure other people are bound to repeat immediately. Instant bedlam should break out. And you and I can be among the first to make a terrified run for the exit."

"Ha! Excellent thinking," Christian pronounced.

"Pairing that insipid North German Protestant with our good-hearted Catholic Austrian countryman is a musical charade, and we are only being good citizens to protest it, since Vienna's main music critic won't. When I think of how the people of Linz cherish their native composer every time I schedule his music." The Maestro of the Bruckner Orchester Linz shook his head in disgust.

"The Viennese are impossible. Not only did they accept that noisy composer from Bonn, Beethoven—you know his name means beet yard—they fell for his worshipper from Hamburg, Brahms. It's inexplicable."

"Yeah. And what about that Vienna critic? She seems to be partial to Brahms," Dieter said.

"Well, as I've said many times, she's unmarried, probably a feminist, probably gay, and probably Jewish."

"You're talking about Stefanie Schreib, of course."

"Who else? People seem to worship her here."

"Well, at least she was somewhat critical of Agatha Endlich's tempi in her review of the second Double B Composers thing."

"Yes, I was reading it in your mother's newspaper; at least that, but you remember I was whispering my critiques into your ear even during the performance."

"Yes, I know," affirmed Dieter, keeping to himself that the loud hisses had jarred him to distraction.

"All right, my boy. Tonight should be quite a performance in more ways than one. I know you can carry it off successfully."

"I'm hoping it will cause them to cancel the final pairing."

"It may do something else."

"Huh?" Dieter was taken aback by his friend's murmured remark, as though he were talking only to himself.

"Oh, nothing. What say we order two fillets mignon? Beef up our strength, so to say, for the main event."

Dieter nodded happy agreement and Maestro Begeist, keeping his dark thoughts to himself, signaled a passing waiter.

48

Five o'clock and Megan was in her hotel room, still blissfully fiddling with the images she would be using for her lecture the following evening. The unexpected bonanza of a photograph of what she was certain was a minor work drawn by Gustav Klimt had suggested a different start for her beginning. Here was a colored drawing dated as early as 1878, when the artist was just a teenager, of a choir rehearsal with what had to be Johannes Brahms at the piano! Freshly bearded, with long dark blond hair, the forty-five-or-so-year-old composer was immediately recognizable. Should Megan begin with this fascinating, unknown image? She still hadn't decided when the phone in her room rang.

"So you're back from your appointments, are you, Tony?" she said without waiting for the caller's voice to sound.

"I am indeed and ready to eat. Are you hungry?"

"Yes," Megan suddenly realized, "I am. And it would probably be wise to eat even a bit earlier than six if we don't want to be rushed before the concert."

"I agree. Which restaurant do you suggest tonight? Something close to the Musikverein again, yes?"

"You bet!"

"Something on the Annagasse, I suspect?"

"Right again. But you have a choice between Austrian food or Italian. Which would you like?"

"Austrian. Does that surprise you?"

"No. It tells me you've walked by the Wienerwald restaurant on the other side of our street near the Kärntner Strasse. It's an oldie. Have you eaten there this trip?"

"No. But I did eat there my first time in Vienna. And I have happy memories of its cozy interior and good food."

"Shall we meet in the lobby in about twenty minutes?" Megan wanted to take her regular PetCam look at her beloved little Button, presently residing at her sister's house. She folded away her just-revised lecture text, which she still read from printout, and not on her laptop—too many things to control! She laughed out loud as she thought of foreign lecture stints in the past when she traveled with four carousels for just two speeches. Showing images in pairs was almost unknown in Europe at that time. Then she plopped down into the lounge chair facing her bed, held up her iPhone, and within seconds was looking at Button. With the time difference of seven hours, it was eleven in the morning in Dallas and he was wide awake, chasing Tina's Japanese Spaniels around the house. Megan waited for them to round the corner again into the living room, where the camera was installed, and watched the racing for a few precious minutes. Then she closed the app, unconsciously patting her cellphone.

A look in the mirror made her decide she should dress up her daytime clothes just a bit. To her all-beige outfit of shoes, slacks, blouse, and vest she added her elegant white-and-beige long scarf. Removing the hood from her elegant black raincoat and stuffing her cloth black hat with narrow brim into the coat's righthand pocket in case of drafts, she took another look in the mirror, and pronounced herself ready. Confirming that the Brahms mystery key was still in her small sling purse, she headed downstairs.

A beaming, flushed-cheeked Tony stood at the reception counter and was facing the elevator door when it opened for Megan on the ground floor.

"You look as if you've had a good day, Tony."

"So it shows? Yes. Lots of info, lots of joviality, lots of Berliner Weisse, Du lieber Augustin, Du."

"Ah ha, so I am guessing you had lunch or maybe just drinks at the Griechenbeisl, am I right?"

"You are absolutely right, Megan. Shall we proceed to the Wienerwald for some sustenance?"

"Absolutely!" The two friends linked arms, pushed the

hotel's heavy glass door open, and strode up the Annagasse to the cheery old restaurant, the name and décor of which was the Vienna Woods. They would catch up on each other's day over cold beer and Wienerschnitzel. Each had much to tell the other, and Megan could hardly wait to show Tony the Brahms bust key.

49

It was a quarter to seven and from her home the Maestra took yet another cellphone peek around her Musikverein dressing room via the newly installed Ring Europe camera Edgar had so thoughtfully installed. She held her phone down so her dog could see the screen.

"See, Fanny, see? This is where *Mutti* will be tonight. You have to stay home, but I'll be back and give you your good night treat. All right?" The dog moaned in happy expectation at the sound of the word "treat."

The new security capability was making a huge difference in how Agatha felt about this evening's performance. She felt comfortable about both symphonies as well. The Bruckner Eighth was one she had conducted several times during her tenure at the Linz Bruckner Orchester, after all. And she had worked particularly hard on the Brahms Third, which she had conducted only once before, also in Linz, funnily enough. The Austrian city, well, all right, Ansfelden specifically, the village where Bruckner was born and which is now a suburb of Linz; that proud city so strongly associated with Bruckner had been surprisingly open to the North German Brahms in her experience.

And now here she was about to conduct the two demanding symphonies by two very dissimilar composers. And two such very different men! Bruckner, considered even by his supporters as somewhat of a simpleton in his persona, despite his virtuosity on the organ, which included a genius for improvisation. And Brahms, even with his contradictory personality traits which included hurtful pronouncements, practical jokes, and jovial barbs, was a man of society, welcome in the highest cultural circles, including the House of Wittgenstein.

Had it been foolish to pair their works? But from what standpoint could it be foolish? The only one Agatha could think of was audience fatigue. No, the Double B Composers series was its own justification. And so far, the respected Stefanie Schreib had not panned her. The music critic had correctly identified and regretted her exaggerations in tempi here and there during Wednesday's concert. Even as she was conducting that evening, Agatha knew her emotions were intruding and she had fought mightily not to be conscious of that reality. On the whole she had succeeded, but Schreib had been spot-on in her critiques.

The Maestra had often wished she knew Schreib in person. From her informed, highly readable reviews she was obviously extremely knowledgeable about music. And she had not been shy about expressing satisfaction that the Vienna Philharmonic's resident conductor was a woman. Agatha had heard all sorts of rumors about the popular critic. She was single—that much was known—but nothing was really known about her private life. Rarely seen in public other than professionally, or when she conducted abroad, she seemed glued to her residence. And what a residence! The entire top floor of an eight-story building owned by her family. And what a location! The building graced Johannesgasse, just off the pedestrian Kärntner Strasse. The stories below were leased to various famous business firms, and the ground floor hosted several different commercial shops. Schreib was within easy walking distance of the Ringstrasse and public transportation, yet it was known she kept a car in the city. Her black Mercedes-Benz Sprinter van, which could hold up to twelve passengers and had tinted privacy windows, was the single vehicle parked in the Johannesgasse building's small inner courtyard.

Well, speaking of cars, it was time for Agatha to change into her conducting clothes, plus an extra item, and then confirm her regular Uber pickup at seven-fifteen for the short drive to the Musikverein. After dropping in on her players in the musicians lounge for a few minutes, she would retreat to her dressing room, unlock it—her new routine—lock it and then again assume her lotus position on the floor, palms out. She would have a brief meditation on the evening's two symphonies: Bruckner's colossal Eighth, with those four Wagner tubas, and Brahms's Third, with its proud personal musical emblem F-A-F, ending in a calm apotheosis with shimmering strings. What bliss!

Pray that she communicates that bliss to the audience.

50

All bases covered, Edgar Wittgenstein confirmed to himself with relief. He had been on his own private investigative prowl of the Musikverein building ever since grabbing a sausage on rye bread with mustard and pickle at the popular Würstlstand in the Albertinaplatz and devouring it in his office. He had checked and locked his and the Maestra's office doors and he had thoroughly searched her dressing room. It was a bare little room as she kept no clothes there. The only item that could be thought of as personal was her baton. And there it lay on the left side of her dressing table inside its rosewood box, always at the ready to be carried to and from the conductor's podium.

The Maestra's baton was slightly unusual and chief stagehand Peter Heimnis, proud to be its carrier, had often studied it, feeling the lightness of the fiberglass shaft, painted white for visibility, and its cork handle, shaped like a small pear. The full length of the baton's shaft was a bit shorter than the standard length by two-and-a-half centimeters, perfect for a man, or in this case a woman, of shorter height. A cork handle was ideal for several reasons: in case of a sweaty palm, it wouldn't slip, thus allowing a conductor to use the baton for longer works of music. And cork provides comfort in the palm as well as an excellent grip. Ah, yes, Heimnis could well understand why the Maestra had chosen this particular baton. He had actually discussed the Maestra's baton choice at length with general director Wittgenstein once.

Edgar was thinking of that discussion now as his eyes wandered around the small dressing room. Looking up at the Ring Europe camera he had installed over the door, he smiled and waved just in case Agatha was watching. Toi, toi, toi, he mouthed. All is secure. No surprises for you, my dear, before tonight's performance.

51

Supper at the Hotel Sacher for the two Brucknerites was ending with the specialty for which the elegant old hotel was known: a *Sachertorte*—that special, simple, dense chocolate cake with two thin layers of apricot jam and coated with dark chocolate icing on the sides and top.

The dinner conversation had focused, not surprisingly, on the merits of the magnificent symphony they were about to hear at the Musikverein, Bruckner's Eighth.

"It's outrageous that orchestras don't perform it more often," Dieter had complained.

"It's a crime against Bruckner. Just because its length is eighty to ninety minutes, give or take a few minutes or so. Audiences are so spoiled nowadays. Eager for intermissions so they can people-watch and hobnob with high society. At least Brahms's Third is that miserable composer's shortest symphony," whined Christian. "Just forty minutes at the most. When I'm conducting it, we get through it in thirty-three minutes."

"You know, the publicity for these ridiculous Double B Composers concerts doesn't even indicate whether the orchestra will be playing from Bruckner's eighteen eighty-seven or his eighteen ninety version."

"Ha!" the older Brucknerite snorted. "We'll be able to tell as soon as the orchestra members are seated because the later version has triple woodwinds during the first three movements."

"Well, I hope it's not the later version because it's notably shorter than the glorious eighteen eighty-seven one. And I will tell you, Christian, that I firmly believe the less dramatic eighteen ninety version was *forced* on Bruckner because of the bourgeoisie Brahms-loving concertgoers of his time." Dieter had gleaned this insight from the Bruckner research he engaged in almost daily at the Musikverein Archive. He wanted to be sure the Maestro, when he retired, would recommend him as superbly knowledgeable about all things Brucknerian.

"Couldn't agree with you more! And what makes me sick is that, either way, Agatha Endlich is competing with me and my Bruckner series. Stealing my thunder. As I've said to you before, who wants to drive two hours up to Linz when you can hear the master right here in Vienna!"

Conversation ended abruptly when the *Sachertorte* slices were served. Each man wanted to concentrate entirely on the divine taste of his piece of cake. Their pace was slow and there was a double smacking of lips when they had finished. Christian glanced at his watch.

"It's time we get to the Musikverein." He waved at their waiter. As Dieter's guest in Wiener Neustadt he certainly wanted to host their delicious dinner in Vienna.

"And now to our incendiary event," said Christian as they strode briskly down the Kärntner Strasse in the direction of the Musikverein.

"You *are* still game, aren't you?" he asked Dieter.

"Game? For our *genius* Anton? I'm all fired up!"

52

It was nearing eight o'clock and Venezuelan organist Fritz Rahm had just entered the Musikverein auditorium where a few other early arrivers were noisily taking their places. Fritz's seat was the aisle seat in the first row of the frontmost parterre seating section and to the conductor's right when facing the orchestra. As soon as the lights were dimmed Fritz would inconspicuously disengage the recently purchased item he had taped to the back of his left leg just above the ankle and below his knee. To position it he had had to slit the black trouser leg, but the slit hardly showed since the item was black, blending in with the material as well as his black sock. The only thing he had to outlast was the first half of the concert as well as the beginning of the second half when, before any Brahms could be heard, the final movement of the composer Anton Bruckner and his goliath Eighth Symphony would be played. It was a perplexing, repetitive symphony which could last eighty minutes or more, the program stated. Fritz would stay in his seat during intermission, taking no chances that his crucial piece of equipment might become dislodged and fall to the floor. He would certainly be stared at, were that to happen. Then another long wait after intermission during the first two movements of the Brahms Third Symphony. Together, the Allegro con brio and the Andante would last around eighteen minutes. Then, some forty-two measures into the beginning of the third movement—the Poco allegretto in a rather unusual 3/8 waltz-like time—and after listeners had had time to hear the first theme, *his great-great-great-grandfather's* theme, begin its repeat, *that* was the moment Fritz would make his dramatic move.

In the meantime, he assessed his surroundings. Two old ladies with a shared, shaky old man between them had just taken possession of the three seats closest to him in the front row and their chatter was as loud and insistent as Bruckner's Wagner tubas were probably going to be. Studying the program, Fritz read that two of those tubas would be tenor and two would be bass. The organist smiled to himself as he pictured how easily their effect could be duplicated on his two-manual pipe organ back home in Caracas. The row behind him was filling up now and Fritz turned to see who might potentially be breathing down his neck. No athletic brawny youths, he hoped. His hopes were fulfilled. More senior, very senior music lovers were arduously working their way down the row to their seats. Fritz looked across the aisle to the middle seating section to his left. Same situation, thank god! Nothing but old people, most of them couples, almost no one under sixty. Excellent. No nearby "heroes" to restrain him. Fritz swiveled in his seat and examined the far back seats of the orchestra floor—ah, ha, still people all mostly over fifty, at least. Excellent.

Yes, he would be thrown out of the auditorium, even arrested perhaps, but it would be well worth it. The original Friedrich Brahms would be avenged. Taken out of the closet never to be put back. And he, the present-day offspring of Friedrich with publicity savvy, had taken care to notify the press and television that "something heart-stopping" would be happening at the Musikverein concert this evening.

53

"You know, now that we've talked about it, I think you're right: I'll *end* my lecture with the drawing, rather than begin with it," Megan told Tony as they entered the Musikverein. During their dinner at the Wienerwald she had peppered her friend with two exciting pieces of news, one about her discovery of a key inside the Brahms bust she'd bought in Elisabet Ney's Austin, and the other about an unknown colored drawing of Brahms at the piano conducting a female choir. Tony had studied the photograph with fascination, and he readily agreed that the image of the choirmaster had to be that of Brahms. Whether or not it was by Ernst or Gustav Klimt he would leave to Megan's expertise. The exciting thing was that the pianist was definitely Brahms.

"Good decision," he said, "let it be the grand climax of your talk. The audience will love it."

"And *I* love the location of our seats," Megan said gratefully as they climbed the stairs to the rear balcony."

"I think the sound in our precise location is the very best in the entire auditorium." Tony had ordered them two middle seats in the raised last row of the balcony which, like the ground floor, had three seating sections. Upstairs, the middle area had ten seats, with five seats lining the two side sections. Downstairs, twelve seats constituted each row of the middle section, while the two flanking side area rows had a total of six seats each.

"Oh, it's just great!" Megan exclaimed after they had taken their seats. "We can see *everything* from here."

"See and *hear*," emphasized Tony, still full of the acoustics conversations he had that morning and afternoon. The two watched as more people took their seats; the great shoebox auditorium was filling up quickly.

"See anyone you know?" Tony asked.

"There certainly could be a few people I know here, but actually spotting them in a crowd like this would be difficult," said Megan. She peered around her, first the balcony extensions down the two long sides of the hall and then the ground floor with its three-section seating. Her eyes scanned the parterre methodically and then finally the raised orchestra stage itself.

"Oh, wow, Tony! There are *three* harps!"

"That's right. Bruckner never used harps in any of his other symphonies, but when he did use them, he went big."

"Just the way he keeps *harping* on his themes."

"Megan, that was beneath you."

The two friends lightly punched each other, then returned to people watching. Another five minutes to go before the instrumentalists took their places.

"Megan? Megan Crespi!" a man's voice above them exclaimed. Megan looked up then smiled in disbelief.

"*Erich!* I can't believe it!" Megan half stood in her seat as she turned and hugged the tall man in a dark blue suit with brown hair and vibrant brown eyes who had uttered her name. A bemused Tony watched the surprise reunion. Of course, his friend would know at least one person in this packed audience.

"Goodness! We haven't seen each other since the Mahler crimes," Megan said, referring to the anti-Semitic outbursts that had shaken Vienna a few years ago. Her art history savvy and knowledge of surmoulage helped identify the main protagonist of the mayhem that followed.

"Tony, this is Vienna's Chief of Police Erich Decker; Erich, this is my friend and colleague Tony Bocello."

The two men shook hands over Megan's head.

"Have you been attending the entire series?" Megan asked, still staring up at the policeman. He immediately squatted down behind her seat and whispered to them both.

"No. But our office was notified by a reporter today that the press had been told, and these are the exact words, 'something heart-stopping' was going to happen here this evening."

"'Something heart-stopping'? That's terrible. But why? Why specifically at *this* concert?" Megan asked.

"We don't know, we don't know. But I thought it best we do not take any chances. I have plain-clothed officers standing and watching in strategic places. Backstage, as well. The threat might pertain to the orchestra or the conductor, or even the audience. Look over there, Megan, there's a friend and fan of yours."

Erich was pointing to a burly, red-haired man standing behind the seats in the righthand side loge in a balcony that stretched all the way down the hall to the magnificent pipe organ towering above the orchestra stage. Megan quickly pulled her "invisible" glasses out of her neck strap holder and peered in the direction Erich indicated.

"Well, I'll be darned, it's Police Officer Niki Jung! Tony, I met him during the Gustav Mahler case in Vienna two years ago. A very nice man."

"The orchestra's beginning to assemble onstage so I better get back to my post," said Erich, taking his leave. "Call me on my cellphone if you see anything, Megan. Or just call me any day while you're here. It would be wonderful to catch up on things." The amiable Chief of Police nodded to Tony, lightly patted Megan on the shoulder, and hurried away.

"What do you say about that, Megan? 'Something heart-stopping.'"

"I can't imagine what it could be. And I hope to god we don't find out."

54

Chief stagehand Peter Heimnis had long since taken the Maestra's baton in its long, slim rosewood case to its podium stand, where he opened the case and laid both sides flat at the ready.

For the past fifteen minutes Maestra Endlich, alone in her locked dressing room, had engaged in her calming yoga routine. And now, at five minutes to eight, she felt centered and ready to go. All should go smoothly this evening. She had labored intensely on the Brahms Third, which she knew well but had only conducted once. As for Bruckner's gargantuan Eighth, she had led it several times in her years at Linz and felt up to the demands it makes. As with other conductors before her, she had positioned the symphony movements so that the final one would be performed *after* intermission. It simply was not fair to ask an audience to sit still for an hour and twenty-plus minutes, to say nothing of her musicians.

For inspiration she thought now of one of her idols, the Australian-born conductor Simone Young. Fifteen years older than Agatha, Simone was extraordinarily talented, acclaimed for both her operatic and symphonic conducting. Her blossoming career had taken her to many of the most important opera houses and symphony orchestras in the world. She had served as chief music director of the Elbphilharmonie Orchestra for ten years. A few months previous to Agatha's Double B Composers series, Simone Young had been, at Agatha's invitation, a guest conductor of the Vienna Philharmonic. The concert was a resounding success. Agatha had been encouraged not only musically, but also sartorially, because Simone's choice of clothes was similar to her own, except in black.

All right. A few more deep breaths and she was off to the podium. Waiting outside her door when she opened it was a smiling, proud Edgar. He offered her his arm as they walked backstage toward the waiting instrumentalists who were tuning to the principal oboe player's A. Why that particular choice, Agatha had asked as a child. Her father's answer was because every string instrument has an A string and of all the instruments in the orchestra, the oboe is the least affected by humidity. She thought of her violinist mother now as she gently withdrew her arm from Edgar's and walked onto the concert stage.

Enthusiastic, warm applause commenced in the two side balconies the moment she was seen. Once she gained center stage, Agatha acknowledged the applause, then turned toward the orchestra, which was positioned in the still-popular, antiphonal Mahler layout, with the two violin sections seated across from each other along stage front. She shook hands with the principal violinist, then crossed in back of the podium, pausing to shake hands with the principal violist and cellist, finally reaching the principal player of the second violins. This was something not done by other conductors and her orchestra loved her for that. As she retraced her steps, her back still to the audience, she blew discreet kisses to the winds and brass and even the percussionists. And then she mounted the podium where her baton and the score to Anton Bruckner's Eighth Symphony awaited her.

The Maestra took up her baton, slowly raised it to shoulder height and stood motionless for a few moments.

Bruckner's mighty Eighth, in C minor like his first two symphonies, was once again about to vibrate in the venerable *Goldener Saal* of Vienna's Musikverein.

55

From her seat in the middle of the back row of the rear balcony Megan had a full view not only of the beautiful gold leaf and marble Musikverein hall and its rapt audience, but also of the orchestra on its raised, multi-level stage. Once an earnest amateur flutist herself, she always looked first at the orchestra flute players, checking whether any of them were female. Ah! Good. One of them *was* a woman, surprise, surprise. She was probably playing a Gemeinhardt flute and it had a gold embouchure. As Megan looked further, she saw the second bassoonist was a woman as well. And, of course, the now usual spattering of women string players. Female harpists were expected and there they were, three of them. Their names were actually on the program, something the orchestra had never done for its first, long-serving woman harpist.

But stop! *Listen to the music*, Megan scolded herself as the Maestra at last gave the initial downbeat to the Allegro moderato. Admittedly unacquainted with the symphony, Megan was surprised by how mysteriously it began with pianissimo tremolo basses, cellos and violas snaking—no other word for it—ever loudly toward a pair of abrupt short themes, one rising, one descending. Then an intentional brief pause before the pattern began again, visiting other keys, slightly rising, then finally dying off only to rise again with jubilant energy, percussions celebrating, harps timidly rejoicing, winds and brasses exultant, and strings elastic in their gymnastics. After an orchestral cataclysm in the middle of the first movement, quotations from the movement's beginning sounded, sometimes moving up and down simultaneously.

Then came what sounded to Megan like a slithering upwards. Yes! Brahms was correct: it did suggest a slithering, circling, slowly rising boa constrictor. The sudden complete pauses that came briefly now and then did not indicate the end of the first movement. Instead, great masses of troubled sound tumbled into the abyss of musical dissonance followed by passages of ascending hope topped by brief arpeggiated harp notes. Whew!

And now back came the rising and falling five-note patterns of the movement's beginning. Would this ever end? Megan had liked what she'd heard in the beginning, and the initial repetitions, but now she was becoming exasperated by them. Ah! The orchestra was approaching a dramatic end as the stomping up and down passages collided mightily. But this wasn't the end of the movement; instead, it died away on a repeated descending motive, ending in the same sort of pianissimo with which the symphony had begun.

Megan looked at her Apple watch. Twenty-three minutes and forty seconds of brief ascending and descending motifs had ceased. She heard the oboe quietly intoning A and a few string players tuning to it. No wonder! Any string instrument, forced into maintaining too long and too many tremolos, could have gone a whit out of tune by the hard, almost continuous bowing involved. The Maestra stood with her head down, eyes staring at the floor. A full forty seconds passed. Then she lifted her baton, gave a radiant smile to the orchestra, and began the second movement.

Unusually, it was a Scherzo rather than an Adagio that came next. It murmured in a continuous rising monothematic theme, just one measure in length, and displayed in three-quarter time with an emphasized quarter note followed by four rapid eighth notes—*one-two*, three, four, five, six, *one-two*, three, four, five six, *one-two*, three, four, five, six, the fifth eighth note dropping down an octave to the sixth note. And finally, after an unleashed orgy of kettle drums, the controlled cacophony stopped in its tracks. Was that it? Was this the end of the second movement? It was.

"That's interesting," Megan whispered to Tony, who had been sitting motionless next to her, transfixed, it would seem.

"Yes?" he murmured, as though coming out of a trance.

"But you know what, Tony? In addition to echoes of Wagner,

which are perfectly understandable considering Bruckner's adoration of him, I also seem to be hearing bits of Gustav Mahler."

"Right you are, Megan. Certainly the younger composer heard and responded to a great deal in Bruckner. He openly admired the rustic genius from Linz. After all, he too came to Vienna from a provincial background, the village of Iglau in Bohemia, as you well know."

"Well, now I'm actually glad to be hearing a bit of Bruckner as it sheds more light on Mahler for me," pronounced Megan, more to herself than to Tony. The pause between movements came to an end as Maestra Endlich raised her baton once more.

The third movement was a slowly articulated Adagio that, Megan gradually realized, used a harmonic rather than thematic development. For her this was a relief from the short, jerky themes of the two previous movements. By the sheer means of interlocking harmony, the upper and lower realms of the orchestra seemed an attempt somehow to merge heaven and earth, time and space. The multi-voiced ecstasy lasted an almost unnoticeable thirty-six minutes.

No wonder the Maestra had decided to perform the final movement, marked "Solenne, non allegro," *after* intermission. God knows everyone was ready to stand up and stretch. But, of course, that's what the deeply religious composer was reaching for, God.

56

"You, the orchestra, were *marvelous*, Agatha, completely, absolutely, totally marvelous!"

Edgar put his arm lightly around the Maestra's shoulder after she strode offstage in the wake of the third ovation given to her and the orchestra's performance of the first half of their third Double B Composers concert.

"Thank you. Thank you. I think the players did splendidly," Agatha said joyously.

"If you carry on this way, we'll have to celebrate late into the night."

"Yes, maybe. But right now I need to sit down. Walk me to my dressing room, Edgar?" Agatha was nodding to a few of the passing orchestra members who were happily smiling at her and giving her a thumbs up.

Edgar steered his Maestra backstage and down the hall to her dressing room. She automatically gripped the doorknob but it didn't turn. Turning to Edgar she laughed.

"I forgot that I locked it. See, I did follow your instructions."

"Excellent. Let's go in." There was a pause on the Maestra's part.

"Umm, Edgar, I did lock it but I don't remember where I put the key afterward."

"In your vest?"

"Oh, good heavens, no. I wouldn't want to be weighed down by something so extraneous as a metal key! I just laid it nearby somewhere. They both turned and looked around. No key evident.

"Wait! Now I remember. I walked on stage with it in my left hand and after I'd finished shaking hands with my principals, I laid it down on the top of my open baton box. That way, I thought, I wouldn't forget it. But I did, didn't I? Bad me." She pulled a long face and they both began laughing. Soon the laughter turned into near hysterics as they both released unacknowledged tension.

"Stay right here, dear. I'll be back presto with the key," Edgar chortled as he turned on his heel and headed for the stage. Peter Heimnis appeared at the opposite end of the hall.

"Is everything all right, Maestra? Shouldn't you be inside resting?"

"Oh, I plan to. Just as soon as Herr Wittgenstein returns with the key. I'm locking my door now. New routine." Agatha was trying to stifle her giggles.

"So Herr General Direktor is now responsible for your security. Well, I don't blame him, considering what was delivered to your dressing room last time. A stink bomb hidden in a bouquet of roses. What a stupid practical joke. I am so very, very sorry that happened, Maestra." Agatha was touched by the chief stagehand's sincerity.

"Here we go!" Edgar's joyful voice sounded from the end of the hall. He was holding the key high above his head.

"Hey, there, Peter," he greeted Heimnis as he reached the Maestra. The man nodded, smiled, and continued on his way.

Once inside with the door firmly locked behind them, something unexpected happened. They instinctively reached for each other and embraced. It was a long embrace; neither was in a hurry to end the comforting hug.

"I am so proud of you," Edgar whispered into Agatha's ear. He had unconsciously used the intimate *Du*. Seamlessly, Agatha returned the compliment, also in the familiar form of address. There was no turning back now. They both realized how close they had become in the past week.

"And from now on you will keep your key in your vest pocket, do you hear?"

"No, no, no, absolutely not. It would destroy my balance at the podium!" Agatha was deadly serious.

"All right. Not to worry. I will be by your side coming and

going and I shall keep your key in my breast pocket, close to my heart, if you allow."

"Yes. Thank you for understanding."

"I'll be waiting for you when intermission is over." Edgar left the room, stepped into the corridor, and gently closed the door.

"Shall we amble downstairs for intermission and merge with the throng, or would you rather stay here?" Dieter asked, stretching his arms out in front of his body as far as he could.

Christian looked at his Wiener Neustadt host with disbelief.

"What? And leave, *destroy* this Bruckner heaven by mingling with ignorant symphony goers? *Odi profanum vulgus et arceo*!"

"Umm, sorry, Christian, I guess my Latin is not up to date."

"'I hate the common people and avoid them.' Horace. And it's a shame Latin isn't taught in the schools any longer. Of course, I stay here during intermission. And you should too, Dieter. It's important that you be noticed by as few persons as possible, considering what you are going to do during the Brahms. Or have you changed your mind?" Christian frowned.

"Definitely not. I just thought a little standing up and moving around might be good for the body." Dieter was aghast that he had ticked off his touchy Maestro who was still staring at him indignantly.

"The body and not the spirit? You'll have enough of that once you've yelled 'FIRE' and we head up for the exit along with, I hope, dozens, then hundreds of other people."

"Yes, yes, quite right, Maestro. What did you think of Endlich's conducting?" he said, hoping to change the subject.

"Not as poor as I thought it would be. She did show an understanding of the master's intentions and occasionally she was able to lead the orchestra as Bruckner would have wished. I give her that. Of course, several years in Linz working with the Bruckner Orchester would have given her some expertise. I would say she has at least studied the master's intentions. There is so much more that I could have conveyed, but for a woman, her comprehension and carry-through were not too bad."

"So, terrestrial competence but not celestial ascendance," Dieter summed up the performance so far.

"Exactly, my boy, exactly."

The younger Brucknerite was relieved. He had regained his older colleague's respect even if he was a Latin ignoramus.

"My goodness, didn't your Musikverein procure us good seats this evening!" It was intermission and Lukas Eifer, looking all the world like Johannes Brahms, with his white moustache and flowing white beard—and keenly aware of the doppelgänger effect—was standing with his back against the wall of the right parterre loge overlooking the orchestra stage. Robb laughed proudly.

"Well, not for nothing have I been deputy director here for all these years. Of course, not for every event can I obtain such fabulous seats, but this time we were lucky. Do you realize that I know almost every one of the players below us? It's just a few of the newest ones whom I've not yet met. The second flutist for example. She has yet to contact me for anything. She's a knockout, don't you think?"

"Umm. I prefer all three of those graceful harpists," Lukas joked.

"I can't understand why Bruckner scored the Eighth for so many harps since they don't play all that much."

"Well, that's Bruckner for you: excess, excess, excess. And we still have the finale to endure after intermission," sighed Lukas.

"Think of the players! At least they have a break."

"Yes, and same for the Maestra," Lukas agreed. "She must really need it. She's doing a great job, I must say. She's really good at contrasting the lights and darks, and so far, she has conveyed Bruckner's 'battle of demons' with great finesse, I'd say."

"I thought so too. She rarely looked down: her eyes were constantly engaging those of the players.

"So you noticed...." Lukas looked at his brother expectantly.

"Noticed what?"

"That she's *memorized* the symphony. Endlich never turned a page of the score. Look down there. You can still see all the sheets are on the right, and to the left the black binder cover is open with not a single sheet on it. See?"

"Oh my god! You're right. Imagine memorizing that humongous symphony."

"I wouldn't do it if you paid me. And we still have one more movement of doubt, death, and consolation to go."

The two brothers were both standing, studying audience members who, like them, preferred remaining in the auditorium to filtering out into the narrow entry hall.

"Hey, Lukas, look all the way to the back balcony. Do you see who I see sitting in the front row? Lukas leaned forward and studied the two men Robb had pointed to. But they were too far away for his eyes.

"You'll have to describe them. I can hardly make them out."

"Sure. One is in his late thirties perhaps, a bit overweight, and clean-shaven except for exaggerated sideburns. The other one is quite a bit older, on the robust side, dark eyebrows, prominent nose, clean-shaven and with a short Prussian haircut."

"Ha! Wouldn't you know *he*'d be here. It's that crazy Bruckner conductor Christian Begeist. He has a hawk nose and haircut just like the composer, but that's all they have in common. I heard him conduct his god once in Linz and all I can say is that he's more Bruckner than Bruckner ever was. Don't know who the younger man with him is. Do you?"

"For sure. We all know him here in the Musikverein. He's Dieter Unfug. An aspiring conductor. Works part time at the string instrument store here. He uses the library often. And he's a dyed-in-the-wool Brucknerite. Goes around quoting what Hugo Wolf wrote about Bruckner and Brahms."

"Which was?"

"What? My big brother doesn't know that composer's famous comment?"

"If I knew it, I've forgotten. Tell me."

"'One single cymbal crash by Bruckner is worth all four symphonies of Brahms with the serenades thrown in.'"

"Outrageous! Well, Hugo Wolf went nuts, didn't he? Died early of syphilitic insanity. Serves him right for belittling Brahms."

"I agree." Robb looked at his watch. Just five minutes to go before they'd have to suffer through the rustic genius's mammoth finale to his Eighth Symphony. Then they could lean back and enter heaven with Brahms.

The Venezuelan organist and great-great-great-grandson of Friedrich Brahms, brother of Johannes Brahms, had not stirred from his seat during the first half of the evening's concert. Nor did he indulge in any intermission break. He simply sat still, checking the black accessory taped to his left leg every now and then and forcing himself to remain calm. The Bruckner music had been sent from hell for him to endure. What was it all about? Why was he so depressed, listening to that sad wailing of sound which became then so inexplicably celebratory? Why so much repetition, not just of brief melody but also jarring reiteration of so many short-lasting rhythms? It was difficult to believe the man was a contemporary of his great-great-great-grandfather and his great-great-great-granduncle. He simply came from another world. The world of a small child let loose on a two manual organ keyboard with lots of enticing knobs to pull out on either side, and with raised floor beams to stomp the hell out of! And Fritz Rahm would have to endure more of the same, he presumed, after intermission. Thank the heavens Brahms's symphony would be coming to the rescue, even though he would have to wait until the third movement and then some ninety-eight plus measures, before his great denouement in front of, counting the instrumentalists and audience, almost two thousand, two hundred persons.

Instead of going downstairs during intermission, Megan and Tony had chosen to remain in the balcony and merely changed locations. They had exited their row of seats and were now standing in the aisle, leaning their backs against the wall and discreetly stretching their limbs.

"You know, Megan, it's almost as though, well, I think Agatha Endlich has *memorized* this Bruckner symphony."

"What makes you say that, Tony? How can you tell?"

"Well, I can't tell physically from here whether or not she's turning the score sheets, but there is something about her interlacing of the thickly woven musical tapestry that tells me she's conducting from memory."

"I take your word for it. Despite the sudden pauses of sound, everything seems so tightly interconnected that silence itself seems to be a continuum of the music."

"Good way to put it, Megan. A musical continuum through sound and silence. Maybe you can stick that sentence into your lecture tomorrow night," he laughed.

"I'll try," laughed Megan.

"I wonder where your Chief of Police friend is. He's not at the post he took during the performance, standing behind our seats," Tony said, changing the subject and looking around.

"Perhaps at the auditorium entrance checking things?"

"Good thought. I see your red-headed policeman is still where he was standing during the performance." Megan, her invisible glasses still on, looked over to where she had spotted Niki Jung before. Yes, he was still standing behind the first balcony loge seats on the right-hand side of the auditorium. From there he had an excellent view of the instrumentalists and the frontmost rows of the auditorium. People were returning to their seats now and she and Tony began sliding down their aisle. Ah! There was Erich. He had resumed his stance just behind them. Megan started to wave, then thought better of it. Not a good idea to attract attention to Vienna's Chief of Police. Especially when a mysterious threat had been made concerning that evening's performance.

The musicians were taking their seats and the oboe's reedy A was already sounding. The final movement of Bruckner's Eighth would take place in a few minutes and then, at last, Brahms's Third.

57

Stefanie Schreib had not stirred from her front row back balcony aisle seat. Predisposed to favor Brahms over Bruckner, she had been blown away by Maestra Endlich's handling of the first three movements of the Linz composer's Eighth Symphony. Yes, she knew the symphony, and had heard it performed before in both Linz and Graz under Maestros Christian Begeist and Lukas Eifer, respectively. But never had it sounded like this! What a boon it was to her spirits, which had cause to be extremely low that evening.

"Pulling out all the stops." She experimented with the phrasing she would write in her concert review later that night. Yes, this organist/composer had pulled out all the stops. But the short silences were somehow just as loud, resounding deafeningly in her head. How to describe the unusual aspect of this particular performance to a knowing and experienced Viennese public? Better to stop fretting and concentrate on the music to come: the fourth and final movement of Bruckner's overwhelming Eighth.

Stefanie shifted slightly in her seat and joined the rest of the audience's enthusiastic applause as the Maestra quickly made her way to the podium. This time she did not acknowledge the applause, nor did she look at the expectant players she was facing. She merely stood, hands joined below her waist, eyes to the ground. The seconds passed slowly; audience and players understood the silence. At last, Endlich picked up her baton, raised it, gave the downbeat, and the four horses of the Apocalypse galloped into the auditorium. Their swift gait was accompanied by ominous rising brass braced by four Wagner tubas, bells up, with their special edgy intrusion.

From then on it was a spiritual journey with many setbacks in the orchestral articulations of despair, hope, and doubt, but nevertheless a journey of life *per aspera ad astra*. Bruckner's message of hard-won consolation came only after the main themes from all four movements simultaneously confronted each other. The symphony's coda, sprinkled here and there with Wagnerian intervals, closed with a prolonged solace, ascending from a hell that raged in the roaring brass, thundering timpani, and sawing strings until its brutally abrupt end.

The city's premier music critic joined the audience in its enthusiastic, standing applause. It was an ending that, to Stefanie's analytical ears, sounded startlingly like the four descending notes of the opening of Bruckner's contemporary Russian composer's first piano concerto. Tchaikovsky. She immediately scolded herself and shamefacedly joined the adoring crowd that simultaneously clapped not just for Bruckner but for the Maestra who had once again brought him to life.

58

Agatha Endlich had left the stage after the Bruckner's final movement to allow her instrumentalists a restorative pause. The string players needed to shake out their fingers and the woodwinds and brass instrumentalists were relieved to breathe normal amounts of air. Even the cymbalist was happy to lay down his large concave brass plates. When the Maestra did reappear, there was something different about her. The hallmark all-white outfit she was known for had a spot of color! Over Endlich's blouse was a celestial blue vest, an obvious homage to the change in mood about to be launched. Appreciative murmurs were heard around the auditorium.

One could almost feel the joyful receptivity of the audience as the Maestra picked up her baton again to usher in the exultant first movement of Brahms's shortest symphony, the Third. Written in F major, but with many excursions into a darkened F minor, it numbers as the ninetieth work of the master and was composed in a single burst of creativity during a summer spent on the northern bank of the Rhine in Wiesbaden when Brahms was fifty.

The symphony's Allegro con brio opens with that famous enunciation of F-A-F, the composer's defiant self-definition as "free but happy." The orchestration's three top notes, however, are F-A-flat-F, shifting the music into the key of F minor, a variance that occurs now and again throughout the movement, sometimes in the treble, sometimes as the base line. The intriguing musical moods would animate the final movement as well.

From his favorite and longtime location at the Musikverein, neurologist Dr. Oliver Rologe, a wiry, white-haired, blue-eyed man in his early sixties, was observing the 145 musicians, some of whom he had heard and watched play for well over twenty years now. Three of them—a bassoonist and two of the string players—had actually been his patients at one time or another. Other orchestra members knew him by sight from his occasional backstage visits during intermissions. As he looked down from his front row seat in the right loge box next to the massive organ pipes he could see not only the instrumentalists, including the fifteen women players the orchestra had been shamed into hiring, but also the engaged audience beyond. Interesting how the look of an audience had changed over the years. People used to dress so formally; now it was wear what you like, and that applied to hairstyle as well. The one thing that had not changed was the quality of performance: his beloved Wiener Philharmoniker had never disappointed him. And what Maestra Endlich was pulling forth from the orchestra with Brahms right now was sublime. Dr. Rologe closed his eyes and listened with rapture.

For two members of the audience sitting in first row balcony seats at the rear of the auditorium, the Brahms symphony was an egregious imposition. A bored Dieter Unfug stole glances at the man sitting stiffly to his right: his facial expression one of disgust, his forehead furrowed, his eyes narrowed, and his lower lip protruding downward. Maestro Christian Begeist would never understand how the Musikverein public could favor Brahms over Bruckner. Or the travesty of scheduling them together on the same program. The Maestro's upper lip now joined his lower lip, resulting in a formidable scowl of scorn and hatred.

Quite to the contrary were the expressions on the faces of two other pairs of listeners. From the top row of the rear balcony, Megan was leaning forward, a happy smile on her face, while Tony relaxed and closed his eyes, the better to allow his ears to receive the splendid sonorities joyfully joining the conversation between F major and F minor that would drive the entire symphony. Now the bucolic second movement was commencing with a lyrical melody for clarinet and a hymn-like texture in the accompaniment—"a little forest shrine," in Clara Schumann's appreciative words to Brahms.

And in the front row of the right loge overlooking the orchestra stage, brothers Lukas and Robb Eifer were sitting back in their seats, hands resting lightly on thighs, and blissfully taking in every note, every tempo, every figuration, every harmony. The conductor in Lukas remained open to what the Maestra was achieving and he appreciated what he heard. A bit different from what he would have done, but nevertheless effective and very Brahmsian in scope and strength.

Directly below the two Eifer brothers, in his aisle seat in the first row to the conductor's right as she faced her orchestra, was a man from Venezuela, the actual great-great-great-grandnephew of the composer whose music was being performed. But not all the music heard by the audience had been composed by Johannes Brahms, he knew. The opening, and major theme of the third movement of this Third Symphony, originated not with Johannes but with his younger brother Friedrich, so shamelessly neglected by history. Soon the some two thousand people in this auditorium would know that, and within seconds the attending press would know, and after that the whole world would know of the brazen theft by unjustly world-renowned Johannes Brahms—a musical thief!

Fritz Rahm only had to wait until the third movement began with its protracted, poignant waltz. Then at measure ninety-eight, when his great-great-great-grandfather Friedrich's original melody was taken up again by the orchestra, he would slip out the object taped to the back of his left leg just above his ankle and below his knee and wait for the beautiful melody's recapitulation. He would allow it to play for eight full measures, then literally spring into action. Not long to wait now. The Andante second movement was just ending.

Maestra Agatha Endlich paused only thirteen seconds before beginning the gentle third movement of Brahms's Third. An expectant, wistful smile lit her face as, turning first to the cellos, she initiated the Poco allegretto. It was a slow, sad waltz in a slightly unusual 3/8 time and was soon joined by the violins, and finally embraced by flutes, oboes, and horns. Instead of the C major of the previous movement, the key was now a poignant C minor. A great musical calm descended upon the main auditorium of the hallowed Musikverein. All seemed at peace as the somewhat bittersweet melody once again slowly sounded.

"*Stop! This music is not by Johannes Brahms! He stole it from his brother*!"

Fritz Rahm jumped to his feet, popping open the collapsible black umbrella previously taped to his leg as he ran up to the raised stage, and jabbed at the startled Maestra with it. Stupefied, the orchestra members stopped playing. On the black umbrella, designated in white, were the opening bars of the movement they were playing. In a flash Fritz hoisted himself up onto the stage in front of the second violins, turned around, and pointing his open umbrella at the benumbed audience, began shouting.

"Johannes Brahms was a thief! A *thief,* I tell you! He *stole* this music from my great-great-great-grandfather, his own *brother*, Friedrich Brahms. *Friedrich, not Johannes Brahms composed this symphony*! *Accept the truth and...*"

Fritz Rahm never completed his sentence. A muscular, red-haired giant of a man had leapt onto the stage from the loge above, thrown his arms around the lunatic, and was wrestling him to the ground in front of some two thousand plus stupefied onlookers.

59

"Should I go ahead and do it, or not?" Dieter Unfug hissed to his Maestro. Christian Begeist, his mouth still open in surprise at what had just occurred onstage, did not seem to hear his colleague's urgent question. He was fixated upon what was happening below. Camera flashes were going off; the press seemed to be at the concert in full force, documenting the struggle still going on. How could they know about such a publicity stunt in advance? It was all so unsettling.

"Do what?" Christian asked, keeping his eyes glued on the action below them.

"You know. Set off our little explosion and yell '*fire!*'"

"Not *now*, you idiot. There's enough bedlam going on. Our adding to it right now wouldn't make sense. Goddamn that blithering idiot down there with his umbrella!"

"Okay, whatever you say." Dieter's feelings were miffed, but Christian didn't notice. Instead, he pointed angrily to the stage.

"Look, look! More police in their civvies. God they're coming out of the walls! Everywhere! This hall is riddled with police. And look. That tall man in the gray suit, he must be the ranking officer. See how he's addressing people onstage and pointing all over the place. See? Two men are guarding the Maestra bitch and it looks like the orchestra members have been commanded to stay in place."

"Yeah, sure looks that way. I guess you're right about not starting our own planned drama."

"I'm damned right," pronounced Christian, "our surprise has been stolen and the police are here now. We might even have been caught if you'd carried out our plan."

"Do you think they'll continue the concert?"

"Damned if I know," Christian snapped as he shielded his eyes from a camera flash that went off near him in their front row balcony seats.

That same question had just been voiced by Megan in the topmost row of that balcony facing the far away stage. She asked Tony what he thought. Both had jumped to their feet, straining to see what was going on after the initial commotion.

"Look! There's your Chief of Police friend, right in the middle of it all. See?"

"Where? Oh, now I see him. The tall man in the gray suit. That's Erich all right. Calm and commanding as ever."

"He certainly was right about what that anonymous caller told the police. You know, that something 'heart-stopping' was going to happen during the concert this evening."

"At least it wasn't a murder or an explosion of some sort," Megan said. "Do you think that crazy man meant to kill the Maestra when he lunged at her with his umbrella?"

"That's what they're going to find out. Although from what we saw and heard up here, it seems he was only intent upon getting his message out that the music wasn't by Brahms, I mean Johannes Brahms."

"Yes. Apparently the kook below is the 'great-great-great-grandson,' if you can believe it, of Johannes's younger brother, Friedrich."

"Right," Tony answered. "Great-great-great-grandson of the brother who was also a composer but, of course, not in Johannes's league."

The two friends from Dallas watched as the tall, handcuffed man, still yelling his message of musical theft, was forcibly walked offstage and police began to disperse. The orchestra members and their Maestra had remained onstage, and now a slender man in his mid-fifties with curly black hair and thick, questioning eyebrows, was consulting with her and the Chief of Police. After a few minutes both men nodded and walked offstage together. The Maestra turned to her players. She seemed to be asking them something. Megan and Tony could see them all vigorously nodding their heads. Agatha Endlich then turned and faced the suddenly hushed audience. She raised her hands, spread them palms out, and spoke.

"Shall we continue with *Johannes* Brahms?"

"Continue, continue!" people from all parts of the auditorium, shouted, and clapped their hands. Others yelled "Johannes, Johannes" in defiance of the message of the crazy man and his black umbrella's message. It seemed that everyone, including the Maestra and her players, desired more than anything else to hear the composer's cruelly interrupted symphony to its final note.

"Third movement it is then! And this time to the end. After that, fourth movement. To the end. All hail to our Johannes!"

Hundreds of people began repeating the Maestra's last sentence and then, as if by signal, suddenly became silent again.

Facing her expectant players, Agatha Endlich gave a smile of encouragement and raised her baton once again.

While Christian Begeist and Dieter Unfug slouched in palpable disgust, the two Eifer brothers nudged each other in relief and contentment as the Musikverein resounded once again with the final two movements of the exquisite Symphony Number Three in F Major by Johannes Brahms.

60

One person did not, could not stay to the very end of the Double B Composers concert. Music critic Stefanie Schreib slipped out right after the dramatically interrupted third movement was replayed. She had a review to write and as she walked the short distance to her home, her brain was turning somersaults. There were both good and not so good aspects of this evening's performance, and she needed to latch onto them before they slipped her mind. A huge personal blow she had received the day before had numbed her emotions, but hopefully not her mind.

She was surprised to see Emma Meier, the live-in housekeeper she employed, come rushing down the hall at the sound of her key in the lock.

"Frau Schreib, Frau Schreib! There is a gentleman waiting for you in the music room. He knocked at the door half an hour ago and asked if you were at a concert, to which I said yes, and then he told me you expected him and that you had asked him to wait for you until you got back home. I hope this is all right?"

"What? I did no such thing, Emma. I don't know who of my friends or acquaintances the man could be. What impudence to intrude into my home like this."

Stefanie slammed her purse on the hall table and angrily, but with a bit of trepidation, entered her spacious music room which was dominated by a Bösendorfer Imperial grand piano. Sitting on the long leather couch opposite it was a distinguished white-haired man with a short black beard. He immediately rose to his feet and introduced himself. His tone was gentle and strangely soothing.

"Frau Schreib, please allow me to introduce myself and kindly forgive my bold invasion of your household. I am just arrived here from Hamburg and I have come here directly from the airport with the hope to meet you."

Stefanie felt confused, angry, and curious all at the same time. Who was this man who spoke with a rolling-r accent and why would he want to see her immediately? How had he gotten her private address in the first place? She found herself unable to speak. She, whose vocabulary was so vast when writing reviews.

Sensing the woman's bafflement, the man motioned to the couch.

"Please, may we not sit down?" Obediently Stefanie lowered herself into the far corner of the couch and her surprise guest took the other. He slipped a photograph out from his breast pocket and held it up for her to see.

"I am a sculptor and this is my studio in Hamburg. Does that by any chance ring a bell with you?" Stefanie gave a noticeable start but remained silent. However, her mind was racing. Hamburg! Auntie Margareta! The commission! The polite but persistent man facing her spoke again.

"This photograph confuses me because something is missing from the studio." Again Stefanie flinched but remained silent.

"Let me come at it another way," Intagliatore said quietly. "The surname of the only other family on the floor of my condominium in Hamburg is Wittgenstein. The young maid of the house is named Felizitas and she is close friends with my housemaid Frau Salem. Does this strike a familiar chord with you, perhaps?"

Stefanie's answer was a sudden burst of sobbing that surprised her as much as it did her interlocutor. Intagliatore waited patiently, at one point even reaching over and lightly patting the weeping woman's shoulder reassuringly. Finally the sculptor added something he hoped would ease the situation.

"You see, *gnädige Frau*, I am attempting to solve a conundrum. My name is Mario Intagliatore, and recently I was given *in advance* a most generously paid commission to fashion a marble bust of Johannes Brahms as he is generally known to history, that is, with a full and flowing beard. I had even visited Italy and selected the marble for the bust. But when I returned to Germany and entered my studio, the clay bust I had modeled for fashioning into marble was missing. That, Frau Schreib, is why I am here. I am forced to believe you are the one who commissioned the bust and I believe you are the one who arranged to have the Wittgenstein maid make away with the plaster. What I cannot understand is why you would not wait until the marble version was cast. Please, I have no intention of asking that you return the bust—you have already paid for it and it is yours. But what I must know is *why*. Why have you settled for the clay when you could have had the marble? Will you not answer this one question?" Finally Stefanie found her voice.

"You deserve an explanation, Herr Intagliatore. And I am beholden to you. You are correct in all you have surmised. The reason I commissioned a bearded bust of Brahms, who as you know, had such a beard when he visited the Palais Wittgenstein here in Vienna, the only reason I did so was to please my father, whose health had been dramatically failing. He and his sister, my Auntie Margareta, are both directly descended from the Vienna branch of the Wittgenstein family..."

"Ah! You *are* a Wittgenstein then. And yet your surname is Schreib."

"That is because my great-grandfather Hans—Johannes—Wittgenstein changed his surname to Schreib after he supposedly disappeared in America. Even though I knew of my heritage, I preferred to remain with the name Schreib, considering the rise of anti-Semitism here in Vienna."

"I see. Yes, it is a terrible thing. But please continue."

"Some weeks ago my father suffered a severe stroke which left him unable to speak. He could gesture, however, and what he kept pointing to was a set of four framed photographs of the bearded Brahms I had recently given him. That is why I commissioned you to create a bust of the master in marble. And that is why I paid in advance, hoping to speed your trip to Italy."

"Which it indeed did," nodded Intagliatore sympathetically. All was becoming clear to him now. But he pressed forward.

"And then?"

"And then this past Monday my father had a second stroke,

not as severe as the first, our physician said, but most probably there would be more, and sooner rather than later. I was desperate to get your bust to him, and my aunt, who keeps an eye on everything that happens in your building, sprang into action. Her maid, Felizitas, is indeed friends with your housekeeper, who, of course, knows nothing of the matter. Late Monday night, and with her brother's help, Felizitas managed to spring the lock of your basement studio door and ferret out the clay bust. It was immediately sent express to Vienna the next morning via Parcel ABC platform. I received it early Wednesday and with it I was able to bring the greatest joy to my poor father...one day...one *day* before he died. Now the bust is locked away in my study." Stefanie began to weep uncontrollably.

"But, but, your father died just *yesterday*?" Intagliatore was horrified. Instinctively, he sprang up, went over to the sobbing woman, and put his arms lightly around her.

The conundrum was solved and his bearded Brahms had brought joy to a soul in need.

61

"Do you think it's really true that crazy, shouting, umbrella man could be related to Brahms, Tony?" asked Megan as they walked back to their hotel from the Musikverein.

"Oh, sure it could be true. Don't you remember, Megan? Although he returned to Hamburg and died there, leaving his few savings to Johannes, poor black sheep Friedrich scuttled off to South America for a couple of years to try to make a name for himself there. I forget which country he went to, but..."

"I know, Megan interrupted happily, pleased to know her memory was still functioning. "He went to Venezuela—Caracas, to be exact."

Tony nodded in agreement, grateful to be reminded of a fact he once knew.

They had reached the Annagasse and, in a few more steps, their hotel.

"What do you think?" Tony asked, pointing to the television in the small lounge to their right. "Shall we try to catch news about what happened at the concert down here or upstairs in our rooms?"

"In our rooms if you don't mind. I'm suddenly feeling my age and fain would lay me down," said Megan with a Scottish flourish.

"Agreed," laughed Tony, "And I'm suddenly also really sleepy."

The elevator was conveniently anchored at lobby level, and after the two friends parted, both did the same thing upon reaching their rooms. They grabbed the TV remotes, collapsed on their beds, and turned on the news. Sure enough, the "wild incident," as it was referred to, was being covered by all the main channels with footage of the Venezuelan man jumping onstage, yelling, and thrusting his umbrella message first at the Maestra and then at the audience. Megan gave a delighted start as she recognized the person who sprang from the low loge box onto the stage and restrained the wild man. It was red-haired policeman Niki Jung! Then Chief of Police Erich Decker appeared, conferring with the Maestra and an authoritative-looking man who stood protectively at her side. What bedlam! The Venezuelan was escorted offstage and focus switched to channel anchors who voiced their own views of what the local press and TV channels received warning of earlier that day— a warning that a "heart-stopping" incident would be taking place at the Musikverein performance that evening.

Enough! Megan said to herself. She still had work to do—practice the lecture she would be giving tomorrow at the Leopold Museum. And she would be careful not to roll her r's too much, a suggestion that had been made after a recent Zoom rehearsal in German about Egon Schiele, the radical Viennese Expressionist artist she was most associated with in the art world. Extraordinarily talented, he had lived a tragically short life, dying at the age of twenty-eight in 1918, not in the trenches of World War I, but of the deadly flu pandemic that ravaged Europe and America as the war came to a close. A terrible harbinger of what the entire world would go through a century later.

It was ironic, Megan mused, thinking of her lecture again, that she would be counselled *not* to roll her r' s. She had *learned* her Viennese-sounding German from the lips of Schiele's two sisters, still living when she began her years of research on the artist in 1963. Oh, how Melanie and Gerti rolled their r's! And, already practiced in r rolling because of her Italian father, Megan had easily picked up the linguistic emphasis and saw no exaggeration in it.

But now as she read through her speech, softly enunciating the German words, a calmness descended upon her. She was practicing, she would be prepared. As with her decades of classroom teaching, her greatest recurring nightmare had always been that *she was not prepared.* Some twenty-five minutes later, her work done, Megan opened her PetCam app and gazed for a full fond minute at Button and his buddies sleeping so soundly around her sister's living room. Then she changed into her pajamas, swallowed her "old age" pills, brushed her teeth, slipped into the welcoming bed, and within minutes was sound asleep. She was prepared.

62

Maestra Endlich had not returned home alone that night after the concert. Edgar Wittgenstein insisted they celebrate her triumph over adversity. In order not to be recognized in public, he drove them to an unpretentious bar near her apartment on the Porzellangasse.

"We absolutely have to raise a glass of champagne in honor of your stellar performance this evening!"

"All right, all right," Agatha laughingly conceded. "Whatever you say, Edgar, my hero, whatever you say. And it's strange, but I don't feel tired at all."

"I don't either."

As they drove slowly past the Beim Solzen Adler bar looking for a parking spot, Edgar suddenly gave a curse.

"Damnation! The place is totally dark, looks closed to me."

"I'm not surprised, Edgar. It's almost midnight after all."

"*That* late already? Where can we go? We absolutely must drink champagne tonight. Do you know any other places around here?"

"Yes. My place. Don't have champagne, but I do have wine—white in the fridge, red on the counter."

A few minutes later the general director and the resident conductor of the Vienna Philharmonic Orchestra were toasting each other with plenteous pours of white wine, and below them, enjoying the sound of their cheerful voices, lay the contented black-and-white collie Fanny. Time passed quickly as they talked to each other across the couch. They had so much to discuss.

"And did you see the expression on Peter Heimnis's face when *you* unlocked *my* dressing room door?" Agatha laughed.

"He must think we're an item by now, with you entrusting your key to me."

"Perhaps he is right," murmured Agatha, her face inscrutable as she took another sip of wine. Edgar glanced at her in silence for a long moment, then raised his glass.

"Here's to our being an item—you and me."

"Oh, Edgar, you have been such a pillar of strength for me, given me encouragement when I needed it most, been there for me..." Tears welled up in Agatha's eyes but she did not cry. She smiled ruefully, unconsciously stroking the contented collie by her side.

"Oh, you dear, dear woman, of course I want to be there for you. Of course I feel protective of you. You are not only talented, not only a superb musician and conductor, you are, you are sweetness itself, you are..."

"Stop it! You're embarrassing me. I can't be all those things! All I do is work and conduct, then work more and conduct more. That's my life, Edgar, there is no more of me, this is what you get."

"And I want no more than to share that life of yours, Agatha. Tell me, could, would you do me the great honor of adding my surname to yours?" With these last words Edgar Wittgenstein slipped off the couch, knelt before a tremulous Agatha, and opened his arms out to her.

That he could love again astonished him as much as his proposal astonished the woman in front of him. Her answer, after some seconds of silence, was considered, slow, and very soft.

"Agatha Wittgenstein Endlich. Yes, Edgar. My answer is yes." She reached for him and they embraced. Not to be left out, Fanny began vigorously licking their cheeks. A joyful calm descended upon Porzellangasse Number 33.

63

An astonishing turn of events had occurred during Mario Intagliatore's visit to Stefanie Schreib the evening before. Just as they finished their conversation and Intagliatore was about to take his leave, the live-in housekeeper employed by Schreib came running down the hall to the music room where they were seated.

"*Frau Schreib! Frau Schreib!* Please come at once. *He's doing it again!*"

Without uttering a word Stefanie sprang up and ran ahead of the housekeeper to one of the bedrooms on the left side of the hall. Mario stood and automatically followed the two rushing women into the bedroom. A young boy with an old face had transformed every inch of his small bedroom into a tightly packed warehouse of food cans, bowls, cups, saucers, and drinking glasses. They were perilously stacked by categories and each item was labeled by type. In addition, shoes, underwear, shirts, trousers, jackets, and coats were carefully folded and heaped on the bed, also meticulously labeled. With his back against the far wall and oblivious to the fact that three people had entered the room, the boy—large for his young age—was conducting the rows of items as though they were a chorus. A long kitchen knife sharpener was his baton.

"*Altos! Louder here! Tenors! Off key, you're off key I tell you!*" he commanded in a voice that had not yet changed.

"Darling! Hans!" Stefanie called, trying to penetrate his consciousness. "It's time to stop conducting now. The chorus has to go home. Go with Emma, now. There's a good boy." Docilely, Hans wove his way through the stacked rows of "orchestra players" and went up to the housemaid, who took the knife sharpener from his hand, patted him on the cheek and led him by the hand off to the kitchen.

"We'll make you some hot chocolate," she was heard telling him as they left.

Stefanie and Mario looked at each other.

"Oh, Signor Intagliatore, I am so sorry.... "

"Tell me, does your Hans have perfect pitch?"

"Well, yes he does, in fact."

"And how long has he exhibited the savant syndrome?"

Stefanie gasped.

"How could you know that?"

"I cannot tell you really. It just seemed suddenly to make so much sense, given that you are a descendant of the Vienna Karl Wittgenstein family. I studied your extraordinary family history at length, once I realized my hermit neighbors in Hamburg are Wittgensteins. And I see you call your son 'Hans.' And so I wonder, could that be in honor of Karl's first-born son Johannes, who disappeared so mysteriously in the New World?"

Mario's question released a torrent of words from Stefanie.

"Yes, oh, yes. I have tried to keep my Hans's savant syndrome a secret ever since he first exhibited symptoms when he was four. His father—whom I did not marry, thank god—exited my life before Hans was born eleven years ago. My mother passed away some years ago and only my father, my aunt in Hamburg, and my two sisters, both in Salzburg, ever knew of his existence or affliction. My sisters take turns hosting him, as my work moors me to the city and I have not the time to care for him as I should, save for summers when he stays with me full time. I take him for refreshing drives in the countryside and have had my car outfitted to protect our privacy and prevent our being spotted by vicious gossips. There! I have told you everything, and I don't know why. I don't know why!"

She burst into tears and Mario instinctively drew her to him, lightly patting her shoulder.

"You told me because the burden is too heavy to bear alone. Your sisters live elsewhere, your aunt lives in Hamburg, your parents, bless their hearts, are gone, and only your housemaid shares your secret here in Vienna. And I presume she is totally discreet."

"Oh, yes, totally discreet. Emma has been in our family for over twenty years." Stefanie attempted to wipe away the tears from her cheeks.

"All right then, now listen. You have a new, and I assure you totally discreet, confidant in me. I only wish I lived in Vienna and not Hamburg. But I am here right now and I am honored to be your helper and your guardian." Mario's warm words brought Stefanie the composure she needed and at her suggestion they returned to the music room.

"Have you had supper?" Stefanie asked.

"On the plane, yes, thank you."

"Then shall we have a sip or two of brandy?"

"What a fine idea. Yes, thank you." Stefanie rose from the couch and walked over to a small bar behind the piano. She poured two brandies and brought them back to the couch. They sipped their drinks slowly and nodded silently to each other. The silence was healing and lasted for several long minutes. Stefanie was the first to break it and she smiled broadly as she spoke.

"And you came here with the sole purpose of solving the mystery of your purloined Brahms bust?"

"Yes. Well, and two other reasons."

"And?"

"A reason I now think might be of interest to you, if you are free tomorrow evening."

"Oh?"

"I suspect that your ancestor Margaret Stonborough-Wittgenstein will be part of the lecture I have come to Vienna to attend. As you no doubt know, her portrait was painted by Gustav Klimt."

"Certainly I do. It's part of our Wittgenstein legend and history."

"Indeed. I recently had the pleasure of meeting tomorrow's speaker, an engaging woman from America with an Italian surname, Crespi. Megan Crespi. She is a Klimt scholar..."

"And of Brahms," interrupted Stefanie. I know her writings on him."

"Well! In that case perhaps you would be interested in attending her lecture at the Leopold Museum with me?"

"I had not thought about doing so, but now, now the idea seems quite attractive. So my answer is yes, but yes provided you come for dinner here before the lecture."

"*Meravigliosa*! What time would you wish me to arrive?"

"I presume the lecture is at eight?" Mario nodded assent.

"Then please come here at five-thirty. We can have a relaxed dinner. At the most, it's just a twenty-minute walk from here to the Leopold Museum."

"Perfect." Mario rose to his feet. "Madame, I know you are the critic for *Der Standard*, and I therefore know you have a review still to write for tomorrow morning's paper. A review which my precipitous being here tonight has no doubt interrupted." In the wake of events Stefanie had actually forgotten her work.

"Oh, my god, yes! And so you also know about the Double B Composers concert series here?"

"Madame, this was my *third* reason for coming to Vienna. Sunday evening's closing concert."

64

Early Saturday morning, upon payment of a very large fine, Fritz Rahm was released from Vienna's city police station at Kopernikusgasse Number 1 and allowed to walk the streets again. A particularly ambitious news reporter from the city's most prominent newspaper had kept watch through the night and was now pursuing the Venezuelan organist as he walked toward the Schottengasse and turned into a shop at Number 4 with a banner that read "JUICE FACTORY." The reporter watched as Rahm ordered a juice smoothie with fruit and ginger shots. When he sat down with his drink the reporter seized the moment and walked up to the fatigued-looking man.

"Hello. My name is Kevvy Gordonovich. I'm a reporter for *Der Standard* and I should very much like to ask you about last night at the Musikverein. Your motivation and goals, so to speak."

A surprised but agreeable Rahm waved the young reporter to the seat opposite him and, gulping down the substantial swig he had just taken, began to speak at length about the reason for his "protest" last night.

"The Fritz Brahms side of the family has always known about Hannes's purloining of thematic material from his younger brother. I have spent the last two weeks at Vienna's major libraries and, of course, in the Musikverein to the archives of which, as you most probably know, Johannes Brahms left all his scores and books—a priceless legacy. But a legacy that also bears witness, even if one searches with a neutral mind, to the many musical ideas, even actual melodic or chromatic quotations taken by the older brother, Johannes, from the younger brother, Friedrich Brahms."

"Yes, the music staves on your umbrella made a most interesting point, and, thanks to the Musikverein's extraordinary acoustics, we in the audience could hear your shouted message."

"Good. I had hoped for that. I had hoped that when I anonymously notified TV channels and the press that there would be a 'heart-stopping' occurrence at the concert last evening. And so there was, you have to admit."

"Yes, there sure was. But I do have a question: why has the world not known this before? Why haven't scholars working with the same archival material come forward with discoveries such as yours?"

"Because they're all cowards! And they worship Johannes Brahms, care nothing for the music of his brother. Some of Friedrich's works—two symphonies, for example, were also published, by Simrock even, but history has ignored them."

"But and I don't mean to contradict you, is it not true that some of your ancestor's compositions have been recorded?"

"Ha! Negligible. Not by major orchestras and no publicity." The reporter was silent, making quick notations in a small notebook he had pulled out. The voluble Venezuelan continued his diatribe.

"And speaking of orchestras, what the hell was your resident conductor thinking when she put together this crazy program series combining a provincial Austrian composer with the internationally known and beloved composer from North Germany who deigned to make Vienna his home?"

"You are saying you do not approve, then, of Maestra Endlich's Double B Composers symphony series?"

"Trash! It is a sacrilege, a *travesty*, and an insult to our family name to pair the two."

"Might I ask: have you contacted Maestra Endlich and expressed your disapproval to her?"

"No. But I just might before she repeats, for the *fourth* time, this ungodly pairing."

"I have just one more question. If, as you say, Friedrich Brahms was so badly treated by his brother Johannes, why did he leave him ten thousand marks in his will when he died prematurely? Died, apparently of syphilis."

Fritz Rahm's face flushed. He jumped up abruptly, pushing their table out into the room.

"*How dare you*?"

Without another word, the son, many generations removed, of Friedrich Brahms stormed out of JUICE FACTORY and disappeared down the Schottengasse.

65

"Hmm. It's a good three hours' drive from here," Megan said, looking at the map the Hertz car rental agent handed her. It was eight o'clock in the morning and she and Tony had just picked up the metallic blue BMW X7 they had reserved for their day trip. Megan laughed when she saw the car: the silver-framed front double grill looked like a huge pair of sunglasses to her. Their destination was Brahms's favorite Austrian summer retreat during the last decade of his life, the spa town on two rivers of Bad Ischl. The famed village had also been the summer home for over sixty years of Austria's Emperor Franz Josef and his wife Sisi.

Megan's lecture at the Leopold Museum was not until eight that evening and she was eager to get out of tourist-packed downtown Vienna for the day and immerse herself in the beautiful Austrian countryside. Tony felt the same way and they had agreed he would drive them back to Vienna and she would do the driving to the famous resort. "It's practically next to Salzburg," she had observed, causing Tony to give a dismissive laugh. He pointed out that visiting the city where Mozart was born meant an hour's further drive west.

"No, I didn't mean we should *go* there, I just meant that we'd be temptingly near Salzburg, 'had we but world enough and time,'" replied Megan, quoting one of her favorite lines, the beginning of Andrew Marvell's poem "To His Coy Mistress."

"So tell me more about the mysterious key you found in that Brahms bust you discovered in Austin," Tony said.

"Well, when I was staying with my friend Tönnies in Hamburg, he showed me his grandfather's collection of old keys and I found a perfect match: my key was made in Vienna in 1890 and it is the key to a man's glove box."

"And are you going to try to find where the glove box is, now that you're here in Austria?"

"You bet I am! I am sure it was Elisabet Ney who hid the key inside the Brahms bust. And that she planned to find out where the matching glove box was the next time she visited Europe."

They had just reached the busy A1 highway and both were quiet for a while, enjoying the increasingly green vistas and rising hills as they neared Austria's beautiful Salzkammergut region, with its Alpine peaks. Finally Megan broke the silence.

"Tony, do you know the photograph taken of Johann Strauss, Junior, standing with Brahms on a wooden porch against a backdrop of trees?"

"Yes, I remember it quite well, as a matter of fact. Both men are shown full-length, facing the camera. Strauss is on the left, wearing a necktie and a vest under his jacket, and looking very dapper. And Brahms is on the right, in his long outdoor jacket, looking very inelegant and pouchy. His bushy white beard is untrimmed whereas Strauss's moustache is densely rakish, as I recall."

"Yes, even though he was eight years older than Brahms, Strauss appears to be the younger man. But did you know the photo was taken in Bad Ischl?"

"No, that I did not know, or at least I don't remember. Are you hoping to find the exact site?"

"Well, yes and no. I'm wondering whether the photo might just possibly have been taken on a balcony porch of the house where Brahms rented the second-floor rooms every summer from eighteen eighty-nine until his death. Or, more likely, and as it is universally identified, the photograph of the two friends was taken on the porch of Strauss's magnificent villa there. But unfortunately that building exists no longer. I just like to leave no stone unturned, or in this case, no porch unbalconied."

"Is the Brahms house still there today, do you know?"

"I hope so. I have two old photographs of it showing a second-story porch on the left side of the house. And that's where we're headed first, if it's all right with you. It's on a curving road leading out of town, Salzburgerstrasse, that snakes above the Traun River and its surrounding mountains. And it's not too far away from the town's river esplanade and a certain Café Walter, which we know was Brahms's favorite site for his morning coffee and gossip."

"How do you know all this, Megan?"

"Just plain old real book research, Tony. The Internet is fine, but I have dozens of books on Brahms at home, both old and recent, and they have tons of information that hasn't reached the cyberworld, and may never. I've always devoured biographies of composers. But not many biographies in my own art history field, come to think of it."

"And yet your work on Schiele and Klimt has provided biographies in addition to analyses of their artworks."

"Umm. I never thought of it that way. It's just that since retiring from teaching—and that makes sixteen years now—my interests have switched from artists to composers. Well, maybe I've always been curious about musicians. On my European travels of the past, when I was young and sprightly, I always did make it a point to visit composers' homes. For example, Sibelius's house in Finland, Grieg's home in Norway, Handel's birth house in Halle, Richard Strauss's fancy villa in Germany's Garmisch-Partenkirchen, Debussy's birth house and Monet's summer house in France. Let's see, oh, yes, Puccini's and Verdi's homes in Italy, Elgar's final residence in England, and, in Austria, ha! Just checking out Beethoven's multiple residences, over sixty of them, could be a fulltime occupation."

"Absolutely," agreed Tony. "It's such a pity that Brahms's Karlsgasse apartment building was torn down a few years after his death."

"Yes, but at least we have the historic photographs of his last three-room apartment there. That was the subject matter of the lecture I just gave in Hamburg, and that's what started me thinking about what Brahms's Bad Ischl rented rooms looked like, and whether or not he had a second-story porch where such a photo could have been taken. For example, there exists a photo of the newly bearded Brahms sitting on a second-story wooden porch of friends in the resort town of Pörtschach am Wörthersee."

As the terrain became increasingly mountainous, the two

friends continued their composers chat and sites associated with them. Three hours danced by and they only realized they had reached their densely wooded destination when a small church on the roadside with the banner *Matthäuskirche von Bad Ischl* signaled they had arrived. With Tony giving directions from the detailed map on his cellphone, Megan drove through the small resort town to the farthermost outskirts and turned onto the Salzburgerstrasse to begin their curving climb upward.

And there it was! Number 51. On the left, halfway up the winding road. The large two-story yellow house with white trim and green-framed windows still stood, and it commanded an amazing vista of both the picturesque old village below and the circling mountains above. A giant triangular attic crowned the house. As they drove slowly past it, there appeared to be no sign whatsoever on the structure indicating Brahms had lived there. They had to have a closer look. Megan drove to the next house on the road, turned into its driveway, backed out, and passing the Brahms house at a crawl, parked on the side of the road just to the left of the house. She and Tony walked up to a small wooden porch jutting out from the second floor on the narrow left side of the house.

Megan was in her element. Looking through her iPhone photographs taken just before leaving Dallas, she studied the wooden porch on which Strauss and Brahms stood in the photograph and then assessed the real-life wooden porch above her. She compared details of the timber balcony struts in front of which Strauss and Brahms stood in the photograph with the overhead porch struts she could clearly see from ground level. They did not match. The narrow spaces between the beams in front of her were simply slender rectangles. Even if she were standing on the porch, the visual result would be the same.

Interesting! This meant for sure that the photograph had not been taken on Brahms's porch, but rather on Strauss's villa porch. There, her downloaded photographs showed, the spaces between the wooden beams were in the shape of elongated tear drops, with six-pointed hollow stars above them. One could even see through them the leafy tree branches beyond. On Megan's phone was an old photograph of the Biedermeier villa where Strauss received the world of the elite during his summers in this beautiful region of Salzkammergut. True, the villa no longer existed, but a wonderful photograph of Strauss standing on its second-story porch did exist and Megan spooled her photos further back to it. The shot of Strauss showed him full-length, standing and facing the photographer, and posing next to his unusually tall standing desk—a desk far higher than that of Brahms. Strauss's left elbow rested on it, and the extended tear drop slits in the struts of his balcony were those also seen in the double photo with Brahms.

Well, if that didn't settle matters, two more images Megan had stored on her phone before leaving America certainly did. They showed Brahms and Strauss's third wife Adele sitting on the same porch at a small circular table having breakfast. Megan laughed as she recalled the famous story of when Adele asked Brahms to autograph her open fan, hoping he would not only sign his name but, as was usual in such gestures, also inscribe a few measures of his best-known music. Brahms did inscribe a few bars on the fan, but they were from her husband's "Blue Danube," and beneath them he had written "Unfortunately NOT by Johannes Brahms."

Porch mystery solved! Although Megan did feel just a tad bit disappointed that Brahms had visited Strauss and not the other way around. On the other hand, did it make sense that Strauss would come to Brahms's rented bachelor lodgings when he owned a villa built for entertaining and performing music? The Waltz King heard his operettas performed every summer in the small town's yearly music festival. And now, along with those delightful ones composed there by Franz Lehar, Bad Ischl had become the "Operetta Capital of the World."

There was one up and coming contemporary composer, Megan thought, who did not mind at all meeting Brahms at Salzburgerstrasse 51 or at the nearby Café Walter or possibly sometimes at the celebrated Zauner Cafe, where they could spend hours talking over pastries and pots of coffee. And that was Gustav Mahler. The two composers admired each other and the younger one, summering at nearby Steinbach am Attersee, and working in his miniscule "composing" hut there, thought nothing of peddling his bicycle the fifteen miles to Bad Ischl.

And, after exploring Brahms's little spa town, the next stopping point for Megan and Tony was indeed Mahler's Steinbach am Attersee. But by automobile, not bicycle.

66

Only when a hungry Fanny nudged her mistress especially hard, did Agatha reluctantly wake up. She gazed around her bedroom sleepily, sat up slowly and looked down at the dear man sharing her bed. What a different world she had woken up to! Edgar was still sound asleep, his perpetually questioning eyebrows arched and a hint of five o'clock shadow on his jaw. What a wonderful turn of events her life had taken. And how surprised she herself had been when, in answer to his sudden proposal to add his surname to hers, she had said yes. And yes, there was an age difference of about fifteen years she guessed, but that was not important. They were both healthy and in the prime of life. And their professions ran along parallel tracks. Edgar had gently become a protective presence in her life, from installing a security camera in her dressing room at the Musikverein to being responsible for the room's key while she was conducting. He was there for her before, during, and after their concerts, and it was he, after all, who came up with the genius idea of presenting a concert series in which each performance would feature music by both Bruckner and Brahms. This coupling of contemporaries idea could be repeated a number of times, she mused lazily, say with Haydn and Mozart, Beethoven and Weber, Czerny and Smetana, Schubert and Mendelssohn, Clara Wieck Schumann and Robert Schumann, Dvořák and Tchaikovsky, Liszt and Bartók, Grieg and Mahler, Ravel and Debussy, Sibelius and Shostakovich, Elgar and Holst. Why the historical combinations were endless! And it was Edgar Wittgenstein, *her* Edgar Wittgenstein who had conceived the fertile idea.

Fertile? Should she take time out of her blossoming career now that she was nearing her forties to conceive a child? Would Edgar wish that?

"What are you thinking about?" smiled the yawning, suddenly awake man next to her.

"Two things simultaneously, actually."

"Simultaneously? Do tell me."

"How your creative Double A Composer series could be continued with other rich pairings."

"What fun. Yes! And the other thing?"

Agatha smiled happily but could not bring herself to answer Edgar's question.

"Go on!" he commanded.

"Whether you and I should also be creative in a personal sense and produce a, have a..."

"A child?"

"Yes. A child."

"Agatha, darling! That would fulfill my greatest desire. A child. A baby Wittgenstein Endlich!" His enthusiasm touched Agatha to the core. She grinned and eased herself back down on the bed beside him.

"Then let's get back to work," she commanded.

Fanny curled up resignedly on the floor next to the bed.

67

"So which would you rather do, stay here for the day or drive to Vienna early enough to have a Chinese dinner before the Leopold Museum lecture?" Dieter Unfug smiled inquiringly at Christian Begeist, his honored guest in Wiener Neustadt. He knew the man's love of Chinese food and thought he would introduce him to one of the city's best and most elegant dining rooms, the China-Restaurant Shanghai on Jasomirgottstrasse in the inner city. Dieter's hovering mother had finally left the two men to themselves in the breakfast room after urging them both to find wives. The older man had immediately immersed himself in the morning paper. He looked up and smiled at his protege's question.

"Actually I'd like to leave early and for what you'll probably think is a very maudlin reason."

"Maudlin?"

"Yes. You know, I'm embarrassed to admit this, but I've never taken the time to visit the Stadtpark and look at the composer memorials there to Schubert, Lehar, and Johann Strauss, Junior."

"Two Franzes and one Junior? But haven't you left somebody out?" Dieter was nonplussed.

"I'm pulling your leg, my boy. Of course, I want to pay my respects to those other composers, but I want to worship and hug, if no one is around, the bronze Bruckner likeness in the Stadtpark. You could say I'm like Bruckner in that respect. You recall the story—and it's true—about, when the remains of Beethoven and Schubert were moved to Vienna's Central Cemetery in eighteen eighty-eight, a reverent Bruckner managed to be there and was allowed to handle and kiss their skulls. Well, I don't want to kiss Bruckner's skull, but I would like to kiss his bronze effigy."

"You had me worried there for a minute, Christian. Fine with me. It's been a long time since I visited the monument to the master. His contemporary, Viktor Tilgner, created it in eighteen ninety-nine. I hate to tell you, however, but the image is set on a white marble plinth so high that we'd have to bring a stepladder along for you actually to embrace him. He's only shown from the torso up. He raises his left index finger and looks over to his right at the miniscule lake before him. What's unusual about the image being in bronze is that it's so textured, the rippled folds of his clothing show. And his hair is cut so short that he looks bald from the ground while his prominent hawk nose looks practically like a sailboat! So, sure, visiting the Stadtpark and its composer memorials would be a great start to our Saturday in Vienna."

"Then we're agreed. Just let me finish reading this really weird review of last night's concert. I truly think the Schreib woman has lost it."

"Oh? How so?"

"She writes more paragraphs about the interruption of the Brahms symphony by that crazy man yelling he was a descendant of Friedrich Brahms—ha, fat chance—than she writes about Bruckner! And when she does, she focusses on the '*pauses*.' Says they are too long. What the hell does she know about the meaningful *silences* in Bruckner symphonies? Even to characterize them as 'pauses' is to misunderstand the master. Those thundering *silences* are the quietude of the Almighty. Why can't she understand that? And she gives only faint praise to the final movement, analyzing just the music, not Schreib's handling of it. A review of a concert is supposed to be just that, a review of the particular performance, not of the symphony being presented."

"I imagine most critics believe they have to educate their readers concerning the structure of the music being played, as well as commenting on a conductor's particular performance."

"Yes. Most music critics write for simpletons. I bet you Schreib wasn't even there for the final movement. Probably sneaked home to get her piece out for today's edition.

"Most likely."

"That explains why she didn't protest when, under the bouncing baton of Endlich the what could be a potential majestic one-hundred-minute duration of the symphony, was only eighty-five hurried minutes."

"I know, Christian. I saw you checking your watch at the end."

"Of course! Just wanted to verify that bitch of a conductor was indeed rushing timeless Bruckner. Hell! I don't want to read any more of what shameless Schreib has to say. She should have taken the Maestra to task, along with that dreadful general director Edgar Wittgenstein—Jewish, you know—who suggested this outrageous Double B Composers series in the first place. Hell, let's get back to Vienna, Dieter, and head for the peace of the Stadtpark and the glory of our bronze Bruckner."

68

Away from his Graz orchestra for almost a week now, Maestro Lukas Eifer was spending a quiet morning in his brother's small but pleasant Vienna apartment, which faced the church of St. Elisabeth on Argentinierstrasse, and was within easy walking distance of the Karlskirche as well as the Musikverein just beyond. After a leisurely breakfast together, Robb excused himself saying he wanted to research something that had come to mind during the Double B Composers concert last night. As deputy director of the Musikverein Library, Archive, and Collections he had access to an enormous trove of historical documents, including Brahms's large estate of letters, books, and music autographs. Robb was on the hunt for one in particular.

"And what will *you* be doing today?" he asked his brother, whose startling resemblance to Brahms never ceased to amaze and amuse him.

"Well, I too have something I'd like to take care of after I'm finished with the paper, so leave me a key on the hall table in case I get back before you do."

"Don't I always?" smiled Robb patiently.

Lukas nodded an absent farewell to his brother and continued reading the review of last evening's concert. Schreib was, as always, most interesting in her comments, expressing approval this time for both composers' symphonies and for their particular performances under the baton of Endlich. She thought the Maestra's placement of the final movement of Bruckner's Eighth after intermission was quite reasonable and she went to lengths to describe Bruckner's orchestration in blocks of sound, suggestive of an organ which, her readers knew, was his primary instrument. Readers were reminded of how the composer himself explained his pauses of deafening silence: "If I have something important to say, I must first take a deep breath!" As for the weird interruption of the third movement of Brahms's Third, the music critic introduced interesting background data on the Venezuelan self-exile of the younger brother of the composer before extending kudos to the Maestra for regaining her composure after the startling event, and her wise repetition of the movement to eager audience demand. All in all, it was a most positive review. Only Lukas wished it had been written about him and *his* interpretation of the great Brahms symphony. But here he was, stuck in Graz, when his life goal was to be conductor of the Vienna Philharmonic. Ah, well, such is life. But then life is full of the unexpected, isn't it, he asked himself, as he left his brother's apartment, conscientiously locking the double bolt door behind him.

There were only two other people in the reading room of the music archive on the second floor when Robb arrived at the Bösendorferstraße 12 back entrance to the Musikverein. One was the perpetual visitor, Dieter Unfug, and the other, a young brunette who looked as though she were a university student. Robb started to walk past her, then stopped in his tracks because of the photograph she was looking at and taking notes on. Dated 1937, it showed Adolf Hitler in military uniform, inside the temple of Walhalla, cap in hands, standing respectfully before a white marble bust of Anton Bruckner.

"Goodness! What on earth is your project, Fräulein?" Robb asked kindly.

"Oh! I'm writing a thesis on Hitler's use of Austrian and German composers to forward his nationalistic cause," the young woman answered, holding up the photograph and smiling.

"That sounds like an interesting if gloomy subject."

"You're right, there! But I think it's important for people of my generation to be reminded about Hitler's enlistment of composers—Wagner especially—to convey what he considered Nordic superiority. And since Hitler was born in Austria, as was

Bruckner, it must have been especially significant for him to bestow his countryman a place of honor at Walhalla. I've found out that Bruckner was the only "Germanic" historical person to have been installed there during the entire period of National Socialism."

"Very good," said Robb, approvingly. "I can think of one image of Hitler that might be useful to you, although it's not in this library."

"Oh, what's that?"

"It's a school photo taken of his class in the year nineteen hundred at the Realschule in Linz, when he was eleven."

"Oh, yes, I've seen that. He's the boy on the extreme right of the top row of students. It's fascinating because the small shadow under his nose eerily foreshadows the trim moustache he would wear as an adult."

"Well, I hadn't thought of *that*. Good! But let me ask you this. Have you identified anyone else in that school photo?"

"No. I was really just looking for images of Hitler."

"Ah ha! Well, considering Hitler's extreme and deadly anti-Semitism as an adult, it might interest you to know that two boys to the left of him on the left, in the row beneath his row, is the young son of the Vienna branch of the Wittgenstein family, Ludwig Wittgenstein, who grew up to become..."

"The famous philosopher!" exclaimed the young woman excitedly.

"Exactly. You might like to make something of the irony attached to this photograph."

"Oh, thank you, thank you, Herr, Herr?"

"Eifer. I'm deputy director of the Library, Archive, and Collections."

"You have made my day, Herr Eifer!"

Robb smiled, nodded his head, and resumed walking toward the file cabinet he had in mind. An apparently engrossed Dieter Unfug never looked up as he passed by. Five minutes later in the privacy of his small office, Robb was deep into the file he had in mind. After a short search he pulled out the music autograph he had wanted. It confirmed what he had thought. Johannes Brahms had first composed the slow, sad waltz theme of the third movement of his 1883 Third Symphony as early as 1870, when his younger brother Fritz was living in Caracas.

Here indeed was something to tell his own brother. And perhaps even the press. The public should know how false the claims of that insane Venezuelan were.

Robb had a final errand and it was one that he had no intention of telling his brother about. He needed to complete it before Lukas returned home. That errand took him downstairs and outside onto Canovagasse, the short street running along the east side of the Musikverein, and he had purposefully saved it for last.

After Lukas had finished reading Schreib's highly interesting review of last evening's Bruckner-Brahms concert, most of which he agreed with, he left his brother's apartment and walked up the Argentinierstrasse to the Schwartzenbergplatz where he could catch the 71 tram out to Vienna's Central Cemetery. He laughed to himself as he remembered that in Vienna, if one says of a person that "he took the 71 tram," it means that the person has died. But not so in this case. A very live Lukas wanted to pay his respects to Brahms and he knew his brother wouldn't be that interested in making the half-hour trip yet once again. He enjoyed the sights of the city as the streetcar slowly made its way out to the huge old cemetery. Graz simply did not ignite the same sense of awe in him as did Vienna, where both he and his brother had been born. Oh, if only his work as conductor could bring him a permanent post in the city of his birth. And yet he had to admit to himself that the Philharmonic's resident conductor was excellent at her job. A true professional. Really, his only hope was that of replacing the Maestra, should she ever become incapacitated.

69

Peter Heimnis answered his cellphone with difficulty that late Saturday afternoon. It was five forty-five and his arms were full of groceries as he helped his disabled wife Luisa into their apartment with the weekly food supplies. He glanced at the ID: "Unknown Caller" it read.

"Heimnis here."

A man's recognizable clipped voice sounded.

"Do you know where your son is right now?"

"What?"

"Do you know where Klaus is?"

"He's here. At home."

"*Is* he? Are you sure?"

"Hold on. Klaus! *Klaus!*" Heimnis slammed the groceries down on the kitchen table and ran from room to room calling his son's name. There was no sign of the boy.

"He is not there, is he," said the man's voice, menacingly.

"Where is he? *Klaus!* Is he with *you*? Who are you? Do you have my boy?"

"*Listen to me*. No more questions. This is what you are going to do and do right now. You will go immediately to Maestra Agatha Endlich's dressing room in the Musikverein, remove her baton with its box and place it on the desk of General Director Edgar Wittgenstein. You may pick it up from there any time after six, tomorrow morning, in plenty of time for the Maestra's concert that evening. That is all. Do you understand me, or must I repeat the instructions?"

“Yes! Yes, I understand. But please, please let our Klaus come back to us!”

“Do as I say *immediately,* and you will see Klaus again.”

Peter Heimnis did not take time to discuss the call with his worried wife. Instead, belting down a substantial sip of whiskey he left the house in the direction of the Musikverein without explanation.

Through the window of *Atelier im Musikverein Wilfried Ramsaier-Gorbach*, a music store, the shelves of which were lined with string instruments—with less requested cellos placed above violins and violas—the unknown caller was watching an impatient young boy opposite the east entrance of the Musikverein across Canovagasse as he paced and waited in vain for someone to meet him there at six o’clock. The man who had called and offered to pay him fifty euros if he would pick up a surprise package from him for his father was unknown to Klaus. And now it was closing in on seven o’clock and no one had shown up. This late for dinner he was going to be in big trouble.

The ID on his cellphone had simply read “Unknown Caller.”

70

As they reached Steinbach am Attersee, the largest lake in the Austrian Alps and less than half hour from Bad Ischl, Megan remembered exactly how to find Mahler's composing hut. She had visited it twice before, the first time with her host whenever she was in Paris, the eminent expert on the composer, Henry-Louis de la Grange, founder of the resource center Médiathèque Musicale Mahler. Back then it had been possible to enter the small one-room hut, photograph the scant furnishings, look out at the view from the small window, and "feel" the lake's inspiration for Mahler's Third Symphony, composed during 1895-1896. But now a noisy camping ground had grown up around the composing hut and it was necessary to pick up a key from the nearby Hotel Föttinger. As Megan and Tony entered the humble little cabin, a recording of the Third Symphony began playing, triggered by the opening of the door. What a lovely touch. As they listened for a while, Tony reminded Megan quietly of what Mahler had said about this symphony: "It has almost ceased to be music; it is hardly anything but sounds of nature."

It was the sights of nature that painter Gustav Klimt pursued during his sixteen summer stays on the Attersee, and the final destination of Megan's Salzkammergut visit was one of the several small lakefront villages where the artist stayed, switching from high society portrait painting to capturing calming landscapes—over forty-five of them done at this particular lake. The closest "Klimt" lakefront village to them was Wissenbach.

Megan parked at a spot she knew overlooked one of the exact views Klimt had painted of the Attersee, and they got out of the car to breathe in and absorb the sight. Both were silent as shifting hues of blue splashed and interlaced before their eyes.

"Ah, *this* is what I needed before talking about Klimt and Music tonight," Megan sighed with appreciation.

"It is wonderful," agreed Tony. He checked his watch. "Shall we eat lunch here or return to Bad Ischl before we start back?"

"Well, we've made our side visits to Mahler and Klimt, so let's return to Brahms now and eat in Bad Ischl. And at his very own Café Zauner."

Half an hour later they were sitting outdoors at Brahms's café consuming Apfelstrudel and toasting the composer from Hamburg and honorary Viennese with glasses of white wine.

They would leave at two and be back in Vienna by five, in time for Megan to take a wee nappie, as she put it. Then a yummy efficient dinner at the Burger King across the street before the evening lecture at the Leopold Museum. A convenient walk, but Megan would have them take a taxi so not to be worn out when she spoke.

Mahler, as well as Brahms, would certainly be part of her Klimt talk. What a trio!

71

An interesting and varied audience was filing into the Leopold Museum's auditorium that evening. A number of students from the University were present, intrigued at hearing about both art and music. One could see some of them pointing excitedly to a local celebrity, greatly respected, rarely seen, but known to all because of the photograph that accompanied her reviews. It was the music critic for *Der Standard*, Stefanie Schreib, and she was accompanied by a tall man distinguished by a head of thick white hair that contrasted with a short black beard. Older attendees, more in the know, also recognized people like the conductor of the Grazer Philharmonisches Orchester, Lukas Eifer, who looked for all the world like a reincarnation of Brahms, and another conductor, the lesser known Christian Begeist, clean-shaven leader of the Bruckner Orchester Linz, and distinctive because his short Prussian haircut was so similar to that of the Linz composer. What few people noticed as the lights went down and the speaker was being introduced, was that the resident conductor of the Vienna Philharmonic, Agatha Endlich, accompanied by a male companion with distinctively arched eyebrows, had slipped into the very back row of the auditorium.

The introduction of Megan by the genial museum director focused on her book about Klimt and her extensive monograph tracing the changing image of Beethoven over two centuries, concluding with Klimt's Beethoven frieze of 1902. Finally the introduction was over and Frau Professor Doktor Crespi from America—from Texas of all places—walked briskly to the lectern. Nodding her head in grateful acknowledgement of the enthusiastically applauding audience, some of whom had heard her speak in Vienna before, she swiftly set out her speech text and placed a small Tascam DR 40 next to it. She was wearing black slacks and shoes, and a tailored black vest covered a black, red, and white long-sleeved cotton blouse. Slipping on her invisible glasses, she looked at the audience, smiled, and brought her first images onto the giant screen behind her. From left to right was a horizontal lineup of four portrait photographs: Gustav Klimt, Gustav Mahler, Johann Strauss, Jr., and Johannes Brahms. Under the identifying names were their birth and death dates. Megan gave her listeners time to take in the images and data, then spoke.

"'Klimt and Music.' Yes, the two go together and in three/four time if you like. His mother was an amateur singer, and his city was the 'Waltz Capital of the World,' thanks to the Strauss dynasty. During the painter's career, even though he cared little for high society, he knew several of the most famous musicians of the epoch." The four photographs disappeared and a single new image came.

"This was not one of them." The audience laughed good-naturedly as they recognized Klimt's well-known portrayal, *Schubert at the Piano* of 1896. On the left, in a flickering candlelit scene, the young composer was shown in profile at the piano, with two earnest female singers standing behind him. Facing the beholder to the left of Schubert stood bachelor Klimt's mistress of the time and mother of two of his children.

"Nor could it be one of Klimt's acquaintances," continued Megan, "since Schubert died at the age of thirty-one in eighteen twenty-eight, just one year and some months after his idol Beethoven's death." Megan added an image on the right.

"Now compare that flickering, 'goldenized' parlor scene with *this* portrait of another pianist, and this time a contemporary musician. It is almost as though we are looking at a photograph of the man, Josef Pembaur, whom Klimt, still in his early realist stage, portrayed in eighteen ninety, complete with rimless glasses and straggly black hair, against a red background, while on the left a giant golden lyre is shown. On the upper right of the painting's very broad gold frame we see a second lyre as well."

After a suitable pause for onlookers to take in the images on the frame, the Schubert and Pembaur portraits disappeared and were instantly replaced by two very similar Klimt images known as "Music I" and "Music II." Both showed, on the left, a young girl dressed in a loose black garment holding up and playing a large golden lyre with its two upright curving arms. In the image on the left, the girl's head was in profile, bent toward her instrument; the portrayal on the right showed the girl, more a sensuous woman now, looking out at the beholder. Megan continued speaking.

"Ah! Here are two more lyres. These flat, two-dimensional pictures, both titled 'Music,' were painted by Klimt in eighteen ninety-five and eighteen ninety-eight, respectively. The one on our right, 'Music Two,' ended up on the entrance supraporta to the Vienna music salon of the Greek industrialist and patron of the arts Nikolaus Dumba, in honor of whom the short two-block street along the west, formal entry side of the Musikverein, is named. Here is the installation photo." A black-and-white photograph now appeared to the right of 'Music Two.'

"And I should really be referring to the instrument as a kithara, as this is the instrument played by the Greek god of the sun, music, and truth: Apollo. In the earlier version on our left, the young woman looks down at her instrument totally engaged, while behind her, and exactly at the level of her derriere, we see the wild-eyed face of Silenius, god of wine and drunkenness. In the later picture his head is to the right of the young maiden. This Dionysian follower is counterbalanced by, facing us on the right in both paintings, a large golden sphinx, suggesting that there is a riddle to be solved in the painting. Are we looking at the opposition between the Apollonian and the Dionysian, between reason and the irrational? In the Vienna of Sigmund Freud, this is not a superfluous question."

Murmurs of agreement sounded around the audience and Megan showed a new group of images on the screen to everyone's instant recognition. Four historic black-and-white photographs showed the interior of the Vienna's Secession exhibition of 1902 in which two major artists celebrated one of history's greatest composers, Beethoven. In the center room, shown on the far right, was Leipzig artist Max Klinger's life-size polychromatic monument presenting the enthroned composer in white marble, stripped to the waist, fists clenched, and leaning forward in thought on his bronze throne toward the giant Empyrean eagle at his feet.

Two framing historic photos on the left showed Klimt's famous three-sided gold-and-silver-embedded Beethoven frieze. On the far-left long wall was a depiction showing the weak imploring the strong—a knight in golden armor. The far-right long wall indicated what would be humankind's reward, the promise of pure joy as intoned by Schiller's "Ode to Joy," and as set to music in the fourth movement of Beethoven's Ninth Symphony. Depicted are a choir of angels and an embracing man and woman—an embrace for the entire world made possible by the arts.

But first, as the grim central panel showed, the hero-knight must traverse the underworld of hostile forces: the ferocious monster Typhon, a gargantuan hairy ape; his three naked, seductive daughters on the left, and the three semi-naked Gorgons on the right, one of them with an enormous belly, symbolizing greed, indulgence, and gluttony.

"*So is this philosophy or pornography?*" Megan asked the audience. Laughter exploded around the room.

"That is exactly what visitors and newspapers of the day asked," explained Megan. After an appropriate pause, she showed the entire Beethoven frieze again, but this time in glorious color. The audience murmured its admiration. Most persons present were aware that the actual, restored frieze was quite nearby, in the basement of Vienna's historic Secession building where it was first shown.

"If it weren't enough to link Beethoven with Klimt and Klinger, there is one more composer we can link to this extraordinary ode to the arts. Can you guess who?"

"Gustav Mahler!" several voices shouted. Megan nodded and a detail of the golden knight appeared on the screen.

"Yes, you are correct, and savvy contemporaries understood that this knight ready to do battle represented Gustav Mahler. The meaning: humanity can be rescued by the arts. But now we have another connection with Mahler as well, because for the grand opening of this extraordinary exhibition, he orchestrated part of the fourth movement of Beethoven's Ninth for just brass and winds, and conducted the ensemble for an awed audience of celebrities. What an evening in Vienna!"

Now two of the opening four images reappeared on the

screen: photographs of Klimt and Mahler. But between them was a photograph of a woman with her dates below.

"Who is this?"

"Alma Mahler!" the knowing audience shouted as if in one voice.

"Yes indeed," Megan confirmed. "A pianist and composer herself, she was pursued by both Gustavs. This you probably know, but you may not be aware of her first impressions of each of them."

Short quotations by Alma appeared underneath the two men. Under womanizing Klimt the text read: "He is an attractive fellow; one can have no idea what a free spirit he is, June, 1898." And under edgy Mahler: "I knew him well by sight; he was a small, fidgety man with a fine head, November 1901."

"Four months after that last observation, on the ninth of March, nineteen-two, the twenty-two-year-old Alma married, not the thirty-nine-year-old sensuous painter Gustav, but the cerebral forty-one-year-old composer—*this* Gustav," Megan's laser pointed to Mahler, " twenty-one years her senior." Two of the university students present clapped spontaneously and the audience laughed good-naturedly at their enthusiasm. Megan shared the laugh, then continued as the initial images of Strauss and Brahms reappeared on the screen.

"But what about Strauss and Brahms? Did they know Klimt? The answer is most likely no. To put it bluntly, they moved in different spheres of society: Klimt in gossipy café circles; the two composers in scandalmongering high society and welcome at the Palais Wittgenstein, or in the spa town Bad Ischl, Emperor Franz Josef's family summer vacation site, for example. Brahms especially, despite his often bearish nature, was a much-prized man of society. The names of his friends speak for a broad spectrum of interests, from the surgeon Theodor Billroth, pioneer of the second school of medicine in Vienna, to the famous anti-Wagner, pro-Brahms music critic Eduard Hanslick."

With these last words, a new image appeared: it was a full-figure photograph of Strauss and Brahms standing side by side on the 'Waltz King's' Bad Ischl villa porch. Megan exchanged knowing glances with Tony, who was sitting in the front row next to the seat she had vacated when taking over the lectern. The previous images disappeared and a new one, writ large, appeared. Smiling, Megan continued.

"However, new evidence has come to me just day before yesterday. and right here in Vienna in the form of this very deft colored pencil drawing," she said, bringing up an image of the photograph left for her at her hotel. She had decided not to end the lecture with it after all, as she had yet another surprise for the audience.

"This drawing dated 'eighteen seventy-eight' and signed simply 'K,' attests to the interesting fact that a teenage Klimt—sixteen, to be exact—then a student at the Kunstgewerbeschule, used to sneak into the Musikverein after school to listen to the Women's Chorus being directed by the man at the piano on the left. Look closely at that pianist's face: he is bearded, has a receding hairline and long dark blond hair falling behind his ears. He appears to be in his early forties. Do any of you know who he might be?

"Johannes Brahms?" asked several members of the audience.

"Yes. I believe it is Brahms. So, although we cannot document Klimt and Brahms meeting at one of the Wittgenstein salons or elsewhere, we now have this fascinating little drawing by a sixteen-year-old Klimt picturing the composer in his prime. And now, speaking of Klimt.... "

Megan beamed up a new color image, a full-length portrait of a stiffly standing, black-haired, bare-shouldered woman dressed in voluminous white silk with hands stiffly linked, left over right. Many members of the audience immediately recognized who it was before being told. It was Klimt's 1905 wedding portrait of the Wittgenstein family's youngest daughter, twenty-two-year-old Margaret—"Gretl"—to Jerome Stonborough of New York.

"Yes, Margaret Stonborough Wittgenstein, who posed for Klimt at his studio during the year nineteen four for this January wedding portrait. And while we may think this is a knock-out portrait, Gretl hated it! Claimed the depiction of her mouth was totally wrong. She even had another artist repaint the mouth." Moans of disapproval came from the audience.

"Yes, sadly. And she never hung it, friends never saw it. But *we* can see it, admire it at Munich's Neue Pinakothek. At least with this portrait we have a Klimt connection with the Wittgenstein family, so perhaps he did actually meet Brahms on some occasion. But that's a big 'perhaps' because, as I said, Klimt moved in the circles of tale-telling café society, not equally gossipy high society, although he was a much sought-after painter *of* high society." Megan paused, then ad-libbed something she had not expected to say.

"And I was privileged to meet one of the society ladies he painted: Friedericke Beer-Monti. First in Vienna, then in New York where we both lived over fifty years ago. It was she who generously and garrulously gave me a rich insight into Viennese society of nineteen hundred. When I asked her what she was doing at that time, her answer was immediate: 'Nothing! Just *living*!'" Members of the audience nodded nostalgically.

Now a large photogravure took up the entire screen—it was Megan's next to last image. Shown was a well-appointed music salon with dark drapes and framed pictures on its walls. The room was dominated by a centrally placed seven-foot-long grand piano seen from the side. Seated at the piano was full-bearded Brahms himself, turning toward the photographer, his left elbow on the music rack, his right hand bent on his right thigh. To the left, bow at the ready, sat the cellist Richard Hausmann and to the right stood a female singer, their hostess. The audience gasped—few people in the auditorium knew of this photograph.

"You are, of course, going to ask, where was this photograph taken? The answer is in Vienna at Apostelgasse twelve. This was the home of the composer's longtime friends, industrialist, music-loving Richard and his talented wife Maria Fellinger, the singer in this photograph. Although they never used the intimate *Du* term, Brahms regularly dined on Sunday evenings with them and their three small children, who called him *Onkel Bahms*." The audience giggled, echoing the r-less pronunciation.

"Maria Fellinger was an amazing woman: a vocalist, a painter, a sculptor, and a photographer to whom we owe many of our images of Brahms in later life. Now, the piano we are looking at was a J. B. Streicher and Sohn, cross-strung, ebonized, and with Viennese action acquired by Richard in eighteen eighty. I emphasize this because, although our music-loving Klimt is not documented as being present at the occasion, in December of eighteen eighty-nine, a cylinder recording was made of *Brahms playing the piano*."

Exclamations of delighted astonishment and disbelief rose from the audience. Only a few persons, including Maestros Lukas Eifer and Christian Begeist and Maestra Agatha Endlich, were not surprised by this piece of information.

"Yes! On December second of that year, the European representative of Thomas Edison, Theo Wangemann, recorded Brahms at the grand piano we see in front of us. Brahms had prepared his Rhapsody in G minor for piano, but as he became more and more impatient at the drawn-out technical preparations for the recording procedure, he played a shortened adaptation for piano of his First Hungarian Dance. He then played his own version of Josef, not Johann, Strauss's *Dragonfly* polka-mazurka. Of Brahms's Hungarian Dance, measures thirteen to seventy-two were recorded."

Gasps of delight came from the audience.

"But," Megan continued sadly, "upon playback, there were so many layers of *noise* that the recording was practically useless. This, in spite of various attempts at filtering and enhancing the cylinder recording. The event became nothing more than a footnote to history."

The audience sighed as one.

"*However*! Recently, employing a state-of-the-art approach to audio signal analysis, two American graduate students at Yale University transcribed the sound by painstakingly removing layers of noise to reveal the music embedded within. Transcription was then followed by careful analysis of the numerous performance nuances, agogic lengthening of time values, inflections, improvised segments and elaborations." Megan glanced at her audience who were beginning to look agog at her agogics. Taking her Tascam she held it up to the microphone.

"Would you like to *hear* the results?"

Every member of the audience voiced an enthusiastic "yes!"

"Yes, let's do. But I must prepare you before you listen: this is still not a rich enough sound; more work must be done to emulate the way the Streicher piano sounded in the Fellinger home. We're not there yet."

Megan then played the results and although the quaking tones were still more noise than sound, it was uncannily personal to hear how Brahms tended to hold some of his quarter and eighth notes a bit longer—his own personal agogics.

Megan played the Brahms-Josef Strauss piece as well, and when it concluded she brought her lecture to an end by showing again the beginning horizontal lineup of the four portrait photographs of Klimt, Mahler, Strauss, Junior, and Brahms.

"So there we have it: an evening with Klimt and Music."

The applause seemed unending, and people began lining up to speak to Megan at the lectern. Remaining in his seat, Tony Bocello discreetly held up two fingers in a V signal.

Purposefully and patiently last in line were a white-haired woman and a girl in her late teens.

"Are you Lisl?" asked Megan smiling before either woman could address her. The young girl blushed and nodded her head.

"And you, then, have to be Frau Margret Grainer," Megan smiled.

"I am. Oh, Frau Professor Doktor Crespi, we are so excited that you placed a photograph of our Klimt drawing in your lecture!"

"I almost screamed with excitement," admitted Lisl.

"I was happy to have it in the lecture because I believe it is a charming documentation of a very young artist's extracurricular interest in music: just right for this talk."

"But you credit it then to Gustav and not Ernst?" a slightly disappointed Frau Grainer asked.

"I do. After all, your great-great-grandfather was only fourteen the year of your fascinating drawing which, in my opinion, is far more advanced than a boy that age could do. Plus the way the K is formed is very close to the way Gustav made his Ks."

"I have brought the drawing with me," said Frau Grainer. "Is this a good place to show it to you?" She had already slipped it, covered in velvet, out of her large bag. A moment later the velvet had been folded back and there was the drawing, its back pressed against the cover of a large book, which framed it, in an awkward manner. The front of the drawing was covered by a sheet of plastic food wrapping. Megan winced.

"The drawing is marvelous. But, Frau Grainer, to prevent any further fading, please take it immediately to an art store and have them fix it up for you with the proper protection."

"Oh, yes, yes, I see what you mean, Frau Professor Doktor. I hadn't thought of that. Oh, yes, right away, tomorrow. Or, I mean, Monday, tomorrow is Sunday."

Lisl spoke up.

"Do you think my grandmother's drawing could be valuable if it's by Gustav rather than by Ernst?"

"Yes. I wouldn't be surprised if a private collector or commercial gallery were to pay up to three thousand euros for it."

The two women appeared dumbfounded. Megan continued.

"If it were I, I'd think first about offering it for sale to your world-famous Albertina Museum: that way many people could see and admire it."

"Do you think the Museum would pay as much as the others?" asked a lustful Lisl.

"That I would not know. But it would be wonderful if the drawing were in the public domain." Megan was amused by Lisl's practical question. Her grandmother cleared her throat and asked the pressing question she had been waiting to ask.

"Then would you be willing, Frau Professor Doktor Crespi, to write us a certification that the drawing is by Gustav Klimt?"

"Oh, no, I'm sorry, that I could not do. We American art historians do not go in for that kind of procedure. I am sorry. But you could show it to the Leopold Museum staff or the Albertina staff and tell them I showed it in the lecture you've just heard and that I presented it as being by Gustav Klimt." A man's voice interrupted the discussion. It was Tony and he tapped Megan lightly on the shoulder.

"We really should get going; they're waiting to close the auditorium."

"Thank you *so* much Frau Professor Doktor Crespi, we are very excited you think our drawing is by Gustav Klimt," Frau Grainer said quickly, turning to go.

"Yes, thank you a lot," echoed Lisl. Megan smiled at them.

"And congratulations on owning such an interesting drawing. Please think about sharing it with the world."

As they hung behind the two departing women, Tony beamed at Megan and whispered.

"Wonderful, my dear, just wonderful. It was a fascinating, lively lecture with such a surprise audio bonus, and everyone loved it."

Megan beamed, tickled that Tony had not known about the most recent transcription results of further research on Brahms's 1889 cylinder recording.

Passing through the doors of the Leopold Museum and into the large and still lively pedestrian area in front of the institution, they were startled to hear two male voices calling to Megan in unison.

"*Megan*! Hallo, Megan! Surprise, surprise!"

Puzzled, Megan and Tony turned toward the sound, and although Tony had no idea who the two men were, Megan certainly did.

"Tönnies! Harry!" she exclaimed with delight. "What are you doing *here*?" She turned to Tony and explained who her Hamburg friends were, introducing them to each other.

"We absolutely *had* to be here for your lecture," Tönnies Helfer said, laughing with pleasure at the success of their surprise.

"Couldn't miss it, even if we did have to come all the way to Vienna to hear you," added a beaming Harry Dunmore.

"Well, this calls for a celebration drink. Where would you like to go?" asked Megan, suddenly feeling her after-lecture weariness lift. After all, it wasn't even ten o'clock yet.

"Hotel Bristol," Tönnies declared without hesitation.

"Hotel Bristol it is then," she joyfully concurred.

72

A fitful, interrupted night had left Robb Eifer exhausted. He had woken up at two in the morning. *How could he have forgotten*? After all his preparations and planning! He would simply have to sneak back to the Musikverein without waking his brother. Lukas was sound asleep on the sofa bed in the living room as he sneaked past him and soundlessly left the apartment. Walking up Argentinierstrasse at this early hour in the morning seemed a bit spooky, but at least there was no traffic as he crossed Lothringerstrasse to the Musikverein. Using his key, he slipped inside through the Bösendorferstrasse 12 entrance. An overhead security camera clocked his entry at exactly two twenty-five in the morning.

73

In the wee hours of Sunday morning, day of Maestra Endlich's final Double B Composers concert, a rosewood baton box was removed from the desk of Edgar Wittgenstein's office high above the hallowed Musikverein concert hall. Eleven minutes later, it was returned to the desk and placed precisely in the position in which it had been found. Late that Sunday evening a staff member discovered that a door opening onto the Bösendorferstrasse 12 entrance to the Musikverein had been left unlocked.

74

Something suddenly awoke Megan very early Sunday morning after a good night's sleep. Exhausted from both the Bad Ischl drive and delivering her Klimt and Music lecture, to say nothing of the jovial nightcap with her friends from Hamburg, she had fallen asleep almost immediately. Now a persistent noise was filling the room. Megan looked around sleepily. Heck! It was her iPhone playing the Intermezzo from Massenet's opera *Thäis*. Someone was trying to reach her, but where was her iPhone? Oh, hell, there it was, across the room on the dressing table, damn it! Throwing back the sheet and pulling herself off the bed, she staggered to her phone and looked indignantly at the Caller ID. It read "Jacquelyn McDonald." God! Doesn't that woman ever figure out the time differences between America and Europe? It's not even seven o'clock yet!

"Hi, Jacquelyn," Megan answered almost reluctantly. "What's up?"

"Hi, Megan. I know it's early for you there, but I absolutely have to tell you about a further discovery I've just made about the Ney/Brahms letter business."

"Okay. What is it?" Megan yawned.

"Well, seems I didn't take quite everything out of the envelope with the key and the letter."

"Oh?"

"Yes. So, listen to this. I was arranging the letter with its envelope on the mat of the large glass display case in which we're going to exhibit the five pages of the letter all spread out." There was a pause as Jacquelyn suddenly coughed, then cleared her throat.

"Yes?"

"And for some reason I held the mailer envelope up to the

overhead light and saw that there was a very small piece of paper, about the size of—let me think—the size of a business card folded in half—inside. I pulled it out very carefully, of course, and there, in Brahms's beautiful, miniscule handwriting, was the word 'Postscriptum.'"

"Oh, wow! What was the PS?"

"It's a little hard to read because the writing is so small, but it says '*Hinweis*'—hint—then a three-letter phrase: '*Ich liebe Zigeuner*.'"

"'I love Gypsies'?"

"Yes. 'I love Gypsies.' That's it. Nothing else. Nada. What do you think, Megan? What on earth could that mean?"

"Well, it has to refer to Brahms's love of Gypsy music. You know, he got that from touring with the flashy Hungarian-Jewish virtuoso violinist Eduard Hoffman, who changed his name to Reményi. They toured North German towns together when Brahms was only twenty and Reményi was twenty-five. There's a wonderful story about their arriving in the small town of Celle to play a concert and finding out at the last minute that their piano was tuned a half-tone flat! But no problem: Brahms simply transposed Beethoven's Violin Sonata in C minor to C sharp minor. Without the music in front of him! And it was Reményi who introduced Brahms to his former classmate at the Vienna Conservatory, Joseph Joachim, also a Hungarian Jew. Joachim became Brahms's friend for life despite emotional ups and downs between them. And by the way, Reményi died *on stage* while giving a vaudeville concert in San Francisco in eighteen ninety-eight." Megan was fully awake now and on all cylinders.

"Wow! But to go back to Brahms, did he compose Gypsy music then, since he wrote 'I love Gypsies'?"

"You bet he did. A year after he settled in Vienna he wrote and published for piano four hands a set of twenty-one 'Hungarian'—code for 'Gypsy' or 'czsardas'— Dances. Most of them feature a slow, melancholy introduction and then fling into an exuberant, fast finish. And later Brahms orchestrated some of them."

"So that would be the mindset behind his coding to Elisabet where she would find his operetta score then? That he loved *Gypsies*?"

Jacquelyn had been listening carefully to Megan's explanation of Brahms's love of Gypsy music.

"Apparently. As for being a clue, the only thing I can think of is what Brahms wrote in his letter to Ney, that Joachim knew *where* the glove box was to which Brahms's key fit. But after he'd written the letter and was ready to trust it to the mail, it occurred to him that Joachim himself might die before Ney had a chance to return to Europe. And that's why he added a Postscriptum 'Hint.'"

"All right then, that's what I'll include in the didactic we're preparing. Thank you, Megan."

"Glad to help. Say, if you're about to display the letter in your museum can I tell colleagues about it now?"

"Sure. Now you can tell anyone you want to. The more who know now, the merrier. News of it should definitely result in an increase of visitors to the museum."

"Good. And I do have a favor to ask of you, Jacquelyn dear."

"Anything. What is it?"

"*Do not call me before eight in the morning.*"

75

"Well, now, don't you look nice and rested," Tony observed as he and Megan sat eating breakfast at the Römischer Kaiser. Their favorite secluded table was free, and they were relaxing over a second cup of coffee.

"Ha! You should have seen me at six twenty- five this morning. That's when I got a call from the director of the Ney Museum."

"Really? What was so important, did he say?"

"It's a *she*, and she did have a very interesting piece of information about Brahms to tell me. And now I can let you know about something I've been dying to tell you ever since we got together here in Vienna. But until now my lips were sealed."

"Sounds scary."

"No, no, not scary, Tony, quite the opposite actually. Something lovely and totally unknown about Brahms all these years."

For the next fifteen minutes Tony listened with growing fascination as Megan, aided by her iPhone photos, narrated the circumstances of finding an old European-style key inside the bust of an unbearded Brahms she had found and bought in an Austin antique store a week ago, and Jacquelyn's later discovery of the love letter written by Brahms to Elisabet Ney. Moving to photographs of the letter's five pages sent by Jacquelyn, she slowly read them out loud. Tony was enchanted.

"Brahms scholars and Brahms fans are absolutely going to love this!" he exclaimed when Megan finished reading the heartfelt sentiments. He had a question.

"And what was the phone call this morning about? Can you tell me?"

"Yes. Jacquelyn told me that when she chanced to hold up the letter's mailer envelope to the light before placing it in a showcase along with the letter, she saw there was a very small slip of paper inside. In Brahms's hand, but in very small script, of course, it announced itself as a postscript with the words 'Hint: I love Gypsies.' That's all. Just 'I love Gypsies.'"

"Oh, so he was referring to his fondness for Gypsy music and/or his own Hungarian Dances," Tony concluded immediately.

"It would seem so at first, but it's a strange way of expressing himself about music. I see it rather as an oblique reference to his 'Gypsy' friend Joachim."

"Well, yes, that makes a lot of sense. So after Brahms's passing, Joachim would be able to tell Elisabet Ney where the operetta score box was hidden, yes?"

"No, I don't think so," Megan answered. "Brahms had already told Ney in his letter that Joachim knew where the 'humble container' was. I think his postscript 'hint' was written just in case Joachim too, were to die before Ney could come to Vienna."

"I see what you mean. And irony of ironies, Joachim would live another ten years after Brahms died. But Brahms couldn't know that, so he was just being sure with the 'hint' slipped into the envelope after he'd written and folded up the long letter."

"Yes, that's what I'm thinking," Megan agreed. It was so important to him that the operetta get to Ney."

"Do you think the short phrase he used—'I love Gypsies'—would have actually served as an *understandable* hint for her?"

"I should think so. They made quite a memorable trio there in Hanover those few days in each other's company."

Tony heaved a breath, folded up his napkin, laid it neatly on the table, and looked at his travel companion questioningly.

"So what is our Brahms destination today, Megan?" Their BMW had been rented for three days, and this was only their second. Without hesitation Megan answered.

"Mürzzuschlag!"

76

Edgar, like many of the other Wittgensteins in his family, was a gourmet cook, and while Agatha was showering and dressing, he had taken creative possession of her kitchen. By the time a pleasantly surprised Agatha appeared, breakfast was on the table. And what an enticing Sunday meal it was: warm *Semmeln*, apricot jam, cold ham cuts, sliced sausage, muesli, a boiled egg each, orange juice, and strong, hot coffee.

"I cannot believe this," a happy Agatha said, slipping into a chair at the kitchen table. How could you have put together such a lavish breakfast?"

"Easily. I just raided your fridge and the kitchen shelves. Found everything I needed. I'm happy you are pleased, dear." Instead of sitting down he knelt before her and kissed her hands.

"Are you still of the same mind about our plans as you were in the wee hours of this morning?"

"Absolutely. We can register for the one at the Standesamt in Alsergrund tomorrow morning; for the other we may have to wait nine months." Agatha giggled like a teenager.

"Would you rather it be a girl or a boy?" Edgar asked blissfully.

"Makes no difference to me. And you?"

"As long as it is a Wittgenstein Endlich, I'll be happy."

The two kissed and continued their joyful warm embrace while neglected rolls, eggs, and coffee turned cold. A matter now of no importance.

77

Mario Intagliatore was enchanted by his second encounter with Stefanie Schreib's boy, who had cheerfully eaten dinner with him and his mother Saturday evening before the Crespi lecture. Mario had asked if he could return Sunday at midday, mix up some clay in the kitchen, and model a bust of the child.

"And this time a clay portrait would be left with me long enough to recreate it in marble—marble that already belongs to you," he had laughed.

Stefanie, who had done her Internet homework on Intagliatore, was flabbergasted. What a marvelous idea. Hans was sure to be fascinated and how flattering to have her son be portrayed by one of the most renowned sculptors of the day.

Mario, in turn, although reasonably sure the needed ingredients would already be in Stefanie's kitchen, took no chances. Just on the safe side, he bought and brought with him a large package of salt and an equally large package of cornstarch.

Once installed in the kitchen, with Hans on a stool looking on curiously, Mario began with two cups of salt and two-and-a-half cups of water in a large saucepan, steadily stirring the mixture over the flames for five minutes. Then he removed the pan from the fire, added a cup of cornstarch and half a cup of cold water, stirred the mixture until it was smooth, and returned it over the flames, cooking it until it became thick.

"Now, *piccolo Signor* Hans, my boy, we must wait until the clay cools down and then we will both go to work. I will make a likeness from the clay of you while you will form your portion of the clay to look like your mother. What do you say to that?"

"But who will do *you*?" asked the boy, totally engaged.

"When you finish doing your mother you can, if you still want to, make a copy of my head. I shall sit very still for you, as you must do now for me."

"May I do your hands too?"

"*Sì ,sì, certo*. As long as our batch of clay lasts, you can make whatever you like."

When the clay was cool and pliable, both Mario and Hans went to work, the eleven-year-old as silent and intent as the sixty-six-year-old. For the next forty minutes, as both modeled the clay in front of them, their silence was only broken once. That was when Hans told his mother something important.

"*Mutti!* When I grow up I want to be Italian!"

78

It was late Sunday afternoon in Wiener Neustadt. The air was clear and the sun still high in the sky. Christian Begeist had brought the relevant Bruckner symphony scores with him from Linz. Seized by the seductive thought that little bitch Maestra Endlich might become indisposed and unable to conduct one evening, he had carefully gone through the score of each Bruckner opus being performed, beginning with last Monday, then Wednesday and Friday, and now the fourth and final program of the ridiculous, insulting Double B Composers series.

What sheer folly it had been for Fräulein Endlich to pit Brahms's measly little Fourth, quoting Bach in its last movement for lack of inspiration, against the master's mighty Ninth! Ah, Bruckner's Ninth. Even if the last movement was not completed—the composer was working on it the day he died—it still held its own as equal to Beethoven's Ninth. Bruckner had dedicated it "to the beloved God," and had marked the hushed opening "*feierlich, misterioso*—solemnly, mysterious." And indeed the symphony's solemn, mysterious sounds quickly drew the performers and listeners into a solemn and mysterious realm, first through the initial tremolo winds and then timpani and trumpet battlefield fanfares as the first movement ends with a chilling, terrifying coda. Ha! Let Brahms try to equal that sense of immensity with his simple, sentimental falling thirds!

Something else was falling acoustically while Christian brooded over the two Bs. It was the voice of Dieter's mother, screaming at her son in the kitchen.

"But I *heard* you drive out of the garage at an ungodly hour last night! Where in the devil's name were you going?"

"No, *Mutter*, you've got it wrong. I was asleep all night. Tucked into my bed."

"You're *lying* to me. I heard your car leave! It must have been two in the morning. And then your noisy car woke me up again; it must have been after four o'clock."

"*Mutter*, what can I say? You make things up in your mind and then you think they're real. You've done this before. . . ."

"Stop! Do not say another word to me. I know what you're up to. Seeing some woman in Vienna! Why don't you just marry some nice girl *here* and settle down. Vienna is an hour away. I need an old age that is peaceful. Why do you make me worry about you so much?" Christian could hear the old woman sobbing dramatically.

"All right, *Mutter*. Stop worrying about me. I must lead my own life. And if that means deciding to take a drive at two in the morning then so be it."

A minute later Dieter joined Christian in the living room and both men rolled their eyes upward.

"Where *were* you last night?" the older man asked in a low whisper. "I also heard your car leaving sometime past midnight."

"Christian, that's for me to know and you *perhaps* to find out."

79

"Why are you so excited about specifically going to Mürzzuschlag as opposed to all the other rich Brahms sites within reach around Austria?" Tony had volunteered to do all the driving and was vocally speculating on Megan's choice as they headed south out of the city and toward the tip of the Semmering Pass. It was a drive of around an hour and twenty minutes. They would be back in plenty of time for the final Double B Composers concert at the Musikverein that evening.

"Let's put it this way," Megan answered slowly. "Spending two summers in eighteen eighty-four and eighty-five at this particular mountain village was instrumental to Brahms's composing and finishing his Fourth Symphony. That's reason enough to visit Mürzzuschlag and absorb its atmosphere. To say nothing of the glorious Alpine scenery as we get closer to it. And then too, there was the fact that Brahms's treasured Fellinger family had a summer house there and that meant there would be a fine piano available and excellent dinners. And finally, although it goes without saying, the fact that there is a Brahms Museum there."

Their route took them south through Wiener Neustadt and Megan asked Tony whether he'd like to stop at the Arnold Schönberg Museum. She had seen it once some years ago but was willing to go again if he wanted to visit it.

"Thanks, but not necessary. I saw it when Charlotte and I were traveling in Austria. It's interesting enough, but I don't need to go again."

"Same case with me," replied Megan. "I visited it just once, perhaps twenty years ago by now, and one time is enough, although it's quite interesting. Especially his painting."

"You do know that Schönberg really revered Brahms, don't you?" Tony asked.

"What? No, I didn't know that. How interesting! *Schönberg* and Brahms?"

"Yes. As early as nineteen thirty-three, just before he fled Hitler for France, and then Los Angeles. It was a program for Radio Frankfurt and he delivered a short analysis of Brahms's art of composing as being ahead of his time. And then in nineteen forty-seven he published the same thoughts in essay form which he titled 'Brahms the Progressive.' Because he grew up in Vienna and was already twenty-three years old when Brahms died, Schönberg believed—rather possessively—that he had a special insight into the master's technique of developing variation—something he also engaged in." Megan's eyes began to glaze over as she tried to follow Tony's excursion into music theory leading to Schönberg's twelve-tone music, although the composer never termed it so himself. Why does there always seem to be math with music?

"Actually," Tony was saying, "it was in large part due to Schönberg that Brahms's music saw a revival in the middle of the twentieth century."

They drove on in silence for a while, savoring the mountainous limestone landscape as they began to ascend the stunning Semmering Pass. Mürzzuschlag—long the skier's paradise of Central Europe—was on the other side, stretching out from a winding river named Mürz. The village had a mere 8,000 inhabitants but in the ski season its hotels hosted hundreds of visitors.

"There's more than one museum here," said Megan, looking up the small town on her phone. One is a history of the Vienna's Southern Railway, another is a Winter Sports museum. Which one would you rather visit first?"

"The Brahms," shouted Tony, laughing. Megan laughed with him. Arriving in town they found a parking space not too far from the museum at Wiener Strasse No. 4, and walked into a long courtyard surrounded by three pale-colored low buildings, each distinguished by a series of arches. Immediately to their left was the all-glass arched entrance to the museum. Standing invitingly outside to the right of the entry door was, true to the original profile image from life by Otto Böhler, a life-size black silhouette of the composer in his characteristic brisk walking mode: hands clasped behind his back, hat, beard, and long jacket pointing forward. Painted on the figure were the inviting words, "On the track of Johannes Brahms." And between the composer's feet trotted the bright red silhouette of a little hedgehog, leading the way to Brahms's favorite Vienna hangout, the Red Hedgehog Tavern. On the hedgehog's prickly body was the designation "Brahms Way." This detail could also be taken by those in the know as a reference to Brahms's prickly nature—quick to take things amiss, but also quick to sudden acts of generosity. Megan had already spotted an array of tempting Brahms souvenirs inside the museum giftshop, but she resisted and instead joined Tony as he entered a room inhabited by a host of the composer's friends in life-size cardboard photographs, some sitting, some standing.

What a marvelous idea! Megan immediately identified a standing Johann Strauss, Jr. and the seated Maria Fellinger, a copy of whose excellent bust of Brahms they had already encountered outside. Standing next to Strauss was Brahms himself. The last seated figure, one person away to the composer's left, was a surprise, and certainly a mistake? It was Bruckner. Knowing the uninhibited animosity of Brahms toward the peasant genius, it didn't make sense to include him here. Or did it? His inclusion certainly made visitors ponder the two composers' works and personalities. Behind Bruckner stood the figures of Empress Elisabeth—Sisi—and Emperor Franz Joseph. What an ensemble!

Following the lead of these figures came a small performance room with short rows of simple white wooden, red-upholstered chairs facing front. Above a wall of small display cases, writ large in red and in Brahms's cursive script, were the words "I live and stroll comfortably in Mürzzuschlag." The beautiful J. B. Streicher & Sohn concert grand that had once been in the Fellinger home in Vienna—site of Brahms's unique piano recording—also occupied this room and was off to one side. A placard said it was used for concerts. Other rooms contained the single wood-framed bed Brahms slept in and a coat stand with his black walking coat and black umbrella.

“Oh, this is so much better than the tiny Brahms room at the Haydn Museum in Vienna,” Megan whispered to Tony, taking what must have been a fiftieth photograph with her “iPhoto” phone.

“There’s certainly plenty to see with all these rooms, photos, and wall exhibits,” Tony agreed after they had made a lingering circuit of the museum rooms. “I’d like to take another look at that weird bronze bust we saw of Brahms earlier, you know, the huge one made by that contemporary artist, what was his name?”

“Josef Pillhofer, who usually shapes things in cubes, and I agree with you, he’s a pill that’s hard to swallow if we want the bust to remind us of Brahms. Let’s do go see it again.”

Without buying souvenirs, a first for Megan, they walked to the outdoor area where the bearded bronze bust reigned on a high and narrow white stone plinth. The bust had been cast in 2004. To both Tony and Megan the head was more about the multi-rippled medium than it was about Brahms. The head looked to be at least thirty inches tall, and yet it was the hand-undulated rippling of the beard and long hair, and not the face, which caught one’s attention. Neither of the two onlookers could bring themselves to like the memorial.

“Let’s go back over to the Maria Fellinger bust so we can leave this Brahms oasis with happy memories,” said Megan finally.

“What? You don’t want to visit the train or winter sports museums?” teased Tony.

“No. But I’d love to have a cold beer and something to eat before we head back to Vienna and the final Double B Composers concert.” Tony was of like mind and after consulting the Internet they decided on a five-star tavern with outdoor seating called Wirtshaus Musiwirt Anbauer. Basking in the warm, sunny weather, sipping beer, and eating fried chicken with plenty of lemon slices, they were not disappointed.

“What do you think the ‘Musi’ in ‘Musiwirt’ means?” Tony asked. “Is it a reference to the muses, or to Music?”

“It’s a teaser, isn’t it? Of course ‘wirt’ means ‘host.’” Just as Megan spoke, something unexpected and totally delightful happened. A woman followed by four men streamed out of the restaurant and headed straight toward them and the nearby diners. The woman was dressed in a dirndl and the men were wearing lederhosen. The latter were also holding musical instruments: a guitar, a clarinet, an accordion, and could it be true? A Wagner tuba! The restaurant clientele were serenaded by the jolly woman and her musicians as the meaning of the word Musi revealed itself.

80

After a relaxed and late lunch, the food once again prepared by Edgar, Agatha asked, almost apologetically, to have some study time for the performance that evening. Edgar had instantly agreed and offered to take Fanny for a long Sunday walk. The arrangement was beneficial for all parties and when Edgar returned, he discreetly settled down with his cellphone in the kitchen, leaving the living room to Agatha, seated with her mini scores at a desk on the far side of the room. As for Fanny, after checking on her mistress, she trotted to the kitchen and settled down contentedly at Edgar's feet. All was well at Porzellangasse 33.

First Edgar answered some of the more important emails to have come in overnight, then he decided to check the Maestra's dressing room at the Musikverein. He opened the Ring Europe app he had installed and studied the room. Everything was in place. No rose bouquets in any corners, thank god! To fill the time, he took a glance at the room's motion history over the past few days. There, of course, was none after the concert on Friday after he and Agatha left, and there should be none at all since. But for Saturday, he saw a notification of movement in the dressing room clocked as commencing at six twenty-two in the evening. What? He tapped *live* and watched with fascination as a person—man or woman was impossible to tell—entered the dressing room, walked straight to the dressing table, then instantly turned and left the room. The person's face was visible for a second. But the camera was on blur mode and it was not possible to make out the intruder's features. Damnation! Who the hell was it? And how did the person have a key to the dressing room? And furthermore, how did the Ring camera get set to blur mode? Did Agatha do that and then forget to turn it back? Edgar turned his back to the living room. He did not want Agatha to notice his agitation. Fanny had, however, and looked up inquiringly.

There was one more notification of movement. It was for this morning at six-eighteen. Edgar tapped *live* and observed a blurred figure enter, take the three steps to the dressing table, then turn and exit. But again the camera was on blur mode. How frustrating! Agatha must have wanted it on blur while she was going through her yoga routine and forgotten to turn it off again. He looked over at her. She was totally immersed in her scores. Best not to ask her, Edgar told himself. If it were not she who had set the camera to blur, then she would become anxious and that's the last thing she needed now—anxiety. No, sweet Agatha must not know of this. He played the two motion sequences of the blurred figure entering and exiting the dressing room over and over, but there was simply nothing more to be discerned about the intruder. Not even verification of whether or not it was the same person. And what was the motive? Why would someone want to enter the Maestra's dressing room? And twice? Was it another vicious-minded prankster? Edgar turned the Ring setting off blur mode and back to normal. Who could have had access to the camera?

Edgar glanced at his watch. It was three o'clock. Plenty of time to go to the Musikverein and check things out in person. Yes, that was the thing to do. He stood up and walked over to Agatha, bringing his face down to hers. She smiled at him, her eyebrows raised inquisitively.

"Darling, I'm thinking I want to drive over to the Musikverein and just check that everything is in order for this evening. All right?"

"Why am I not surprised you want to do that?" Agatha laughed. "Will you be back in time for dinner? Oh my god, aren't we sounding like an old married couple already!"

Edgar joined in her laughter.

"You can rely on that, my sweet. I should be back within the hour. And no more kitchen today, I'll bring us something already prepared."

81

Sunday's glorious weather had benefitted all Austria, and as the late evening sun began to sink below the horizon, a host of eager concertgoers was filing past images of Johann Sebastian Bach and Christoph Willibald Gluck and ultimately into the *Grosser Saal* of Vienna's venerable Musikverein. The sophisticated audience had gathered to hear the final performance of the unusual series that presented not one but two symphonies. One by Anton Bruckner, his only symphony in D minor—the "tragic key"—and the other by Johannes Brahms, also in a minor key, in this case E minor. The older composer by nine years, Bruckner would be represented by his unfinished Ninth Symphony; Brahms, by his last symphony, the Fourth—both mighty legacies to the world of music and both known to Musikverein audiences.

There was one thing, however, that had changed about the Musikverein. There was a visible presence of police inside and outside the building. And, unknown to most persons, there had already been good reason for the presence of law enforcement. Half an hour before the auditorium doors opened to the public, a deranged man had entered the building from the musicians entrance on Canovagasse, run up the stairways straight to the locked Archive rooms while shouting to one and all: "Brahms has sent me! Brahms has sent me! Open the door! Open this door!" One of the few staff members within hearing distance immediately alerted the police and the intruder was escorted out of the building and into a squad car where he continued yelling that he had been sent by Brahms. The man was not unknown to the police. They had arrested him two evenings earlier. He was from Venezuela and his name was Fritz Rahm.

82

Three hours earlier, Edgar's minute scrutiny of Agatha's dressing room and of the corridor outside leading to the stage had turned up nothing. He had also checked the other rooms off the corridor. Everything in the Maestra's was in order and nothing was missing. Not that there was much of anything to be missing, given that she kept no wardrobe in the closet and only a few cosmetics in the one drawer of her dressing table. On the left side of the table her baton in its rosewood box was laid out as usual, preparatory to the chief stagehand's placing it on the Maestra's podium some half hour before performance. It had its own small stand to the left of the large score stand. Before leaving Agatha's dressing room, Edgar made sure to check the surveillance camera was not on blur mode. Satisfied that nothing was amiss, he left the Musikverein and returned to Porzellangasse and his two charges, as he now lovingly thought of them.

With a few delicious tidbits for Fanny, Edgar and Agatha had an early and leisurely dinner of tender roast beef accompanied by delicious fried onions and roasted potatoes, courtesy of the nearby Gasthaus Wickerl. By seven-forty, two of the feasters were entering the Musikverein via the musicians entrance. Both were fully prepared for the revelations Bruckner and Brahms would bring this very special Sunday evening.

83

Peter Heimnis did not need to set the surveillance camera to blur this time. His entry into the Maestra's dressing room was legitimate and part of his job at this time of the evening on a performance night. It was his and his responsibility alone to carry the conductor's baton in its box to the podium and leave the box open on the smaller of the two stands there. This was always done half an hour before performance time so not to disturb the Maestra as she collected her thoughts in the privacy of her dressing room. Regarding his previous two entries—the one clocked at 6:58 last evening, the other at 7:03 this morning—they had been necessary due to the unfortunate bind he was in concerning his son's safety. He, of course, had turned the surveillance camera to blur mode where it would be impossible to identify who had entered the room. When Klaus returned home to his worried parents a quarter after seven last night, he was in a very agitated mood. The boy explained how he had waited in vain for a man who had called him and said he'd give him fifty euros to pick up a surprise package for his father.

"And you didn't think that was strange?" Peter had almost shouted at his son.

"No, I thought it was great! A surprise package for you and fifty euros for me. And then he never even showed up or called or anything. And now *I'm* in trouble!"

And now as Peter stood backstage supervising things for the last concert of the Double B Composers series, he realized all of a sudden that he was feeling uncommonly tired. Also his lungs seemed to be heaving abnormally. He compensated by sipping a few drops of whiskey from his hip flask. After all, he was still reeling from the kidnapping scare he and his wife had gone through the night before. Would they ever find out who the man was and why he wanted him to remove the Maestra's baton, place it in the General Director's office, and then return it to the dressing room the next morning?

84

"Oh, look, there's your nice Officer Decker, same place as before," Tony murmured to Megan as they moved toward their seats in the raised last row of the *Goldener Saal* rear balcony. The seats were the two middle ones they had occupied before. Megan twisted around to her left and nodded her head at him ever so slightly. She did not want to bring attention to Vienna's Chief of Police by waving. Megan and Tony had both noticed the presence of police outside and inside the grand old concert house.

"Let's hope that's enough to be preventative in case we have another show-stopping disaster ahead of us," Tony had commented.

Another pair of concertgoers was occupying the same seats they had had before. Up from Wiener Neustadt were Maestro Christian Begeist and his younger colleague Dieter Unfug. Already seated in the first-row center of the back balcony, they were scanning the audience below and reaffirming that the best aisle of escape was on their right.

"So, Dieter, same plan as before, then. But a different Brahms symphony. During which movement do you plan to set off your little smoke bomb?"

"I'm damn well not going to wait until the third movement again, that's for sure. No, it'll be right away, during all those whimpering falling and climbing thirds of the first movement. Ha! I'm going to jump up about thirty measures in, yell 'Fire' as I jerk the ring, and drop the smoking cannister onto the audience below. I'll keep on yelling 'Fire, fire' and pointing, and you join me as we start a stampede for the exit. Result: bedlam. Good?"

"Sounds most effective. Excellent idea to do it right at the beginning. How long does the smoke last, did you say?"

"Could be as long as ninety seconds."

"Plenty of time for panic. Good."

Backstage, in the corridor leading away from the Maestra's dressing room, Peter Heimnis was standing with his back against the wall. Something had come over him making him feel increasingly weak, slightly dizzy, and out of breath. Gasping for air, he slowly slid down until he was sitting on the corridor floor. Ah, that was better. No one around. He would simply take a lie-down right where he was.

The brothers Lukas and Robb Eifer were back in their seats at the front of the rightmost loge box overlooking the stage. Lukas had conducted both symphonies on the program and was holding forth enthusiastically on their respective merits.

"To pair Bruckner's Ninth, which he was still seeking to finish on the very day he died, to pair it with Brahms's Fourth, happily completed in Mürzzuschlag, is truly brilliant. Each composer's final great symphony. What a perfect double homage."

"Well, certainly the contrast will be paramount, but what I don't understand is why the Maestra, in Friday's concert and now this evening, has jumped from Bruckner's Fourth Symphony to his Eighth and Ninth. How do you explain the gap? Why wouldn't she pick one between the Fourth and the Eighth before moving full steam to his last and unfinished symphony?"

"I'd surmise that Endlich's decision was based on presenting only the very best. She realized the middle symphonies have their weak, or shall I dare to say, excruciating points, The Fifth, for example, is riddled with fugues, double fugues, and quadruple fugues. Exhausting for the listener, unless you are Bach." A mirthful grin came over Robb's face: his brother was never afraid to be blunt.

"And the Sixth?"

"The Sixth. Good lord, man! You know what's called 'the Bruckner Rhythm,' don't you?" Robb looked at his brother blankly.

"It's two quarter notes plus a quarter triplet or a quarter triplet plus two quarter notes and it absolutely *swallows* the music! The exhausted instrumentalists might leave even before the public does."

"You make a good case, but what about the Seventh? That's a really popular symphony, you have to admit. Even I have heard it several times."

"That's the point. Audiences have a musical guidepost with this one. Wagner had died of a heart attack in February of eighteen eighty-three, and as his adorer-in-chief, Bruckner finished up his symphony—for the first time—that year by inserting Wagner tubas in his honor and crowning the symphony with a doleful Adagio that, if you look at the score, comes to its climax at the rehearsal letter W—you know, W for Wagner."

"I didn't know that."

"Why should you? But the point is, Bruckner's Seventh was, during his lifetime, very popular and still is very much so two centuries later. And that would be exactly the reason why Agatha didn't program it, jumping straight to the lesser-known but titanic Eighth, with huge demands on the musicians as well as the listeners, and climaxing with the main themes from all four movements sounding at once. What musical daring! And you heard for yourself how astounded and receptive the audience was Friday evening."

"That I did, dear brother of mine. That I did."

"So let's just sit back and enjoy this double climax: Bruckner's and Brahms's final symphonic messages. Each sublime its own way. Each sounding the end of an epoch."

Unfortunately, Mario Intagliatore's seat, hastily reserved just before he left Hamburg, was in the third row of one of the left parterre loges, far from Stefanie Schreib in her usual front row aisle seat in the back balcony. He could just make out her figure, although she couldn't see him. But she had told him where they could meet after the concert. By the bust of Clara Schumann. Stefanie's directions had been lengthy: the white marble effigy was on the landing of the upstairs staircase to the *Goldener Saal* on the right side, next to where the second section of the staircase begins, with its equal access to the smaller *Brahms Saal*. Mario was thrilled he would soon hear from the lips of the music critic of *Der Standard* the judgment of this ambitious concert before its public appearance in tomorrow's newspaper.

The orchestra had finished its finetuning, the oboe was silent, and players and public alike awaited with anticipation the entrance of Maestra Agatha Endlich.

85

A warm, welcoming applause sounded from the far-right loges of the *Goldener Saal* as those sitting there were the first to spot the Maestra make her way to the stage. The clapping surged like a roaring wave as she walked past the first violins to the podium, turned and shook hands with the concertmaster, then the section leaders of the violas, cellos, second violins, and a kiss thrust to the string basses along the back. Only then, after returning to the podium and mounting it, did she turn and gracefully acknowledge the adoring audience. Putting one hand to her heart, she gestured to the various sections of the auditorium in grateful acknowledgement. Then, since the applause did not abate, she blew kisses to her enthusiastic well-wishers. By now many of the concertgoers were standing. Cheers and loud whistles sounded throughout the auditorium with its marvelous acoustics.

Edgar Wittgenstein was standing in the wings clapping as well, filled with pride and love. He watched Agatha blow a final kiss then turn to the orchestra. She was wearing the all-white outfit with its discreet sprinkling of Swarovski crystals that had become sartorially famous. Total silence fell upon the house. The Maestra lifted her baton from its rosewood box, took a deep breath, and raised it. She never gave the downbeat. Instead, the baton dropped from her hand. Bracing herself against the podium bar she leaned over to recover it. The effort made her suddenly vomit and she lurched from the podium to the stage floor, all her limbs twitching.

For a moment there was total silence. Stunned, no one moved. Then the concertmaster jumped up and knelt over the unconscious Maestra whose entire body was now jerking in spasms.

Edgar Wittgenstein had witnessed everything from the wings and he was at Agatha's side seconds after the concertmaster was. He took one look and shouted at the audience.

"Physician! Physician! Is there a physician in the house?" he implored.

A voice from the right loge next to the organ pipes shouted "I'm coming! *Don't touch h*er!" It was Dr. Oliver Rologe, a man known to many of the orchestra players. He was actually climbing over the balcony rail. The long drop below would have placed him behind the second violinists, two of whom had quickly abandoned their instruments and were reaching up to brace his fall. The maneuver, against all odds, was successful and within seconds Rologe was at the unconscious Maestra's side. She presented all the signs of nerve gas poisoning: pupil constriction, runny nose, mouth drooling, spasmodic vomiting, excessive sweating, rapid breathing, coughing, and evacuation of the bladder and bowels.

"*What is it?* What has *happened* to her?" Edgar was imploring the expressionless doctor to explain. There was his darling Agatha lying unconscious on the floor!

From their different seats in the front parterre close to the narrow flower hedge separating the low stage from the audience, two more physicians joined the one onstage, each whispering his identity and specialty to the kneeling doctor. Without lifting his eyes to theirs, Rologe murmured his specialty and diagnosis to them.

"Neurologist. Nerve poisoning—probably sarin. Probably absorbed through the skin, perhaps also nostrils and eyes. Or her clothing. Convulsions continuous. There's an outside chance we can save her. Depends totally on how much she's absorbed. As you know, a nerve agent does not directly kill. Rather, it turns our own nervous systems against us within seconds."

"Right," said the older of the two doctors, a cardiologist. "Need to get her clothes off immediately."

"Shouldn't we carry her offstage first?" asked the younger doctor, an oncologist.

"For god's sake! We can't touch her. But we've got to get the clothes off *as soon as possible*, no time to waste," commanded Dr. Rologe. He turned to Edgar Wittgenstein.

"Are you in charge here? Call a hospital immediately, but in the meantime we need to strip and scrub this woman *right now*! Can you get us the basics? *Gloves?* Scissors water, soap, sponges?"

"I'll try." Edgar jumped up and turned to the concerned instrumentalists. He spoke in a commanding voice.

"Please, everyone, to avoid confusion, I ask that you *stay in place*." Then he turned to the audience and made the same request. Low murmurs of assent and concern filled the hall and came from both constituents.

The General Director of the Musikverein bounded offstage, issued commands to staffers, made one quick phone call, and within minutes had organized most of the items required. The call had been to Vienna's Military Medical Center. Sanitary equipment and a preloaded vial of pralidoxime and atropine were being dispatched at once.

86

"*God*! *What a gift!* Dieter. I've got to get down to the orchestra and let them know I'm here. That I'll conduct the Bruckner for them." Maestro Christian Begeist had jumped to his feet.

"Right, Maestro! Go for it!" Dieter Unfug looked at his wide-eyed mentor and nodded vigorously. In his mind he went through a sequence of likely events: Begeist would save the day for the Wiener Philharmonic; he would be offered the position of resident conductor, and he, Unfug, would be asked to replace him as conductor of the Bruckner Orchester Linz. What a perfect scenario. A scenario he had long hoped for, dreamt of, and planned for.

To the voiced indignation of those seated around him Begeist stormed his way along the front balcony row and to the aisle. Dashing up it to the exit he disappeared down the stairs to the parterre.

A uniformed policeman stopped him as he breathlessly entered the auditorium.

"*Halt! Sir!* You've been told to stay in place," he said to the robust, clean-shaven man with a prominent nose and Prussian haircut. "That applies to everybody."

"Yes, yes, I know. But I am to conduct the orchestra!"

"That may be, but for now nobody moves."

"You don't understand! I need to be there on stage with the orchestra."

"You will remain here until things have been resolved," the policeman said firmly, blocking Begeist's way.

Members of the audience seated near the two arguing men were beginning to turn in their seats and gawk at the scene. They gasped when the arguing man with a prominent nose shoved the police officer aside and ran down the left parterre aisle toward the stage. He was shouting at the top of his voice.

"Orchestra members! Do not despair! It is I, Christian Begeist, Maestro of the Bruckner Orchester Linz! I will conduct you!" He was almost to the stage, with the policeman in hot pursuit, when Chief of Police Eric Decker lunged from where he had been standing in front of the stage and intercepted him. It took only seconds for the raving man to be cuffed and handed off to the pursuing officer. The audience could still hear him ranting as he was forcibly led out of the auditorium through the left stage door.

From his front row balcony seat Dieter was leaning forward and watching the ruckus with fascination and joy. If his Maestro had gone off his rocker, then he would hardly be appointed conductor of Vienna's Philharmonic. Who would have thought the Maestro could be his own worst enemy? Their Maestro disgraced in such a public manner, the city of Linz might need to have another conductor lead its Bruckner Orchester immediately. And who better than he, Dieter Unfug, former assistant conductor there? It was a win-win situation. A rare smile flitted across his features.

87

Four rug-draped music stands, their trays raised as high as possible, had been placed to form a rectangle around the unconscious Maestra and the three physicians attending her. A privacy of sorts was thus accorded them as they awaited the crucial delivery from the city's Military Medical Center. Temporarily distracted by the loud, self-serving appearance of the Linz Maestro, Edgar Wittgenstein stood again at Agatha's side listening to the doctors' murmured conversation.

"Why is the combination of pralidoxime and atropine effective?" the younger physician was asking his elders. Oliver Rologe was the first to answer.

"Sarin intake, and I'm presuming that's the nerve agent we're dealing with here, doesn't kill directly. But within seconds it turns the nervous system against the recipient. It twists the signaling between nerves, and tells them to do things they normally do, but with altered, usually greater frequency. Pralidoxime will reverse muscle paralysis and atropine will reduce uncontrollable secretions of the nose, mouth, bladder, bowels, and lungs to improve breathing."

"*Do not touch that baton!*" Dr. Rologe suddenly shouted at Officer Decker, who was bending over the podium to pick up the Maestra's abandoned baton.

"It could be contaminated," Rologe explained. "For god's sake it could even be connected to the sarin exposure!"

This instantly registered with the Chief of Police and he summoned one of his men to take care of safely transporting the baton to forensics.

"Ah! Here's the delivery now, thank god!" exclaimed the older physician who had raced up from his seat to help.

Edgar had given explicit instructions to the military medics concerning exactly where to enter the concert hall for the quickest route backstage. And now dashing on stage from the left wing was a young woman in uniform. She ran to the three men kneeling over the Maestra and gave a toothbrush-size plastic case to Oliver Rologe, whose hand was already out and open to receive it. She helped each physician pull on a pair of surgical gloves and as soon as Rologe was outfitted, he touched the Maestra for the first time, gently turning her over on her right side and pulling down her stained white slacks. Removing the hypodermic needle from its box, he injected the powerful combined dosage into her left thigh. The military woman expertly flipped a white sheet over the recumbent victim as two men in military uniform arrived with a gurney. Dr. Rologe acknowledged the two volunteer physicians with a nod and followed the gurney as it was speedily rolled offstage and toward a waiting ambulance.

Edgar desperately wanted to follow, but realized it was up to him to decide and announce what the waiting orchestra and audience ought to do next. Should the concert be played? Would it not be disrespectful? Yet here, right in front of him, were some two thousand expectant people who had paid for the concert and who deserved to hear it. But certainly the new young assistant conductor, hired only last spring, was not up to the job. Nor was the now elderly concertmaster. Such a pairing of Bruckner's Ninth and Brahms's Fourth required years of experience and close knowledge of both symphonies and composers. Edgar was aware that a most competent and well-known conductor, Maestro Lukas Eifer, was in the audience. He had spotted him earlier, sitting with his brother, Musikverein colleague Robb Eifer. In fact, Robb had recently introduced them to each other. But would it be fair to lay such a burden on him? And so suddenly?

He could ask.

Turning first to the audience, he began speaking. The extraordinary acoustics of the concert hall carried his words far and wide.

"Ladies and gentlemen! We all regret the misfortune that has struck our Maestra. But she is in good hands now and I know she would want the concert to proceed. How do you feel about this?"

"Continue!" "Go on with it!" "Yes!" were the shouts from the audience that immediately followed Edgar's question. Orchestra members began stamping their feet in a roar of agreement.

"In that case we are fortunate to have in our midst the conductor of the Grazer Philharmonisches Orchester, a man experienced in conducting both Bruckner *and* Brahms, Maestro Lukas Eifer." As clapping recommenced, Edgar turned to the rightmost loge overlooking the stage and extended both his hands.

"Will you do it for us, Maestro?" All clapping ceased and expectant silence reigned as heads swiveled to the loge in question. A tense silence followed, seeming to last an eternity. At last the white bearded man who appeared to be the living image of Johannes Brahms stood up and nodded his head once.

"Yes," he answered simply while his proud brother enthusiastically joined in the applause that immediately burst forth from all corners of the great hall.

Some minutes later, after speaking with the concert master, Maestro Lukas Eifer from Graz mounted the podium. It, its railing, and the two music stands had been thoroughly cleaned and sanitized by the military medical crew. The fallen baton, along with its redwood case, had been requisitioned by Erich Decker for forensic analysis.

The sixty-three-year-old Maestro, who preferred conducting with his hands, smiled encouragingly at the orchestra members and raised his right hand. The downbeat came and for the next two hours the audience rapturously absorbed the two symphonies Lukas had previously described to his brother as "Each sublime its own way. Each sounding the end of an epoch."

88

It was a concert to end all concerts. Although Edgar Wittgenstein had slipped away to keep watch over Agatha at the Military Medical Center, everyone—instrumentalists and listeners—had given their total concentration to the historic performance at hand. During intermission complete strangers spoke to each other as though they were old friends; young and old chatted away, praising the composers, the music, the orchestra, and the conductor. What a happy turn of events.

It was true that backstage during intermission two of the orchestra players had come across a man sleeping on the corridor floor. It had been impossible to wake him, but he was soon identified as chief stagehand Peter Heimnis. Deciding he had probably passed out from an overdose of the whisky he famously kept in a hip flask, the two men carried him to the musicians lounge and gently laid him out on one of the couches to sleep it off.

89

"Here I am!" Stefanie Schreib was waving at Mario, trying to catch his attention.

"Ah! Sorry to be so long but I couldn't find the Clara Schumann bust in spite of your detailed directions. Had to ask an usher," Mario said, a bit out of breath as he joined her.

"Wasn't that an incredible evening?" he continued. "Disaster followed by sublimity."

"Ah, thank you, Mario! You've just given me the opening line for my review."

"Have I? I'm honored."

"And I'm honored you want to cast my son's bust in bronze."

"Yes, especially since it will occasion the need to return to Vienna with it and see you again." Mario smiled.

"When do you return to Hamburg?"

"Tomorrow morning, I'm afraid. But I shall take you up on your suggestion that I introduce myself to your Aunt Margareta and let her be the first to see the completed bronze of little Hans."

"You never know. Now that the Double B Composers series is over, perhaps Hans and I will take a driving trip up to Hamburg. After all, it would make sense that you see your model in the flesh once more before you cast his features in bronze."

"What a wonderful idea! Please do so!"

"Give me your telephone number then."

"Oh yes, and yours also."

The couple entered the data on their cellphones and grinned happily at each other. Stefanie was the first to speak.

"And now I must rush home! So much to write about tonight!"

"And I shall gallop alongside of you if you allow. I faithfully swear not to come in. I understand you must work."

"Thank you for understanding."

Mario offered the music critic for *Der Standard* his arm and the two walked briskly away from an approving Clara Schumann bust, out of the Musikverein, and toward Stefanie's home.

90

"I am so sorry you didn't get a chance to meet the poor Maestra," Megan said, as she and Tony walked back to the Römischer Kaiser after the catastrophic yet thrilling Double B Composers concert.

"Yes, I was really looking forward to our meeting. I wanted to convey to her how proud Dallas is of her. But of course it was only right that the Musikverein cancelled the series' after-concert party."

"And after all that planning too. But to have had it with Maestro Eifer would have been wrong, somehow."

"Tasteless," agreed Tony.

"Do you have anything planned for tomorrow?" Monday would be the last day in Vienna for both of them. They had arranged to be on the same Tuesday morning flight for their return to Dallas.

"Yes, I do," Tony answered. "You'll probably laugh, but I want to see some art. My music business trips never leave me time to visit museums."

"I understand," Megan laughed. "I'm probably seeing old friends tomorrow afternoon, but, if you like, we could go to a couple of museums together in the morning."

"Yes! I'd love to be led through the Belvedere Museum by my favorite art historian."

"Thank you. Let's just check and make sure it's open on Mondays." Megan pulled out her iPhone and checked. The data confirmed it was open on Mondays.

"Great! So shall we have an early breakfast together and head out?"

"That depends on what you mean by 'early.'"

"Seven or so?"

Megan's face expressed horror and disbelief.

"Eight-thirty would be the absolute earliest I could do it. Remember, early morning is when, still in zombie mode, I do my daily exercises." Tony laughed.

"No exceptions? After all we're not in Vienna every day, or every week, or every year either."

"All right. For *you* I'll make an exception. How about eight?"

"Eight it is then and thank you for making such a rare exception."

"That's only because you are an exceptional person."

"Why, thank you, Megan."

The elevator was at lobby level and a few minutes later they were in their rooms, both more than ready to go to bed. It had been, to say the least, a day of contrasts crowned by high drama—mountainous outdoor Mürzzuschlag versus indoor Musikverein performance of Bruckner and Brahms, beginning with tragedy and ending in glory. Neither one had the stomach to look at television coverage of the horrendous evening.

91

Backstage, Chief Erich Decker had thoroughly interviewed the character he called in his mind "the mad Maestro." He then released the rambling man from Linz to the custody of his self-identified fellow conductor and local host, Dieter Unfug. The latter, keeping his thoughts to himself for now, drove them back to Wiener Neustadt. All during the ride Christian continued to rave about how this had been his opportunity to save Bruckner and conduct a performance of him that the audience, the world, would never forget. Why hadn't he been allowed to mount the podium? True, people were fussing around the prone Agatha Endlich who hadn't even given the initial downbeat of the great Ninth Symphony. Instead, she had carelessly dropped her baton and tripped and fallen when she lunged forward to recover it. So typical of a woman! Think before you leap! How noble he had been, defying the order to stay in place and rushing down to the stage, alerting the abandoned orchestra that he was there to conduct them. To save the dire situation caused by a careless woman! Instead, he had been stopped by the ignorant police! What did Dieter think?

Dieter kept his eyes on the road and his thoughts to himself, only murmuring acknowledgement that he was listening. It was too late to put the disgraced man he had worshipped until now on a train back to Linz, but it would be the first thing he insisted upon doing tomorrow when the man could pick up his suitcase and his Bruckner scores. Christian Begeist's ego had done him in and he, Dieter Unfug, wanted no more of the man who had brought shame on himself. And, along with the predictable television and press coverage, he would make sure that the board of directors of the Bruckner Orchester Linz would be fully informed of this embarrassing incident.

Time to pick a new Maestro.

92

Robb was so proud of his brother he could burst. Lukas had given an inspirational interpretation of Bruckner's Ninth, conveying the musical enormities that caused its composer to dedicate the symphony "to God." And then the Maestro, who looked so much like Brahms, had conducted that composer's Fourth Symphony so masterfully that it was cathartic, causing the audience to jump to its feet and call him back to the podium three times.

Now, after they took their leave of excited orchestra members who had crowded around Maestro Eifer backstage, they were walking briskly down Argentinierstrasse back to Robb's place.

Immediately upon entering the apartment Lukas threw himself on the living room couch and uttered a long sigh of exhaustion.

"We did it!" he said contentedly. "We did it."

"*You* did it. Bravo, my brother, bravo. And now, in celebration of your extraordinary accomplishment of directing players you hadn't had a chance to rehearse with, I have a gift for you."

"Oh? What's that?"

"It's hidden in my closet. I'll get it for you right now."

"Hmm. Does it have anything to do with your leaving here in the middle of the night last night?"

"Oh my god! You knew!"

"I knew."

"Why didn't you say anything?"

"I was too sleepy; thought it must be a dream. So what was that all about?"

"You'll see!" Robb disappeared down the hall to his bedroom.

Lukas pulled himself up from his slumped position on the couch and sat up expectantly, his feet on the floor. What did his unpredictable brother have in store for him now?

He knew the moment Robb rounded the corner back into the living room. A violin! Robb was holding a beautiful dark brown violin in his left hand and a bow in his right.

"For *you*! To take back with you to Graz."

"Are you mad?" Lukas was touched and thrilled.

"Yes. I want you to have a violin available in both Graz and Vienna."

"What a thought!" Lukas was clearly delighted. "Here, let me hold it." He reached out his left hand, carefully grasped the instrument by the neck and stood it in his lap. He looked keenly at the front, up and down. Then turned the instrument around and examined its back.

"It's a beautiful very fine grain spruce, of course," he said approvingly. "Hand me the bow and let's hear how it sounds." Robb obliged and Lukas started to tune the instrument. It didn't need tuning.

"Great. It's ready to go! Have *you* been plaing it?" Robb was almost as good a violinist as his brother.

"Of course! I had to test the instrument, after all."

Lukas tightened the bow strings slightly and began to play the instrument, giving eloquent voice to Bach's Sonata No. 1 in G minor for solo violin.

"A very good instrument indeed!" Lukas stopped and smiled in approval. "Don't tell me it's China-made. Is it German-made? I know it's not Italian."

"You're right, it's not Chinese and it certainly isn't Italian—I couldn't afford one of those. It is indeed German-made." Lukas played the violin again for a minute, then stopped and smiled inquiringly at his brother.

"Markneukirchen?"

"Right again! I bought it from a conservatory student who came into the Archive. His parents had just given him a Guarneri from Cremona and he was eager to sell his German violin. And I was able to get it for a good price."

"So now you must tell me! Is that why you left here in the middle of the night? Where did you go?"

"To the Musikverein and to my office. I'd simply forgotten to pick it up. If it was to be a surprise, I couldn't bring the violin home with me last night after we heard that lecture on Klimt and Music together. I'd planned to return for it a little while after we'd walked back here. Pretend I had left something at the office. But I forgot. When I woke up suddenly in the middle of the night, or I should say morning—must have been around two—I realized I could sneak out, get it, and still keep it a surprise. I'd planned to give it to you just before you return to Graz tomorrow."

"But what a gift, Robb!"

"But what a brother, Lukas. You *thrilled* them this evening."

"Well, after just a very few minutes, the orchestra and I became one. It was fabulous. A wonderful collaboration."

"If the Maestra doesn't recover, or even worse, should she die, I bet the Philharmonic will invite *you* to be its resident conductor," Robb pronounced in what sounded like a fait accompli.

93

Chief Erich Decker's men were in the process of making a thorough examination of all the rooms and corridors backstage. Decker was on the verge of leaving the Musikverein after tying up a few final details when one of his men, with one of the musicians in tow, came running after him.

"Sir! Wait! This man tells me that the chief stagehand, Peter Heimnis, is lying in the musicians lounge unconscious. Apparently he and one other orchestra player had found him passed out on the floor of a backstage corridor floor during intermission and they carried him there. They figured he was drunk, as everyone knows Peter—that's his name, Peter Heimnis—is an alcoholic. He carries whiskey around with him in a hip flask. But he's still out and we can't wake him. Also he's shit on himself."

Decker's eyes narrowed. He was putting two and two together and getting sarin. Possible sarin poisoning, as with the Maestra. He called the Military Medical Hospital a second time and waited until its dispatch team arrived. That was their job; his job would be to interrogate Peter Heimnis if and when he came to.

94

At six o'clock on Monday morning Massenet's *Méditation* intermezzo for solo violin and orchestra from *Thaïs*, composed just three years before the death of Brahms, sounded loudly on Megan's iPhone. Half lulled, half angry, Megan dragged the throbbing device from the bedtable to her ear.

"Yes?" Her voice conveyed her irritation. An apologetic voice sounded in her ear.

"Megan! It's Jacquelyn. I know I promised not to call you so early in the morning but this just couldn't wait! I have to tell you something and it could be important."

"Go on," said a resigned, sleepy Megan.

"Well! Remember how I told you about finding that little 'Hint' note by Brahms still in the key and letter mailer?"

"Of course I remember." Exasperation overtook drowsiness.

"Well! Remember how I translated Brahms's handwriting? 'I love Gypsies.'"

"Yes. '*Ich liebe Zigeuner*.'"

"Well, guess what?"

"*What*?" Curiosity vied with exasperation.

"Well, I misread the sentence. That last word is not '*Zigeuner*.' It is '*Zigarren*.' Cigars. Brahms loved *cigars*, not Gypsies! '*Ich liebe Zigarren*. Well, he loved Gypsies too, I guess, but that's not what this hint note is about. It's about loving cigars. And I'm sorry to have made a mistake in reading his handwriting. It could be important, and that's why I wanted you to know right away, regardless of the hour."

Megan was totally awake now, and far from continuing to be annoyed, she was thrilled. Yes, Brahms had sent Elisabet Ney a three-word *hint* to the whereabouts of the score he had composed in honor of their tryst. And the words, newly examined, were "I love cigars." What a shift in meaning! And what an idea had immediately formed in Megan's mind!

"Jacquelyn, you have made what could be an important discovery and I'm glad you called me, even if it is at an ungodly hour."

"Oh, thank goodness! Let me know if you find anything, won't you?"

"Of course."

"And do you forgive me?"

"No."

95

"Megan! You're already here?" Tony had come down for breakfast early, hoping to read one of the hotel's gratis newspapers about last night's events at the Musikverein. But there was Megan, already canceling her coffee with cream. She beamed at him.

"Well, good morning. Yes, I'm here early because I got another one of those early calls from the director of the Ney Museum, Jacquelyn McDonald. But, again, she had good reason to call, and as soon as you've been to the buffet and get back here with your breakfast makings, I'll tell you some very exciting news. News that's going to completely change our morning, maybe even afternoon plans."

"What? I can't wait to hear what's so important."

While Tony was helping himself to a substantial breakfast, Megan made a quick phone call and the outcome was exactly what she hoped it would be. So much so that the moment Tony was seated she began talking.

"Do you remember I told you about the amazing five-page love letter Brahms wrote Elisabet Ney?"

"I do."

"And that Jacquelyn called me later to say she had discovered a 'Hint' note in the mailer envelope? Three words written by Brahms that said, 'I love Gypsies'?"

"Certainly I remember. We talked about the Hungarians Eduard Reményi and Joseph Joachim in that regard."

"Yes. And rightly so. *If*, that is, the note was about Gypsies. But what if the word 'Gypsies' had been misread and the word was actually 'cigars'?"

"*Cigars?*"

"Yes, cigars. Does that suggest anything to you?" Tony thought for a moment, then shrugged his shoulders. But he took a stab.

"Well, we know that Brahms was a heavy cigar smoker," he offered.

"Yes, *and....?*"

"And what?"

"Never you mind. Perhaps it's better to surprise you. Especially if I am wrong. Then you'd think I and the ruckus I'm going to make this morning are crazy. But I don't think I am wrong."

"So do we have time to eat breakfast in a relaxed way?"

"Absolutely. We have plenty of time. Museums don't open until ten."

"I thought you said our morning plans were going to be completely changed."

"Yes, I did. But for now just relax, eat slowly, have a second cup of coffee, wait, and see. I can tell you this much: someone is coming, at my request, to meet us here at nine forty-five."

"Will you tell me who at least?"

"I'd rather it be a surprise. But when you see who it is, you may be able to figure out what I hope is going to happen."

"So *Zigarren*, and not *Zigeuener*, that's the key word?"

"Yep. That's the key. Cigars, not Gypsies."

96

Edgar Wittgenstein had spent the night by Agatha's bedside at the Militär-Medizinisches Zentrum on Brünnerstrasse, not far from Vienna's Central Cemetery. The proximity of the two was not lost on him and his anxiety was increased by the occasional entry into the hospital room by non-communicative medical personnel who simply checked Agatha's respirator readings along with her vital signs and exited. Edgar had been given one duty by the first physician to see her, after learning he would be staying with the patient overnight. Using the surgical gloves supplied in a box on the bedtable, he was to rinse the patient's eyes with water for ten to fifteen minutes every hour. This he did faithfully through the night. Finally, just before seven in the morning, Agatha partially opened her eyes. The sight of Edgar caused her eyebrows to rise and although she could not talk because of the respirator, they could at least touch hands as Edgar joyously bent over her.

Shortly after this, a physician Edgar had not seen before entered the room, nodded genially to him, studied the respirator readings in silence, then bent over the patient.

"Good morning. We can take you off respirator now," he said, gently beginning to remove the apparatus. That done, he pulled the other chair in the room up to the side of the bed and sat down facing Agatha and Edgar.

"Good morning, Frau Endlich. I am Doctor Gerhard Beistand. Are you aware of what brought you here to our hospital?"

Agatha shook her head very slowly.

"What is the last thing you remember?"

“Bruck...ner,” Agatha said with effort.

“She is the resident conductor of our Vienna Philharmonic,” supplied Edgar. “When she raised her baton to begin the concert, it dropped to the floor, as did she moments later.”

“Yes, terrible. I’ve seen the admitting report. We are treating her for sarin inhalation. She was extremely fortunate to have received medical treatment at the acquirement site, as well as here,” The doctor had spoken very quietly. He turned to Agatha again.

“Do you remember, Maestra Endlich, raising your baton to conduct?”

“Bruck...ner,” Agatha murmured again, her forehead contracting with the effort.

“And do you remember what happened after you picked up your baton?”

“Af...ter?”

“Do you know who the man across the bed is?” The physician smiled encouragingly at her.

“Ed...gar. Ed...gar.” The hint of a smile crossed Agatha’s lips and Edgar gently stroked her forehead.

Yes, my darling, it’s your Edgar and I have been with you all this time.”

“All...time?”

“Since you were brought here from the Musikverein last night.”

“Mu...sik...ver...ein.” Again she seemed almost to smile.

“And do you know where you are now, Maestra?” The physician gently asked.

“Whe...now? Ed...gar. Hos...pi...tal.”

The physician quietly pushed his chair back, stood up, and bending over Agatha spoke in quiet tones to her.

“Yes, you are safe in the hospital and you are recovering. You will feel better soon. I shall be back to see you soon again.”

Dr. Beistand moved to the door and when he was out of Agatha’s sight, beckoned Edgar to join him.

“She is recovering nicely, physiologically, but it may take a little longer for her fully to recover mentally and emotionally. She may have insomnia, fatigue, and vision problems for quite some time. This, unfortunately, can be some of the longtime consequences of sarin poisoning, as we have discovered from following the victims of the nineteen ninety-five sarin subway attack in Tokyo."

"Well, regardless, I shall be there for her. Thank you, Doctor, you are the first person who has paused to take a personal interest in one of your patients here."

97

After hearing once again from Dieter Unfug's mother that he should get married and settle down, Christian Eifer was more than happy that early Monday morning when his host abruptly offered to drive him to the train station for his return to Linz. Actually Dieter did not so much offer as state he would be driving Christian to catch his train. The older Maestro continued to be obsessed with the fact that he had not been permitted to conduct the evening before, and Dieter had had more than enough of that.

Half an hour later the two parted with scarcely a word spoken, never to cross each other's path again. News of Maestro Eifer's embarrassing public display had somehow already reached the board of directors of the Bruckner Orchester Linz and the board acted immediately. The Maestro was informed that it was time for him either to retire or resign— his choice. Eifer decided upon neither and instead embarked on a very public lawsuit which was ultimately decided against him. He lost his reputation and most of his investments, something which at least made computing his income taxes less arduous in the future.

98

Another visitor to the Militär-Medizinisches Zentrum that early morning was Chief of Police Erich Decker. He wanted to interrogate the Musikverein's chief stagehand, one Peter Heimnis. The man had shown signs of nerve gas poisoning, and the physician with whom he spoke before seeing the suspect informed him that sarin had been the agent that rendered him unconscious. Most likely Heimnis had inhaled the nerve gas. However, it could also have entered his body through his nostrils or his eyes or his skin. But it was a low-level exposure and overnight a respirator had done its work and the man was resting quietly. Yes, he was definitely up to being questioned. The hospital would be releasing him that evening unless there were any complications. Decker entered the room where Heimnis had been quarantined.

"Herr Peter Heimnis?" The man's eyes opened wide at the sight of a uniformed police officer and he strove to rise to a sitting position.

"Yes, sir."

"I am Chief of Police Officer Erich Decker and I am here to ask you a few questions. Do you feel well enough to answer them?"

"Yes, sir."

"Your doctors have determined that you have come into contact with sarin. Do you know how that could have happened?"

"I'm sorry, sir. What is sarin?" Is he playing dumb, Decker asked himself? He played along.

"Sarin is an extremely dangerous nerve agent. And last evening at the Musikverein you were discovered by two members of the orchestra, passed out and unconscious on the floor."

"What?"

"It is I who asks the 'whats' here." Decker was losing patience with the man. "What were you doing that could have brought you into contact with sarin?"

"Just my regular duties, sir. I'd taken the Maestra's baton to the podium half an hour before the concert began and after that I was supervising things backstage. I do remember feeling super tired and having a bit of trouble breathing. That's when I had just a small sip of whiskey. And after that I remember nothing. Just waking up here in the hospital during the night."

"What was the exact time you entered Maestra Endlich's dressing room to carry her baton to the podium?"

"At seven-thirty, the time I always do."

"Yes. That matches the time and person recorded on the dressing room video cam. And why did you enter the dressing room at six twenty-two Saturday evening and again at eighteen past six yesterday morning?"

"*What*? I wasn't at the Musikverein at those times!"

"Do not mess with me, Herr Heimnis. Our video technician has sharp-focused the two blur images enough to recognize your small stature, and your short white hair, all of which matches your 'official' seven-thirty entry yesterday evening before the concert."

"I, I don't know what you're talking about."

"Was it to remove overnight and then return the Maestra's baton in the early morning?"

"No!"

"Herr Heimnis, we have reason to believe that you, like the Maestra, have come into contact with sarin. Analysis of the baton shows that the porous cork handle was saturated with the nerve agent sarin. This leads us to conclude that you took the baton in its case to a site where the baton could be dipped into sarin and that, afterward, you returned the saturated baton, protected in its case, to the dressing room. Unfortunately for you, you were not afforded complete protection and the fatigue and shortness of breath you likely soon experienced were caused by the sarin you yourself had come into contact with."

"Please, Officer, I had nothing to do with any of that!"

"Do not deny this. We know exactly *where* you did this. In the office of the General Director. We have found a used surgical mask and a pair of nerve gas exhibiting surgical gloves in the waste basket under his desk. There is the proof! I therefore must charge you, Herr Peter Heimnis..."

"Wait! No, no, no! Stop! Yes, I did do some of those things, but I *had* to! We, my wife, and I, thought our son had been kidnapped! A man called me Saturday at dinner time and told me he had my son and if we wanted him back, I would have to follow his instructions to the letter. He told me to do what you said I've done, and I did so, scared out of my mind we'd never see our boy again." Peter Heimnis looked at the officer imploringly. There seemed to be no doubt as to his sincerity.

"And did this mysterious man return your son to you?"

"Yes and no. Klaus returned by himself. He hadn't been kidnapped after all. Just instructed by an anonymous phone caller to wait outside the Musikverein on Canovagasse for a package for me, and that he would receive fifty euros for doing so. The caller never showed up. It was just a trick to get him out of the house and away from home at dinnertime so my wife and I would be panicked. Klaus came back sometime after seven o'clock, seven- thirty I think it was, and by then I had already carried out the order given to me to take the Maestra's baton and leave it in the General Director's office. I could return it to the Maestra's dressing room any time after six the next morning. And I did. And that's what you saw me doing on the camera. A man scared to death, taking and then returning an innocent enough object. Oh, please! You've got to believe me!"

"I am listening. Give me your home number so I can question your wife, and if she tells the same story I will be more inclined to believe you."

"*Peter!* A woman's anxious voice sounded behind them. It was the man's wife and she looked desperate. A nervous teenage boy was at her side.

"Only now have we found out from the Musikverein where you were taken! Klaus and I have been sick with worry! What has happened to you, darling?"

A mute Peter held up both hands and looked imploringly at the man who had been questioning him. Officer Decker took over and explained to Frau Heimnis and her frightened son the thread of events that had led from the Musikverein disaster of the night before to the hospital. The explanation was welcome but the tension remained. Decker decided upon further questioning now that the whole family was assembled.

"Herr Heimnis, Frau Heimnis, can you actually have no idea who the man was that ordered you to carry Maestra's baton to and from the General Director's office?"

Peter Heimnis shook his head helplessly.

"Papa! Tell about the bad man who gave me stink roses to give Maestra!"

"Oh? What's this?" Decker stared at Klaus. The boy looked at his father imploringly.

"It's true about the man. I had not connected the two before. But it must be the same person," Peter Heimnis said, becoming animated. He explained the peculiar mission given him to have his son pick up a bouquet of roses from in front of the Hotel Bristol flower shop and deliver it to the Maestra in her dressing room just before the second Double B Composers concert. How it turned out to contain a stink bomb set on a timer so that the odor would swamp the room when she returned there after the performance. He had come upon her and General Director Wittgenstein just after they had opened the door and the stench had already entered the hall. Stopping them, he had gone into the room ahead of them and discovered the exploded stink bomb.

"And how does your son know about this?"

"Because Papa sent me to Bristol Hotel to get roses from the man for Maestra," Klaus explained before his father could. "And late that night Papa woke me up and scolded me so hard because he thought *I* put the stink in the flowers. And I did *not*!" Klaus began to cry. Decker put his hands on the boy's shoulders and looked into his eyes.

"I understand it is not your fault, son. Can you tell me what this man looked like?"

"He had dark glasses and a hoodie on so I didn't see his face much, but I could see long hair growing down next to his ears. He looked real weird."

"Ah ha. Sideburns. That is very helpful, Klaus, yes, very helpful." Decker was thinking of the Musikverein's security camera's sequence of a man wearing a hoodie entering the building at three-eleven Sunday morning and departing twenty-three minutes later at three thirty-four.

"Officer, I think I should tell you that this mystery man did give me a first, innocent assignment of which I thought nothing at the time, but which may be useful." Peter Heimnis was now fully focused on the recent events concerning the Maestra that had taken place over the past week. He realized his own avarice was partly to blame for enabling some of the strange events that had occurred.

"And that is?"

"Well, I have to admit that in each instance, until what we thought was the kidnapping of Klaus, money for me or my son was involved. First, during the initial concert of the series I was directed by this mystery caller, who obviously knew all about me and my family, to leave a sealed envelope addressed to the Maestra on her desk upstairs at the Musikverein. I was mailed one hundred euros for doing this simple thing. I didn't ask why; I was just thrilled to receive the money. My wife's medical expenses have hit the roof lately. Then when the second call came in, instructing me to send Klaus to the Hotel Bristol flower shop for the bouquet, another one hundred euros was paid in short order and by mail to my home again." Peter looked at his distressed son.

"Dear Klaus, I do apologize for having immediately blamed you concerning the stink bomb. Please believe me." He stretched out his hand toward his son. Klaus took it and Peter, exhausted by the strain, closed his eyes and let his head sink onto his chest. The effort of the past few minutes had caught up with him. His son realized he had something to add to what his parents had thought was a kidnapping.

"Herr Officer," he said, "I should tell you that the offer of money—fifty euros—and a surprise gift for my father—are what convinced me to go meet the no-show mystery man Saturday night when I got in so much trouble for coming home so late for dinner."

Decker assessed the situation and decided he had learned what could be learned.

"What you and your father have told me is very helpful and I need bother you no more. It is good to see a family that is as close and caring as yours." Then a thought struck him and he spoke again.

"But just before I go, Herr Heimnis, can you tell me *who* of your colleagues at the Musikverein might be behind all this? Leaving you as well as the Maestra exposed to nerve gas?" There was a very long silence. Heimnis rolled his eyes upward and seemed to be thinking hard. At last he spoke up, slowly shaking his head.

"No, Officer, I cannot think of anyone who would do such a thing," he murmured as his wife and son began to weep again.

Uncharacteristically, Erich Decker stayed a few more minutes, explaining to the frightened mother and son what he knew about the sarin poisoning of the Maestra that had also laid low their husband and father. Then he left abruptly; he had two more suspects to question. Oddly enough, both were conductors.

99

"Who in god's name could that be at this hour of the morning?" muttered Robb Eifer. He had just returned from driving his brother to the train station. Lukas had regretfully left his brother and Vienna to return to Graz, but this time with a violin.

When Robb opened his front door, he was amazed to see Officer Erich Decker. Recognizing him from last evening's disastrous event, he sputtered a question. "Oh my god! Has anything else happened at the Musikverein?"

"No. I'm here because I need to ask you a question."

"Sure. Won't you sit down, Officer?"

"Not right now. Let me ask you directly: what were you doing at the Musikverein at two twenty-five in the morning before yesterday's concert? The security camera shows you entered, then, some nine minutes later, at two thirty-four, exited holding a violin case. *Why* were you there at such an hour and *what* was in the instrument case?"

"Oh! Yes, I can see why that might look odd, even suspicious. It was on account of my brother, the conductor who took over directing the concert at the Musikverein last evening."

"Lukas Eifer—you are related to him then?"

"Yes. Wasn't he magnificent, saving the concert like that with no preparation?"

"No dispute there. But you haven't answered my question. I hope you understand how serious this is. The Maestra was the victim of a poisonous nerve agent, sarin, as was the chief stagehand Peter Heimnis. Again, *why* were you at the concert hall at two twenty-five in the morning?"

"To get something I'd totally forgotten to bring home with me after the concert: a violin I'd bought as a surprise gift for Lukas."

"Can you show me the violin?"

"No. He took it back with him to Graz this morning. Now he has access to a violin in both Graz and here, as he keeps his first one with me."

"Can I reach him by phone right now to verify what you say?"

"Sure. Here, let me call him for you, and you can ask him yourself. I just hope he can receive calls on the train."

Robb placed the call and it was answered almost immediately. Without saying a word Robb handed his cellphone to the officer.

"Maestro, this is Chief of Police Erich Decker calling from Vienna. Can you verify that you received a gift from your brother yesterday? And if so, what is it?"

"Yes, Officer. He surprised me with a violin!"

"Thank you. That is all I needed to know. And may I add, Maestro, that your performance last evening was magnificent!"

Without waiting for an answer Decker hung up and handed the phone back to Eifer.

"So, Officer, am I now off your list of suspects, I hope?"

"Yes. For the time being. I do have another question to ask you. I know you are deputy director of library and archival collections at the Musikverein. Would you know anything about the man who was with that crazy conductor who ran down the aisle last evening after the Maestra collapsed, shouting *he* would conduct the orchestra? He approached me when I was about to release the man, telling me he was the conductor's host and that he would take care of him. Said he was a conductor too."

"Ha! You've asked the right man. His name is Dieter Unfug and he lives in Wiener Neustadt. He's unemployed as a conductor, spends hours in our library at least four or five times a week, has a key to the building, and I discovered quite recently, when I visited that string instrument sales and repair store in our Musikverein looking for a violin for my brother, he works part time there."

"And where is 'there'?"

"Oh! Sorry. Canovagasse Four A, the *Atelier im Musikverein Wilfried Ramsaier-Gorbach*."

"Good. That is precisely what I needed to know. In addition to filming your own entry and exit there, the Musikverein's security cameras recorded a man in a hoodie entering the building at Bösendorferstrasse twelve at three-eleven yesterday morning and leaving exactly twenty-three minutes later at three thirty-four. Apparently this man accessed your General Director's office. We found an abandoned surgical mask and a pair of surgical gloves in the waste basket by his desk. Something one would need if working with a nerve agent like sarin. Looks to me like we might have our man. I'll direct my office to arrest this Dieter Unfug as a suspect in the attempted murder of Maestra Endlich and to bring him in for questioning. If we don't find him in your library or at the string shop today, I'll have the Wiener Neustadt police pick him up and bring him here for interrogation. Turns out it may be a real plus that you bought your brother a violin and can prove it."

Officer Erich Decker nodded briefly at Robb, then turned on his heel and found his way to the door. He had one more person to see this early morning.

100

A very tired Stefanie Schreib woke up at eight as usual, regardless of the fact that she had worked on her review of last evening's disrupted but divine concert until two in the morning. There was so much to cover. After several tryouts of sequence placing, she had decided to proceed chronologically after all and narrate events just as they had happened instead of going directly to the music played. Her description of the event that literally felled Maestra Endlich captured the surprise and drama. She wrote about the immediate aftermath: the daring drop from his balcony seat to the orchestra stage of loyal concertgoer, physician Oliver Rologe, and the subsequent arrival of medics from the Military Medical Center. She described the calming actions of Herr General Direktor Edgar Wittgenstein, and how he included both orchestra and concertgoers in the decision, culminating with the appeal to a well-known member of the audience, Maestro Lukas Eifer, to conduct the music. And that he did with a masterly hand, inspiring instrumentalists and concertgoers alike with absolutely mastery of both the Bruckner and the Brahms. What an evening of physical chaos followed by sounds of the sublime!

Her first call this morning would be to the Military Medical Center for word of poor Agatha Endlich's condition.

101

"It's almost ten! They're going to throw us out of the breakfast room in a few minutes, Megan. Won't you please tell me who we're waiting for?" Tony had had just about enough of secrets and mystery. And just about enough of coffee. He was on his third cup.

"And here he is!" exclaimed Megan, looking past Tony and smiling broadly.

Tony swiveled around in his seat. A tall, uniformed man was standing to his left. Tony had seen him before. Oh, yes, Megan's police chief friend Erich Decker.

"Thank you so much for coming, Erich," Megan said. "I don't think you two have met formally: Tony, this is Chief of Police Erich Decker; Erich, this is my dear Dallas friend and colleague, Tony Bocello. You met and shook hands with each other in the rear balcony of the Musikverein last Friday evening."

The two men smiled and shook hands again, then Erich took the chair opposite Megan, whose back was comfortably against the wall. She picked up the conversation.

"Erich has agreed to take time out of his busy day to accompany us to the Haydn Museum where, with his intervention, I am going to examine something in the Brahms Room. Can you guess what, Tony?"

"I don't know what's there. A piano? A painting?"

Without answering, Megan burrowed into her sling purse and pulled something out.

"No. Think again." She held up the small brass key of Austin discovery and pretended to be unlocking something.

"Oh, good lord! Brahms's side table where he kept his cigars."

"Exactly." Megan grinned triumphantly. "I told Erich about the hint Brahms sent Ney, those three words: '*Ich liebe Zigarren.*'"

Erich laughed. "Which your museum friend initially read as '*Ich liebe Zigeuner.*' Quite a difference between the two."

A very patient waitress came up to them, a cup and coffee pot in her hands. The cozy breakfast room was deserted except for them.

"Care for coffee, Herr Officer?" she asked, smiling at the uniformed man.

"Aren't you just about to close?"

"Not to worry, sir."

"In that case, yes, thank you. That's exactly what I need right now. It's been a super busy morning already."

"I may sound ignorant," said Tony to Megan, "but why did you want Officer Decker to come with us, if we're off to the Haydn Museum?" Both Megan and Erich answered at once.

"Administration."

"Don't you see, Tony," Megan explained, "if you and I—American tourists—entered the museum and told them we wanted to examine the sewing table in the Brahms Room, we would immediately be denied access. But if Erich makes the request..."

"Ha! Lead on, Officer Decker, lead on!"

Erich's squad car was just outside—one of the perks of his profession—and off they went. The same priority applied when they pulled up at the museum. They had scarcely gotten inside the door when they were greeted by the museum's director. His tone was cordial as introductions were made and he led them immediately to the Brahms Room without their having to explain what they wished to see.

"How can this be?" Megan whispered to Erich.

"I called ahead," he whispered back.

There were no other visitors in the Brahms Room, and after they had entered, the director stood blocking the entry so no one else could enter.

"If I may ask," he said, "I know which of these objects you wish to examine, but I do not know exactly why. Why?"

"Of course I am happy to explain to you," said Megan. "A just discovered letter, containing a key, Brahms wrote a month before he died to a woman he had known and loved in his youth refers to a musical composition he had recently written in honor of their love and in a genre he had never undertaken before. An operetta in celebration of their love. Now such a work by him is unknown to history. Brahms referred to its whereabouts as being in, and I quote verbatim: 'a small container to which only you, my eternal darling, have the key.'

And now, through sheer happenstance, I have that key." As she spoke Megan slipped the key discovered in the Austin Brahms bust out of her vest pocket and held it up dramatically. The museum director gasped.

"And so this round sewing table on top of which the master kept his cigars—this is where you think the score to his operetta might be hidden?" He pointed to a sizeable table, the round top of which was inlaid in three different grains of circling blond wood. There was no accompanying coverlet.

"Yes, I do, because as an afterthought he wrote a three-word hint concerning its whereabouts. The three words are 'I love cigars.'"

"Oh! Right on!" The museum director was now almost as excited as his guests. "Let's get to it then. I presume we should turn it over and look for a hidden drawer or something."

"That's what we're hoping," Megan replied.

No sooner said than done. Officer Decker carefully picked up the heavy circular table and with Tony's help slowly turned it over. There was no drawer of any kind. Just an attached empty black cloth bag for storing sewing materials. Disappointment rivaled disbelief as the four expectant persons stared at the table's underside. And Megan experienced a further disappointment. She distinctly remembered that, as she had studied it in Max Kalbeck's photograph, the table appeared to have *three* ornate legs, not four as here. And it was of a smaller size than the one in front of her. Also where was the fringed velvet coverlet in Kalbeck's photograph? Hugely disappointing. Finally Megan spoke.

"Herr Direktor, are you quite certain that this is *the* sewing table shown in Kalbeck's contemporary photograph of Brahms's living room—slash—music room as shown right here on this wall?"

She pointed to a copy of the black and white photograph taken just days after Brahms's death.

"Well, yes and no. When the Brahms Room was created here in the Haydn Museum to display mostly objects from his Karlsgasse apartment—the clavichord here is Haydn's, not his—we sent a small round rotted tapestry-covered table we believed to have been in the composer's bedroom to the Brahms Museum in Mürzzuschlag. We just couldn't display every single item we'd received."

Megan and Tony looked at each other in disbelief. They'd just *been* in Mürzzuschlag, just *been* to the Brahms Museum there! There was nothing like a round sewing table on display.

"Let me write down for you the name and phone number of my colleague at that museum and perhaps you can talk with her, hear what she has to say, if anything, about the table," said the director consolingly.

Wordlessly, with just a nod of her head, Megan accepted the piece of paper with the data on it. She roused herself to thank the director and, as Haydn was unable to console them at that moment, they left the museum. Vienna's Chief of Police was surprised to find he shared the deep disappointment of his two American friends.

After making sure they had all fastened their seatbelts, Erich started to pull out into the street, then stopped, allowed the patrol car to roll back, and turned off the ignition.

"What are your plans for the rest of the day?" he asked his passengers.

"Nothing definite, really," answered Megan. "We were going to go to the Belvedere Museum this morning and I'd planned to see two old friends late this afternoon. Tony?"

"Visit a few more museums by myself, I guess."

"All right, my friends. It's simply wrong to end our museum investigation this way. Let me make two calls."

While Tony and Megan waited in suspense, they listened to Erich as he assumed his Chief of Police identity. The first call was to his office and his questions were terse.

"Is he in custody then? And you found him where? All right. No. I'll deal with him when I get back. Good work." Erich looked at his two passengers and nodded his head to their questioning looks.

"Yes, Dieter Unfug was picked up in Wiener Neustadt, arrested, and brought to Vienna and is being held at our main station as prime suspect in the attempted murder of Maestra Agatha Endlich."

Erich's second call, after borrowing the number from Megan, was to the director of the Brahms Museum in Mürzzuschlag. She was there. Yes, the museum was open on Mondays. And yes, they owned a small round table that had originally belonged to Brahms, from his bedroom most likely. It was not on display at the moment. Erich thanked her, hung up, and turned to his two Americans.

"Hold on. We're off to Mürzzuschlag. Change of plans. Taking the Süd Autobahn/A Four, we should reach the Brahms Museum in just a little over an hour."

Erich's prediction was correct and he again used his official vehicle to park directly in front of a museum. This time, however, it could only be in front of the large inner courtyard that contained the Brahms Museum. An excited Tony led the way to the arched glass door building on their left and within minutes after the man at the sales desk called upstairs, an unsmiling Frau Doktor Priscilla Pfau appeared in the entry room. She guided her guests down to the basement where a number of furniture items that had seen better days were stored. On the way Megan spotted part of a large white wooden balcony railing identified in the accompanying didactic as "Balcony transferred here from Brahms's lodgings at Bad Ischl." The wooden struts differed dramatically from those at Strauss's villa porch, but neither did they match what she and Tony had examined in person on the Brahms house there. So! That explained her Bad Ischl balcony investigation at least. The balcony they had seen was not the original balcony.

"Now let's see. I think the old bed table is over here," said Doktor Pfau, walking to a section in the back of the basement on their right.

"Yes, here it is. Ancient and derelict as you can see."

Megan tried not to show how thrilled she was. Here was that small round table with three ornate legs about which she had spoken in Hamburg. And still covering its top was the now faded but still recognizable velvet coverlet, complete with long fringes.

Noting Megan's intense stare and misinterpreting it as one of disgust, the museum director hastened to explain.

"Oh, yes, that disgusting ancient coverlet. We couldn't remove it. It's rotted and completely stuck to the tabletop. Didn't want to rip it off, so we just left it on." She nodded at Megan whose facial expression had changed from serious to joyful. Ah, these unpredictable Americans.

"Can we turn the table over," Megan requested, her heart in her throat and the Austin key in her hand.

"If you must."

Repeating his action at the Brahms Room in Vienna's Haydn Museum, Erich gingerly picked up the sewing table, which was a little heavier than one would have thought, and Tony helped him turn it over, the coverlet's stiff fringes collapsing backwards as they did so. Supporting the circular base of the sewing box, which measured some twenty-four inches in circumference, were the three beveled legs partially disclosed in Max Kalbeck's photograph of 1897. There was nothing more. No hidden score crammed between the legs. No man's glove box.

"Turn the table back up," insisted Megan tersely. The men did so, setting it down soundly on its three legs. The odor from the coverlet was nauseatingly unpleasant. Nevertheless, Megan thoroughly felt with her fingers around its circumference. It became obvious that it and tabletop were now one, so closely did they adhere to each other.

"Pull the table top off if you can. Never mind the coverlet, it will peel off with the top," an increasingly tense Megan urged. She did not so much as glance at the bored museum director who had other things to do with her time than watch people from snooty Vienna play with old pieces of discarded furniture in her basement. With all his strength Erich simultaneously pulled and twisted the top. That worked. Off came the top with its stinking cover revealing a compartmentalized circular area still containing—frozen in time—needles, thread, thimble, scissors, and three cigars.

"*Lift up that layer*. There may be a false bottom," Megan commanded. Erich obeyed. In front of them was a hinged, rectangular man's glove box. Megan smothered a gasp. The box dimensions appeared to be around fourteen inches long, eleven inches wide, and nine inches high. In the middle of one long side was a small ivory keyhole. Without a word Megan leaned over, fit the key into the lock and, taking a deep breath, slowly turned it. It engaged and the box top was released. Inside, immediately visible, was a thick music autograph, its many pages flattened down and tied with string. The title, in Brahms's familiar handwriting, was discernable through the constraining strings.

It read *Waltzerfreude bei Wittgenstein*. An operetta!

"Wow, Erich, I really have to admire the way you didn't give that Priscilla Pfau director any chance to wonder whether or not you had the right to remove the Brahms score from her museum's moldy basement," said Tony as the squad car left Mürzzuschlag behind.

"I don't know what a legal scholar would have to say about it, but I believe an item of such scholarly interest, such cultural worth, needs to be taken back to Brahms's Vienna immediately. Let the legalities lie where they may, but I know we're doing the right thing." Erich gave a short self-affirming grunt.

"When you think," said Tony, "that this unique work by Brahms was moldering in the basement of a provincial museum for decades, it makes your hair stand on end." The trio moaned. Erich turned serious again.

"And your guidance, Megan, in urging that this precious autograph should be immediately deposited with the Musikverein's Archive, to which Brahms himself left all of his own historic and personal documents, this was certainly the right thing to do. I truly don't think anyone can find fault with that."

"Thank you. The Musikverein is absolutely the perfect place for this unique autograph." Megan resumed what she had been doing. She was carefully studying the second page of the precious Brahms score which was placed securely on her lap as she sat in the back of the car.

"Listen to this! Here are listed the main characters who 'waltz' at the Wittgenstein salons. Clara Schumann, Joseph Joachim, Johann Strauss, Junior, Richard Strauss, Gustav Mahler, Alexander Zemlinsky, Arnold Schönberg, Eduard Hanslick, Ilse Conrat, and, of course, the principals, Elisabet Ney and Johannes Brahms! And, I see here, some famous singers and instrumentalists like, yes, here's the clarinetist Richard Muhlfeld, and Brahms's good friend the surgeon Theodor Billroth, who was a very fine amateur pianist and violinist. My goodness, the whole Viennese musical scene is here!"

"What a view, a 'sound' book, of society at that time," Tony said, enchanted. "Is Klimt mentioned?"

"Umm, no, I don't see his name here."

"This discovery is so important," Erich proclaimed. "The world must learn about this! We all need good news, and this is surely that."

"And here's a charming scene," Megan pronounced, carefully opening the score a number of pages later and studying the text. "It's about how Brahms 'baptizes,' with sprinkles of champagne, the shy little Wittgenstein son Hans—you know, the one who mysteriously disappeared while on a visit to America. Oh, and here are more children—those of Maria Fellinger and her husband. And here's the future sculptor of Brahms's grave monument, Ilse Conrat. How totally charming!"

After another half hour of driving and listening to Megan's articulation of scenes from the operetta, Erich suddenly had an idea, one he did not tell his passengers in advance, but upon which he acted immediately. He called the Musikverein and asked to be connected with Robb Eifer. When the man answered, Erich put the call on loudspeaker.

"Library, archives, and collections. Robb Eifer speaking."

"Robb Eifer, this is Chief of Police Erich Decker. We spoke earlier today."

"Dear god! Have I done something wrong after all? Surely you don't still suspect me of bringing sarin into the Musikverein?"

"No, I do not." Erich relaxed his stern tone of voice and became jubilant.

"It is I who am bringing something into the Musikverein. And it is of such import that I am asking you to notify the press and TV stations to be there when I arrive in forty-five minutes with two American scholars who just discovered, languishing in a basement at Mürzzuschlag, *a complete autograph by Johannes Brahms*."

"Oh my god! A Fifth Symphony?"

"No. An operetta."

"What? An *operetta*?"

"Yes, an operetta. With the name 'Wittgenstein' in its title. All will be revealed when we arrive. Just have the press and TV there. We shall be pulling up at the Bösendorferstrasse entrance. See you then."

Ever happy to bring Vienna police good press coverage, all went as Erich had envisioned. The two American scholars were enthusiastically interviewed by the press and cable stations. Herr Doktor Anthony Bocello, former president of the Dallas Symphony Orchestra, framed the place of vocal music within Brahms's oeuvre and why it was such a surprise that the composer, known for a consoling *German Requiem*, would henceforth also be famous for an enchanting operetta titled *Waltzerfreude bei Wittgenstein*. And Frau Professor Doktor Crespi happily described the events leading up to the discovery of the unique operetta by Brahms, detailing the famous guests at the glittering Wittgenstein salons of the 1880s and '90s. Crespi allowed the press to scan the images on her iPhone of Brahms's five-page letter to Elisabet Ney—good publicity for the Austin Museum—and she encouraged them to contact the director, Jacquelyn McDonald, for further details.

Elsewhere in response to the happy news dominating the evening newspapers and television news, an elated phone call was made by Robb Eifer to his brother Lukas in Graz, while Stefanie Schreib wrote a special celebratory column for *Der Standard*. And Edgar Wittgenstein murmured the extraordinary news into the ears of a recovering Agatha Endlich who, nine months later, gave birth to a strong, healthy child named Clio, muse of history.

History and the entire music world's concept of Johannes Brahms the composer and Johannes Brahms the man was now and forever changed because of the chance discovery of a Brahms bust in an Austin antique store.

Readers Guide

1. Megan Crespi, a retired professor of art history and musicologist who now solves art crimes, and her younger sister Tina Crespi, a dedicated veterinarian based in Dallas, are browsing in an antique shop in Austin, Texas. Megan holds up a battered bronze bust and tells Tina she thinks it is a bust of the composer Johannes Brahms. On what is this based and how does Megan prove her point? What happens when they leave the shop with the bust and load it into their vehicle?

2. High above the blue Danube near Regensburg, the white temple of Walhalla honoring historic German luminaries marked the first year of the twenty-first century with the installation of a bust of Johannes Brahms. Who is the creator of the marble head and why is it controversial? What particular reaction did the head inspire? Do you agree or disagree with what a vandal did to the bust of Brahms?

3. The day before Megan gave her speech, they had visited Formosa, the Neoclassical-Germanic castle with its two-story crenelated square tower that had been sculptor Elisabet Ney's home and studio and was now a museum. What famous personages had Ney sculpted in Europe before she migrated with her husband to America? What is the exciting possibility that Megan wants to research? To whom does she make a call?

4. Edgar Wittgenstein, the multi-talented general manager of the Vienna Philharmonic, is sitting with closed eyes in the loge of the

city's Musikverein, venerable home of the famed orchestra. Why is he so blissful and what novel suggestion of his has been implemented? Who is conducting this evening's performance? Which composers are being performed and for what reason?

5. The sunny breakfast room of sculptor Mario Intagliatore's capacious apartment overlooks Hamburg's newly completed, glistening white promenade along the Elbe River. From where has the artist just returned and with what exciting new technique had he become acquainted on his trip? Do we know what his latest commission is?

6. At the turn of the nineteenth century, the Wittgenstein family in Vienna was one of the wealthiest in Europe. It was also Jewish, which meant that it received its share of prejudice. The pater familias, Karl, was a steel tycoon whose wife, Leopoldine, half-Jewish by blood and Roman Catholic by faith, eventually gave him nine children. Which two became very famous and what were their professions? The family home, known as the Wittgenstein Palais, was just steps from which well-known Vienna building? What was the layout of the extraordinary music room and who were among the famous guests performing there? Who was Johannes "Hans" Wittgenstein and do we know what happened to him?

7. As they continue to discuss Ney on their drive back to Dallas, what does Tina tell her sister to do? When Megan talks to the Ney Museum's director, Jacquelyn McDonald, what intriguing document in the museum's collection comes to their attention? Do we think something will come of it when Megan leaves on Tuesday for lectures in Hamburg and Vienna?

8. When sculptor Mario Intagliatore starts to unlock the door to his basement studio and it swings open, what does he discover? Does his housekeeper have any explanation?

9. Tuesday evening as they both finish work, Edgar Wittgenstein thinks it might be nice to relax a bit over dinner with the innovative

young conductor who was open to unorthodox suggestions such as the one he had made concerning pairing Bruckner and Brahms. Agatha accepts his invitation. To which unusual nearby restaurant do they walk and what are their interesting biographies as each relates to the other? Are either of them married or with a partner? What shocking thing happens when Agatha returns to her office alone?

10. Back in Dallas on Monday, Megan prepares for tomorrow's flight to Hamburg. What are her packing priorities and are they evenly divided? What important items does she keep in her expandable black sling bag? Why does reference to Eleanor Roosevelt come up? What, to Megan, are her most important wardrobe items?

11. A frustrated Mario Intagliatore has decided not to contact the police about the theft in his Hamburg studio. Why is that? What has he done to give himself and his housekeeper peace of mind? And to what is he looking forward to doing on Wednesday afternoon?

12. We learn about the amazing life of one of the Wittgenstein family members and the Brahms legend he passes down to his own children and grandchildren. What is the legend and which descendant has found a prize position in Vienna?

13. Conductor Lukas Eifer is happily musing over the many things he has in common with Brahms. What are they? Of which orchestra in competition with the Vienna Philharmonic is he the conductor? He wonders whether Maestra Endlich will really be able to complete the grilling schedule. Do we?

14. Stefanie Schreib's *Der Standard* review of Maestra Endlich's novel concert pairing the first symphonies of Bruckner and Brahms appears early Tuesday morning. Although usually reserved with her praise—some readers might say even stingy—her approving comments on the conductor's interpretation of both symphonies border on extravagance. What features does she dwell upon specifically with each composer? And what is the readers' response?

15. Conductor Christian Begeist's copy of Schreib's review has landed in the waste basket. It is a good shot, considering that he had suddenly tossed it over his back from his seat on the couch. Why is he so perturbed and why does he, conductor of the Bruckner Orchester in Linz, the composer's birthplace, feel so threatened by Agatha Endlich? What were the exact words he murmured to her when he went backstage after her Monday performance to "congratulate" her?

16. It was a long flight from Dallas with three airport changes, but Megan does not feel at all tired. On the second, overnight lap of the trip from D.C. to Frankfurt, she works on her new book. What is the topic of this book? Megan reflects on the important artist she felt compelled to teach to all her twentieth-century classes at Columbia and Southern Methodist University. Who is this artist? Megan reflects on her own early life as a refugee. What happened to cause this? She ponders her experience with Hungarian refugees. Where and when were they? What is the legacy that has made her such a collector of books?

17. Intagliatore successfully supervises the transfer of his Brahms bust copy before the afternoon symposium on the composer. Where on the Hamburg University campus is it placed and what is so unusual about the building? Does the bust of Brahms have a beard or is it *ohne Bart*?

18. Agatha calls Edgar at work early Wednesday morning and asks if he can come to her home. How does she sound? When Edgar arrives, what does she show him? What do they discuss might lie behind the disturbing document and which measures is Edgar going to take to ensure Agatha's safety during the evening concert of Bruckner and Brahms?

19. Megan's final flight arrives on time in Hamburg and waiting for her is an old friend who has offered her his guestroom while she overnights in his city. Who is this friend? They discuss the word "Elphi." To what does that word refer? What is their schedule for the day and evening?

20. Maestra Endlich reaches the Musikverein for her second Bruckner/Brahms performance that Wednesday evening, her self-confidence restored, the silly threat about pairing the two symphonists forgotten. How does she dress for her concerts and what is her pre-conducting routine? How does she differentiate to herself the two symphonies she will be conducting that evening? An abrupt knock on the door interrupts her reflections. What happens next? Should we be suspicious?

21. After lunch at home, Tönnies drives Megan to the site where the Brahms symposium is being held. What and where is it, and what is unusual about the auditorium where Megan will be speaking? Megan is the keynote speaker and she uses images. What does her lecture entitled "The Visual Brahms" address and who are the idols and what are some of the images? Something unusual happens during Megan's presentation. How does she handle it and with which spontaneous idea does she challenge the audience at the end of her speech?

22. Brahms's Second Symphony has come to a triumphant end and the audience brings the Maestra back to the rostrum three times. The Double B Composer series was, once again, a success. Edgar walks Agatha back to her dressing room. What happens when she opens the door? And what does the chief stagehand Peter Heimnis find when he enters the room? What is Agatha's unusual response? Do you think we should take what has happened seriously, or is it merely a poor joke?

23. Megan and Tönnies are at an Italian restaurant inside the Elphi enjoying a pre-concert dinner of vitello tonnato and talking about their families and their parents' addiction to smoking. Why does this bring the conversation around to Brahms? When they finally enter the main auditorium, Megan is nonplussed. What does the concert hall look like? After they have taken their seats and discussed a comic incident having to do with the first performance of the Brahms Requiem, a man suddenly addresses them. Who is he and what is his background? Does Megan know him?

24. Home again in her apartment on the Johannesgasse in Vienna's inner city, Stefanie Schreib is penning the finishing touches to her review of the second Double B Composer concerts. What does she have to say about Maestra Endlich's performance? And which descriptive word does she refrain from using? What else do we learn about?

25. That Wednesday evening after the Bruckner/Brahms concert Maestro Lukas Eifer is pleased he has decided not to return to Graz until the following Monday. What does he think of the Double B Composer concerts so far? Does he prefer one composer over the other? What is the attitude of his brother Robb?

26. After the fabulous Brahms Requiem concert at Elphi, the trio heads to Tönnies's home for a nightcap. What does Megan finally do at his request? What does "Core, Cor 'ngrato" mean? And is there any connection with Brahms? We learn a bit about the medical careers of both men. How can they be characterized?

27. Jacquelyn McDonald, director of the Elisabet Ney Museum, has not let the grass grow under her feet. Intrigued by her friend Megan Crespi's theory that a bronze bust she found in an Austin antique store was that of composer Johannes Brahms as a young man, she embarks on a thorough search of the museum's file cabinets looking for any archival documents that might substantiate Megan's theory. What else does her laborious search encompass and does she find anything?

28. Thursday's edition of the morning paper is out. Will Fräulein Schreib take that miserable woman conductor to task? Maestro Christian Begeist is reading the review of last night's second Bruckner/Brahms concert. What does the review say about Maestra Endlich's performance? Does Begeist agree? Which composer does he prefer over the other and where does Begeist live?

29. Megan is still sound asleep at eight-thirty that Thursday morning when the cheerful voice of her host sounds outside her bedroom

door. What does he have for her and what does she want to visit in the city before her plane leaves for Vienna that afternoon? Who is Eduard Hanslick and what is his relation to Brahms and to Richard Wagner? Megan and Tönnies come across a life-size marble bust of Brahms by his friend Ilse Conrat. What else did she sculpt pertaining to the composer and what is so sad about her personal history?

30. After practicing a bit of meditation to calm down, Ney Museum director Jacquelyn McDonald begins the exciting process of examining what she has discovered. What has she found? What happens next and what is a hoverboard?

31. Intagliatore's housekeeper has prepared a delicious lunch for him and his two guests, Megan Crespi and Tönnies Helfer, and they discuss many things including Brahms's childhood trauma. What was it? Which Brahms family member do they mention? Their sculptor host is eager to show the two his basement studio. What do they talk about once there?

32. In Wiener Neustadt, Brucknerite *Maestro* Christian Begeist meets his fellow Brucknerite host Dieter Unfug for lunch at the restaurant Am Wasserturm. What is it next to and how is it decorated? They order Tafelspitz, then turn their attention to a small package Dieter has picked up from the post office. What does it contain and how will it be used?

33. Megan and Tönnies say farewell at the Hamburg airport. Where is she off to and what is her travel outfit? When she reaches her arrival point, she takes a taxi to her favorite hotel. What is its name and who is there waiting for her?

34. Jacquelyn McDonald returns to her office, the threat to her institution resolved. At last she has a chance to read the five-page letter from Brahms to Ney. What does the five-page letter address and why is this such an important discovery? What does Jacquelyn do next?

35. Megan and Tony Bocello are having dinner at Salieri's and their talk turns to why some concert halls have better acoustics than others. What are the reasons? Which auditoriums has Tony already visited on this trip? And which tasty Italian dish have they ordered?

36. Megan is awakened at six-thirty the next morning. How? Why? What is the extraordinary information she receives and from whom?

37. On leave in Vienna from Caracas Cathedral, Venezuelan organist Fritz Rahm has two aims, one investigative, one explosive. What are they? What is Fritz Rahm's heritage?

38. Robb is shocked that his brother Lukas has never been to the Brahms Room in Vienna's Haydn Museum. They go there Friday morning. What does the room contain and whom do they meet there?

39. Edgar surprises Agatha by showing up at her door at noon. He has a large sack with him. What three items has he brought for Agatha? What is her reaction?

40. On the drive up to Vienna that Friday afternoon, the two conductors Christian Begeist and Dieter Unfug make a stop at an historic town. What is it and how does visiting a certain composer's house affect their spirits?

41. Because the weather is so beautiful, Megan's impromptu lunch at Salieri's with Maestro Lukas Eifer and his brother Robb is consumed outdoors. What are the topics of their far-ranging conversation?

42. Peter Heimnis is shocked to see that a video camera has been installed in the Maestra's dressing room. What does he decide to do about it? And do we get the impression he likes or dislikes the Maestra?

43. Back at the hotel the receptionist has an envelope that was left for Megan. It contains a handwritten letter and a photograph. What do we learn from both items and what does Megan discover?

44. After lunch together, Edgar leaves for the Musikverein and Agatha, feeling strong again, glances through the scores of the Bruckner and Brahms symphonies she will be conducting this evening. Which ones are they and how do they differ from each other?

45. After weeks of work looking through the unpublished scores of his great-great-great-granduncle, Venezuelan organist Fritz Rahm finds what he has been looking for. What is it and do we have any idea what Fritz will do with what he has found?

46. Tony has his Friday morning meeting with the Musikverein's acoustic engineer. Who is he and what do they discuss? Tony's afternoon appointment is with Edgar Wittgenstein. At what interesting locale does it take place and what important developments do they discuss?

47. The two Brucknerite conductors, one employed, the other seeking a position, are enjoying an early dinner at Vienna's renowned Hotel Sacher just off the Kärntner Ring, a convenient ten-minute walk to the third Double B Concert. What are they discussing and what do they have for dessert?

48. Five o'clock on Friday evening finds Megan in her hotel room blissfully fiddling with the images she would be using for her lecture the next evening. What is the new image she will be adding? Tony calls her and they agree to have an early dinner before the third Bruckner-Brahms concert that evening. Where do they decide to go? And what does Megan do just before they meet in the hotel lobby?

49. It is a quarter to seven and from her home Agatha takes yet another cellphone peek at her dressing room via the new Ring Europe camera that Edgar so thoughtfully installed. To whom does she show the image? Agatha thinks about the critic who has mostly praised her performances. Who is it? And what little is known about this person's private life?

50. Edgar Wittgenstein has been on his own private investigative prowl of the Musikverein building before tonight's third Double B Composer concert. He thinks about a conversation he had once with Peter Heimnis. What particular item did they discuss?

51. The two Brucknerites are having supper before the concert at the Hotel Sacher. What is the hotel's world-famous dessert and what did they discuss during dinner?

52. It is nearing eight o'clock and Venezuelan organist Fritz Rahm has just entered the Musikverein auditorium where a few other early arrivers are noisily taking their places. Fritz's seat is an aisle seat in the first row, to the conductor's right. Do we know what is Fritz planning to do and do we know when he will make his move?

53. Megan and Tony are entering the crowded lobby of the Musikverein. What has she just decided to do concerning her lecture tomorrow evening? Where are their seats and what does Tony say is particularly good about them? Suddenly a man's voice utters her name. Who is he and why is he at the concert?

54. For the past fifteen minutes Maestra Endlich, alone in her locked dressing room, has engaged in her calming yoga routine. Peter Heimnis had long since taken her baton to the conductor's desk, and now, at five minutes to eight, she feels centered and ready to go. Which symphonies will she be conducting this evening and of whom does she think for inspiration?

55. From her balcony seat during the Double B Composers, Megan has a full view of the orchestra. Which instrumentalists does she seek out first and why? How did the Bruckner Eighth Symphony begin, forte or piano? Why would Brahms describe Bruckner's music as being like a "boa-constrictor"? In addition to shades of Wagner, what younger composer does Megan seem to hear in Bruckner's music? And why has the Maestra scheduled the final movement to be played after intermission?

56. Agatha walks offstage for intermission after a third ovation from the audience. Who is waiting for her and what do they do next? Why is this action delayed briefly? What new arrangement do she and Edgar make on the spot? What are their thoughts concerning the music just played? We learn the widely differing reactions of some of the audience members. Who are they and have we met them before?

57. Stefanie Schreib was blown away by Maestra Endlich's handling of the first three movements of Bruckner's lengthy Eighth Symphony. After intermission the symphony's final movement is performed. How would you characterize the music and what is the reaction of Schreib and that of the audience?

58. When Maestra Endlich returns to the stage after conducting the final movement of Bruckner's Ninth, there is something different about her. What is it and to what could it be related? Our narrative circles the Musikverein hall and visits three pairs of characters. Who are they and where are they seated? Do we know of any other person or persons attending the concert? The orchestra begins Brahms's Third Symphony and the audience is entranced. But in the middle of the slow waltz of the third movement something totally unexpected occurs. What is it? Is anyone hurt? And what decision does the Maestra make?

59. During the ruckus at the Musikverein, the two Brucknerites are discussing whether or not to go through with their own plan for the evening. The police and press photographers seem to be everywhere. After conferring with the chief of police and others, the Maestra turns and asks her audience if the performance should continue. What is the answer and is everyone happy with it?

60. Music critic Stefanie Schreib has slipped out of the concert early in order to write her review for tomorrow morning's paper. What happens when she returns home? Is this a sad or happy turn of events?

61. Megan and Tony walk back to their hotel after the Double B Composers concert that had been so bizarrely interrupted. In their hotel rooms they both check out television coverage of the event. Does Megan do anything else before going to sleep?

62. Maestra Endlich has not returned home alone that night after the concert. Edgar Wittgenstein has insisted they celebrate her triumph over adversity with champagne. Where do they try to go and where do they end up? What unexpected event happens that makes them, as well as Fanny, the collie, happy?

63. An astonishing turn of events has occurred during Mario Intagliatore's visit to Stefanie Schreib the evening before. What is it and whom does it involve?

64. When Fritz Rahm is released by the police, someone follows him to the café where he goes for a juice smoothie. Who is it and what is discussed with Rahm? And what brings the discussion to a sudden close?

65. Megan's Saturday lecture at the Leopold Museum is not until eight that evening and she is eager to get out of tourist-packed downtown Vienna for the day and immerse herself in the beautiful Austrian countryside. To which Brahms-related important site do Megan and Tony drive and what does Megan hope to confirm once there? How does her iPhone play a role?

66. We look in on Agatha and Edgar. How has their relationship changed and is this a glad or sad turn of events? What goal do they set for themselves and how soon might it be accomplished?

67. Christian Begeist confesses to his Wiener Neustadt host that what he'd like to do most today is to visit Vienna's Stadtpark. What does he want to do there? Reading Stefanie Schreib's review of Friday's concert, he expresses several stunning views. What are they?

68. Lukas Eifer asks his brother Robb, who has an errand at the Musikverein, to leave him a key to his Vienna apartment as he too has something he would like to do in the city. What does he learn from reading Schreib's review of last night's Double B Composers concert and do we learn what he wishes to do today? One of the two persons in the Musikverein library when Robb arrives is studying a photograph of Adolf Hitler standing before a white marble bust of Bruckner. What are the circumstances underlying this image and which other photograph does Robb direct the student to study?

69. An unknown caller to Peter Heimnis indicates to him that his son Klaus has been kidnapped. What does he tell Heimnis he must do to regain his son? Where is the boy? Do we know?

70. To whose composing hut in Steinbach am Attersee do Megan and Tony drive? Which symphony was composed there? It was the sights of nature that painter Gustav Klimt pursued during his sixteen summer stays on the Attersee, and Megan drives on to the small lakefront village of Wissenbach to enjoy the exact same view as painted by the artist. Which lecture is Megan giving this evening concerning Klimt and will this view be one of the items discussed?

71. An interesting and varied audience is filing into the Leopold Museum's auditorium that evening. A number of students from the University are present, intrigued at hearing about both art and music. What is the intriguing title of the lecture and whom do we spot attending the event? Why does one couple slip into the back row of the auditorium just as the lights go down? Which four persons does Megan's speech address in addition to Klimt? Do we find out who knew whom? Megan shows her next-to-last image. Whose music salon is it and who are the three musicians in the photograph? What surprising business does the European representative of Thomas Edison conduct in this room? Which two events take place after the lecture is over?

72. A fitful night wakes Robb Eifer up at two in the morning. *How could he have forgotten*? After all his preparations and planning!

Where is he going when he sneaks out of his apartment trying not to wake his brother?

73. In the wee hours of Sunday morning, the day of Maestra Endlich's final Double B Composers concert, a rosewood baton box is removed from the desk of Edgar Wittgenstein's office. It is returned eleven minutes later. Have we any idea what is going on?

74. Ney Museum director Jacquelyn McDonald telephones Megan at an ungodly hour. She has found a Postscriptum in the key and letter mailer sent to Ney by Brahms. It reads *Ich liebe Zigeuner*. How does Megan interpret its meaning and application?

75. Over breakfast Megan tells Tony about the phone call she received from Jacquelyn. How is Brahms's violinist friend Joseph Joachim involved in her analysis?

76. "Are you still of the same mind about our plans as you were in the wee hours of this morning?" Edgar asks Agatha over Sunday breakfast. What are the plans?

77. "And this time a clay portrait would be left with me long enough to recreate it in marble—marble that already belongs to you." Who is saying this and to whom? Which things happen next and why are they so touching?

78. Seized by the seductive thought "that little bitch Endlich" might become indisposed and unable to conduct one evening, Begeist has carefully gone through the score of each Bruckner opus being performed, beginning with last Monday, then Wednesday and Friday, and now the fourth and final program of the ridiculous, insulting Double B Composers series. But something equally intriguing is going on in the kitchen of his Wiener Neustadt host and his mother. What is it?

79. "Why are you so excited about specifically going to Mürzzuschlag as opposed to all the other rich Brahms sites within reach around

Austria?" Tony asks Megan as they head south out of the city and toward the tip of the breathtaking Semmering Pass. What is there about this small village that makes it crucial for them to visit?

80. While Agatha studies the two scores for the final Double B Composers concert, Edgar makes a disturbing discovery via her Ring Europe surveillance camera. Where is that camera and what does Edgar decide to do about what he has witnessed?

81. In the *Grosser Saal* of Vienna's venerable Musikverein a sophisticated audience has gathered to hear the final performance of the unusual series that presented not one but two symphonies. One by Anton Bruckner, his only symphony in D minor—the "tragic key"—and the other by Johannes Brahms, also in a minor key, in this case E minor. The older composer by nine years, Bruckner would be represented by his unfinished Ninth Symphony; Brahms, by his last symphony, the Fourth—both mighty legacies to the world of music and both known to Musikverein audiences. There was one thing that had, however, changed about the Musikverein. How does this turn out to be useful during the shocking event that occurs next?

82. Edgar's minute scrutiny of Agatha's dressing room and of the corridor outside leading to the stage had turned up nothing. With what does he return to Agatha?

83. As Peter Heimnis stands backstage supervising preparations for the last concert of the Double B Composers series, he suddenly realizes that he is feeling uncommonly tired. Also his lungs seem to be heaving abnormally. How does he compensate? Would he ever find out why and who was the man was who wanted him to remove the Maestra's baton, place it in the General Director's office, and then return it to the dressing room the next morning?

84. Several pairs of concertgoers are present for the final Musikverein concert this Sunday evening. Who are they and do they share similar interests?

85. Edgar Wittgenstein is standing in the wings clapping along with the audience, filled with pride and love. He watches Agatha blow a final kiss then turn to the orchestra. She is wearing the all-white outfit with its discreet sprinkling of Swarovski diamonds that has become sartorially famous. Total silence falls upon the house. The Maestra lifts her baton from its rosewood box, takes a deep breath, and raises it. What unthinkable thing happens next?

86. Maestro Begeist runs to the orchestra stage. What is his motive and does he succeed?

87. "Why is the combination of pralidoxime and atropine effective?" This is the question asked and answered on stage by Dr. Oliver Rologe. What is the physician's specialty and how has he reached the stage? How does Lukas Eifer play a role?

88. Why is this evening's performance a concert to end all concerts? And what has been discovered backstage?

89. After the concert Mario Intagliatore offers the music critic for *Der Standard* his arm and the two walk briskly away from an approving Clara Schumann bust and out of the Musikverein. Where are they headed and who is the critic?

90. For Megan and Tony it has been, to say the least, a day of contrasts crowned by high drama— mountainous outdoor Mürzzuschlag versus indoor Musikverein performance of Bruckner and Brahms, beginning with tragedy and ending in glory. Neither has the stomach to look at television coverage of the horrendous evening. What prevents Megan from meeting her friend for breakfast the following morning at seven?

91. What is the embarrassing incident that Dieter Unfug makes sure the board of directors of the Bruckner Orchester Linz knows about?

92. Robb has a wonderful surprise for his hero brother after they arrive back at his apartment. What is it and what is Lukas's reaction?

93. Chief Erich Decker is on the verge of leaving the Musikverein after tying up a few final details when one of his men, with one of the musicians in tow, comes running after him. What have they discovered backstage? And what is it that Decker figures out when he puts two and two together?

94. Megan is once again awakened at an ungodly hour by a phone call from Jacquelyn. What is the revelatory message she has for Megan this time? How does it change the name of the game?

95. Over breakfast, Megan reveals Jacquelyn's amazing find to Tony. How does it change everything?

96. Why and who are at the Militär-Medizinisches Zentrum on Brünner Strasse in Vienna?

97. After hearing once again from Dieter Unfug's mother that he should get married and settle down, Christian Begeist is more than happy early Monday morning when his host abruptly offers to drive him to the train station for his return to Linz. What surprise is in store for him when he returns there?

98. Another visitor to the Militär-Medizinisches Zentrum that early morning is Chief of Police Erich Decker. Why is he there and who shows up to confirm a suspect's story? What are the insights he gleans?

99. When Robb opens his front door after driving his brother to the train station, he is amazed to see Officer Erich Decker. What is the specific question Decker has for him and how does Robb divert suspicion from himself? Decker then seeks information about a certain Maestro who had attended last evening's concert. Is this helpful to us as readers?

100. A very tired Stefanie Schreib wakes up at eight as usual, regardless of the fact that she had worked on her review of last

evening's disrupted but divine concert until two in the morning. There is so much to cover. What does she discuss?

101. Chief Erich Decker shows up at Megan and Tony's hotel while they are having a long, drawn-out breakfast. He has agreed to take time out of his busy day to accompany them to the Haydn Museum where, with his intervention, Megan is going to examine something in the Brahms Room. Do we have any idea what? Why does she hold up the small brass key found in the Brahms bust at Austin? How does the latest information from Jacquelyn figure so decisively now? When they are not successful in their quest, Erich, now as curious as the two Americans, decides he will drive them in his squad car back to Mürzzuschlag to examine something that the director of the Haydn Museum has admitted is stored and rotting in the basement. What extraordinary find does the trio make after they arrive? Why do press and television anchors await them in Vienna after Erich calls the Musikverein? What do Tony and Megan have to say about the amazing discovery that will forever change the history of Brahms the composer and Brahms the man? Do we agree?

www.ingramcontent.com/pod-product-compliance
Lightning Source LLC
Chambersburg PA
CBHW010747310726
48980CB00004B/390

9781632934390